PENGUIN BOOKS

Believers to the Bright Coast

Vincent O'Sullivan is a major New Zealand writer. An award-winning novelist and short story writer (he won the Montana Award for *Let the River Stand* in 1994), he is also highly regarded as a playwright, poet, critic and editor. He has edited a number of major New Zealand anthologies. Vincent O'Sullivan lives in Wellington, where he teaches at Victoria University.

Believers to the Bright Coast

Vincent O'Sullivan

PENGUIN BOOKS

PENGUIN

Penguin Books (NZ) Ltd, cnr Airborne and Rosedale Roads, Albany,
Auckland 1310, New Zealand
Penguin Books Ltd, 27 Wrights Lane, London W8 5TZ, England
Penguin USA, 375 Hudson Street, New York, NY 10014, United States
Penguin Books Australia Ltd, 487 Maroondah Highway, Ringwood,
Australia 3134
Penguin Books Canada Ltd, 10 Alcorn Avenue, Toronto, Ontario,
Canada M4V 3B2

Penguin Books Ltd, Registered Offices: Harmondsworth, Middlesex, England

1 3 5 7 9 10 8 6 4 2

First published by Penguin Books (NZ) Ltd, 1998

Copyright © Vincent O'Sullivan, 1998

The right of Vincent O'Sullivan to be identified as the author of this work
in terms of section 96 of the Copyright Act 1994 is hereby asserted.

All rights reserved. Without limiting the rights under copyright reserved above,
no part of this publication may be reproduced, stored in or introduced
into a retrieval system, or transmitted, in any form or by any means
(electronic, mechanical, photocopying, recording or otherwise), without
the prior written permission of both the copyright owner and
the above publisher of this book.

Designed by Mary Egan
Typeset by Egan-Reid Ltd
Printed in Australia by Australian Print Group, Maryborough

For Barbie Jean and Bruce

Dr Crippen was hanged in 1910 for the murder of his wife, the music-hall *artiste* Belle Elmore. He was arrested with his lover, who was dressed as a boy, on board an Atlantic liner, while attempting to escape to his homeland, the United States. There were many conflicting reports on what became of his young mistress after the trial. One was that she was last seen outside Pentonville gaol on the morning of his execution. Another was that she emigrated to the Antipodes.

Mother Suzanne Aubert established one of her homes for the sick and the disabled in Herne Bay, Auckland, and was assisted by a number of young sisters who worked under her direction.

These few facts remain facts in the novel. Beyond those few, the rest is fiction.

Before the beginning

TOM HOPAI KNELT ON ONE KNEE, SO CLOSE BESIDE HER SHE COULD feel his breath on her neck. He edged his thumbnail against the tiny orange creature with black spots on its shiny back. The ladybird rested on top of a little hot hill of melting tar.

'See?' Lucy said. She looked past the boy beside her to her brother, who couldn't stand Tom wasting time with her like that. He stood, frowning down at both of them. She was too dumb at school to read even, and all this fuss about everything, bloody ladybirds and spiders and the birdcage in her bedroom with a canary that looked like the cat had half chewed it anyway. It made him sick to look at, never mind its shitty knobbled tray and the stink even with the window open.

His friend's thumb pushed very softly and the creature didn't move. Tom said, 'It's dead all right. That.'

Lucy threw down the twig she had tamped at the tar with. She stood up and brushed the dirt from her knees and smoothed down her tartan skirt. She told Tom Hopai, 'All right, then.'

'So we can go then, can we?' Jackie said. Like it was a miracle. 'At last?'

'Don't talk like Dad,' Lucy said. Very quietly. It was such a bold thing for her to say.

Lucy liked it when Tom stood behind Jackie and grinned at her. It was good when he came over from the Hopai farm because Jackie liked him too and laid off telling her what to do all the time. Her brother didn't show off so much either, because Tom was better than he was at hooking eels from under the bank and finding nests and thinking of things to do. She rubbed the smallest speck of tar from her finger onto her skirt and thought it would never show, not seeing she did it so carefully where the black lines of the tartan crossed and made a blob of their own. She followed along behind the boys.

'Oh dear,' she said suddenly. Wouldn't you know it, she thought, she had forgotten that nasty straw sunhat *again*. It was on the rocker on the back verandah and her dad would see it there for sure. Her dad was very strict about hats.

'Ever see me go to work without mine, have you?' he asked. She would shake her head and know how she'd forget it again and yes, she always did. Her hair was thick and streaky-gold like her mother's but no one listened when she said, 'The sun can't even get through,' and patted her head. But she laughed now when Tom Hopai told her, 'You're like us jokers, Lucy. Sun never hurts us two.'

The girl's head nodded sideways. 'Only Jackie here,' she said. 'He looks boiled.'

Jackie walked away. If they were going to talk like that, he thought, well blow them. His own skin was so pale next to Lucy's, Mum made him spread oil over it before she let him out.

'Ten years old and oil on you,' Lucy said.

Then Tom said, 'The creek?' and Jackie said, 'All right, the creek's okay.' Not that the water above the smooth round stones was enough to cover your ankles. It hadn't rained since school broke up. 'This keeps on,' Tom's father said, 'we're puckarood.'

Tom's father was a farmer and lived next door with Lucy's auntie. Sometimes after tea her mother and dad shouted about that and he said he'd go and live in a house in town by himself, don't push him too far. He was sick of living on charity by God he was, and her mother said, Live in that butter box they called the station, would he, and deprive his children of all this? Then Mum's arm moved round in half a circle like everything from there beside the open kitchen door to as far off as the hills and the trees no bigger than you'd drawn on a scrap of paper was what she meant. Deprive her children of that.

The boys called back for Lucy to get a move on, and went behind the huge framework of the barn. She wouldn't like the game down at the creek, she knew that already. The boys would give her stupid names like Lonely Feather and make her sit inside the falling green streamers of the willow that was nothing like a tent although they called it that. They ran round and fired sticks at each other and Jackie slapped himself as if that made him a horse or something.

'I'll tell if you don't keep up with us,' Jackie called back at her. She knew his face would be turning red and stupid the way it did when her auntie laughed and said, 'Dead ringer of the sergeant, goodness me!' Although her mother always stuck up for him. 'He's quick as a whip, that boy,' she said.

Lucy wished she hadn't come. But that was when she looked up and saw what the boys couldn't see because they were behind the barn. She saw the figures silvery and wobbly where the heat rose up off the ground and looked like water. They moved towards her like they had no legs, just floating above the paddock, walking on the light. The man's shirt was shining white and the lady next to him leaned on his arm. It was like a picture in a book. 'They're the angels,' she said. Lucy's breath caught at her words. Her heart thumped as if she had a rabbit down her shirt. Then Jackie came back round the corner of the barn and stopped in the big pool of shadow. He saw his sister's arm held out straight and her finger pointing across the paddocks to the hills. He stood still and Lucy thought, He can't see them, I'm the only one can see them. Then Jackie leaped and yelped like a dog struck by a stone. He started off back towards the house and telling his lies from then on, because he never said it was Lucy's finger told him to look in the first place. As if she hadn't seen them first and even called them angels, before anybody knew a thing.

Also known as Mrs Cooper

I stand on the corner of Brewery Road, and look across the road, to above the long stone wall. No one bothers me. There are so many other people about who attend to the same thing. I stand holding as firmly in my sight as I can the peaked roof that covers where he will be, this moment, as calm as ever, with only me in his mind. He will be as courteous as ever, even to those who lead him up the steps.

I take notice of the sky, because the doctor too always noticed it. It is overcast, as fixed and dull as canvas, and a light wind blows coldly from the east. The tall packed houses are colourless. The lives that stack inside them seem so unreal, so very far, and the paint on the railings, even, was not the paint of the ordinary world as I walked the short distance from Offord Street, where I spent the night in a boarding house, and said no to the Scottish landlady, I would not take breakfast.

Everything I want to own is in a leather bag only a little bigger than a handbag. When I came to the Caledonian Road I stopped in the cavern beneath the railway bridge and leaned against the damp stone. From there, beneath the bridge, it is no great distance to the walls, the peaked roofs, the small windows with their bars that you see up high, beneath the roofline. I had thought I would be so calm. He would so want me to be calm. 'That is how you will defeat them.' He had told me that. Yet now I hear my own rasping breath, and feel the pelting of my heart beneath the dragging weight of my coat. I must

17

now go on for his sake, I tell myself. I must go on for him. And I walk on and am at the edge of the crowd, which is silent and alert and expectant. The faces are tilted towards the long iron roof. We saw wolves once, in a deep stone pit, their muzzles lifted, watching those who watched back. Their eyes were pale as spit. We watched them without speaking, drawn together because of them. Because they were so utterly themselves and so were we. We said nothing but the doctor stroked my wrist.

I am wearing my wig for the first time. Beneath it my hair is cut short as a nun's. I wear my wig and a deep brown coat that was my Gran's and is too large for me. It is to make me look larger and older. I also wear boots unlike any I have worn before, so I feel as though my feet are lifting weights. I feel that I shuffle like a slattern. That is what I want. The newspapers so liked to say 'she dresses to advantage'. It was in the eyes of the court, and in the eyes of those who stood to watch me outside the court. She is the handsome young woman who dotes on a middle-aged monster. They would like to touch me themselves, even the women would like to touch me. They liked to think of me undressed. Undressed with him.

At Brewery Road I stand against the doorway of a public house. There is the heavy smell of malt, of fermenting things, from further along the street. And there is such expectancy and quiet for those few minutes. There is a young woman in a bright dress who holds a child that begins to cry, and she places it against her breast beneath a shawl, without taking her eyes from the long roof and the parapet on the square building in front of it, close behind the wall. And there is a stirring in the crowd, a sigh, a sudden lifted murmur of satisfaction when the high door suddenly opens, and a man in uniform tacks a square of white paper to the wood. There is a sigh of disappointment that the prison bell is not slowly tolled. A tall man says to the woman beside him, who is standing on her toes to look over the crowd, 'There's another two in there waiting to be topped. That's why there's no flamin' bell.'

I feel a deep stillness beyond all this. A stillness which lasts so briefly, and yet while it does it is as if nothing will move again, and there is only calm. Then I see a man, a newspaper man I suppose, who is watching me. His hand raises and tips for a moment the brim of his squat round hat. I cross the road quickly and he edges past the people beside him, and comes after me. I turn through the archway of a large brick building that leads through to a courtyard, and from that into another beyond, and then into a third. Each yard is enclosed by the walls and windows of apartments. I stand back in the recess of a doorway in the last square. The man, who has removed his hat, and reveals a deep imprint where it pressed against his brow, looks about the empty, silent space, and goes back the way he came. I move quickly through several alleyways, until I stand alone on the Roman Way, the first road of all. I walk to the corner and cross past the Methodist chapel with its coloured bricks and the fancy windows that look nothing like England. Then I follow the high iron railings that enclose green fields. I walk so quickly the bars of the fence blur at my side. I am thinking only that it is important to take a train to the docks as soon as I can, that any business I have with this country is now over for ever. I keep everything else from pushing into my mind.

Two or three times I touch the wig that I fear is beginning to slip. The heavy boots are now troubling me. The laces in one of them bite against me like a cord. I turn at the end of the railings into a street I don't know. The curtains are so still, the grey houses so ordinary, I am struck simply by that. A cat leaps from the top of a flight of steps, startled as I pass it. A child in its night clothes watches me from a window. Both her hands are pressed against the glass. But already I see the tower of St Pancras Station, away to my right, and I feel I am at home. The high pale clock, as much as anything in London, has been with me since I was a child.

There is no one on the pavement ahead of me except an old woman trying to raise an umbrella in the soft scattering of rain. For the first time I turn, but there is only a distant figure moving in the other direction. The last man in England who recognised me is left behind. And I think there is nothing that only a little time ago I might have valued, there is no God nor country nor person that is any more part of me now than this ugly pale wig, which at least helps me make

~ough London. St Pancras is there in front of me, now I
         into the station road. And I say over to myself that I will
       ~ur own truth. Peter's truth and mine. They cannot deprive
me of that. I intend to live that truth, although when I walk between
the marble pillars into the booking hall of the huge station I know
there can never again be a time when the way I use that word will
touch the other world that set itself against us, those lies and
judgements and clanging doors that killed my gentle lover in October,
on a cold grey morning, October 1910.

I have never heard an American voice before the doctor leans down to
Emily and says to her, 'Now take it easy there, little lady.' I stand at the
bedroom door, so that his back is towards me. But as he speaks I see his
strangely small hand against the navy flannel of my cousin's gown. The
doctor's hair is pale and thin. When he stands and turns, the light from
beyond the closed net curtains glazes across his spectacles. He is talking
to me, talking to Gran who stands beside me, and I cannot yet see his
eyes. His voice is very calm and I watch his hands fold against the watch
chain on his waistcoat. The waistcoat is a shiny green material that
runs with light and changes and is almost black when he turns so his
back is now towards the window. My uncle, who sees him only as he
walks through the sitting room, who saw no more of him than his
quick clear movement and the shiny metal corners of his leather case,
says once the front door has closed and Gran come back, the aspidistra
curving from its polished copper pot behind her, 'You could tell that
little strutter's foreign without so much as him opening his mouth.'
Then my uncle's hand slaps down on the opened newspaper, flattening
it across his knee.

It is only by chance that the doctor is visiting Mr Groves's house
when Emily takes ill. Mr Groves is our neighbour, a huge slow-moving
man whose wife is religious, and so a friend of Gran's. A friend in
God, to use my grandmother's phrase — an important distinction from
a friend she might choose for herself. She does not in fact like Mrs
Groves, who claims to have once seen a floating baby in a darkened

room and to have heard voices that are not according to nature. My Gran knows God is down to earth and does not go in for vaudeville. But she is patient with her neighbour, who plays the harmonium in the local chapel, and bakes great batches of food and feeds her selected poor as well as her lumbering spouse. Mr Groves is an inventor, a clever man in a street of very ordinary folk. 'The inventions are all *in here*,' Mrs Groves explains. In the head. In the 'spiritual capacity'. Although it is in a shed in his little yard that Mr Groves experiments and mixes and invents the medicines the American doctor is interested in, and so visits occasionally to place his orders — as he did the morning when Emily fell sideways with her sudden pain and Gran called across the fence between our terrace houses to Mrs Groves. And Gran came back and stood beside the plant whose leaves she sometimes oiled, although she had heard that was a thing you should never do, it closed the natural pores. She stands beside it now while my uncle sneers at the doctor who had advised from the front door, 'I'd recommend you get your own doctor quite quickly, ma'am, I'm more on the laboratory side of things.'

'Dapper little Yankee,' my uncle says.

Two bright spots flush on my grandmother's cheeks. They appear there only when she is upset or angry. When God lets her down. She turns sharply to my uncle, who looks back at her over the glasses that are held together with twine, and laughs good-humouredly when she throws at him, 'He is a man who has used his gifts. There's a grace in him that others would know nought enough of.' And then, to neither my uncle nor to me, she says softly, 'If only she had told us.'

Later in the day they will take Emily away. Mrs Groves will be standing beside me, telling me while Gran sits with Emily in the black cab that moves down the street, and neighbours on their summer steps or at opened doors look after its dark twinkling further and further off, 'It's already too late when it gets that late, as Mr Groves will tell you.' She enjoys telling me more. 'It's like a pea in a pod. When the casing breaks it's too late already, see.' It is called peritonitis, my uncle says. 'It's the will of one greater than ourselves,' Mrs Groves corrects him.

I am sixteen, and a smart girl. Not that smart's enough, my Gran likes to say; a girl finds there's more to this life than being good at her books. Once when she tells me that, loud enough for my uncle to hear from the next room, he calls out, 'Another pearl from the Yorkshire oracle, is it?'

He and Gran do not get on. The spots rise on her cheeks that day as well. 'There's the finger of God even on those as don't feel it,' she calls back. We hear his quiet laugh, the page of his sporting paper turned and slapped flat. 'Ballocks, woman,' he says.

As I go into the kitchen where he sits close against the range he winks at me and whistles under his breath. His fingers run down a column of horses' names. 'Cheltenham,' he tells me. 'That's a track for sprinters.' And he takes a coin from the pocket of the shirt inside his dressing gown and hands it across to me, without speaking. It is for me to take to Mr Sam Nathan's betting premises, or rather to the door in the side lane, where frail dark Mrs Nathan, 'as close to Jezebel as you'll ever come', my uncle sometimes says of her, opens the door a matter only of inches, takes the written note I hand her, and closes the door again with as few words as my uncle entrusts his messages to me in the first place.

My uncle is great on foreigners. Even Gran and furthest Yorkshire. 'Those Vikings or whatever they are from up there,' he says, 'those left-over Picts.' He nods towards Gran, winding her up, knowing she will hear and yet think he intends her not to. The tip of his tongue sits very pink between his teeth as he nods and waits for her snapped reply. He leans forward, takes his weight briefly on his walking stick, and eases back. He looks at me and suddenly he begins to cry. His eyes are closed tight, yet the tears sneak between the lids.

'Their nerves,' Mrs Groves has confided in me, several times. She draws closer towards me than I like, and there is something hot on her breath. 'Their nerves is often the ultimate tragedy.'

I like him more than anyone, next to Emily. I like his scorn and his fun and his pretence that betting on horses is a conspiracy against grace and to be condemned, and I like his crying because he is not ashamed of his tears. He never says he is sorry for them, or sorry for himself. He is forty years old and until you come to his crushed legs you know what Gran means when she sometimes says, 'He was a figure of a man. Before and all.' Before the swinging slingload of Danish timber slips its winch in the Limehouse dock where her Stanley is foreman, and buckles him to this awkward shape. He sits by the coal range summer and winter. He reads only newspapers, and he and Gran argue when it is time for the stacked piles of them to be thrown out. He never married, and never drank, and so is able to pay Gran for living with us. 'He was a great one for jokes,' she says of him. The jokes are still there, though they have become more bitter, more directed at herself. 'The finger of God,' she says. 'He knows what that is, all right.' She would die rather than say so, but she is glad he is living with us. She is happy to serve his every need. The finger expects that much of her, sure and all.

There is Gran in our household then, and my uncle, and Emily who is my cousin. Her mother is never spoken of, and nor is mine. It is only her boys, and us, who matter to Gran. My own father died in India, on a day so beautiful, so she had heard, you wouldn't credit what men could get up to with their killing and the rest of it. One of his friends had come to see her when the trouble there was over. That is what he said to Gran, about the day being so beautiful. A day when the sky didn't have a cloud in it. The man was small and dark and hard to understand, because Gran had never before heard a Welshman talk. The earth out there, the Welshman said, was dry and yellow like they never got at home and sometimes you could see you'd think to the end of the world. There is a photograph of my father on the wall in the parlour. He had moved his crossed leg while the photograph was being taken, so there was this blur that made me wonder as a child why he was wearing a dress you could nearly see through. I heard so often what my father's friend told Gran about the day he died, and when I hear my father mentioned I imagine always the same picture in my mind. I am standing on a very high hill, and the earth as far as you can see is yellow and dusty, and a tiny figure in red lies on the ground, and another figure stands beside him. There is no one else in the empty brightness.

There is another photograph, one of my mother, that is kept in a drawer. I do not know how old she was when it was taken, but it is well before I was born. Already she looks sickly. Gran says you could tell by looking at her that her lungs weren't made to last.

'And now our Em,' Gran says, the night after the doctor stood beside her bed. I still see his hand so white against her gown. 'God won't put me through this again,' Gran sighs.

Her Bible says so much about love she cannot believe the pain God sends instead. I am the one who will one day say the words she cannot bring herself to say, calling Him to account. I shall say them because, although I do not know it, they in fact begin that day, when the doctor smiles at me. It is so slight a smile I am hardly sure it is there. I have gone with him to the door, and he stands, one foot raised on the step, his hand on the black iron railing. He takes a small card from a leather wallet and hands it to me. 'You're very welcome to call in on me sometime.' Gran had already told him I was in an office only a little way from Oxford Street. He taps his deep collar while he looks at me and says, 'That would be a neighbourly thing to do.'

When I go back to the kitchen Gran is holding the handle of the boiling kettle with a folded cloth. She says to me without turning, 'I want you to go round to Purchese Street. See if Dr Smith is there.' And my uncle calls through from where he sits with his folded papers. 'What did he say?' Uncle Stanley calls again. Gran stands at the doorway to tell him, the cloth still in her hand. She touches the side of her own stomach, laying her hand flat across it. 'He felt her stomach here,' she says. 'She couldn't stand the least touch just there.' It is as if she has said something that embarrasses us all. My uncle slaps down again at his paper and Gran says sharply, as though I intend to contradict her, 'Well, just go then, will you, girl? I'll feel a road more at ease with one of our own looking at her. Touching her.'

Then the second American voice is hers, but so unlike the doctor's I do not take in at first they are from the same country. She is as loud as he is quiet, as flashy as the doctor is restrained. It is two years further on. I am working for the doctor in Oxford Street. I am already, he says, quite indispensable to this little concern of ours. He speaks of the business with a quiet pride, considering that the Munyon Homeopathic Home Remedy Company will later be described as on the margins of quackery, at the theatrical end of medicine. I will try to explain to Sir Richard Muir that the doctor is sincere in this, as he is in everything else. And the famous prosecutor will look at me, and say simply, as if he explains to a child, What on earth has sincerity got to do with it? I will come to hate him. I shall think, twenty years further on, as I look across almost empty farmland to the white fringe of the coast and the empty sea, glittering as a knife, while the cicadas begin that awful racket behind me, I will remember how Sir Richard plucks at one corner of his gown, and draws out for the world the story that it holds its breath to hear. It is he who will tell the world about Miss Belle.

'Miss Belle,' she says, 'is certainly the name I prefer to be known by.' These are the first words she speaks to me. She leans in close against me. She lets her hand play across the top of my Corona. Her rings rattle against the keys. The peppermint on her breath comes at me almost as a cloth put across my face. I am struck, at once, by how loudly she speaks. Later on I notice that she speaks at that same level whether she stands, as now, only a few feet from me, or at the other end of the long storeroom. Her voice ropes people in to her, the doctor jokes, much as a good cowman brings down cattle at any distance. He tells me that with his soft smile, minutes after his wife leaves. He taps with his beautifully square fingernail against the rim of an enamel basin where he has been mixing a grey paste. He explains to me that shortly Miss Belle may be taking her rightful place on the stage. 'It's been a mighty long spell for her,' he says. After all it is quite some time since that complication with Miss Marie Lloyd. 'Nineteen-o what was it?' he says. 'That's long enough for anyone to forgive, surely to goodness.' He pauses and looks across at me, his eyes large and frank behind his spectacles. 'But one thing you learn about theatre business,' he smiles, 'you learn not to cross Miss Lloyd.'

Miss Belle has so many clothes I cannot believe it. She wears boots with more silver on them, as my Gran would say, than the Pope of Rome could count on a good day. I have never before known anyone from the stage. I wonder how much difference there is between the way she appears in ordinary life, the way she performs simply for the doctor or myself, or old Mr Lewis the accountant, or the quiet New Zealander who is the dentist in the partnership, and how she would act were she engaged in what she calls 'a suitable role'. I know she is vulgar, that my Gran would class her as a right bit of brass, but I cannot stop admiring her. Her lovely skin is what strikes you first. It seems as though there is a blush always just beneath it, on her fine arms as much as at her throat or the top of her bosom, which her clothes manage to make the most of. And there is the sense too of something so generous, so sprawling in her vitality, as she paces about the office or the storeroom. She throws herself back on the doctor's tilting chair, her legs flung out in front of her, while she removes her hat with a quick drawing of the long pin with a huge pearl on its end. I can see why men flock at her, why the doctor too is held by that energy even as he is repelled by it. It is some months, of course, before I dare to admit I have understood that. She is an animal that provokes — that very phrase comes to me as though it is another voice than my own that says it and I merely overhear. And the doctor apprehends that I understand.

To see that as clearly as I shall come to see it is hardly a gift. 'Don't try to see things too clearly, miss,' my Gran used to reprimand, when I asked as a child the questions for which she had phrases, and commandments, but no real answers.

'If God loves us why do we die so ugly?' I asked as a five- or six-year-old. I was playing in the yard with my cousin when Mrs Groves's mother looked at us across the fence. She held two boiled sweets towards us in a swollen paw. Emily ran off and told Gran what I had said. 'There's smarter'n you, remember, girl!' my grandmother warned. She disliked things that seemed to come at her, unexpected. 'You'll not find your clever ones close against the Throne.'

I think of Gran at times as I look at Miss Belle's proclaiming flesh as pride and glory. But it is a thing that comes merely to my mind, it has nothing to do with what I feel. For already Gran's just Father is as remote from me as Gran herself, who after Emily's death, and then my Uncle Stanley's within six months, had gone back to Scarborough, a quickly aged and broken woman whose sayings no longer comforted but merely filled in time, as she waited for life to ease its grip on her as well.

Before she left for the north, my Gran gave me sixty pounds which came from my uncle's provident fund, and told me that for all the spats we might have had I must listen to her now because she spoke God's truth. She knew she had been severe with me for my own good, but now the harvest had come to ripeness, for she knew beyond all doubting I was a sensible girl. How very right she was. I am so sensible I still have forty-five pounds of what I was left, a whole year later. I pay board at Mrs Freeman's in Fisher Street, and dress as neatly as I do on what I save from my wages. I know I look best when I seem subdued, when my long, dark grey coat swishes back from maroon or deep green skirts, and my paleness which had worried Gran shows to such advantage beneath my piled hair. I am good at what Gran called 'making do'. I make most of what I wear, apart from my hats. Mrs Freeman is glad to let me use her sewing machine in return for the hours I spend with her little girl. Her husband is usually on some ship in places his wife is never sure of, and she works in the kitchen at the Chelsea Hospital now her child has someone with her in the evenings. At first she made some effort to conceal from me the food she steals from the hospital, the small parcels of two or three sausages, or the occasional apple for her girl. 'It would only be wasted,' she says. 'It would be a crime to waste it.'

She is surprised that I so obviously do not disapprove. I tell her, meaning it to be a joke, that I heard it said so often as a child that I was born with a defective moral sense, there must be something in it, mustn't there? But Mrs Freeman does not smile when I say that to her. She looks puzzled, as if I am the one who has confessed, not she. 'It's an uphill fight, I can tell you that,' she says. 'Holding things together.' So I am serious when I talk to her, and when I speak with her little girl. The child is called Audrey and is four years old, a grim, small-faced girl who slaps her rag dolls for an amazing range of offences. She and her mother both bore me, if I admit the truth. Sometimes when I look up from what I am reading I catch one of them, or even both, looking at me so sternly, so coldly, I wonder what it is I do that so offends them. As if they know what it is I think of them, that I long to be somewhere else.

I have heard a lady at a meeting in the Edgeware Road say that with only a little less than what I earn a young woman is on the edge of a slope where she can lose control of her destiny. As if you can grow up in Clarkenwell and need to be told that! That will not happen to me. That is one thing I know for certain. I know too, without any fuss about it, that I give people the impression I have life in hand. I know the doctor admires my quickness and my neatness. Mr Lewis says he would rather I do the accounts with him than any young man he knows. Mr Holland the dentist has even asked me have I ever thought of emigrating? He tells me of his own country which is large and empty. He says, almost as if it was his own doing, that in his country women already vote. I am not as much interested as he would like me to be in a place that sounds as rough and tumble as it is far off. I laugh with him, though. I say, 'That's a very long way to go to be allowed to behave like a man.' He insists on the freedom the place would give me. 'Truly,' he says, a word he likes to repeat. I have no idea, he tells me. And the natives, he assures me, will no longer eat you.

'Then why?' I begin to ask him. 'Why leave?'

'Ah,' he says. He raises both hands, one of which holds one of his dreadful little instruments. 'How,' he asks, 'are you ever going to talk sense into the young?'

There is something good-humoured but forlorn in how he says it. I glimpse behind his words the tall, pale woman who very occasionally climbs the stairs to his surgery. She glances at me, but does not speak. It is hard to think of Mrs Holland as a passionate person, even in youth. Or of Miss Belle not being so! As soon as she meets me, after she squeezes my arm for the first time to say we are girls together and breathes peppermint so close to me and asks me do I have a feller, surely I must, Miss Belle takes quite a shine to me. The doctor tells me, 'My wife thinks you're quite the little number.' I know she is taken by what I suppose is the contrast between the two of us. She looks at my dark skirt and its matching cut-away jacket, and my felt hat with the pink rose that I would never tell her in a hundred years was sold to me at half price by Mrs Freeman's sister, who bought it but never wore it, put off by her relative saying a rose like that could never go with auburn hair. 'A picture!' Miss Belle declares when she sees me in it. 'The girl we all want to be!' She swings her full skirt slightly and begins on words from a song. 'Down Lovers' Walk,' she grins at me. And the doctor, who stands a little behind her, that quiet smile on his face, tells me it is a number that was quite a hit a year or so ago, he could assure me of that, she performed it at the Bedford Music Hall, High Street, Camden Town. 'Quite a triumph in its own right,' he says again.

I have only known Miss Belle a short time when she stands behind me as I type, and takes my own hair up in both her hands, raising it as if she weighs it. She lets it run across her wrists. 'My God,' she calls to Mr Lewis, who has looked across from the bench where he is pasting labels on boxes of ointment. 'I could sink my face in this. Have you ever seen anything so gorgeous?'

I am as surprised by how frankly she says this to me as I am by the way the doctor talks of his wife. 'She isn't one to pull her punches,' he smiles. 'She's a healthy woman, our Belle. She's inclined to take life at a rush.'

Mr Lewis says once, just after she has swished through the storeroom and the doctor followed behind her, 'You have to remember where they come from. Remember that and they're very nice.' And then after a silence while he tears the wrapping from a packet of fresh labels, 'There's a dab of Buffalo Bill in American women, wouldn't you say?' He is so obviously enchanted by her colourful prancing about. He believes too that the doctor is run by her. 'What man wouldn't be?' The doctor though is more decisive than Mr Lewis thinks, and Miss Belle is a good deal worried that at thirty-four her career is, as she has said of the diet she began and then soon gave up, 'taking her nowhere fast'.

This last week she has come into the office twice, the first time in her lavender jacket that she swears she is ashamed to be seen in, to think it fitted her perfectly only twelve months back. She is close to tears. Then two days later she is there again, radiant, as the doctor compliments her, in a pink frock with broad white panels. It is spring, after all, and Miss Belle must take a part in it. She is so full of goodwill towards a world she approves of. When she flings through the door the doctor is on the low step-ladder, checking stock against a mail order. It is warm enough for a light sweat to raise across his forehead. He passes a hand across his brow as his wife calls up to him that it's such a pity he is missing out on all this, the day, she says, the day out there is one in a million. He smiles at her and smooths down his waistcoat. In the centre of the dark shelves and the benches and the stacked cartons of patent medicines Miss Belle indeed makes the rest of us look drab.

'You've brought it inside with you,' the doctor says, 'we don't need to go outside to see the spring.'

Miss Belle twirls in front of us, billowing out her skirt. The buttons on her American boots glitter as she turns. The doctor's index finger runs quietly across one side of his moustache as he considers what next he should say. 'Yes, that's charming, Belle,' he says. She smirks, not at him, but at me, and when she speaks it is to Mr Lewis and myself. 'My,' she declares, 'you're turning him into a regular Englishman, you know that? There was a time he'd have told me I was mighty pretty, but now will you listen to him! "Charming"!' And to the doctor she says, 'You're so subdued!' Then she kisses him on the forehead before she spins away, laughing to include us all.

The doctor's finger moves between his tall collar and his skin. He clears his throat, as though he intends to speak. But Miss Belle swoops down on me. She stands with her hands on the back of my chair. I can feel her breath on my hair. She looks at the letter I have in the machine and begins to read it aloud. 'Dear Sir, In reply to your question about persistent abdominal discomfort.'

The doctor, colouring up, attempts to cut her off. 'Please,' he says to her. For all his courtesy it is clear that he is angry.

'My,' she says, 'some folks!' She smiles at Mr Lewis and myself, roping us into youth and fun against her husband's earnestness.

'It's a matter of privacy,' he says. 'People write in confidence.'

'I can't even read the person's name. What's more private than that?'

The doctor says nothing in reply, but returns to the list he holds between his fingers. The slip of yellow paper is shaking as he holds it. He counts and lets fall from his cupped hand a stream of pills into a row of small red boxes. That is the only sound for several seconds. Until Miss Belle raises both her hands to her shoulders, the palms facing outwards, rolls her head from side to side, and says to Mr Lewis, who laughs back at her, 'Lordy me!' And to the doctor she says, 'It's hardly fun-time in this place, is it, Peter? It's all so *businesslike*.'

Then the New Zealand dentist is there suddenly at the doorway in his long green smock and rubber gloves. He asks the doctor will he step into his surgery for a moment, it should not take more than that. A problem, he says, with an impacted wisdom tooth, a plate has prevented its natural growth for years. Mr Holland nods apologetically towards Miss Belle. And so the spell is broken. But I know that for a few moments at least I feel it too. It is a kind of shimmering that goes out from her, a current the doctor resists yet is compelled by, as surely as a swimmer is held in a tide that is too much for him. Later, and far from here, when I come to learn more of perversions, the drag that pulls some men and even women into dark spaces where their own wills are quite subdued, or actually lost, I shall think of this morning. Miss Belle with both hands raised. The doctor smiling not towards but *away* from her, resisting. I shall come back again and again to my first picking up the tension that burns between them, in that plain room with its broad skylight and its stretch of dirty glass. I feel myself held too by whatever it is that I do not yet understand — the performer and her audience, the mistress and her fear she is losing a slave.

But so gaily again, now the doctor has gone through with Mr Holland, Miss Belle wheels to me and tells me, 'You need some good fresh air if ever a girl did!' She takes my hand, her warm plump fingers lacing with mine like those of an older child dragging another out to play. I find myself laughing back at her. Mr Lewis smiles across at us. He tells me, 'Go on, girl. A splendid day like this!' He removes his spectacles and rubs them on the square of cloth he carries in his breast pocket, a thing he does when he is moved.

'Isola's,' Miss Belle announces. 'The ices at Isola's! It's next thing to round the corner.'

Out in Oxford Street she takes my arm and directs me through the traffic. A swirl of warm air dashes at her clothes, she shrieks as she pats herself down against the billowing cloth. People turn to look and smile. We are runaway girls together now, that is what we are playing at. 'Well, pretty near round the corner,' she says. It is more than ten minutes' walk until we are in the streets near the British Museum. We weave and glide between cabs and drays and motors. A cabbie calls out to her as she flourishes us in front of him. 'Cheeky!' she banters back at him. She shakes her gloved finger and his face splits open in a wet red grin. I think the whole world must be looking at us, yet my shyness seems absorbed into her own high spirits. I call out in exaggeration too when a barrel rolls down a plank beside us and whacks against the pavement. Then we are in one of the quieter streets of bookstalls and single strollers, and Miss Belle is no longer on quite such display. She is explaining to me now, as friend to friend, about the bumpiness of her career. The mighty mean-spirited way of the halls over here, she says, compared to how things were done back home. 'Don't they understand we are all *artistes* together? Can you imagine not understanding *that*?'

She speaks of the doctor being the soul of sympathy itself: he is so devoted to her career there isn't the singlest other thing she could ask for that way, she assures me of that. Not a thing she could ask him that he wouldn't do for her. And as Miss Belle confides to me she continues to hold my hand, to pat my sleeve with her emphasising fingers, to laugh so close against me I wonder if this is what it must be like to be a man, to have a woman dance attendance. Yet although we walk along so obviously as friends, as intimate friends, I am subdued again. Her presence is so commanding, so full. So sensual, even to me. I feel I must seem so dull beside this drift of peppermint and chatter. As she directs me to turn left and into the tearoom and waves her hand ahead of her, I feel that she is offering me the world, running me off from work, from what Gran would call my rightful place, and tempting me with her own glamour and indolence.

At once Miss Belle dominates the large room with its white cane chairs and glass-topped tables. A group of elderly musicians in an alcove of tubbed palms continues to look at her. She jokes with the foreign waiter about quite where is the most agreeable place to sit. We take one table then change it for another. And somehow in the time from Oxford Street to here, in the dash through traffic and her constant smiling at the world, engaging its approval, and in the first few minutes in the lovely quieter stir of Isola's, Miss Belle has told me so much I had not known about her. About the sister she still writes to in New York, and her first sight of Peter, would I credit this one now, at a Sunday meeting, a hoe-down for young professional Christians! She herself was Catholic, of course, Miss Belle says, Polish would I believe it! But this girlfriend of hers took on this crazy notion of getting folks together from different churches. Lord knows how the doctor got there, she couldn't rightly remember. As if anyone from Michigan was likely to have a real religion to begin with! But there they were, forced to drink this appalling gingerpop and sing Methodist hymns as well, supposing you want to count *that* as Christian, and then this preacher saying prayers, honest to goodness, they were the kind Luther could have written, all faith and no works, I must know what she means? She was about ready to strangle that girlfriend, I'd believe that one, wouldn't I? And then she noticed this young balding man beside her, solemn as a barn-owl when she first caught sight of him, but he's not singing a line, not saying a word, and Miss Belle just turned to him in desperation you might as well call it, and told him, Brother, you've just got to get me out of this place.

'And you know what he says?' Miss Belle asks me. Her eyes are opened so wide I could imagine her telling it on stage. 'You'll appreciate how you could very well look at Peter and you might even think there was nothing interests him except the names for bones and things? Just a doctor through and through, I mean, and nothing else? Well when I said that to him about getting me out of there, he looks at me fair and square and says to me so deadpan it could be Sam Mayo saying it, you must have seen his routine? He says, "So there is a Providence after all!" '

Miss Belle finishes her story as she unbuttons her gloves and draws them off and smooths them across her lap. Her eyes flick over to the men in the string orchestra and then to the waiter who stands ready to approach us, and then she says to me, 'Well ask yourself. What young woman with her heart set on the theatre wouldn't go for a downbeat man like that?' Her mouth opens wide as she laughs, she is happy because I laugh back with her. She enjoys the men watching her as she laughs.

Miss Belle orders for both of us. 'Tasters,' she says, when the coloured glass dishes of ice cream are placed in front of us. 'Back home we call them sundaes. And do they ever have the edge on this lot!'

She then confides in me how she is waiting this very minute for a fellow *artiste* she is working up quite a little number with. She sighs good-naturedly and tells me again the way her career has taken a setback twice since coming over here. She didn't hold one bit with political disputes being brought on stage, but there you are! She wasn't the only one, was she, who was willing to perform when most of the *artistes* withdrew over some dispute or other? But next thing Miss Lloyd is persecuting her season after season, vindictive as you like. Her plump finger dips into the ice and runs the smooth vanilla across her lips. Her eyes keep coming and going to the doorway, until a gentleman in a black jacket and grey check trousers enters and comes towards us. He is perhaps thirty years old, although I am not good at guessing ages. Miss Belle introduces us. She does not say I work for the doctor, but declares that I am her special friend. 'Youth!' the man says, picking up the drama of it, the mature, confident woman and her timid younger admirer. And the man makes rather a thing of bowing to me, as he speaks in one of the deepest voices I have ever heard. Miss Belle is on to my surprise. She gives her quick loud laugh, and tells me Dash is one of the primest villains in all the halls, isn't that so? 'He has only to raise an eyebrow and the virtuous faint.' But her friend, who now realises I have nothing to do with the theatre, finds me dull, I'm sure, and begins to talk business with Miss Belle. They exchange the names of songs and discuss the timing of movements, and she explains to me how they are working on an act together that will really eventuate into something. And does she mean something!

'Well,' the man says. As if it is up to him to act modest. He lifts what I already know is a famous eyebrow.

'It *will* be, Dash,' she says. And to me she confides she is *très fortunée* to have so talented a partner. Dash taps a cigarette on the silver case he slants in the palm of his hand, and for a second its polished surface serves as a mirror as well.

I ask him does he sing in the act they are working up? Surely he must sing with a voice like that? He looks away from Miss Belle for the first time. He considers my face, my body, in one sweeping glance. He then smiles at me very deliberately, as if telling me I may not be quite so dull as he had thought. 'Oh yes,' he says, very casually. 'Sing. Dance. Juggle. Comic turns. Tragic roles. Anything,' he says, and he and Miss Belle are immensely tickled at this, 'anything except juvenile leads.'

I see he is making fun of me. Miss Belle leans towards me and says, 'Dash can no more stop playing the fool than he can stop breathing.' She raps his hand at the very idea of it. 'Now stop it,' she orders him. 'At once.'

I see then, very clearly, that Miss Belle has brought me to the tearooms to set her off, to provide what dressmakers call an 'accessory'. I am so obviously younger, my hair is so much finer, yet no one — no man at any rate — would think of giving me a second glance beside her radiance, beside the personality that seems to flare off her like a bright deflected light. There is something so unrefined about her which men delight in as well. Later I will read or hear that she was 'loud', that she was 'drawn in too generous lines'. She is those things, of course: her figure is too full, she herself is aware of that. So her wide frank smile, her 'daisy eyes' as she holds your glance, are saying to you — are saying to men, is what I mean — that there may be so much more, who knows what limits there may be to her largesse? (A word the doctor teaches me, that.)

Her friend makes no attempt to hide his fascination with her. He is held, I see, especially by the wetness of her lips, her habit of running her tongue across them as she leans forward, telling him to 'Listen, Dash. Now just you pay attention.' There is an urge towards her that she blatantly returns as she claps her hands, then half conceals her face and peeps at him between the bars of her fingers while he finishes a story about another performer.

The man takes a small notebook from inside his jacket, and licks the end of a pencil before he begins to write on a page that seems already to be hatched over and over with words and figures. While he attends to this Miss Belle turns to me and says surely I'll take another ice, a growing girl? I point above the tearoom's door to the clock with its heavy wooden rim. She rushes her fingers to her mouth. 'That man will have me horsewhipped!' she declares. 'Keeping you out all this time!' But we laugh together at the thought of it, the doctor becoming violent about anything.

A week or so after that excursion to Isola's the doctor tells me, 'I'm afraid Miss Belle feels badly down.' It is a warm afternoon, and I sit at the typewriting machine with my jacket draped across the back of my chair. My maroon blouse rustles softly as I move. The office and the long storeroom seem awfully quiet. Mr Lewis is down at the docks for the afternoon, tracing with the Customs people an assignment of goods from St Louis. (The doctor's advertising makes much of his American ingredients.) There is almost the feeling of a holiday. It is one of those rare times when there are only the two of us, in the doctor's words, 'holding the fort'. Even Mr Holland the dentist is not there this afternoon. He has had to call on a colleague in Dean Street, as he is suffering from toothache. The doctor and I think this is amusing, but Mr Holland does not easily see a joke at the best of times. Miss Belle told me once, 'His sense of humour was frozen all that way down south. Can you imagine anyone laughing at anything that far away?' She batted her eyelids fast at the thought of it.

The doctor is sitting on Mr Lewis's high stool a few feet away from my desk. His fingers move as though washing themselves in the fob pocket of his waistcoat.

'Well now,' he says, very slowly.

I like it when he talks like this, shyly and yet so at ease with me, his reticence no longer a trouble between us. He tells me about 'home', where he began. I imagine the long plains, the soft gold of a huge harvest moving in the slightest wind. You see it for hour after hour, he says, on your way out west. 'Space,' he says, 'there are few gifts to touch it.' It is strange that when he thinks back like this he speaks only of places or of what the weather is like, the way Miss Belle will tell you of people and little else. 'The taste of New Yorkers!' I have heard her say. 'Jew boy comics or nigger minstrels. Ikey and Rastus. Can you just see me fitting in with either of those?' When the doctor pauses and squeezes his bottom lip I still have in mind the spaces that go on for ever and the wind from a huge hollow sky, and the small wooden railroad stations you speed by and try to imagine what life must be like in towns so small and remote as Ledville and Thomastown and Fortune's Creek. Then the doctor says, looking down at his hands, 'My little lady is certainly down to it, the way things have panned out.'

The old argument in the halls has flared out again. Miss Lloyd, he says, pursues Belle's career, she nips it in the bud. 'I am not at all convinced that the person she has chosen for her partner is a person of reputation. That adds to her difficulty, I believe.' He does not tell me, as witnesses will eventually tell the courtroom, how Miss Belle subjects the doctor to awful rages when they are alone in their tall grey ugly house in Camden Town. He does not speak against her to me, now or at any other time. But looks up at me. He has removed his spectacles, and it is like looking at the face of a boy. That is when he touches my hand for the first time. We say nothing for several minutes. It comes to me so suddenly, as if a door is flung open. I see his utter dejection. Then we hear Mr Lewis on the landing, and the doctor replaces his spectacles. He stands at the window, looking down into the street. When Mr Lewis reaches his felt hat to one of the curled pegs behind the door, the doctor tells him quietly there is warmer weather expected. 'I'll be mighty surprised if it isn't sweltering in here before too long.'

In the courtroom there will be other men as well. There will be Mr George Miller, an Englishman brought all the way back from East Chicago, Indiana, who had decided on real estate because it was more profitable than show business. He will insist, 'It was not because I was a failure on the stage.' He answers another question. 'We first met at a house in Torrington Square in December 1899. Her husband was in

America at that time, as far as I understand. I would visit her two or three times a week.' He visited her sometimes in the afternoons and sometimes in the evenings.

I will sit in the courtroom and wonder at how long ago, how dusty and remote, all this detail seems. It is the year my uncle took Emily and me to the gardens at Kew. It was my birthday. It was a day when rain took us by surprise. We ran across a green slope and all I could think was that the rain would spoil my new muff. I think of that day and I lose the thread of the barrister's questioning, but I take in Mr Miller's awkwardness, his dabbing with a yellow handkerchief at his neatly clipped beard. Even though he is guiltless and quite safe, his eyes dart about the court, his answers are hesitant. The lawyer does not let up in his questions. 'Were those affectionate letters?' He will read out from them: 'Love and kisses to Brown Eyes.' It is on the hoardings that afternoon. George Miller will look at the gowned man in front of him and tell him weakly, 'My intentions were not of the kind you are perhaps speaking of.'

I try not to move in the courtroom, to give no inkling of what I may think, whatever evidence is given. The public gallery seems to look at no one but myself, or at the doctor, whose expression does not alter, who out of consideration so seldom even glances across at me.

'Did she discourage such expressions?' they will ask the sweating actor. The letters are ten years dead, but they will excite the court. Oh there will be such intense closeness as we sit there, a few feet from each other. Our closeness is the very defiance that others may not see it. We will not allow them to catch us holding each other's eye, to see the link between us so they might paw at it, pass it from one to the other, from the hoardings to the whole of England. My hair is still short as a boy's. How they love to look at that! As they wait to hear of me in my boy's clothes. They will strain to hear of me on the ship's deck as the wind whips back my jacket and the captain sees the safety pins that make him certain these are not my proper clothes. They will want to hear the tapping of the telegraph from Scotland Yard while the doctor and I sleep in our cabin and the inspector on another ship is gaining the distance between. They are excited that we are lovers yet I seem to be a boy. They crane forward. The silence will be as sacred as in an abbey when the doctor answers what they ask him, when the police present their case. 'These are human remains.' We will be proud of each other, the doctor and I. We do not let each other down in front of them. We will give them nothing to feed on.

Miss Belle's photographs are in the papers a hundred times. She is more famous than she ever dreamed, than even Miss Marie Lloyd could stop her being! But the doctor will not finish for them the story they grow tense to hear. The rage with him is for that — how he denies their final gasp. They will never hear how he removes his cuff-links and hears the small clink as he places them on the mantelpiece, nor see him roll his shirt sleeves to his elbows, hear his hands as they move across the instruments in their tray. They will wait to hear what he will never give them. But they will love to guess that this was how he must have done it, and this is how he disposed of her, and how we were lovers even as his instruments nicked and slid, and he made me dress as a boy to get away. The gentlest of men will become a name children use to scare younger children. 'He will get you!' they will say, hiding behind curtains, leaping suddenly out.

Before those long days in the courtroom are over, my new life will have begun. There will be nothing, once Peter goes, that I have respect for. I will soon enough forget Mrs Freeman, grimly delighted that her righteousness is seen by the world as she counts the nights I was not at home. Or Mr Lewis, so old, so unconnected in his answers. Or the dentist, whose country I go to because I can think of nowhere further. There is nothing I regret. I am sorry only that there is not a God for me to say that to as well. To say, There is nothing you can do to make me regret. And nothing to make me love you, even if you are there. The sentence my Gran could never bring herself to say.

I am more than halfway across the Indian Ocean. I keep to myself, but I cannot avoid entirely the kindness or the normal curiosity of other passengers. I wear a wedding ring and say my husband was a merchant in Scarborough, the only other town in England that I have some idea of. I hint that I have inherited a little money and have a craving for another world, at least for a time. I draw out these facts when I am cornered by the need for what, after all, is a far more likely story than my own.

I dress always in dark colours, although my own hair is now like pale straw. I look, even to myself, so unlike the dark, long-haired girl of the newspapers, or the boy in the sketches. I have invented for myself a life which is easy enough to tell, because it is quite true. It is simply not my own. I talk as though I were Emily, had she stayed alive. I have the same husband who was almost hers, who had the same life as that young man until an accident in my version, rather than the emigration of fact, took him off. It is quite understood when I spend so much time in my cabin or, when the weather so suddenly improved, sitting alone in one of the *Scharnhorst's* canvas chairs, looking out to the endlessness of sea. I have deliberately chosen a German ship to travel on, in the hope there might be fewer passengers from England. This is only partly the case. There are Irish families going to Australia, a number of Germans, rich New Zealanders returning home, but also a sprinkling of English, whose voices are the loudest above the click of the deck games, the thump of quoits.

There are two couples who travel as friends. They play cards together, and croquet with flat wooden discs. The men, in white flannels, are happy enough to toss a rope circle across a net for hours at a time, while the women, their legs extended on long low chairs, read beneath their huge hats. When the sun shines they glance up as I walk past, and their faces seem a mass of moving freckles beneath the brims of straw. In the afternoons they rest in their cabins, and in the early evenings the women stroll arm in arm on the cooling decks, and the men lean at the stern rail, where stewards bring them drinks. One of the women is called Mrs Goddard. She is perhaps ten years older than myself. She has pretty red hair, and a gap between her front teeth that makes her look like a young girl. Her friend is older, cleverer, not so attractive. Everyone seems to know that the older woman, Mrs Calder, is very rich, and that her blond, much younger husband owns a farm in Queensland that is half the size of Wales. These are the people I sometimes talk with, although only because they make such a point of friendliness. Mrs Goddard's husband is forty. I know that for certain, because of a small party for his birthday and the glass of champagne he brought to me personally. He leaned above my deck chair, raised his panama hat in a deep, good-natured flourish, and said he would not feel his age so much if I shared a birthday toast with them. It was late afternoon and the sun dazzled in the glass he held towards me. His wife and his friends call him Bill. He is so careful in his speech that I suspect there may be another accent behind the one he speaks with. Or at other times you may think he is reconsidering, from moment to moment, what it is he wants to say.

Early on, four or five days out from Southampton, he asked me did I fancy bridge? I would be most welcome to join them should I care for a rubber or two. I tell him it is very kind of him, but I am quite happy as I am. And I do not play cards, in any case. But I watch them across the lounge as they play among themselves. His own wife, he said, plays only under compulsion. She would be far happier with her novels — Mrs Robbins and other improving authors, he said, raising his eyebrows a little. They look so serious as they play, but occasionally the blond man says something that makes them smile. When the game is over they laugh while Mrs Calder draws the cards together and shuffles them. One of the men raises a finger towards the stewards who stand in a row against one wall, their trays in front of them like lowered shields. I am held simply by how normal, how ordinary such lives seem to be.

I leave the lounge and stand against the rail. Already the grey low skies have broken. England is far behind us. I think of the doctor and myself on that other ship. I feel the slow regular lift of the deck beneath me. I hear the humming engines, a piece of loose metal vibrating somewhere above us in our cabin as we lie together through the nights. His hand strokes and strokes at my neck, my shoulder, against the grain of my close-cropped hair. The Atlantic was seldom anything but cold and grey, and the smoky lift of spray as the waves peaked. Here already it is so intensely blue, and sometimes as still as if painted on a plate. As the moon increases, the deck becomes a long pale slab. The emptiness of the deck, and the cut of the shadows across it, excites and calms me at the same time.

I have been standing for ten minutes perhaps when from a dark clot of shadow I hear the whispering of a man and woman, their sounds of furtiveness and rush. It is Mrs Goddard's husband and their rich dark friend. She clings against him as they move across a narrow flag of moonlight into another block of shadow. I feel nothing as I see them, beyond noting my own profound indifference. I hear their breathing, and one quick cry that makes me think of that strange shrillness you sometimes hear at night from a tree outside a window, a sound that thickens the silence about it. I move slightly, and the man hushes the woman. He picks up that someone is there, no more than a few yards from their rapid coupling. I hear his quick sigh of warning, of irritation. But until he stands and looks from his office window into the lane that leads from Queen Street, he will have no idea of what I may have heard or who it is that is aware of them, for the darkness is deep as a ditch beneath the lifeboat where I am standing. I go back to my cabin and lie thinking of Peter. The ship dips softly, and the panelling creaks about me.

I become more friendly with his wife. The older woman is pleasant to me, but makes little effort, as Mrs Goddard does, to draw me closer. There is nothing in me that interests her. She is not the kind of woman to conceal a fact like that. But she does tell me her husband is a grazier, an Australian, although she herself intends to sail on, to stay for a time with relatives in Auckland. She seems remote from the pale six-year-old son whose green eyes drill at things. Yet the boy seems happier to be near her than with his father who fusses about him, attempting to draw him into games which clearly bore him. He likes to stand by his mother and lean against her, and stroke the material of her dresses. He runs his fingers along the pheasant's feather in a hat she sometimes places beside her deck chair.

Mrs Goddard tells me about the country we are sailing to. She has no regrets about leaving behind her 'all that', as she calls the England where she and her husband have been for several months. She had admired and checked from her list the things that were important to see, the cathedrals and landscapes, the race meetings and the garden parties, the celebrations for the Coronation. But she now counted the days to be back where life really was.

'Even our garden,' she smiles at me. 'It's nothing so grand at all but I am so looking forward to being in it again.'

She tells me she was once a teacher. She says she knows how fortunate she has been in marrying Bill, but she would give anything to go back to the classroom again, to the children. 'Not that Bill will hear of it.' And she asks me what do I intend to do?

I lie about relatives I have in the south, in the town I can speak of with passing knowledge only because of Mr Holland. I am not sure, I say, if I shall stay so very long. My trip is to take my mind off other things.

'I know,' Mrs Goddard says. She lets her hand rest for a moment on mine.

'If I stay on I could be a secretary. I am used to being independent.' And I think of the slight gift that I have, which Emily had so much more of, and I say, 'I am quite good at drawing. At design. I could get work perhaps with some paper. Some printer.'

She does not say so, but I see she does not believe I might make a living from that. Most of such work seems to be done by men, she says. And then, 'Would you like to draw me?' she asks. 'Bill of course would pay you.'

'I could never do you justice,' I tell her. We laugh to cover my reluctance, and she does not raise the matter again.

Another time we sit watching the long spectacular evening a few days to the north of her country. We are comfortably silent together. Mr Goddard stands at the rail in front of us, smoking a cigar that he crackles first against his ear before striking a match on the sole of his boot. When his wife speaks, she tells me that if I do decide to stay on in Auckland, or decide to come back there, after the south, I must indeed get in touch. It is not an impulsive offer. I know she warms to me, and that we could easily enough become friends. I have only to cover the little space between us. But she knows, I am quite certain, that I shall not take up her kindness. I have no difficulty in deciding that. For I know, quite as much as I have put so much of myself away, that part of my defence, part of what is so essential if I am to survive, is to guard my loneliness at whatever cost. The doctor's final gift to me, I suppose, is that. I am as decisive as I am cold. I think of him handing me the sunset brooch.

A few days later she embraces me and says goodbye. There is sunshine and a blustery wind that snaps the little flags strung out above the deck. The colours on the low hills around the harbour are strangely bright, the landscape is sprinkled with small square buildings. I think of a child's rough drawing. I see that Mrs Goddard is crying. Her husband has turned aside and looks at the long tin roofs of the sheds along the wharf. He waves down to someone among the crowd gathered below. Snatches of band music keep coming and going with the gusts of wind. I feel a rush of exhilaration that takes me by surprise. It has nothing to do with happiness. It is sheer relief, the fact that I am no longer part of England. It is as if I hear an actual snap of what binds me to back there. Then I am following a porter down the gangway to the waiting cabs.

After so long at sea, the air seems heavy with horse dung, the reek of oil and tar, the clogging of chaff and swirling dust. I wave to the Goddards as they drive off with several cabloads of friends. I nod to other passengers I came to know a little on the voyage out. And in ten minutes I am in my sitting room in the Imperial Hotel. There are noises from the street when the maid opens the long window. Boys' voices call through the tocking of hooves on the road; there is the ringing sound of the horse-drawn trams in their metal grooves. I am alone, in the centre of whatever world there is. I have survived this far at any rate. I say that sentence out loud. 'I have survived, my love.'

I am happy at the Imperial. 'Value for money,' I had heard a man on board declare one evening. 'You'll get your money's worth even if you get no frills.' I had remembered the name and asked to be taken there.

There are long green velvet curtains in my sitting room, and a matching settee. There are paintings of Scotland on the walls. Things seem familiar and yet are not so. More people speak as though they were not from home than those who do. I am not sure why this surprises me. I feel this is meant to be England over again, but unpacked it feels so different, so much less stable, under a sky that flickers and changes a dozen times a day. I sit in a little ferry and cross the harbour to a place that has a green, and a promenade, and an English church, but it is like someone has sketched it in and got it wrong. Outside a wooden school there is an archway still from the Coronation. I know this sense of unreality is in me, of course, not in those who live here. And I am glad for the difference. I must make my life here, give it what shape I can, as certainly as those two young men I walk past in a side street are hammering at the frame of a new small house that looks like nothing I have seen before. I think of a box with windows.

In my first few days I walk and walk. I take in as many parts of the town as I can, as if I must see it all, draw into me what is so new, as quickly as I can. For all the Goddards told me on the way out, I notice there are long sunken valleys and dull stretches where the poor are crammed, as well as the handsome hillsides, the streets of trees where the large white houses tell you yes, it was worth coming this far, it would hardly have been like this had they stayed at home. But it seems there is a strange muddle, even as they talk to you. They do not explain how it is possible to be servile and superior at the same time. They look at you, especially if you have a little money, as if they are taking in the real thing. I don't know how else to put it. Yet they feel sorry for you as well, because you have just arrived. I have no one to talk to about this, so I may indeed be wrong. At one level I know so clearly where I am, and feel at ease. At another I am quite unsure how much I must change for this place to be mine, to grasp what Mr Holland saw when he laid his instruments down and looked onto the wet bustle of Oxford Street and said, 'A young woman would have more scope there. Truly.'

One evening, on a sloping street behind the scaffolding for the new Town Hall, on a corner below a public house and a stretch of Chinese shops, I pass several women who are whores. I hear them talk among themselves as I walk up the hill. Apart from their flashy clothes, their behaviour seems that of ordinary women. When I pass them again, half an hour later, they are tarting it up with a group of men, 'shiyacking', as I will come to hear it called. One of them raises her skirts almost to her knees, enjoying it the more, I think, because she has spotted my respectable glance. 'You won't get a bargain like this again, sonny,' she tells the man who had stopped a few feet from her and then walked on. She calls after him, 'Make do with the old dutch then, God help her!'

I cross the road and stand in the shadows where the new building rises. I watch her and the other women between the plane trees that rise from the footpath. It is like one of those revelations in the Bible my Gran was fond of referring to. As if a voice spoke from above me, or whatever! I remember as I escaped from Pentonville Road to Market Street and walked by the high iron fence that it was *their* world I was still living in, yet it had nothing to do with *mine*. Mine had been ripped from me twenty minutes before. It was as if a hood was taken from my eyes, and I saw things without the words they have always stuck there. The lies that make it easy for them. And I know now as I look across at the whores on their scrap of footpath, the shadows from the trees mobbing across them, that the need for women like that will be eternal. It is neither good nor bad, but simply as things are. And so it comes to me, that quickly, what my 'living' here is to be. 'And the Lord said, Samuel.' That leaps into my mind, even before I have stepped from the doorway back onto the footpath. It is the name I give the first premises I buy. 'Samuel Cottage', in Newton Road.

I return to Grey Street the next day, a little earlier in the evening, before the streetlights go on and the lamps are lit in the Chinese shops and the little smear of romance falls across the whores. At first I see only a couple in Salvation Army uniform, striding up the hill. Then a young woman stands near the laneway at the side of the Carpenters' Arms. She is rummaging in a draw-top bag that hangs from her arm. Her dress is pale green and her high boots have white buttons along the sides. I see that she is coughing, and that what she looks for is a handkerchief. She holds it like a ball, crammed against her mouth. She speaks to two men who pass her, but neither gives any sign that they have heard her. Later she will tell me that if she 'gets a few out of the way' in the afternoon, or the early evening like this, she need not hang about until the public houses are closing, which of course is the time to take your pickings. By then, with the late air, she says, she is coughing so bad she has had men leave her room before they're even through. 'Being sick doesn't fit the picture, does it?' She is sardonic and bright and bitter. 'One thing mind, a cough like this you don't put weight on, do you? There's as many as like you bony as there are who go for the bouncy ones.'

I walk up to the woman and stop in front of her. She looks at me, neither startled nor surprised, but simply waiting for whatever I have to say. 'You wouldn't believe the women who speak to you either sometimes,' she will tell me too, in time. 'The things they'll put to you.'

I place several notes in her hand. 'I want to talk to you,' I tell her. 'My hotel's the best place.'

I take to her, I suppose, because there is no subservience about her. She falls into step beside me. She makes no effort to talk. I realise even this is business for her. She will do simply what she is paid for. I say to the maid as we pass on the stairs at the Imperial, 'Bring up tea for us, will you?' Then I close the sitting room door and she sits in the armchair before I have a chance to invite her.

'This is nice all right,' she says.

I tell her my name, and she tells me hers is Greta. Then we wait until the tea things are on the small table between us. I ask her is she hungry.

'You lot like to imagine women like me are always hungry.' She says it with a sense of humour, more than accusation.

'I've no idea what to imagine,' I say.

'Then don't try,' she says. 'We do this for a job. That's the only difference. That lot sign a bit of paper and give it away.' She laughs with a self-awareness that surprises me. She enjoys looking at the room. She is more interested in that than she is in the food, or in me.

'Are you from the church?' she asks me.

I smile for the first time. 'Me?' I say. 'I'm from no one except myself.'

She seems not to take in what I say. 'Are you giving me money so I'll feel ashamed?' She looks at me, her grey eyes steady on mine. 'They don't realise, do they, shame isn't something you keep on the boil just to make them feel good.'

So I tell her, 'I want to ask you some questions and I'll pay you again when we've finished talking.'

'Talk's all you want to do?'

'Yes,' I say. Later I will be amused as I remember this, how I was so new to the game as not to understand what she meant.

'Christ,' she says, her eyes still holding mine. It is what she thinks I want. 'The money's for talking stuff to you, is it?' Then the words tumbling from her, the talk of splashing and mounting and hot ruts. She asks me, 'Those are the words you want?' And her beginning to cough as she keeps speaking, the obscenities clotting and jetting into the handkerchief she has drawn from under the cuff of her sleeve and is now jamming close against her mouth, leaning forward as though she will vomit across her fists. When the spasm passes, there are tears of strain in her eyes. She leans back against the padded head of the chair.

'That's not what I want,' I tell her. She waits until I am more precise. 'I want to know how much. How much you get.'

'How much they pay?'

'As a rule.'

'There's no "as a rule" about it. Six bob, say, with your clothes still on. Eight with nothing. More the longer they stay. The prices drop the older you get.'

'You're still young,' I say.

'Twenty-eight. That's getting on. Compared with you, I'd say.'

'Where?' I ask her. 'Where do you work?' I am surprised at myself. How coldly I can ask these questions, although I am not, God knows, cold towards the woman herself.

'That green cottage near the bottom of Vincent Street. There's an entrance from the lane at the back so the neighbours don't nark on you. And a landlord who doesn't want his slice in kind.'

It's a good set-up, she explains. She'd had a lolly shop in Parnell but the cops did their short beat outside and scared business off. She pays ten shillings a week for her room. It is twice what it's worth but like she says, who's calling the tune? She doesn't charge more for a shot, as she calls it, in case the cops tumble to her. The more you charge the heavier they'll lean.

'Who looks after you if you get sick?'

Greta looks at me and laughs. 'You are a do-gooder, aren't you, then?'

'I'd like to know how to buy and sell you for a better price. How it might be better for you.'

For the first time, she looks at me seriously. 'Are you running a drum?'

I answer her question with one of my own. 'Are different men after different things?'

'Only the frills. It comes to the same thing.'

'Special payments, then?'

'For special things.'

'Tell me. Exactly.'

'I have to go,' she says. 'I've missed the best time as it is.'

I know I have made her uncomfortable, that I puzzle her, and that is what she wants to avoid. I tell her I would like to see her again.

'That's what men say.' She says this with a smile that warns me not to pity her, not to invest in what is not my concern.

'A businessman, then. You can think of me as that if you want to.'

At the door she says, 'I'm sorry I have that cough.'

'You've seen a doctor, have you?'

'I don't need one to tell me what it is.' And again that slight, hesitant laugh, less bitter than at first I had taken it for. It is more a dry, hard amusement at the absurdity of how things are. I understand what she is saying. She knows too she is not a woman I would have working for me, however much I pitied her. She may have a few more months on her corner, and she then will sink. From sight, as we say. She knows what is passing through my mind. She says, 'That'll be all then, will it?' I give her a guinea more than I had promised. I can hear the soft brush of her sleeve against the wallpaper, even after she turns at the landing and I no longer see her.

Emily took me another time by train to Alexandra Palace. We left the station at Wood Green and walked up the slope to the great glass building. It was like a ship, I thought. There was a race meeting on the course below the hill, another course my uncle fancied for sprinters. There was also a fair — canvas booths and barrel organs and men who linked arms so another man stood on their shoulders, then a girl in a pink dress stood on top of him. We lay on the grass and heard the noise of the crowd below us heave and rise when the horses pounded into the straight. The beat of the racing horses was lost in the swelling roar. I remember it rained, and we ran under the glass dome that was so huge to a child. Then the sun came out and we walked back to the stalls and the man with no legs swinging himself like a pendulum on a wooden frame, who sang with a voice so deep it was hard to believe it was true. And after the rain the cut grass smeared across my new shoes and soaked them, and I began to cry. But Emily was happy because her young man sauntered up to us as if by chance. She did not even have to say to me that I was not to mention him to Gran. Emily swung her big blue hat from one hand and her fellow held the other. When I looked up to him he winked at me or moved his mouth like it was pulled down at one corner with a hook. His name was Harry. He came back with us in the train, and when he left us at the station he touched the edge of his little brown hat with one finger.

Just before we had got on the train we passed two women with their faces painted up as if for a joke. They stood near the wooden overbridge and smiled to people as they passed. Harry said something to Emily and she smacked his arm with her opened hand and told him 'Don't!' But she laughed as well and I looked back at the two women, who kept on smiling at people, and I noticed other people were laughing too, like Emily. As if it was all a game. And I have no idea how I knew, but it was as certain as if someone had shouted out to look at those there tarts. Tarts, as I already knew, were ladies who hold up their dresses for money, who let men put their hands there. Who nobody wants to talk to because if you're a tart no man ever wants to marry you, ever. Some of them got sick or even died from what they did. I have no idea how I knew all that. There must have been talk at school. When I looked back at the gaudy women, a soldier had put his own hat on the head of one of them and she took it off and skidded it out above the crowd and people cheered. 'Stop gawping back!' Emily had said and tugged me after her. I knew she didn't want me watching. And the two women kept grinning all the time like their mouths were fixed on. It is so strong a memory. And one of them holds a flag in her hand, a small Union Jack on a stick. My first glimpse of what we call the trade. And how different!

My first house is a wooden cottage above Newton Road. There are four girls. There is no room for more. Only three are here at any one time. We take half each of what they earn. They like me because I am straight as a die, as Miriam some time later says, and they know I will not let anyone put one across them. They cannot quite make me out, but that is fine with me. The girls call me Missus. I don't try to be their friend, and I know they are not quite as easy together when I am there as when I am not — yet they know they will not get a fairer deal than I give them.

It is amazing how the word spreads. We have enough custom to pick and choose. In two months' time we have no one calling who is not on a regular basis. It is amazing, too, how simple life seems. There are roster sheets and days for the laundry cart to call and the day Mr Sefton the accountant comes by and Mr Reynolds the jeweller on Tuesday and Mr Quin from the police is Saturday morning, and so everything has its place in a routine. It is as though I run a school.

'This place ticks over like a charm,' Carol says. 'You wouldn't believe what some of the places are like.'

I tell them, 'Don't take any tripe from anyone and don't think of yourselves as trash.'

'You got to use the right words for things, Missus,' Carol says. She is short and nuggety and the toughest of the girls. She has a boy at school, although I know that only after she leaves and another girl tells me. 'No point trying to pull the wool on that one.'

I tell them, 'You've decided on what you'll do for a living the way men decide on their jobs. It's simple as that.'

'Come off it, Missus!' Carol says. 'You got your nipples tugged round like mine's been this week you'd know it's not like that!'

'Nipples if you're lucky, don't you mean?' Ruby tells her. They joke together. It amuses them when I say not to think of themselves like that.

I watch them and say why can't they see what I'm saying to them? 'The words are nothing if you don't believe in them.'

'It's the words half of them come for. That's right, Carol?'

'Reckon I've talked as many off as any other way,' Carol says. There is a touch of pity, I think, in how they think of me.

Miriam is the one who says very little. She is tall and the picture of health, yet the least in demand with the regular men. She is also the one who will do anything. She puzzles me as the others do not. Although she is the one who will wear the different clothes they ask her to, who will allow herself to be tied or thrashed, and will give her body to whatever demand is made of her, she is oddly untouched by any of it. Nor does money seem to obsess her as it does Carol, and to a lesser degree Ruby. 'I love counting the takings,' Carol says. 'I'd piss on the lot of them for another quid.'

Her talk smears across the other girls. The filthier she can talk about it the more in command she is. I notice in time how many of the women work out their own tricks for doing that, for claiming that somehow they stand apart from what they do, that one way or another they hold the trump card. Only Miriam is quite indifferent. She will accept whatever goes, the degradation, the abuse, as if this is acting anyway, why bother to get worked up? I think Miriam's body is put apart from her somehow. It is pummelled and ridden as though it is someone else's but happens to have her name. I do not pretend to understand. She is more intelligent than any of the others — much more than I am, I know. In the quieter patches while the other girls sew or play the gramophone I have bought them, turning over and over their few favourite songs, John McCormick or Dame Nellie Melba or Harry Lauder, Miriam will sit and read. To look at her you would think she teaches a school.

I make a point of listening to whatever they want to tell me, without pressing them to confide. They do, of course. The dark girl who is married and works only in the afternoons has told me more, I suppose, than any other woman. Carol tells me how her father came at her when she was fourteen, her mum spewing through the wall from too much gin. 'You can guess what that was for too,' she says. 'She duffed more often than a rabbit.' Miriam is the one who scarcely says a thing. Yet she is the one who will take on customers the other girls refuse. I give her the room furthest from the small sitting room where they spend so much of their time, and I insist the gramophone is played when the rowdier ones are with her.

'You've got a lot of delicacy for a lady in this game,' Carol says to me one day, pushing me as far as she dares to go. She resents it that I am younger than she is. That I'm hard as flint, as I've heard her say.

'I'm not on the game,' I tell her. 'You are, Carol. I'm in business.'

One evening Miriam comes into the sitting room rubbing her forearm, her face glowing as if she had been running.

'Christ,' Carol says to her, 'you must of fair walloped that bloody sod.'

Miriam ignores her and addresses herself to me. 'I don't want any more tonight,' she says. 'I'll go home early.'

She does not explain herself, ever. I do not expect her to. Over the years, she is the one who stays with me longest. I have no idea if my affection for her means so much as a jot. But I am jumping ahead, by decades.

I have been in Samuel Cottage for three years when I decide to take another house. Ruby told me there was a cousin of hers on the game as well, who told her months ago Ma Murfitt was pretty near ready to toss it in. 'That old trollop,' Ruby said, 'she's been running shops since Adam first fancied a bit.' She winks at me and I have no idea what it is she means. A tall Australian girl then tells me Ma was famous because she kept on putting it across until she was close on seventy. She says, 'Like someone who owns a mine and works in it themselves. Don't come every day, do they?' Which, I suppose, is a sneer at me. But I like her tarty directness, and I am interested in what they tell me about Ma Murfitt.

'Thought no more about it than having another cup of tea,' Ruby says. She laughs as she tells me. 'Miserable old bitch though. Paid the girls thirty percent.' Ma was a Catholic too, it seems, like Miss Belle. 'No business over Easter. And December whatever it is. Our Lady's birthday.' Ruby says the story went round that during Lent she made the girls wear purple veils on their heads even when they were ballocky. But the latest of it anyway, Ma has this head sherang from the police in her own front room, handing over the kick-back for the force, when Ruby's cousin who's taking in the tray with the double malt and the two tumblers sees Ma's face go blue as if a sock's been jammed in her windpipe and she keels over from the table, dead as old mutton.

'That whole side of the gully,' Ruby says, 'there won't be a decent knock shop between here and Newmarket.' She is, of course, angling to run it for me.

That night I tell Miriam when she is the only one without a customer, and we sit in the tiny sitting room and she leans with her chin on her hands above the gramophone. She says, 'I could keep an eye on this place if you did take on Mrs Murfitt's.' As though she spoke, say, of watching a cake shop. She looks at me very solemnly, and she reminds me of Emily, before she smiles. I do not, though, want to feel more towards her than I do. I am not prepared for friendship. I do not want what they call normality, its wiles and works, its robes and ropes, the lie of its sincerity. My courage, such as it is, is to stand against those blandishments. The doctor told me once of a man he saw from a train in the middle of Oklahoma. It was flat, he said, flat as an upturned iron, a landscape that ran from one horizon to another, and all he could see in it from the passing train was a single man, tall and black, in the middle of that overwhelming space. The man seemed to do nothing; he stood near nothing he might have worked with to explain his being there; there was no road nor building nor fence even in sight. But the man held his hat in front of his overalls and watched the train racket by a hundred yards in front of him and neither waved nor moved, and the doctor said he was the vision of what we truly would like to be. He said how he had envied him, so certain in his world, so untouched, so distant from others. Miriam smiles at me as though at a friend, for the first time. For a moment she is not a whore and I am not the woman she works for, who sells her body and pays her half of what it earns. And I think of Emily's deep lovely stare before she laughed, and the doctor telling me that, about the man he saw from the train, in a space so huge that words like field or farm or countryside were little things, the breath of a passing moment, while the image of the man was large as his mind could hold.

Two of the girls who worked for Ma come to see me some days later. When I open the door they look at me and mistake me for one of the girls and ask can they talk with the lady from England? They say they'd like to work for me. They know I am fair and I'll take no nonsense from anyone. 'You got a good name, Missus,' one of them tells me. I notice the rash on the inside of the arm of one of them, and think, But I won't be taking you on, girl. I tell them I shall think about it.

'I haven't got the money, Miriam,' I say. 'Not quite enough.'

She smoothes out one of the doilies she works on. Then there is the quick glint of the crochet hook. Her face is so mild, so composed, I am fascinated, as I always am, simply to look at her. She is like a statue in a church. And she says, 'There must be someone you can lean on, mustn't there? Someone you've got the drop on?' She smiles quietly. She knows the advice she is giving me is sound, but she chooses to give it in the phrases Carol might have used. We both understand that, and smile.

Sir William's secretary, who I know instantly dislikes me, suspects I am there from a charity. Sir William is known for his support of different causes. 'Put a Sally hat on, you'll do even better,' Miriam had joked.

'Is it regarding some bequest?' the secretary asks.

'No. It is simply a private matter.'

The woman, whose name I later hear is Miss Clifford, watches me for some flicker that will put me clearly in one of her categories. I am wearing clothes as dull as I mostly wore on board ship, but my blouse is crimson. He will know I have entered the world a little but that I am still to some extent withdrawn. As I know how in these years since we talked he has prospered and become a public figure. I wear no jewellery, although for a moment before I left I held the sunset brooch in my hand as a kind of good luck charm.

'You know Sir William?' the woman says.

'Yes. He and Lady Goddard.'

Then it occurs to me it is my accent she dislikes. She says, 'I'll see if he is in.'

'I know he is in,' I say. I had seen a large green Buick in the lane beside the building, a man in a peaked cap leaning against the mudguard reading a folded paper and moving a pencil beneath what he read. I guessed whose car it must be.

'May I tell him who is calling?'

'You might say a family friend.'

'I'll have to see.'

'If you would,' I tell her.

'I'll have to see if he's *free*.'

The woman enters a door with a mottled glass panel. I see her outline against the glass. It is like the shape of something below the surface of water. Then she opens the door and stands where both the man inside the office and myself take in her smile. 'If you'd come this way, madam,' she says. As I pass her, our clothes actually brushing for a moment, I smell her perspiration, and a sweetish scent as well, something she hopes will cover it.

He is as urbane as I expect. He stands and comes around his large dark desk. I congratulate him on his title. He waves his hand and smiles, and tells me, 'My wife was so disappointed she never heard from you.' His wife in a silver frame on his desk. The photograph holds nothing of her vitality and fun. We talk a little about how long it seems since those leisurely still days crossing the Indian Ocean. He says he has been so busy since then he has scarcely had time to think. 'Apart from profits and losses,' he smiles. 'These ledgers.' His hand flips casually on the thick opened book in front of him. 'Those columns are my cage, you might very well say.' He looks at me directly. 'I see our antipodean air agrees with you.' His hair has gone quite grey since I saw him. I know he is aware of my noticing it.

I ask after Mrs Calder.

'Oh? You remember my wife's friend?' He says she now lives over here permanently, which is good at least for Annie.

'And her little boy?'

He moves the framed photograph a fraction, and says her boy, and the husband, are on the station still in Queensland. 'They become so attached to their land. Australians.' There is the slightest pause, and then a tapping on the frosted glass.

Miss Clifford brings us tea. We sit in two leather chairs. There is a glimpse of harbour, but I am surprised by the narrowness of the view. The aspect from Miss Clifford's room is more attractive. Sir William picks up my thought and gestures to outside the window.

'Views distract,' he says. 'There's nothing to do in here except work. Otherwise I never would.'

We both know it is time to come to the point. I say no, thank you, to more tea. He has the silver pot already poised above my cup. I say, 'I believe you own several houses in Mt Eden?' His glance at me is then so sharp, so drained of anything except an almost animal alertness, that for the moment I fear I have made a mistake in coming to him. So I tell him, directly, I am interested in renting one of them. The one nearest to town. I tell him I have heard the lady who rented it recently died.

He crosses to his desk, and I hear the soft rustle as his fingers move in a cigar box. He attends to the end of the cigar he takes up, then places the cutter back beside the box.

'Charming houses, although few enough would agree with me.'

'Charming?' I had not expected that.

'Proportion of the windows. The verandahs. It's the locality, unfortunately, people are aware of. That's what they buy. Not the look of the place. But you'll have noticed all that.'

'I've noticed the girls there,' I say.

Sir William lights his cigar with an elaborate attention, listening to its crackle against his ear, running his tongue along the stem, before he turns to me in a cloud of exhaled smoke.

'Are you a reformer?' he says, 'these days?' There is a change in the tone of the room.

'No,' I say. It is up to him to guess — or has he already done so?

'A blackmailer?'

I laugh, so that he knows I am not there to be unpleasant. But I know, suddenly — I cannot even tell why I am certain of it — that he realises I know about him and his wife's friend. And that she now lives here because their affair goes on. I guess too that he will protect that part of his life with an instinctive savagery, if he must.

He turns from the window and stands above me. I cannot make out the expression on his face, with that glare of light behind him. He is a dark shape in the smear of blue cigar smoke. I take in his relief when I tell him, simply, that I already run one whorehouse and I know Ma Murfitt's has come onto the market. 'I'd like the chance of getting it.' I say this in as neutral a way, I hope, as if speaking of a parsonage.

Sir William moves quickly from the window. He returns to the big armchair opposite mine, and sits and crosses his legs.

'You're a survivor, I see that,' he says.

I continue to look at him.

Then on another tack he says, 'I never quite believed the story you told us on board. Or at least Margaret didn't, and she convinced me.' He uses the name of his wife's friend very deliberately. It is an invitation to tell him more about myself.

I say, 'I don't want you to question me in any way.'

'Not question *you*!' He makes no effort to cover his irritation.

I assure him I am not the sort of woman to do anything rash. 'I want to lie as low as possible. No attention is the best attention. For all of us.'

'We've not yet agreed to anything,' he says.

'Not yet.' He understands, I think, that there is no compelling reason to prevent my doing anything.

What we then agree is that he will rent me the house. He will give me as reasonable a rent as the market allows. It will all be transacted through another party. He denies that he knew what Ma Murfitt was up to when he first let the place to her. It is important I keep his name quite clear. 'They wait for you to make a mistake,' he says. 'They love to catch us out.' I have no idea who he means. And we say nothing of what might at the worst be done with the knowledge each holds about the other.

He advises me, as I take up my purse from beside the chair and put on my gloves, 'If you're expanding your operations.' He smiles at the word he has chosen. 'If you're expanding,' he says again, 'it might not be a bad idea to employ a man. A kind of night watchman. Not all clients are gentlemen, as you may even know.'

'You're recommending someone?' I say.

'I will send a man who may be of some use. Only if you think so, naturally.' Sir William takes in my hesitation. 'He's an old bruiser,' he assures me. 'He's a brainless man you could twist entirely, that's all. But he'd sort out any trouble. He could do your garden as well!' And as though he also takes up another of my thoughts, he says, 'You needn't worry about him with the young ladies. There will be no problem there.'

We are standing again at the doorway. Sir William has lowered his voice, presumably aware of Miss Clifford's attentiveness. He says, as he picks at a speck of ash on his sleeve, 'You of course know Inspector Quin?'

'Only by name.'

'Not a bad thing to know him. Personally.' His hand is on the large glass doorknob. He repeats to me the name of a solicitor who will 'attend to all this'. Sir William shakes hands with me. We understand there is an agreement set in concrete. My unspoken assurance to him is that I shall not see him again.

Two years later, I buy another house, in Boston Road, and Ruby moves in there to manage for me. It is cheek by jowl with the prison, and is popular with the warders. 'The best insurance you'll ever get,' Ruby tells me. 'Got the force in the palm of our hands, you might as well say.' She also tells me we could do with a couple of native girls. There is nothing some men go for more than that. I mention this to Dr Savage, but his advice is not to touch them. 'Once you get your first girl with TB and that's put round you'll be out of business.'

Dr Savage is a tall, precise man who detests what I do but knows his vocation is to confront nature as it is. The girls believe he is cold and superior to them and at first they object to the inspections I insist on. 'I'd rather give it away to those prison buggers than have old Savage with his prodding about.' But it is Ruby I convince first. When she compares 'us', as the cottages are called among ourselves, with what she knows or hears of other houses, she sees the point of what I impose. 'Mind you,' she says, 'it's a wonder any bloke comes within sniffing distance. Those bastards in O'Neill Street where I used to work burned incense. You hardly knew you weren't in a temple or something. This place all you get a whiff of is mercury and whatever that other stuff is. Makes me think of embalmers. You might as well toss the beds out and bring in marble slabs.'

'You got customers'd fancy a bit of that, haven't you Miriam?' Carol provokes.

Miriam's eyes rise from her book. She looks at Carol without speaking.

'Sorry,' Ruby says. 'Sorry. I could have sworn that was Miriam who'd flog a nigger's arse for five bob, but it looks like the Mother Superior. My mistake.'

Miriam places her fingers in the folded wings of the book, and goes from the room.

'I don't get that high-and-mighty carry on of hers,' Ruby says. 'Do you, Missus? I just don't get it.'

'If we fight among ourselves,' I say.

The war, of course, will be the making of us financially. By its end I even have a home of my own. It is tall and grey and respectable, opposite a red brick church. It is here Miriam and Ruby and I meet to discuss the business. It is here they both like to come on their free days, and we play at ordinary women. Often I am here by myself. Darkie has a small wooden building out the back. His slightly backward son is sometimes there as well. Darkie who was a logger and a two-bit scrapper, and is now my protector. 'You'll need a man,' Sir William had said. At first sight he is a shambling, angry man of fifty, perhaps Irish, maybe Welsh, dark and nuggety and crude, derived from some stock he neither knows about nor cares for. 'I'm like Moses,' he tells me once, when I ask him where he came from. 'Find the buggers who knocked me up, then I'll know as well.' But he would sit in front of an oncoming tram if I told him it would make me happy. Darkie is my guard and my slave. He often spends evenings at one of the houses, where he disapproves of the girls. A good thing, Ruby says, it keeps him from wanting the occasional privilege. 'Not that I think he's up to it. Know what I mean?'

And so, the years. I have put on weight, although Miriam tells me I am still what she calls a looker. Now the girls seem so much younger than myself. There have been how many dozens of them? Carol dies in a fire on holiday in Sydney, Ruby is almost murdered in Samuel Cottage by a crazed soldier soon after the war. So many Beryls and Roses and Noras. Miriam, my only dear one. Most of them I remember, with neither affection nor dislike. I am fair and considerate, and I know I have given a better life to most of them than almost certainly they would have had without me. They keep on calling me Missus, or Mrs C. I am almost legendary, I suppose, as Ma Murfitt once was. I feel that nothing can now touch me, nothing move me. That what I determined that morning as I walked by the flickering black rails in Market Street I have indeed brought off. At least I have defied them, and on my own terms.

And day by day, I have been diverted. The business side of it — the squabbles, the very rare moment when I have feared exposure — have had a lift, you might say, about them. The absurd pecking order among the girls themselves. They are at the very borders you might think of the respectable world, and yet their plotting, their snobberies, their lust for edging ahead, for their brief dominance over men who might as well be hiring horses. Pride or vanity will always intervene, even among the plainest and the stupid. The sad human certainty that 'this is so for all the others. But *I* am special.' I think of how even Ruby, for all her watersider's tongue, the most cynical of all, would put on an act when Inspector Quin called round, like any other man, simply for trade. She would dab at her hair in the mirror, she would flatter him so that the others would say, Did you see how the Inspector fell for Ruby, did you? Just as behind the Inspector there is his own fantasy of power, the figure of Sir William, drawing on his cigar until it burns vivid as a coal between his lips. 'Sir' is what so entrances Inspector Quin. We are all like that. The circles we touch and nudge, like those big rings magicians clash for halls of gawping children, until *look*! One ring has actually passed into another! I imagine the intricate business of quietly spoken telephone calls, folded papers, the shrouded words and loaded hints, as one world overlaps with another, Sir William at his window, I with my whores. Sir William with his bankers, his judges, Inspector Quin's uniforms and cells. I at least see things as they are, name them as they are.

The Inspector sits with his cup and saucer like a child's miniature between his huge white hands. He directs at me his wide porcelain smile. Julie the Tahitian rubs her bust against him as she passes, brushing his balding head with its strands of hair slicked down so carefully across it. But I take this in, as I try to do everything, without the wrappings — can I put it like that? Without the lies, the self-deceptions, that fit on most things closely as a hood. Without that blur of sentiment and self-importance, the buzz that hangs over almost everything, like flies in summer seething across you are not quite sure what. Think clearly, I remind myself, don't let things blur. I can do that at least for Peter.

So what is the truth, you might ask? I have no answer for a question as meaningless as that. But from what I know, at least I can speak of fact. It is a man scrabbling at a woman's clothes in the shadows of a lifeboat as a ship cleaves through a piercingly brilliant night. There is the whisper as he fumbles at her, into her, the quick intense betrayal of two other beings who sleep or lie awake in the gentle, creaking rock of their cabins perhaps fifty feet from where the rutting against the rails racks off in rasping breaths, in the quick reassemblings of deceit. And since then, how much of my life has been tied into the words of coupling and its bargaining? The selling off of parts. The endless routines of sluicings, hygiene, sudden scares, the running of taps, the chink of basins, all hours of day and night. The garments hefted off and ripped, the girls afterwards slung back on the sofas, pale as dolls. What the world of the prosecution, the impassive judge, would like to call depravity and so put out of mind! Yet look, my trade insists to them, every single day. Look from your benches and your varnished seats. *This* is human nature. Beyond your clubs and churches and colleges and halls. This rut and gasp, this gush, this filth you condemn yet spend half your lives imagining, pursuing. Is not this at the centre of all your pretence? At the end of your wildest dreams, you ladies too with your high collars and your lowered hat brims, who hope as you lean forward in the galleries that the doctor may raise his eyes by chance and look into yours?

'What does life mean without God, then?' Gran used to ask, the spots rising on her cheeks at my uncle's cool provoking. Open any of my doors, I would tell her now. Hear that frantic gasp, do you? See that parody of epilepsy in every room, over and over again? That is as real as touching your finger to a flame. But then see them rise from that, one by one, like the resurrection. Put on their clothes, walk back into rooms where fuck will no more be said than a madman throws a bomb, where they sit and say, Let us talk about justice, let me tell you of God. We cockroaches who clamber one across another, let us talk of love.

Once I said to Miriam, an evening when she came back to the red sitting room, her cheek and one side of her neck rubbed raw by the grinding beard of her last encounter, and picked up the book she had left face down on the gramophone so as not to lose her place. I said, perhaps the most offensive of all things I could say, yet with an innocence which did nothing to prevent it hurting her, 'How can you put up with it?'

'The fucking?' she said.

'The make-believe. The lies.'

Miriam looked at me with what I know was contempt, however much she tried to cover it with her rough laugh. She said, 'I wouldn't worry too much about it if I were you, Missus.' The only time she had ever called me that, the name the other girls used. The name that placed us exactly, as even more did the next thing she said. 'Just make sure we get our fair whack when you tot it up.' Telling me I am the one in charge, but do not presume. *You are never one of us.*

She was right, of course. As I know there must be a level on which the girls even hate me. They know they are safer with me than in any house in the city. But I am not the one, am I, who finds myself several times a day in a darkened room, in the brown thick light from the drawn holland blinds, with a male I may detest or fear yet still lie beneath and feel his breath, his mechanical prod, the urging tangle of his words, while I know I am as interchangeable with the girl in the next room, in the next street, as the pegs on the wire stretched across the back verandah? They will take the birthday cakes I always have for them, the presents, the care that they regard me for, yet liking me is quite another thing. I am always *beyond*, I know that. I am always on the other side.

Sometimes, perhaps once or twice a year, I wake in sudden fright. There is always a time, a matter of seconds, until I swim back to myself. Until I know why the empty terror began. It is with the knocking on a door. I stand in my boy's clothes, the sunset brooch the doctor has given me grasped so tightly in my hand that for days I carry a cut on my palm from its spike. I am in my boy's shirt, behind the beating on the cabin door, and the doctor's hand moving from between my thighs. 'Hide it somewhere, love,' he says. The sunset brooch. Hide it, he tells me, for when I need it. And then I am awake and I look across the court, which presses at us like a zoo, and his gaze is waiting to hold mine. And I am proud not merely of him, but of *us*. Because *we* are what they hate.

Until the nun.

It is a morning of thin rain and sun when I leave Molly O'Connell's dress shop around the corner from Pitt Street and collide against the woman on the safety zone. She is older, and is wearing her ridiculous get-up. She smiles at me and holds my eye for what — two or three seconds? And so becomes part of my life. At first I will be irritated by what she means. Then later I will resent the contempt I assume she must have for me.

The first time Darkie sees me talking to her he will tell me, 'Jesus, Missus, you talk to that sort you'll talk to anybody!' Yes Darkie, I tell him, who on earth does she think she is? He will look at me, puzzled by whatever is going on. But then Darkie's life, I think, has been spent in something very like bewilderment, which he breaks up as crystal in the right light can fracture into different flashing points. One of the flashing bits is rage and another is his filthy tongue, and a third is loyalty to balance that fierce hatred when another part flares out. 'I've the very man for the job.' Wasn't that what Sir William had said? And a week later this shambling man with a gleam on his chin where a snick from shaving had hardened into a dark bead crunched along the gravel path at the side of Samuel Cottage, and Ruby, who had seen him through the patterned curtain, turned to one of the other girls and told her, 'You can take this rooster. I'm too young to turn it up for grandpa.' But when he sat in the sitting room he showed no more interest in duffing them than if they were bags of chaff. So Carol told me later. For he simply looked at them with no interest whatever, and after several minutes which the girls rather than he himself began to find awkward, he asked them, 'Is she there or isn't she? The old slag who runs the place?' And when Carol had come to get me and told me what a choice one we had in there to deal with, he looked at me and said as if he had merely come to do the garden, 'You'd better fill me in about what this lurk's supposed to be.'

'Stopping anyone who causes trouble,' I told him. 'Keeping an eye on things.' We had walked through to the verandah.

'Making a job of them?'

'What?' I said.

'Slapping the buggers up. Ones who get out of hand?'

'Is that what you do?'

'So they don't come at it again.' He then belted the top of the verandah rail with his opened palm, so fiercely I stood back at the impact of it, and the wood sprang loose from one of the struts. 'Didn't Shylock tell you that?' And I thought for the first time, Of course, of course he is, Sir William is a Jew.

Darkie has belted and slapped and talked too loud from that day until now. After a few weeks I tell him the girls would rather he didn't come into the sitting room. It is supposed to be reserved, I explain. A place where they can relax, stretch their legs out, I say.

'Try to get them together again you mean,' he says. He apologises when he sees his joke offends me. But he takes no offence himself that they want him to keep out or to be quieter when he comes into the kitchen in the evening and bolts the door closed. And Ruby says to me a little later, 'You know, Missus, old Darkie there, he wouldn't touch it if you gave it to him on a toasting fork. He's the perfect man for the job.'

I tell Ruby to lay off about him. I say, 'He thinks of you lot like daughters. He'd jump off the roof if you asked him to.'

'He's an uncouth old pig,' Liz says. She is a new girl who stays with us no more than a few months. 'He hates women's guts.'

It is towards the end of the war when I buy my own house in St Benedict's Street. It is in a line of tall attached houses of a kind you don't see often in this city of wooden crates, cottages, those few grand edifices with their verandahs along three sides. (Sir William's house I saw once in the *Weekly News*. There was a lawn with a monkey puzzle tree sixty feet high. The white house — the half of it you could see — was elegant and cold. There was a rocking horse on the verandah that made no sense, as I knew there were no children.)

I have tried to get Miriam to come and live there too, and not spend her life entirely in Samuel Cottage. I tell her there is no need for her to keep working. I say to her, 'Think how long we have known each other, Miriam. Ten years at least. We're friends. We don't just work together.'

'I know we're friends,' she says.

'Then isn't that enough?'

She puts her hand for a moment across mine. 'I'm fine so long as I'm here,' she says. 'In *this* house. Try to see that.'

I have no real idea of what she means. In any case there are now only two younger women with her in Newton Road. It is so quiet that at times you might think it is a family home. The house has not in any true sense been 'open' since Carol moved out, marrying an Australian who said what did being on the game for a bit matter any more? He had killed people for nothing he believed in. Next to that, he said, what's a bit of rutting? I remember him in the red sitting room. I had bought champagne. He was a wiry man with a strange, broad accent. He said, without bravado or offence, 'We're all so covered in shit, Missus, it's like we're pure as snow. Who's going to say I'm wrong?' We liked him but we were glad when he left. Miriam was the one who said, 'God help Carol then. No one wants to live with truth that close in your face.'

Miriam. In a way I have become obsessed with her. She jokes with me, 'You're not old enough to be my mother,' when I insist that she at least leave the house for an evening.

'A weekend,' I say, 'we could go somewhere together?'

She spends so much of her time alone, apart from the men who more and more seem not to want normal fare, as I rather stupidly put it. I sometimes see the marks on her legs, the rope burns on her wrists.

'Two hours a day,' she says, dismissing it. 'I never do more than two hours a day.'

She talks mostly to young Spicer, who is nothing like his father. He is a foot taller than Darkie, so much slower-witted. She pampers him, almost like a mascot. I hear them laughing in her room as I wait for her among the velvets and potted plants of the sitting room where we take supper every night. The other two girls prefer to sit in the kitchen where they make endless pots of tea, and lean towards the shiny embroidered circle in the middle of the wireless I have bought them. It is a kind that has only just come out. The girls leaning towards it remind me of women who pray, leaning forward in their chapel.

I say to Miriam, 'You're a great one for admirers!' It is the evening when Spicer has brought the lace for her, and Darkie, shagged leg and all as he likes to remind you, has gone down to the bus depot to pick up a sack of nectarines one of Miriam's regulars has sent her from

Waiuku. I have piled the fruit into a large dish for her, and carried it through to her room. The lovely colours of the nectarines and the glowing yellow of the plate.

I say, 'There, doesn't that look something?'

Miriam scarcely gives it a glance. She is standing at an opened drawer in the long chest where she keeps her things. She is holding a cane switch that has splintered and frayed at one end.

'I'll need a new one of these, won't I, see?' She runs a finger along the exhausted wood. 'There's hardly a session left in this one.' That is all she says.

She has never told me so, but of course Miriam is quite as old as I am (and I am older now, by years, than Miss Belle when she first sailed into the office on Oxford Street, the one day she ever wore the sunset brooch, her teeth so white I thought nothing in nature is as brilliant as that, before she spoke and I realised she too was an American). She makes no effort not to look her age, yet I quite see — I imagine I can see — what it is in her that makes the boy so infatuated. The younger, so carefully made-up women seem not to touch Spicer at all. He is polite, as he always is, but they are no more than shop-girls, say — than women he might speak to but scarcely notice. But Miriam absorbs him. It is the sense, is it — I try to explain it, but can do so only clumsily — the sense that you will never, could never possibly know more of her than what you see? That even in those costumes of hers, the dark heavy revealing strips of leather, the tall animal confidence as she sometimes walks through to the sitting room to ask me to change a note while a man waits in her room, and she is unconcerned who sees her in the shoes that so elevate her, the buckles and the thongs crossed along her thighs, that none of this reveals who Miriam is, any more than it conceals. I do not even have the words to say what, in any case, I only half understand. As if this woman I have come so to care for is somehow nowhere at all, not there, not absolutely, in the body I have seen so often and am, I suppose, fascinated by as well. And yet she is nowhere else either, if not exactly there. As if her surface and her depths (her soul, my other friend would say) are no longer simply where they should be, and yet how can they be anywhere else?

I see Spicer sometimes touch her arm, lay his opened hand on her knee, and yet there is nothing in it of the kind of touching my houses exist for. It is something I know Peter would have understood. She would let Spicer do as he liked, I suppose, should he ask her. Although I am not sure even of that. Or that Spicer would want to ask. But adores is the word, the only word, for how the boy thinks of her.

So the years have flitted past, as we say. How I come back to saying that. There have been books written about the doctor. About us. I see them mentioned in the papers, and one of them I look at in the library in St Mary's Bay Road. I sit at a large table, with my back to the room, and read about myself. Peter's face looks back at me from the page, so mild, so inoffensive — a gentleness that has something to do with what excites the readers, for the book's edges are grey with handling. The *disposal*, I suppose, as they like to think of it. It is a favourite word in the book. And Miss Belle, so much plainer, more coarse than I remember her. It must be a photograph she had taken for her agent. She wears a costume from another century that shows her shoulders, her bust, as dull expanses without their living vividness. I know how they love to imagine that as well, those large confined breasts, her handsome arms, the provocation she excelled at. And then the mild man who must have stood in utter silence as she lay unmoving, at last, in front of him. And the story too, the details they like, of our running off, my haircut, my man's suit too large for me, a handsome boy. So I sit on, my hand resting across the book, and I am no longer simply there. I stand in my black socks and the long white shirt buttoned to my throat, and nothing more. The doctor's hand brushing so lightly against my leg, his nails, their merest tips, at the inside of my thighs. His fingers move in reverence, that is the only word that comes to mind. I lay my forehead against the wiry cloth of his jacket. His other hand moves now against the grain of my shortened hair, and across my neck. I shudder, so strongly and suddenly, in the summer warmth of the Institute reading room that I quickly turn. Thank God there is only one woman there, her back towards me as she stands before the shelves. I close the book and for a moment touch its cover, his name spelled out so large. Then I walk into the dazzle of the street. I raise my hand to shade my eyes against the glaring bulk of the Post Office across the road. My heart pelts, as if my years of control, of subterfuge, have brought me no further than this, only minutes from the creaking cabin and the rapping on its door. His hand for a moment warm and certain as it spanned my neck.

I walk the length of Ponsonby Road, back through the dip and the rise of Newton Gully, before I am — what was my Gran's phrase? — *collected*. My wits collected. Darkie flourishes his clippers at the small hedge in front of the house. He stands back as I click the latch of the gate. He makes a show of drawing his naked arm across his forehead and says, 'Hotter every day, Missus.' And I laugh, because it has struck me for the first time that here I am in my forties, and I have been called nothing else for nearly twenty years! I tell him, 'I don't know how we'll survive if it keeps on like this, Darkie.'

He shows the puffed pale cushion of his bad gums, and tells me, 'We'll survive by doing nothing then. That's not a bad lurk.'

I don't quite know what he means, but 'Will we?' I say.

'Always works, that one.'

I enter the hallway with its rose-patterned strip of lino, the smell of polished boards along its sides. And I am thirty pounds heavier, my God. As if we need more of a disguise than time! I think of that girl in the book who was slim and elegant, her boots high on her calves, her hair close against her face as she turns from the thrusting camera. The doctor's head had come close against hers, that first time, in the soiled London light, beneath the gash of dirty glass in the warehouse roof. There is nothing really after that, I remember, except love, and then those who want to kill it. There is so much, so quickly. I and she, the girl in the book. There is happiness packed so close, there is the knock, and he takes her hand. He places the sunset brooch inside it. He has told her already what it is worth, how its jewels will keep her going, should she ever need it. He kisses her on the cheek and opens the cabin door. He tells her the last thing, while she buttons her clothes, his hand on the door's brass handle. 'Bear up there, little lady!' The captain enters the cabin and removes his shining peaked cap. The Inspector from Scotland Yard who becomes famous steps in behind him. There is hardly room in the cabin for all those who want to enter. It is so long ago, yet it is so easy to think of myself as her, to think there is no time at all between then and now.

'I can understand that,' the nun says.

Marie-Claire

I AM ON THE TOP OF A SAND DUNE, FACING THE WIND FROM THE NORTH. I am not sure whether to run, to come to the line of folding surf against the long curve of the beach. I think I would rather go back to the hotel, to the man with the gold braiding on his shoulders, who will open the thick glass door and call me 'Mademoiselle' as no one has ever done before, apart from my grandfather when he is joking. I would then dash up the stairs where the sound of my boots is lost in the mossy carpet, and sit alone in my room, the sunlight glimmering along the brass fender, glinting on the bed ends, making me think of the burning iron that heretics had to carry to prove their peace with God. I have read about them in a book that was once my mother's. She had written something beside it on the margin, but I cannot read her writing, which seems to me, at this age, a deliberate scribble. Writing that is meant to keep me on the other side.

But I do not go back to my hotel and the room I so enjoy. My brother has already run barefooted ahead of me, his legs blurring in the high bright light, a scrambling spider as he crawls another dune, then flies down the far side, running towards the sea. I sit down and pull off my black boots, and roll the dark woollen stockings from my pale legs, and take off after him. The sand is warm and slippery and lovely against my naked feet, and the wind ruffles at my skirt. I feel such exhilaration as I rise on the next incline of the dunes, my feet all but floundering to a standstill in the deep sifting of the sand. Then I feel myself flicker across the last level stretch towards my brother. He is facing me, his arms held out from his sides, the sleeves of his loose white shirt whirring swiftly in the wind, and behind him the distance — so vast to me at ten years old, at the ocean's edge. There is a great arc of bending white water pouring against the land, spray riding in a haze above its tumult. I am calling out suddenly, my words whisked away on the wind. My brother leans forward. He is like a bird, I think, on his skinny tilted legs. 'What?' he is calling to me. 'What?'

My memory stops there. I have no recollection of our walk back to the hotel, or of much else we may have done for the rest of our holiday, and my father scarcely survives at all from those ten days. I have some fleeting image of the dining room, the white cloths almost stiff as cardboard, and the silver napkin rings of the special guests, the ones who stayed there longer than the rest of us, who had no homes, I thought, except hotels. There was a small group of musicians playing while we ate, in a space that must have been well lit, because the hands of the players are so clear, the quick shot of light on their moving cuffs. My brother eats enthusiastically, which my father always approved of. His boy might be thin but at least he was healthy. They often laugh together. I sit on my hands until when I remove them from beneath my thighs they are raw red, and sometimes tingling with pins and needles, and when I look up at the waiter who stands beside me, I look at him so intently that my father frowns at me and coughs. Then I gaze in front of me at the bowl of such clear soup that I see the pattern on the bottom of the plate, a small sprig of flowers that later I will think is like tea-tree. For I am given a child's plate, not the wide white ones my father and brother eat from, although my brother is only a year older than me. My hands push hard against the wooden sides of the chair while I imagine I can make my weight press down more heavily on them, deaden the feeling even more. I am aware of the potted tree only a few inches above my head, a wide green hand, and through the pale liquid in front of me the sprig of tiny flowers rocks with the movement of the table. And the music — at least now — is always the one tune, over and over, the German tune so much in fashion, which my English grandfather liked to whistle, those notes which are the earliest I remember, apart from hymns. Yet I must have eaten as sensibly as my brother. For I am a healthy girl in an orange-faded photograph, a girl a little too heavy, a sensual mouth I expect an unsympathetic eye might detect, and a smile which I cannot fathom, although it is my own. A girl of ten who liked running on the beach, who watched her brother's every movement with admiration, who seemed not to be disturbed that unlike most girls she no longer has a mother, and yet remembers so little of her father from that holiday, the most important thing in her life until then. Those days under the pouring movement of the skies, beside the heaving sea, and over there was as surely England, as it was France if I turned and faced the other way.

My father is an agent for an English company in Lyons, although his office is in Sens, and we live more remotely still — in Villeneuve-sur-Yonne. He is efficient and brisk, if you happen to meet him through business, but privately he worries that he be thought sentimental, which he is. I realise even as a child that he is a little afraid of the world. He would do anything love is capable of — which is not so very much — to prevent his son and daughter being wounded by how things are. He believes it is a world that seems to offer one so much, then arbitrarily dashes that promise from one's grasp. Yet he is far too considerate, far too deliberately secular, to hint at such things as we come in on summer evenings from playing near the river, our eyes tired and gritty from the day's sun and the pushing wind, or when we have come in late — after nine, indeed! — from an evening with our grandfather at the fairground, among the grinding thump of the great mechanical organ, while the wooden horses rise and fall with their splotchy haunches, their flax tails, their blood red flaring nostrils deep as egg cups. He will never so much as hint to us, bright and wind-burned as we are, what he is so convinced of at these very moments — that all things will pass, that delight is precious and rare. And so we must both love and mourn for it while it is there. Father's way is to intimate all this by sighs, by rubbing his eyes with his middle finger and thumb, holding us with his sad naked stare before replacing his elegant pince-nez, its crinkled black ribbon attached to the lapel of his jacket. He will look at us and say, 'My dears, you make me very happy.'

In my teens I believe too, without giving it a great deal of thought, in my father's remote and surely lonely celibate life. When I am at the river settlement more than twenty years further on, on a Sunday morning when I am sent to call the children in their stiff European suits from clambering in the shaking marvellous dapple of the orchard, I sit on a large abandoned wagon wheel to read the letter François has sent me. I know it will be about our father's will. The image of my father has set so long before: a youngish middle-aged man in sombre clothes, who observed the world pass in its vanity with an easy, comforting melancholy. Who, in my childhood, seemed always to check papers in unknown languages through the tilt of spectacles where his desk-lamp shone in two bright pips. And now my brother's letter, which will be worried, nervy, as all his letters are. He too is set in those few determining pictures we carry from the past, my thin-legged spidery sibling on the side of a Normandy dune, his weight flung on one leg and then on the other, graceless and near-exhausted as he shouts and reaches the top, the sea there, his glittering reward. The sea, the sea!

In the sweet warm light, with the children now whooping down past the dormitory towards a wagon making heavy weather of the slope from the yellow banks, I look again at the stamp on the envelope, the sower with her hand flung out behind her, the arc I imagine of dispensing seed, and the address in broad purple strokes. 'Nouvelle Zélande' is underlined with a flourish, as though for a moment the exoticism as he thinks it of that distant and resented place had flared into my brother's wrist, the swirled line declaiming where his civilised world decidedly signed off. They all mean so much less to me, I know, than they do to him, 'these painful facts', he calls them. He is saddened to tell me, with as much delicacy as he can manage without being quite obscure, what had shocked him so profoundly. I fold the letter with no feeling much of any kind. Perhaps a little pity for my father. 'You have no sentiment,' my father told me once, as I stood, a sixteen-year-old, defying not his commands but his mind, refusing to share his opinion of the Church. 'No finer responses.'

I think of that as I fold the letter, running my thumb on the embossed seal of François' business firm. The two pages, written I know with as much embarrassment as care, inform me that what we might reasonably have expected to be our parents' considerable estate does not exist, for either of us, beyond a token bequest. There were three women, François said. It seems one or another of them had been there for those decades from our holiday in Normandy, when Father had taken up with the first of them as we spent our days on the dunes in that piled silver light. Strange, I suppose, that the news scarcely touched me, certainly not in any sense that disturbed or disappointed me. Yet my brother, who believes himself such a pragmatist, was galled with what was so clearly a moral rather than financial hurt. And so it comes home to me, as I sit in the orchard, above the dark tugging arc of the river between its sombre banks, that what someone like François so frets about as 'morality' hardly comes into my thinking. I mean, I do not *judge* in the way such sternness seems to demand. My place is here. My belief in God is utter. I do what I have chosen to do. As for my judging others — how can that come into it?

I walk up the slope, through the heavy summer grass, into the coppery tang of the long kitchen. Mother looks up from the jars she is filling from an enamel jug so large she has difficulty supporting it. 'You can stick the labels on the ones I've done,' she says. Then she adds, thinking aloud as she often does, 'Measles may seem little enough today, Sister. It's the next generation we have to think of.'

A child runs past the table and his foot catches on one of the thick wooden legs. Two of the jars fall sideways, their contents slopped across the table's scrubbed white top. Mother bellows after him in Maori. And then to me, in her own tongue, which more and more, as she now says, she uses only to pray, as if only God any longer seems to understand decent French, 'It's the will of God I suppose that we show endless patience. Endless.'

I love her, I admire her so much at this moment, I think I shall never be happier with her than I am now. This is not because of mere natural warmth between us. It can never quite be that. With this small aging woman and her sudden irritations, her certainty of being 'called' in a way no others of us dare to presume, her vast passion to knock a stupid world into shape, there is always distance of a sort. It is her *activity* I love, her refusal to accept that nature any more than the law of bishops or judges is to be taken as the final word. I think here at least I understand her, her will to confront all things in total truth, to leave things better than she found them. If that means nudging even the Divine Will — well, sometimes one may have to do that as well! Her spiritual depth is her refusal to concede. 'That is all God asks of us,' she says at times, her face tilted above her clasped hands as she advises those of us who are younger, so much less wise, although wisdom is a word she shies away from. The religious life is a matter of looking at things squarely, looking straight. And how do we do that, Mother? 'Learning what to put right,' she says, 'then doing it.' Or on another occasion, on the long verandah, 'Realising we have one world at a time. Make a fist of the one we are in.' She likes to clip our spiritual wings — can I put it like that?

My name for religious purposes — as if there are any others — is Sister Martine. François, who takes after our father in his energetic secularism, addresses his letters to me as 'M-C. Depoux', as though those old initials, with our family name, might at least in his own mind make my hair grow once again to the brilliant cape it was, or somehow remove the habit which Father told me was insulting my body for the sake of a most unlikely pay-off. 'Heavenly cover,' he sardonically called it, an insurance broker's joke. Or perhaps my brother may be nowhere near so imaginative as that. He may address me like this simply to defy the conventions of the life I chose. Or more likely still, to spare himself the embarrassment of his staff being reminded of how 'the scientific century', as Father called it, was so let down by the frail female of the family. How a freemason, and later a Dreyfusard, is so related to this distant Pacific fragment of the *Ancien Régime!* It is so hard to imagine what remains, if anything, of that anxious tender boy who took his lead from me until we were well in our teens. I remember how angered he became that I could write so much better than he could ever manage as he puzzled over his exercises. That is how I see him now, still more a boy than a man of almost forty, puzzling over having to write 'Jerusalem, Wanganui River'.

Marie-Claire Depoux was a clever enough girl. She was trim, like her English mother, with the loveliest hair, her father would tell her, of any child on either side of the Yonne, 'even if you stood on the tower of Notre Dame, and looked every way.' He was also — even before the 'catastrophe' — disconcerted by her far more than he could ever quite say. By her broad attentive stare, to begin with, which became a social embarrassment in her even as a child. He would tell her in public places that it was not the thing to do, to look at people for so long. He asked his sister, with whom the girl was sometimes sent to stay, to watch her particularly. Would she do what she could — it was so hard for a man, a widower, to say those things as they should be said — do what she could to curb that curiosity which at times transfixed the child? She would try, her aunt said. And to the girl — on a pleasure boat on the river, in a church in Paris, where the women's hats, if you remember the style at that time, were such a forest of amazing breadth and colour — her aunt would remark that to stare was not the thing, that *ladies* never stared. Her father continued to be irked by it. 'It is primordial,' he said. His favourite word for what society could not bring to heel.

I have this habit of thinking of myself, especially at such distance or such a time ago as that, as though this 'she' is not quite myself. I realise how this is an egotism of an inordinate kind, that there is always vanity in it, this fancying yourself as though one part of you performs while the other is your audience. I mention it once to my friend, as I seem to mention so much that I speak of to no one else. She laughs and says, 'My girls do that. Some of them. They think the creature in the mirror is more exciting than themselves.' I smile back at her; I say perhaps that is so. But it is not, I know, the vanity of mere prance. It is a way to look at myself with the hardness I look at another. I know 'looking hard' is something I shared with Aubert. No excuses, she liked to say. No beating about the bush. 'God is the greatest pragmatist,' she said.

Marie-Claire was eighteen when she broke the secretiveness of her thinking, and insisted to her father that what she has chosen to do, she will do. For the first time, she saw him pale with anger. 'Hugger mugger,' he said to her. It was the week after she had refused an offer of marriage from one of his colleague's clever, handsome sons. 'Hugger mugger with your religious fantasies — all these years, and not a word until now!'

She repeated her father's words, the odd phrase that he grasped at in his anger. 'Hugger mugger with God, that's all.'

He told her she had failed as a daughter and a woman. She was too cold, he said, too intellectual. 'A woman,' he lamented, 'is the better for being warm.' His eyes, however, dropped before hers, and he turned the bronze inkwell on his desk.

She thought how he was not in any sense a vicious or difficult man, simply rather a shallow one. And she was within a fraction of leaning forward, of putting her arms about the alpaca jacket, or kissing him, trying to explain, 'It is not a choice of you or *Him*, my dear. Choosing Him includes you too.' But the moment passed, and François tapped at the door, and their father shouted back to leave them alone, will he, for God's sake? And she regretted for ever that she neither said that to her father nor embraced him.

It was soon after that I travelled with my grandfather to Lyons, to begin my training. He was a dear, idealistic Englishman, who loved France without ever truly understanding her. His dream was the France of revolution, of liberal politics, of the men he met in a dull, smoky café in rue Carnot, who said when they were younger they too had been firebrands, and who now exchanged books and papers like conspirators. Proudhon, he would say, now there was the man to sort them out. He did not know — he did not want to know — that France, for all her faults, is irredeemably Catholic. (I think, even as I say it, what a curious adjective to use!) He places his hand across mine as the train moves through the placid countryside and the small towns. He says the names of stations as we stop or skim past them. He believes, I am sure, that this is a secular litany, a roll-call of the world I have given up, a requiem for my lost youth! I do not say to him that the self-denying cage he thinks I am entering is in fact a place of glorious egotism, a place where the only two things that can ever matter to me will perhaps not always be at ease, but certainly together without distraction: myself and God. But suppose I could say that, would he not ask me, 'Then why the *Church*? God if you have to, but why *that*?' And I would not know how to tell him, as I might say to him later on, 'Because, dear Grandfather, we are all born into history, and must do what we can with that. There is nowhere else, no other doorway but the one in front of us.'

It will be a long time before I can say that. The gift we may come to only at knifepoint. So I look from the window at the flashing slip of vines and clustered houses, and the broad fields where — another theme of my grandfather's — the marvellous pagan Celts set up their stones, their regime of sky and quartered time and cosmic centre, before the Franks rode in with the sweeping swords of barbarism. I watch the lovely country without regret, and smile at him. Had I listened to him, condescended to him less — had I even thought, when he recited the lines I only half attended to from his favourite English poet, that he too may have had a view of life which was as valid as mine. (I will be sixty-four when I come to admit as much. I will be sitting in the aura of my own decay, behind a slow-witted driver and a woman who is worse, most people would think, than a whore. The eyes of a maniac will attempt to hold mine.)

My grandfather, in his gentle but insistent voice, recites the history of the city we approach. He tells me, finally, as the train moves beneath the great iron bow of the station, 'You are part of all that, *ma fille*.' All that, the human flow he means, which after all is all we have, and I choose to step aside from it. He says he may be the last man I will ever talk with in utter liberty. It is so typical of him that this is his final appeal. It is not the flesh I give up, as I suspect Father so regrets. It is not the mere social expectations of François. My grandfather, so self-indulgent, so English, so easily fearful in his rationalism, appeals to something else. To the words, the speech, that may no longer be mine — the things I am no longer free even to say.

I know now, of course, that I gloried in what I thought was my uniqueness. It is not that very different, I expect, whether we are nuns or anything else: we all do much the same. We run our solitary drama, the tangling of one human will in our uneven contest with the divine, but are we ever as extraordinary, as unique, as we like to believe? Soeur Martine, arrayed in white as the young bride of Christ. Young and beautiful. I quite exulted in that, although I would not for the world have admitted so. 'She gives up more than most,' I imagine I overhear. When the blades of the scissors run cold against my neck, and my hair like a living creature slides down my back, I shiver with a gust of feeling that takes me by surprise. It is the moment we postulants wait for, so rich in symbols, the moment, so we believe, when our families will sob, for that is the moment when we indeed give ourselves to one world while they remain in another.

Much later I suspect that so much of my *frisson* was pure theatre. I have no qualms that I may not have been sincere. But was there not more than a dash of spiritual pride in my certainty that I was so much stronger than those two resentful and disparaging men, in the pews set apart for relatives, might ever be? (Two men, as only my grandfather and François agreed to come. My father refused. I have wounded him, he says, but that is not the point. He would not come and watch at the moment when I so implacably wounded myself.) But, thank God, there was so much more beyond my weakness and my vanity. So much immeasurably beyond them, as the dark wire of the horizon was beyond the little sand dune where I stood that day as a girl. The immense encompassing reality of God diminished my flicker of pride to what it was — a glint on a single wave towards that horizon, a momentary crest that flamed only because of what it reflected so minutely.

I suppose if I were obliged to say so — an unlikely thing — I would say most of what I have done in my life comes down to two things. Or that is what I would like to be able to say. Whatever the bigger things, the theological virtues, the divine scheme or whatever, life as we live it, day by day, is this: it is to say things as they are, and then act as best we can in that fragment of time that has been allotted to us. Truth and action. Action and truth. There is no precedence between them. Everything else adheres to those.

And so when Kate says to me once, in that frankness she too easily thinks will offend, 'What does your life add up to?' I tell her — I shock her telling her — that so much of it is the dreariness of service, so much of it, too, is pus and defecation, pustule and chancre, dribbling age and regret, the endless regret of being born into a fallen world. She laughs uncomfortably as I tell her that. She calls through to one of her girls to bring us tea. The girl, a few minutes later, carries through a tray with pink cups. There is a band of gold around their rims, down the centre of their handles. She blushes, I can see, that a *nun* is here, of all places! She has thrown a shawl across her shoulders to prevent my catching the low plunge of her frock. As if flesh in its healthiness will somehow shock me!

'The last truths,' Kate says. 'Isn't that what you call them?'

'The four last things?'

She does not ask me what they are. But, 'What is it like?' she says. 'Spiritual intensity?' As she raises the polished teapot and holds the cup with its reflecting streaks towards me, she is smiling but no longer mocking. And I know my answer disappoints her, as I know it would more than disappoint the community I live with. All but Aubert in fact, who would not agree, but at least would understand.

I tell Kate, 'I don't know what you might mean by spiritual, if you try to imagine it apart from' — I move my hand towards the door, the outside street, the world generally, I suppose — 'apart from simply this. I mean we live in one world, always, which is spiritual and here as well. I don't know why we so long to separate them.'

I had once tried to say as much during a retreat, to a Redemptorist father. I told him the clutter of the world was where I most felt God.

'In serving Him there?' he said.

'No!' I said, 'I mean I know Him *there*, because that is where He is. Not behind it, I mean, somehow waiting for this bit to get over with.'

I knew I expressed it badly. I knew words would never do what I wanted them to — how could they? But the priest seemed put out. He said, stroking his knee impatiently, 'I don't believe I heard that, Sister.'

85

'It is the total arc of life,' I tried to say. 'We live along that arc, it burns at every minute, its total length, from the intensity of whatever point we are at that moment.'

'I advise you, Sister,' he said, 'to beware of spiritual pride.' And he instructed me that the greatest sincerity in even the most ardent of souls will not for long survive the corrosions of striking out on one's own. As if the traditions of the Church, the wisdom of its direction, are somehow not enough. I was surprised that my words had caused him such distress.

It was a few days after my twenty-third birthday when I sailed into a harbour so sheeted in squalls that it was another two days before the wind fell and you could open a door without an enormous hand pushing you back inside. And then, it was there, my new country! The fact that it was so ugly, so without taste or finish, did not bother me in the least. Sister Regine, a dull, extremely pious girl from the South, who travelled out with me on the same ship, cried for several nights after our first trips into the city in the heavy, lumbering tram. She saw only the unfinished streets, the ripped-open hills, the houses like wooden crates, the gape of a people whose faith of course was not ours, as they looked at us as they would at grotesques from a fair. Good people, I now know, but in those days, before we had even makeshift competence with their language, they struck us as coarse-grained, ill-dressed peasants, as Regine said, done up as though for their Sunday stroll. But Regine is at once given two ill babies to care for, so that within days she is too tired to complain about so mere a thing as the local people's looks! I am overheard, nonetheless, as I try to buoy her up.

'There's a kind of freedom, surely,' I tell her. 'There must be, mustn't there, being among things we don't care for?'

Regine looks at me, without taking in my meaning. But Aubert puts me in my place. 'Don't worry yourself with philosophy, child. Get on with the work we are here to do.'

She herself hands me the bucket and the chunk of yellow soap.

After the children's dormitory, when I feel I must have earned at last a little rest, and one of my knuckles is bleeding from where it caught on a metal screw angled out from near the floor, she directs me at once to the ward where the aging ill look out across a little stretch of lawn towards high ugly slopes, scarred where trees have recently been cut and dragged down. This whole country, I think, is a jaw that has been ripped by a mad dentist! Some of the sick lie all day and look at nothing else, or when the cloud is low, at the endless shred and streaming along the tops. I do not know how the poor souls can be anything but depressed, there is such melancholy in those awful hills. I shall never become used to them.

By the end of that first day I am what now I would call well and truly whacked. In the next few weeks Aubert varies my work, so that there is no tough or unpleasant job I have not done for days at a time — except, I feel, use the skills I have, the actual tending of the sick that I am trained to do. (Years later she will joke at what a challenge to her my fiendish pride had been!) She decided that the great bins for coal at the back of the kitchen must be repainted inside and out, which meant that I was blackened scrubbing out the bins even before the coal-tar paint was applied. I wore a kind of overall made from sacking, and a hood from the same cut-up sugar bags, a caricature version of a bulky friar. I had never held a painter's brush in my life, any more than I had realised how coal dust will get through any number of layers of clothing, so that even to clean the grey rim left in the bath is another trial. Yet I do not, for all that, find such labour quite the ordeal Aubert intends for me.

Regine, at one point, comes as she believes to console me, to tell me quietly she prays for me, she understands how difficult it must be.

'It is a matter of offering it up,' she says, her large intense eyes following me, so that I think without any intention of unkindness of that slow heavy look of animals as you walk by them in a barn. And I laugh, and realise too late that I have hurt her when I say, 'This is a bit of a game that's going on, that's all.' She is hurt, because her chance to commiserate is not quite working out. And because there is an implied rebuke of Mother, whom I believe is testing my will. Regine says, 'You must remember that from our novitiate, Martine? Obedience does not require that we attempt to explain why.'

I take up the brush with its heavy clogging paint and say, shortly enough I suppose to hurt her over again, 'I'm sorry I'm not more upset for you.'

And so it comes home to me, more vividly then than it has at any other time, that the big sacrifices, as the world thinks of them, are not the challenges of religious life so much as these, the pinpricks, the irritations from those who are so close to one, who serve God as purposely as one does oneself. I shall never want to rob a bank, to kill, to choose a man before God, to offend anyone with premeditation or malice. But I know, standing in my sacking gown, with paint smeared across my nails, across my swollen knuckle, that when Regine speaks to me in attempted comfort, I am facing the kind of threat that most truly eats at my soul.

I think Aubert hints at something rather like this, in her offhand yet careful way, when a few nights later she asks me into the small parlour where she has set two cups and the shortbread biscuits she so fancies. She says nothing of the test she has put me through. She pours tea for me, and places the cup on the oil cloth in front of me. She takes two biscuits and eats the first before she speaks.

'I expect these are my alcoholism. These and sugar,' she says, sinking a heaped spoon into her black tea. She watches the rush of darkening liquid through the piled sweetness. And she takes me by surprise with her next remark. It assumes, for one thing, that I am much cleverer than I am, although I recognise the name from the books on my grandfather's shelves. Or perhaps it is simply her way of telling me it is a life of service I have chosen, not one of meditation. Certainly I will come to know, over the years, how slightingly she thinks of mere contemplative orders. So it is activity she is telling me about, the immense point and satisfaction in that, when she says, 'I have often thought, Sister, a few buckets of water and a bout of decent scrubbing may have done wonders for Schopenhauer.' But there is something of a joke in her saying so. For she quite apprehends that I have been enlivened, and not in the least depressed, by the work she has given me for the past few days. It is a way of saying I have passed muster, I suppose (although that phrase too I will not know to use for several years), something beyond simply my choice of vocation, I mean, for certainly there were tests enough in Lyons to weed us out. This was a further, a more private thing of Aubert's, which she would never, for example, have put to Regine or to quiet, anaemic Agnes, who will live out less than eighteen months before we stand in the chill high air of Howick, and bury her from a wooden church that looks like a barn. As we stand at her grave, the ancient Latin words of *Salve Regina* are torn away in ribbons, in scraps, by the gusts of wind.

It may seem strange that I speak so much about Regine, and yet have so little natural affection for her. Although it is not a thing I have read about, or even heard talked of, I believe that in religious life there is always a twin — can I call it that? A double, another we feel so close to, yet so different from, a mirror that gives us back something so foreign to ourselves, and yet we know that difference is in fact in us, as much as in the other. It is difficult for us not to become obsessed with that person, by strong affection or even stronger dislike. We will notice things in her we would never be disturbed by in another. We will find ourselves on trial, as it were, simply by being in her presence. When we stand together, work in the same kitchen, share our few enough moments of recreation, Regine is the one who gives the impression of endurance, of toughness — the farmer's daughter fresh from her apple barrels and her cheesecloths. Yet she is also the timid one who craves to be directed, who easily becomes depressed. She is hopeless with the dying, and I am soon the one preferred at deathbeds. She is thought to be so sensitive and I so matter-of-fact. But I know her distress is for herself and not those she attends, and my coolness, as Regine herself calls it, is that I know for compassion to be effective one's own discomfort is put aside. It is my competence, not my tears, that the dying have most need for. Regine speaks to me of what she calls her 'weakness', and yet there is such subtle pride in it! That was her Cross, Mother had told her: that her will, her considered vocation, led her to serve the ill and the deformed, though she would derive such little satisfaction from it. Regine repeats this to me, like a girl repeating a compliment.

Aubert senses something of what I think, yet it is what I try so hard, so genuinely, not to think. She will say so, much later, when Aubert herself is very old and I am middle-aged. We stand at the end of the verandah at the Herne Bay home. The lawns have been cut that afternoon, the air is sweet with early summer. Regine, who has been reading in a cane chair, is a few yards away from us, in one of her troubled, sweating sleeps. Aubert asks me to fetch a seat for her. She looks out across the cut fields of the convent school opposite until I bring a stool for her from the other end of the verandah. She then turns, and the light slips across her spectacles, and I think how old she has become, how at last that extraordinary vitality is burning down.

'If we might presume to anticipate, Sister,' she says to me, 'anticipate for argument's sake, Regine's reward will be so much greater than ours. It has been earned at so much greater cost.'

'Yes,' I say. 'I see that, Mother.'

'With greater effort. Which is another way, is it not, of saying with greater love?'

We both know the argument is not quite so simple as that. But I am happy to hear Regine praised, and accept the justice of the mild reprimand that is part of what Aubert says. By now, of course, Regine has been a thorn to me for half a lifetime. I cannot imagine life without her. I think, at times, that she has defined my spiritual life far more than any other being. Although I am not including Kate as I say that. And yet why not? I hear another voice demanding. Do I not have the courage to admit as much as that?

There is never much room for sentimentality with Aubert, but I put my hand on her shoulder as I stand behind her, and she is content enough to let it rest there. Her own two hands are on the verandah rail in front of her. They are like the hands of a very old child. The ring on her right hand is worn almost to the thinness of wire. I think of another time — I cannot have been in the country so very long — when a large group of us sat out here. It must have been a feast day, for so many of the community to be taking things so easily in mid-afternoon. I think of it as early summer, on a day not so different from this. Some of us were sewing, and others reading, and old Soeur Pierre, who came, as she sometimes confided, from noble stock, moved her needle in the circle of an embroidery frame where she worked with remarkable precision.

'Bishop Cleary,' she remarked, when she saw how I watched the deft plying of her fingers and the needle's quick bright glint, 'has asked if I have time for doing lacework for a gift for the Nuncio.'

Another of the sisters, I expect to please the aging Pierre, then remembered how she had read that the Little Flower herself enjoyed few things more than needlework — enjoyed it so much, in fact, that she at times had scruples that she did so. And Regine, who read as much on St Thérèse as she could find, looked puzzled and said, 'I'd not heard that about her, Sister.' But at the mention of the Lisieux saint, Aubert snorted with open impatience. Or contempt, I would call it, now that I am less troubled than I was as a younger woman, to use words correctly. (How long it has taken me to realise language is the harshest and the finest knife we can use, running it close against the bone of how things are. And my father's own precise mind, I think: how he would be revolted at how imprecisely I have just put it! His scorn was great for 'image mongers', as he called them — his phrase when Grandfather quoted from his English poet, 'the hounds of spring', and the swinging lines he tapped to with his cane. Or when he glanced at what I might be reading. 'Ark of the Covenant', he would say, 'Star of the Sea'. Say those phrases not with malice, but with a true regret that people needed to say anything only in terms of something else. 'The poetic mind,' he teased Grandfather. 'One day it will be like the appendix. We will wonder why we have it, simply to cause us pain.' Or again, as he said to me, 'My dear girl, can you not see you are worshipping a *turn of phrase*? The human decencies are more substantial than to need *maquillage!*') Aubert could not resist butting in, now St Thérèse was raised. 'A pity she didn't do a bit more work for the poor. They were there, you know. She had only to go as far as the gate.' Regine's face flushed at the very words. Pierre, so mild in her noble descent, tugged sharply at her needle, there was the faintest snap of tautened thread.

Yet Aubert is a touch riled as she picks up my amusement at what she has said.

'Sister Martine, you will make afternoon tea now for the sisters?'

And as I walk, reprimanded, through to the cool vault of the polish-smelling hall, I hear her follow up, 'And you, Regine. Would you sing for us? Please?'

From the broad white space of the kitchen, I sense the sisters on the verandah, their pause, the welling of regrets they so seldom concede, as Regine's fine voice enchants them from their rounds of illness and decay, decrepitude and imbecility, with the clarity of her ancient words from the country she will never see again. And it comes to me with a sudden bitter melancholy that I am thinking of them, the sisters, as 'they' and not as 'we'. Dear God, I say. I see my fists folded on the bench with sheer remorse. Dear God, shall I never lose my egotism, even now, after so many years?

And all that itself so many years ago now. Aubert gone. And Regine. I think of the two of us, little more than girls, lying one above the other in the cabin bunks as we sail towards our new home, the dip and creak of the timbers, the thrumming engines that carry us on. Two French girls with all the optimism of their choice.

Spicer comes to the kitchen door each morning at 6.45, so precisely I know the time by his knock as much as I do, a few minutes later, by the distant tinkle of the bell in the sisters' chapel at the elevation of the Host. Whichever of the community is on kitchen duty will hear Mass later, with one of the aging priests who says it for the patients.

He is a silent, hard-working young man who has difficulty with words. I have sometimes seen him with an older, darker man in Symonds Street as I walk with one of the younger sisters who pushes the pram that is the emblem almost of the Order, the pram that leaves the driveway empty and returns laden down with the groceries, the pieces of cloth, whatever strikes the city's good and generous people as useful to us. At first some of the sisters find a deep embarrassment in what they take to be begging. Aubert, of course, thinks of it quite differently. 'The privilege is *theirs*,' she says. 'Those who contribute are the true recipients, not us.' I have heard her say to the younger sisters half a dozen times that the embarrassment should be elsewhere — with those who give us nothing. Those, as she says, who shy off, embarrassed by the chance for charity, as they would shy off, just as embarrassed, should Christ walk up to them and hold out his wounded hands.

'I seen you with the pram,' Spicer in fact says to me, a few weeks after his first hammering against the flyscreen. And his first words on that first morning, 'I'm here for the slops,' the same every morning year after year, until the awkward boy is a tall young man. Mr Coffey arranged his helping about the place, saying to me once, as he tapped the side of his head, 'He's no Joe Ward, mind. But he'll do. He'll do all right for the slops. He'll manage the cart all right.' Spicer places the bins of rubbish on the wooden cart and drags it behind him across the paddocks. The pigs set up their yelping grunts the moment they see him move out from behind the hedge at the end of the kitchen garden. 'Feed them all day, they'd still hog at it,' he says. He says he hates them, the greedy slobs, although he describes them sometimes more vividly, and realises he has just committed language, as Regine calls it. So he looks down for a moment as he wipes the back of his hand across his chin and says, 'No offence.'

The scraps then, the clotted porridge, the crusts, the clogging dollops of cold stew, the slushed mass of vegetable peelings and cores and leftovers, are collected each morning as in a kind of ritual — the same words, the same awkwardness when I try to draw from him more words than he is prepared to give. Part of it, I expect, is our strangeness. He could know us for twenty years, I think, and still think we were unknowable, and totally crazy. I have heard him, from behind the hedge as he bellows to his two cows, driving them to the small stall where he ropes them against a headboard, abusing them, calling them fat no-good bleeding whores, dumber, he tells them, than that lot in there, meaning the sisters he will quickly walk by rather than speak to or do more than give his quick sideways nod. I suppose it is something of a triumph for me that he speaks the little he does. It is more, by far, than the others ever draw from him.

'Is that young man a mute?' our new Superior will ask, with a dash of irritation.

'No, Mother,' I explain to her. 'I think he is simply terrified of nuns.'

She clicks her tongue. 'A fairly normal Protestant, in that case,' she says. And then, catching herself, not wishing to sound unfair, she revises her words. 'A fairly normal man.'

There are times — a very few — when I am aware that he looks at me closely as I move about the kitchen. As if there may be something he will catch in my face when I am off guard, which will explain me to him, somehow give myself away. But the moment my eyes meet his he is flustered, and hefts the bin against his side: 'Better go then, eh.'

I know, too, that it is the woman in me, not just the nun, that puzzles him. One day, when he has cut his hand on a loose nail on the bin, I dab the wound with cotton wool and bandage it for him. 'A little more and it would need stitches, Spicer.' And as I turn his hand I feel, as though it were an actual lamp, his attention fall upon my cheek, my closeness. I remember a tall ungainly boy when I was fifteen or sixteen, a judge's son, who sat behind us in church, who stood at odd corners when I walked from school. 'He's gone on you,' my brother teased me. It is what my grandfather, with the best of intentions to rescue me from pure illusion, also had in mind when he walked with me in the long alley of plane trees from the riverside back to La Porte de Joigny, and asked, 'Do you know quite what you are giving up?' And the dear kindly man's exasperation, so that he swung at the grass tops with his cane, when I said to him, 'You can only "give up" what you want, Grandfather. Otherwise there is hardly merit in it.' Spicer is fascinated with me, but I am realist enough to know it is hardly admiration! I know that to 'woman' he would want to add monster — that is what fascinates him. That a normal-looking woman is also *this!* I have the feeling that I am repellent to him. I realise that is part of sex, the dark unfathomable current that is always there, whether we say so or not, between men and women. The distaste as much as its endless dragging force.

(Spicer, who will be so important to us, as the trees in the narrow drive flick in a rush above us and the branches clash along the sides of where we sit. His knuckles white against the wheel he grips. This hesitant and slow-witted boy who smiles slightly at me from beneath his cap with the shiny leather brim. Who calls me 'Sister' for the first time because a man, as he has heard, should protect women in adversity. He is trying to make me think how at ease he is, how I can depend on him completely. But I am close enough to smell his fear.)

It is one of the most important events of my life, however little I might think so at the time. I am standing on the safety zone where Pitt Street turns into Karangahape Road. I am feeling not quite well, which is unusual for me. I had woken with a headache, and there is a dull pressure where my headpiece presses in against my temple. If I had mentioned it, Sister Edmund in the infirmary would have insisted on one of her tonics, and if there is one thing I dislike it is fuss about my health. My large black bag is swelled with the material the manager at Barker and Pollock's has just given to the Home — twenty yards of blue gingham for the children's summer frocks. He will give me the same amount again the next time I am in Newton. He told me how he admired Aubert's stand in supporting the unfortunate girls who turned up at her door, unmarried.

'It's not wowsers I mind,' he said, 'it's hypocrites. Your lot as much as mine. At least your woman isn't one of those.'

It is only September, but already warm. Two men on the roof of the hotel on the corner across the street move against the sky. The brilliance and the dark figures stay imprinted behind my lids as I close my eyes. As a rule I would walk at least half the distance back to the Home. For the first time I am using my age as an excuse. My hair, in these last six months, has the flecks of grey that make me realise how truly my father's daughter I am. How far can I explain myself in terms of that distant, indulgent man? The same jawline, the same steady wide-set eyes, and now the hair as well.

'The English explain everything,' my grandfather had told me once. I held his hand, I could not have been more than eight years old, at the zoo in Lyons. I had said how looking at animals was nasty, because it was sort of like looking at ourselves. 'Nothing is nasty in nature, Marie-Claire,' Grandfather said. 'We are all part of it to the same extent, exactly.'

'Who said so?' I asked him.

And my grandfather told me, 'An Englishman called Mr Darwin.'

That comes into my mind, that memory from a day so many years before, when I had scraped my leg against an iron fence as we were leaving the last enclosure at the zoo and the inexplicable sense of distress as I saw the dark smear against my white woollen stocking.

Again I close my eyes for a moment against the glare, and there is an unexpected tug on my handbag. I open my eyes to see a gloved hand drop its gift of rolled notes onto the parcels of cloth. I smile and say 'God bless you' to the handsome, compact woman with a flow of dark hair, who steps past me and crosses from the safety zone to the footpath. I notice not much more than that she is energetic and hesitant together, and that her clothes are almost as dark as my own. She is gone in the press of people.

There is nothing so unusual in receiving gifts of that kind. People — they are almost always of another faith — who would feel awkward in approaching us directly will slip money into our hands, or place in the pram some gift of groceries or toys or shoes or even once, I remember, a tight roll of chickenwire as I passed the broad curved verandah of Mr Shroff's Hardware at the top of Victoria Street. Aubert takes such things as a matter of course, as scarcely her business, although from time to time she will add to our prayers in chapel a request for God's favour on 'those good people known only to You, benefactors of Compassion'. I am always a little surprised, and wonder at what prompts such gifts. Regine, when we once discussed it, said surely it was some sudden passing of the Holy Ghost, an impulse to assist God's work? Perhaps there is more of my father in me than I would like, for I said to her it may certainly be that as well, but there are quite human reasons too: there is guilt and pity and shame and a sense of bargaining with God, there is gratitude and hope, there are a dozen explanations for why people might be moved to help us. 'Not everything need be a miracle, Sister.' And Regine, with her infuriating persistence, said, 'How do you know?' As Kate in time, with good humour and scepticism, will ask me that same question of God, of my vocation, of love and evil. 'How do you know?' she will insist. And I suppose it is scarcely apostolic of me as I say, 'I shall never be able to answer you, my dear, in a way that could possibly satisfy you. But that is not the point. Not the final point.'

'And what is?' That too will come from her with such insistence. And her disappointment, I know, when all I have to offer her is to say, 'There is an obligation only for things to have meaning for oneself. That is as much as we can hope.'

I do not say the word 'grace' to her any more than I would say 'sin'. Another soul is always too remote to lock down with words that are mine but may not be hers. My own faith is irrefutable as rock. That is *my* certainty, *my* grace. But there is no reason why my part in God's larger scheme should comprehend another's part in it. As if a thing might make sense only on condition I understand it!

'You're next thing to a heretic yourself,' Kate will tease me much later, after I have told her a little of what I think.

'Yes, don't I just look one!' I laugh with her.

And of course, there is 'Mrs Cooper' between us, before we can speak as directly as we do. Yet in another way she is so clearly there, from the beginning. I think of the woman's dark sweep of hair, her quick precise stepping with the crowd on the footpath, and her being caught, in perhaps fifteen seconds, so definitely in my mind.

Back at the Home I give the bank notes to Sister Edwina, a plump practical West Coaster, as it is always said about her — although what is the West Coast? Irish. Coal mines. Endless rains. I refuse to admit that anyone can be defined by so few phrases. The French — I know we are summed up just as neatly, just as absurdly. It is what takes place *between* those easy definitions that in the end place us most truly. 'She is French, but . . .' 'She is West Coast, but . . .' I always listen for what comes after 'but' when anyone is talked of. That is where you look for people. On the border. At the edges. Where the expected adjectives break down. ('Don't ramble!' Kate sometimes says, when I start like this. She is like the Redemptorist from years ago, on that retreat. 'Don't speculate, Sister,' he had said. 'Enough human wisdom has been defined, isn't that so, for you to be comfortable within its borders?')

So I give the packed, rolled notes to Edwina. She keeps our accounts with such competence the co-adjutor flattered her in front of us all on Mother's feast day. He should have her running the diocese, he said, he would sleep easier for knowing everything was in its place. Edwina quickly counts the money, takes a key from a chain on her belt, unlocks a drawer, places the notes away, and relocks it. She enters the amount in a ledger. She then turns back to another page, and runs her finger down a list of items.

'Straw hats,' she says, 'a windfall like this. Now with summer coming on. Shoes and straw hats. God knows the poor creatures can do with a bit of smartening up.' She means those who lie afflicted with encephalitis, the retarded mites, the imbeciles who will never learn to say a sentence let alone write one, the young incurables who thanks to the money we had not expected will now sit and lie and tumble in blue smocks and new straw hats and shiny shoes, and make visitors grimly face their existence for all of five minutes. I like the fact, without knowing why, that this is where Edwina will spend the woman's money. In decorating the hopeless, as some would call them, rather than the dozen more useful things it might well go on.

Edwina's forefinger bulges her cheek as she probes at a back tooth.

'Does it hurt?' I ask her.

She ignores my question and comes back at me obliquely. She takes the finger from her mouth and rubs it dry against her knee. 'Let me tell you something, Martine,' she says. 'If it wasn't for the fact that I believe in Hell, I would take that money and spend it all on chocolate.'

Kate likes me to tell her about Aubert. 'I like the sound of her,' she says. 'I like the way she said damn you to everyone, all her life.'

'Except God,' I say.

Kate tells me not to be absurd. As if she does not understand that.

Aubert, I find, comes into my mind so much. It is seven years since she died, how many more since she left us for those years in Rome and was given the run round, isn't that what they say? By the bishops and the Curia and whoever else believed she was not up to an Order of her own! The years when she languished in what must indeed have seemed like the eternal city, when she wrote her long encouraging letters back to us in Herne Bay, in Jerusalem, in Island Bay, reminding us of what she had always told us, that it was only work that mattered, while she was forced to waste so much of her final years convincing the Vatican accountants, the rubber-stampers and the line-rulers, the uncomprehending men who suspected her of spiritual pride. The handiest thing to throw at a woman whose vision was larger than their own.

'I wouldn't have made a bad nun,' Kate says.

'Let's keep fantasy out of it,' I tell her. We smile at each other.

Edwina is now dead as well. The communion of saints. It is such a distant phrase when we are young! I will have been here forty years in January. I said, didn't I, how my hair is practically grey? I do not look much without my habit, believe me. And since the diagnosis, since old Dr Flynn removed his rimless spectacles to rub his eyes, and looked at me with his alert, shy glance — he was as young as myself the first time I met him — and spoke to me with the frankness of a friend. It is my vanity, strangely, that gives me the most trouble. We are schooled for so long, we are reminded each day, that death's implacable reality is why we choose to serve as we do. We know too you cannot spend a lifetime with the ill and be unaware of this — that so few, at the last, are spared the pangs of physical fear. Our revulsion at the thought of our own demise, however firm our faith. Christ feared on the Cross, even He. So I suppose that fear will come to me too, before too long.

Dr Flynn said to me, he knew I would want him to speak with utter frankness. I replied that whether I wanted it or not, he *must.* Then with the same fountain pen he has used since I first knew him, its gold band inscribed from his family for his graduation, he sketched the few necessary lines, a picture of how things were, and how they would be. 'There is always room for error, of course.'

While '*It is all so very simple,*' I was thinking, '*it is all so trivial.*' And I was held by the incongruity that what came into my mind was vanity of the emptiest kind. For even as Dr Flynn's pen stroked the outline of my ovaries, hatched across the corruption already there, I thought with the rapidity of instinct, *I do not want to be so thin that the ring slips from my finger, that the bones of my wrist show through like domes when I raise my hands and try to hold a cup.* I am seared with shame that when the chips are down, as Spicer says, this is what comes into my mind, an image that flashes without my will or my control. Not thoughts of God, or of those I love, but of how I shall look! And I recall then something Regine told me, not long before she died. She was quite unflustered by her disease. Whenever the weather allowed it she sat in a cane chair in the sunlight, her hands in her lap. In my condescension, I remember, I thought how fortunate she was never to be troubled by thinking, to be as simple still as she must have been as a novice. I sat by her, when I could find the time. She seemed greatly to enjoy our speaking together in our own tongue. I remember too a young priest who visited once, the secretary to a Vatican official while Aubert was under scrutiny. He was from a village not twenty miles from where François now lives. He knew the pâtisserie between the rue de Valprofonde and the école, he said the man with the eye-patch, the Algerian, still sold birds at the northern corner of the market! It was enchantment, to talk with him. But he laughed at one expression I used, and said I was like something preserved in Pompeii, no one had said that in his lifetime! I've no doubt there was something comic in the two of us, Regine and I, still speaking the language of girls in our failing bodies. I said to her, 'Regine, I envy your calmness. I don't know anyone who deserves it more.'

Ten minutes later, after one of the younger sisters had herded her troop across the road to a concert in the Mercy Sisters' school hall, Regine said without turning to me, 'There is one thing, Martine, that comes back into my mind. That won't give me any peace.' She is back on her family's farm, below the white cliffs that hang like stiff huge curtains. It is before she even decides on the novitiate. Her father is much older than her mother, who is half Italian. For years she and her mother have talked, without believing it will happen, of one day travelling south, to visit relatives in San Remo. She has no idea, Regine says, of what Italy really is, but it is everything, nevertheless, that her father's stern melancholy is not. 'Although I loved him,' she says. 'I would stand near him all day while he turned the big cheeses or handled the muslin sieves, hoping he would notice me and put his hand on my head. And yet one day.' She looks at me with a burning frankness that makes me pity her, makes me wish her not to trust me to this extent. 'One day one of the farm boys runs shouting into the house and my mother screams out, and rushes to the barn, and a little later they carry Father back. He is lying on an old door, I remember, that had leaned in the barn for ever, with sticks underneath it for the men to hold.' Regine is not looking at me. She picks at the black mittens on her hands. All I am thinking, still, is that I do not want this confidence, that there is such injustice in her being pained by what she remembers from so long ago. But she brings herself to tell me. 'I knew Father was dead before they brought him into the house, all the time they were walking across from the barn. It seemed to take ages, like it was a procession, and yet I know the men were walking fast under the weight they carried. Father was a huge man, did I tell you that? And all the time. All the time I felt this — this *joie*, that is the only word, and I was thinking, At last, at last we can go to Italy!' Regine looks at me then, and smiles. 'There!' she says. And as though putting her guilt behind her, 'Remember the novice mistress in Lyons? *No secrets*, she used to tell us. As though we might be hiding jewels!' She is laughing suddenly at the thought of it, while I am thinking, simply, 'All this time and I have never known her.'

Dr Flynn removed his long green gown and folded his spectacles, and looked for a moment towards the fragment of lawn through the netting in front of his window. As though he need delay with me, before speaking the truth. It is later in the day, in fact late in the evening, after rosary in the Chapel, and the Litany of the Blessed Virgin, when I lie in my room and perhaps for the first night in many years switch off the light without reading a page or two from one of the books near my bed — the Imitation, the volume of Teresa of Avila, a travel book about the Holy Land approved for recreation. And so there I am. I lie in the darkened room and watch the dim white curtain stir above the slightly opened window and then hang so still, its long folds motionless as marble. I lie and think of Dr Flynn's thin tired face, the indent of his glasses printed on his cheeks, his hesitancy before he spoke. And I realise that it was Dr Flynn himself he was so moved by, rather than by me. He was thinking how he had worked with me for so many years, that he had once remarked (yes, a nun can notice that!) on my 'young admirableness'. That was almost one of Aubert's own near flattering phrases, when she realised I had a knack for pharmacy that was not so far behind her own. Oh, he was taken with my mind as well. That quickness as much as my physical grace that had made my father and my brother, and my grandfather especially, believe it such a waste when I insisted how God had chosen me, when I said it was hardly my part to quarrel with a choice so much higher than my own. (Towards the end, you find you can say anything about yourself, even the complimentary things.) Yes, I know as I lie in the darkness that gradually permits me to make out outlines, one shade from another, to feel at home where I have always been, however strange it is for me to lie and brood like this — I know it was Dr Flynn himself he grieved for, even as we spoke as frankly as we might about another body, neither his nor mine, which lay between us. He spoke of the swelling protruding like the curve of an infant's head from my side. He had no need to spell out the rest — that in say six months' time he would examine me, my distended abdomen, and the rest of me weakened, shrivelling, as though my strength were poured into the growth that was fed by my decline. (I quite know what might be made of how I put that! My secret yearnings, my hidden regrets for what I have never known. It is in fact no more than the kind of image my father so detested. But think what you like. There is nothing that might ever be said that bothers me, not now.)

He makes no effort to comfort me, my old friend. He offers no false hope. We know each other too well for him to offend me with pretence. We have, I suppose, been together at the deaths of scores of patients in those years we worked side by side. That brief curt nod that meant yes, he had done all that he might, it was now in my domain, should I want to call the priest. His eyes meeting mine, how many dozens of times, at such moments? There is an intimacy in that, which is difficult to explain. For in spite of his name, Dr Flynn is not a Catholic, and I even doubt there is much at all that he believes. So there is that as well, that curious closeness of being so far apart, faced with the eternal facts. (Even with Kate, I would hardly attempt to spell out *that*!)

And so now, that afternoon, rubbing either side of his nose with his nicotine-yellowed fingers, and then his hand running loosely over the folded insect — so it strikes me — of his gold-framed spectacles as they lie before him on his desk. Until I say to him, say it to console him, 'There is nothing to be done about it, my dear friend.' And as if he takes his courage from mine, only then does he look at me directly, taking up my own words. 'No, dear friend, there is not.' And with a cunning I may once have been ashamed of but now — how quickly! — I am not even troubled by, I tell him there is one favour he might do me. 'Without any doubt,' he says. I think he already suspects that what I shall ask of him will be 'irregular'. (How Father's language lingers on in me!) For I am now asking him to lie, as I am prepared to lie myself, and I am not touched by the merest flicker of remorse.

As I leave the doctor's room, with its wine-coloured carpet that absorbs all steps, the buoyant and the condemned, to the same sinking hush, I turn and smile back at Dr Flynn. I doubt that he sees it. The two ovals of his now replaced spectacles glint as the afternoon, blustery beyond the bow window, washes across them when he tilts his head. I think at once of the pebbles of Aubert's own glasses, and my sitting beside her, a year or so before she died. On the white verandah, half an hour before the sun went down in a flurry of burning cloud. She had so seldom sat merely looking at things that I think she was surprised at how marvellous it was to take the sunset at its own pace. I started to say something. I began to quote one of my grandfather's favourite lines, I've no idea where from. Yet I must have heard it dozens of times as a child. It was almost a reflex with him, what I realise now was a response not to what he saw but to what he knew he should feel. But before I had finished half a line Aubert's hand seized mine, almost roughly.

'You,' she said. 'Keep quiet and look.'

My first lie, the one that has lasted for several years, is that Kate is somehow other than she is. My friend, I say, is not to be defined by that, there is surely in everyone a place beyond the palisades of condemnation or necessity? Yet she is a woman who owns brothels, who supervises prostitutes, who makes her living from selling bodies for the vilest of sins. And how, you say, am I to justify such friendship? Since the growing trouble with my side, with my guessing at what it is so long before Dr Flynn sketches it on his blotter, it is a question that asks itself over and over. And my answer, too, is there as if in some way independent of myself. I do not justify it. I do not try to explain. It is part of me, much as the colour of my eyes, or now, the pressure of my swelling. You do not look at the sunset, as Aubert and I did that evening from the verandah, and divide off this part of it from that, with some grid, some net, that is in our minds. You do not confront the eternal fact of God, the extensiveness of His love, and say, 'Here I please Him, there I do not,' as though my boundaries, my little divisions, touch that burning sea. And I too, in His image, am what I am, entire. That is how He will find me — of a piece. What I feel for Kate is part of that.

She had put the banknotes in my bag on pure impulse. She came out of the tiny shop along from the hotel on the corner, whose single window was a glitter of buckles and buttons and the gleam of leather belts, and above them the cards of looped laces and shining ribbons. It is next to an ironmonger's, and the difference between the shops in some small way amused me — all that business and usefulness of one, the smells of oil and tin as you passed the opened door, and then the frippery, so close there, in the silly window. 'The girls love those things,' she told me, very much later. 'Most women do.'

She had left the shop, and before she stepped from the pavement to cross the road she saw this God-forsaken nun, as she had thought, standing on the safety zone, leaning into the silver-painted parapet at the end, looking dead beat. She knew I would have been entering shop after shop, begging for those who were not up to begging for themselves. She was moved by anger, she said, not kindness. She felt provoked by the indignity of what I was obliged to do. She knew when I left the tram at the Three Lamps I would trudge along Jervois Road rather than spend another tramfare. And why is she by herself? she thought. Aren't they always scrounging about in pairs? She imagined, as do so many people, the wards of monstrous children, the orphans forced she believed to endless prayer, the demented old, the sisters yoked for ever to the service of physical distress, irreversible decay. She imagined a kind of veneer of dedication, a sentimental slick across such vileness, so that we exulted in the baseness of what we did. She said her cheeks were hot with anger for the duplicity of God, putting one across women like myself, saying here is the world He had made a hash of, now give your own lives, utterly, to picking up the pieces. She saw us as saintly phantoms, rewarded with endless spurious content. She is as amazed as I am, once we are friends, that we have ever got so far as this. She will, by and by, at the worst of times, I suppose one must call it, she will say, almost desperate that I assure her, console her, 'It must be worth it, mustn't it?' And the awful but not despairing thing I will think at that moment, when truth, if you like, is the only space I have left to live in. 'The love of God,' I will tell her, 'never promised to make things easier at the end.'

I was surprised, and then deeply hurt, when one day the new Superior took me from my work in the dispensary, and put me in charge of interviews, admissions, contact with families, generally keeping up, as she put it, with whatever concerned us in the city and the country that might in any way impinge on our lives. 'It's a different world now,' she says. 'We need to keep up with it.' This is well after the war, when she is worried that our work is less appreciated than it was.

'Prayer has never let us down,' one of the sisters says. I can hear Aubert's voice, from years ago, replying to Regine, who had said precisely that. 'Prayer is splendid for the soul,' she said. 'But it will not buy soap unless we take a hand in it.'

I cannot imagine that Sir William Goddard gives much of his

precious time to thoughts of the spiritual life. As I say that, of course, I acknowledge again the risk of guesswork about anyone. Even the very ill, when personality crumples smaller and smaller, like a handkerchief rolled up in a clenched fist, can quite take one by surprise with some stray remark, some darting flare of temperament that you would never guess at. (My garrulous English grandfather, whose idea of paradise surely would have been a good café, a constant audience and superior brandy, had asked that a rabbit — so François wrote me — a grey rabbit bought from a pet shop be placed in his bedroom through his quick last illness.) But Sir William. To all appearances Sir William is as much at ease with how the world is, with managing it successfully, as I can imagine a man quite being. When he stands with his hands clasped behind his back, the fingers of one hand are always flicking, snapping, even when he is speaking quietly, apparently so at ease. This is something you see only if you are not the person talking to him. It is then you understand how he is a man who is impatient even as he charms. For he works at that, indeed. Even with a nun older than himself.

He sits in the comfortable chair on the other side of my desk. I know his name, of course. He is prayed for among the list of 'special benefactors'. His eyes move quickly from the large crucifix behind me to the neatness of my desk, my folded hands, the paperweight which is a medallion struck for Leo XIII set in a circle of enlarging glass. I know from the way he takes us in — the room, myself — watches me carefully as I speak, that he is not a Catholic. Years before, when I first met his ailing and now long-dead wife, I was surprised, I am not sure why, at her simple directness. As though she were at a remove from the wealth and elegance of what she wore. Her husband now smiles at me, folds a fist on either knee, and says he will come to the point at once, he appreciates the value of my time. I know there are men — businessmen, I suppose I mean — who believe that if a nun is silent, she is thinking on a different plane to himself. So I say nothing and smile at him, as I used to smile at the three male generations of my family round the dinner table, unsettling them with my silence.

I must know, Sir William says, I would be aware that the trust for which he is signatory has contributed to the Homes in the past? Island Bay, he says, as well as Auckland? And then, holding my eye, no nonsense between us, man as it were to man: 'You're *au fait* of course with medical conditions?'

'Of course.' I repeat his own words. His favourite phrase, I know that already.

He says it is an unfortunate case, the one he wishes to raise. A regrettable case. He knows I — the Home — must have moral views about the disease?

I see he dislikes the words he is obliged to use. I assure him everything to do with the Home is in utter confidence.

'It's a large favour to ask. The woman of course won't recover.'

'Dr Flynn will examine her again.'

'I believe, at this stage, recovery is out of the question?' He wants me to reassure him.

'Physical recovery, yes.' And I dislike myself for that, as though my business is with verities beyond those he would understand. I dislike the pretentiousness, and the pause it gives him. And thinking perhaps that I still carry some doubt about whether we would accept the woman, he asks should he speak to the bishop? Would that ease our way? 'It is only a five-minute drive to the palace in New Street.'

And I say, smiling still, but so tartly I know I have picked up some of my manner from Aubert, 'Bishops and palaces, Sir William, before we accept the afflicted? I don't think so.'

'In that condition?' he persists.

I tell him I could show him several similar cases within twenty yards of where we sit.

'I can give you more details, should you wish.'

'Dr Flynn's report is adequate.'

'Socially, I suppose I mean. What I know of her. What I've been told.'

'All stories are similar enough, aren't they?' I say to him. 'With syphilis?'

He is relieved, I know, that business is now concluded. He takes his hat and his long white scarf from the rack inside the front door.

107

He then stands on the verandah, turning the hat in his hands. Spicer, who is crouched before a lawnmower turned on its side, examining its loosened wheel, sees us step from the doorway, and seems to dash at the sight of us. I wonder, for a moment, at the strangeness of his look, his scuttle beyond the corner of the house. Sir William does not so much as notice him. He glances towards the gates, where a handsome motor waits for him. Its driver stands with his arms crossed, leaning against the shining curve of its front, and watches young Sister Eugenie with several of the children descending the hill.

Sir William looks at me and smiles. 'It was less difficult than I expected.'

'Are we that off-putting?' I have a hint of teasing in my voice.

'Thank you,' he says. He takes my hand in his, which surprises me by its softness and its warmth. My own seems hard and dry inside his clasp. He places his dark hat firmly on his head. But at the steps he turns, and adds that I can have total confidence in the woman who will bring the patient in tomorrow — total confidence. 'She will tell you all you need to know.'

The driver quickly throws down his cigarette, and holds open the door for the distinguished man. It looks as though he steps into a dark rich cabinet. Half a minute later the children turn and exclaim and wave as the motor passes them. Both Sir William and the driver wave back. The driver presses several times on the dull, bellowing horn that excites the children to whoop back. From where I am, as I close the doorway on the polished hallway, I hear young Eugenie calling to her children to be calm, to be sensible children, and then she is comforting one of the retarded ones, who is bawling now that the marvellous vehicle has turned the corner and left the street as it ordinarily is. I think of the last thing Sir William had said before he slipped from the hallway, his dark hat wheeling slowly in his hands, the pale silk inside it taking the light and losing it. 'You will find her very sensible. Mrs Cooper.'

There are still almost thirty minutes until the sisters' afternoon tea. I sit in the empty chapel, idly enough, I admit. I make little attempt to pray beyond a few rote phrases. But I know by now, and quite accept the fact, that prayer is scarcely my strong point. *Laborare est orare*. I take comfort from that! I am glad simply to sit here and close my eyes.

From outside the chapel there is the chirr of Spicer pushing his fixed mower up and down the lawn. I imagine the quick green rainbow of the grass from the machine. I think how strangely things come together. In this past half hour I have spoken with a man of such privilege and wealth that a driver runs him about the city, while another young man who speaks differently from anyone else, yet is not a fool, nevertheless runs from the very sight of him. And the orphans, like a chorus, weren't they, a chorus in an opera say, whose work is to exclaim at life as it goes by! And I had turned a pencil in my fingers and arranged for a syphilitic woman to come into our care. In so short a time this crowded fragment of existence, this muddle of chance and birth and luck, all so ordinary enough; and yet was it not declaring too, how even with faith, and more than that, with love, chaos is only just kept out of sight? What an effort it always was, such an effort to keep the mosaic in place — does that make sense? I mean, not to let one's mind flounder in confusion. I pray now, I know I *must* pray, for a clarity that is deeper than to see things as they seemingly are. To work harder, to strike against that muddle. I want clarity so much, so that I might do things better. So I may, I suppose, say at last to God, I have done what I might that outlines are not blurred, that nothing is seen as wasted, that value flares in all things, simply because they exist.

Miriam — that is the woman's name — already is in the final stage. She has a rash running from her ear to the white collar of her dress, and along both arms. I cannot be certain that she knows how ill she is, but I suspect she does. She is self-contained in a way I cannot describe. In a week's time she will be a favourite with some of the older patients, because she listens to them and makes them laugh. But she will also have days when she refuses to leave her room. When she will sit in the big chair in front of the window, and look at Spicer when he carries the buckets to the paddock for the pigs, and stroke her dressing gown for hours at a time, the way the senile so often do.

Only once does Mrs Cooper give her grief its rein. It is the day, months later, when Miriam can no longer speak, nor perhaps even hear. She is propped up high like a doll, her arms laid in front of her along the blue counterpane. We are back in my office. Mrs Cooper says to me, although it comes from nothing we had said before, 'We have to have lies, don't we, to keep us going?' And she is leaning against me then, as I stand beside her. Leaning into me from where she sits in the chair from which Sir William had ruled all things, as he imagined. Her head is heavy against my thigh and I feel the rack of her sobs as though some kind of shock is passing from her body into mine, a current of pure grief. I put my hand on her head, and her fingers move to entwine with mine. One grieves like this so seldom in one's life. It is the grief for all things perverse and diminishing and unbearable. It is the way one cries for so much more than is ever understood.

'Mrs Cooper,' I say quietly.

This, then, was Mrs Cooper. She was frank and warm, and once she moved beyond her natural enough contempt for a woman who had concealed herself, as she supposed, from life, there was no barrier between us.

That last day she told me what she knew of Miriam. She explained the life she lived. She made no secret of what her own part was, in a world of sexual fact. She told me without shame and without boasting. She said, 'A long time ago I took a vow — if you can accept it as that — that I would never be subdued by what the world wanted to impose on me as right or wrong. That I would be true to how I saw things for myself.'

I avoid answering her directly, yet Mrs Cooper understands, with caution as well on her part, that we must speak in utter confidence between us.

'I took the same vow,' I tell her. 'If you can accept it as that.'

'She'll die?' she says. 'There is no question of that?' I notice how still she sits, as though by nature she has that quiet at her centre which we sisters are always assumed to have and that I have worked so hard to pretend to. 'There's nothing that can save her?'

'No,' I say. 'You know what is likely to happen?'

'Of course.' And then, 'No. Not in detail. No.'

I tell her. I speak, I know, as though I am reading from a textbook as I describe the tertiary stage. The manifestations. The uncertainty of how long, how painful it may be. 'We'll do all we can to spare her.'

Mrs Cooper's breath grates harshly as she comes back at me, 'You'd better, for Christ's sake!'

'As is everything we do,' I say. I am ashamed of that, too, at how glibly I have turned her words. I feel the warmth rise to my cheeks. I tell her, 'I'm sorry if I sound sanctimonious.' I raise my eyebrows at her, enough for her to know we are both caught in roles of one kind or another. She as much as I.

I am strangely upset after that meeting. Perhaps it is because I recognise Mrs Cooper, and she gives no inkling that she has seen me before. It is not vanity, though. It is deeper than that. For a few moments, I remember, after the roll of notes with their thick rubber band dropped into my bag, after that arc of hair spread out, rayed out, a kind of black monstrance (I think of it uncomfortably as that), *ostensoir*, as we say at home, one of my favourite words since childhood — I suppose I had thought that here was that kind of brief illumination we sometimes have through ordinary mortal things, the loveliness of a thing merely for its own sake, because it *is*, no more than that. And she had forgotten. It had meant nothing to her at all.

I am anxious to find something to do. I walk through to the dispensary, where Sister Julian has taken over the work that I loved. The green-painted room is empty, the brown blind drawn over its broad square panes. Two of the blue jars are wrongly placed. I return them to where they should be. I am getting old and fussy, I tell myself. I must make a point of not reprimanding her. This lust for discipline — as a young nun I always thought how that was the final trial of the religious life! I sit on the high stool at the corner of one of the benches, beside the thick journals, the smaller books of instruction written in Aubert's clear, scholarly hand. I feel an unaccustomed depression. My mind is on the drabness we run the risk of decaying into. I take in, for the first time with any attention, the dark-framed photograph of some jubilee, the black and white of clergy, the massed school children, the distinguished faithful as they crush into the Domain. How boring photographs always are! The bones, I think of it. They are the bones of what we were on that day, under that pelting or that brilliant sky, as our clothes pressed too tight or we stood and thought of lunch, of the grubbiness of Father so-and-so's soutane, the prayers intoned with devotion or merest rote: all that was *life*, the richness of what was going on, and now it is this scrap of dots and forgotten dullness. I run my finger inside my veil. I have never been one for 'moods'. But my skin is cool, my pulse even.

The young sister opens the door, flinging herself into the room, laughing, calling to whoever she has just left in the corridor. She turns, her face bright with living, with that very second. She is startled as she closes the door and sees me sitting on the bench. 'Goodness, Sister,' she says. 'Are you all right?'

I tap the exercise books, the leather journals, piled beside me. 'I was sitting here thinking of Mother,' I tell her.

I know as I say it that I am not quite telling the truth. But it is better if she believes that is why I am here. I could scarcely say to her, I have waited a lifetime, my dear, for some kind of significance. And now, today, this afternoon, after so many years of near contentment, I know what the saints mean when they speak of dryness of the spirit. I know that is what lies in store. And I doubt if I am up to it.

It is nowhere as bad as that, in fact. I realise — how quick and unwelcome all this realising is, at my age! — that I would very likely have been a tiresome, overdramatic woman, had I not chosen this life. I would not have cared for the woman I might otherwise have been.

Yet things change so fast. Mrs Cooper visits Miriam several times a week. Dr Flynn says it is not a word he goes in for, but Godsend is on the tip of his tongue. 'You know what the last stages can be like,' he says.

Not every visit, but at least once a week, Mrs Cooper stays for tea with me in my office. She tells me, frankly, how she loathes God.

'Or loathe Him because you think He isn't there?'

She looks at me for quite some time, as though making up her mind whether to risk offending me. But it is not God she wants to talk of. She says, her eyes suddenly lowered and the *chink, chink* of her spoon against the side of her cup, 'I want us to be friends.'

'Yes,' I say.

She takes her time again. She puts her cup down heavily on the carpet beside her and says, 'Look. Let's never say anything to each other because we *have* to, is that all right?'

I run my hand vaguely over my habit. 'Because of this?'

'I don't think of you as that. Not just that. I don't think of Miriam as a whore. I don't want you to think of me as — well, anything.' She stops there. She looks at me and says, as if it matters to her what I answer, 'I hate being told what I am.'

'I've no idea —'

'I own houses of prostitution. You know that.'

And I say to her, with all honesty, and with dreadful innocent condescension, 'I know you're not an evil woman.'

She laughs at that. She drives the fingers of one hand up through her thick hair and shakes her head slightly, and tells me, 'That's a beginning then, isn't it?'

This must be the fourth or fifth time we have talked. I look forward to her coming. I know she enjoys talking with me. And this afternoon as she leaves she pauses just inside the door to the verandah. She looks, as she has done before, at the copy of a famous painting Bishop Redwood gave Aubert.

'What's that?' Mrs Cooper says. 'I'm not up on painting.'

'It's by Raphael,' I tell her. 'It's supposed to be a good copy.'

She looks at the plump arms, the fat child scrabbling across the Virgin. 'It looks like she runs a restaurant,' Mrs Cooper says. And she laughs when she sees she hasn't offended me.

'I won't tell the sisters that.'

Then she turns to me on the step. 'We met before,' she tells me. 'I gave you some money once at a tramstop. There's no reason why you should remember.'

Miriam goes so much faster than is expected. There are spells for a few days at a time, and then for six or seven days, when she seems unaware of who speaks to her, of where she is. Kate — Mrs Cooper has asked me to call her that — sits by her, and holds her hand, and there is an occasional spasm in Miriam's fingers. I suspect these are involuntary, but Kate takes them as deliberate. When they occur she speaks to the other woman. I have given instructions to the nursing sisters to leave them alone at such times. 'We have no notion how God may move people,' I say.

That is lame, even to me. I know I mean something like that, and I am more or less correct. But those are not the words to say. It is drawing this woman and her dying friend too eagerly towards where I am comfortable. I wish I knew how I could move more towards them, to do that, at least. But I am here, by habit I suppose, with the words we use that always limit us, whoever we are. And so I make God sound *mine*, as though He is a closed fist I do not want opened. Scruples, the spiritual director used to tell us in the novitiate, scruples are an act of pride, of self-importance. Is every flicker of my mind such an affront to God? Monsignor Levesque would put his knuckles under his fat gourmet's chin and laugh at us, until we laughed back. I was too healthy, too certain, really to know what it was he spoke of or tried to jolly us out of. But is that my trouble now, I wonder? Dear God, if only Aubert were still here to talk to! Her common sense would soon whack me out of this.

Kate's anger at times has nowhere to go, except towards me. At least I can be of some use in that. She wants me to justify what is happening, to talk of God's will or whatever might give her a wall to kick against.

'Why Miriam?' she demands.

She waits for me, I know, to tell her sex must reap its punishment, but I refuse to comfort her with that. Nor is it what I believe.

'Because of the war,' I say.

'The war?'

'Because men consorted as they did in Egypt. Wherever. That is where the disease began. For most people here.'

'That's no sort of answer,' she says.

'It is Dr Flynn's. And men cleverer than Dr Flynn.'

Another time she accuses me of denying what I believe. 'You think there is a reason for this, but you will never say so. You are afraid to admit even that.'

'If there is a God, there is a plan. But that is not to say I know it.'

'Then why are you here?'

'I know my part of the plan,' I say. 'That's all I can know.'

We sit in my office while this goes on. The rest of the community, I suspect, think she takes too much of my time. Or that I fancy myself as in some way spiritually guiding her. I cannot explain, and so make no attempt to. I lie awake, as I have never done, and go over what Kate has said to me and what I say to her. Until one afternoon she throws her tea cup against the wall. It shatters with a quick snap, and the liquid shakes out in a dark broken flow. The wall runs with it, towards the fragments of the cup on the polished boards. Neither of us moves. There is such quiet in the room that we hear the soft dripping from where some of the tea splashed up against the frame of an Italian print. She makes no attempt to gather the fragments, to apologise for what she has done. She has no idea of what I feel, even about this.

Then without bothering to look at me she says, 'I have not lost my temper for twenty years. There were people who did things against me then, and I swore they would never make me despair. Make me think for a minute they were right. I hated them with a coldness that would never distress me. Now look what you have made me do.'

Young Julian, who is the sister on night duty, wakes me at three o'clock in the morning. It is a month, perhaps, since the broken cup, longer since Miriam has spoken a word of English. No one knows what it is she speaks, after weeks of silence. Dr Flynn thought it might be Polish. He asked a bootmaker from a shop at the top of Blake Street to come and tell us what it was the woman said. But the squat, heavy man who was terrified at being in a place of such illness said it was not Polish that Miriam spoke, nor Russian, nor Czech. He knew at least that it was none of these. Nor did Kate have any idea. Miriam had never told so much as a detail about her family, or wherever it was she might now be harking back to — the language one can only suppose she first heard when love, please God, was a thing she knew for what it was.

Julian wakes me by shaking my shoulder until I am sitting, startled. 'It is three in the morning,' I say to her. The green phosphorescent dots on my alarm clock stand so solid in the dark. She leans towards me and I pick up the fear in her young voice.

'I am the only one there,' she says. 'I think you should come.'

It is the morning after the day when the small figures are taken from the crib in the chapel. Petty thefts have occurred for some time, as they always must have in institutions like ours. A year or two ago one of the white surplices, with its deep border of lace, disappeared from the press where the vestments are kept. Last night the sacristan said two of the figures had gone. The child and St Joseph, from the crib. It is unlikely that it was one of the orphans, or one of the retarded, although who knows the secret promptings of a child? 'Don't ask them,' I advised the sister who reported it. 'It will upset them all if they think we suspect them.'

I go with Julian to the sick room, where the end is almost come.

An hour later, as I put on my long black coat and walk out into the sharp air, I think how such trivial events lie beside those of greatest moment. Statues — toys — are stolen; a woman dies in agony; an aging nun walks into the remains of the night, a slit of mild silky grey already there in the lower sky, across the school playground and through the lane into John Street, then up the slope of Vermont Street, past the Marist Brothers school whose asphalt spaces spread out, pale and bare, in the expanding light. As I turn into Ponsonby Road, it is as though bonfires have been lit beyond the rows of modest houses, their roofs black against the flare of the new day. The air rings with the clamour of birds in the big trees. A young man with a kind of hood pulled behind his head runs past me, his arms punching out as though at some opponent who feints in front of him. 'Sister,' he grunts to me as he runs past.

'Good morning,' I say to him. Someone has told me before — it must be Dr Flynn — that he is a sportsman of some kind, a hero with the local children. And I remember. A school fair the Sisters of Mercy organised in New Street, and he was standing there, I am sure, that same young man. He laced big gloves on the tiny fists of the children, let them pummel against his huge raised hands while behind him a wheel whirled on a wooden stand and slowed to coloured strips, and a piece of card tocked slower and slower against the nails at the rim of the wheel, and a cry went up that the young man was the winner. 'Give the champ his ham,' the man calls from the platform. Strange that I remember that. And I am thinking still, as well, of the jumbled images of the previous night, the stolen carved figures, the woman talking on in God knows what tongue, her handsome face, her throat and breasts, glazed in final sweat, jerked at last to what we must believe is peace.

Then the sky is again surprisingly dark. I am almost at the brick Police Station when the quick rattle stirs in the plane trees, and I feel the rain. The clock across on the building where the dentist does the sisters' teeth shows not quite six. In the smear of rain a baker's van moves shiny as a toy. The horse's head and back are steaming. I cross the empty, bald main road. A charwoman letting herself through a wooden gate at the back of the Star Hotel pauses with her hand on the upraised latch, watching me until I pass. I hear the latch fall behind me, and the gate scrape as she draws it back. I walk down the steep slope of Newton Road, into the warren of small wooden houses. It is another ten minutes until I begin the rise on the other side of the valley, St Benedict's riding high above it, making me think of a tall red ship.

Kate's house is in the same street as the church, beyond the presbytery where I see the hall light burning behind the panes of coloured glass above the door. Her house is tall and narrow, painted a light grey. The knocker, which is shaped like a curved fish, rings out more loudly than I expect. Inside there is the quick thud a cat makes, startled and jumping from a chair. There is then so long a silence that I knock again. Almost at once, a dark man opens the door to me. I apologise to him, I say I thought, surely, Mrs Cooper lived at this number? I see past him to the end of the hall. It is clear that I have woken him from where he slept on a kind of couch, a blanket thrown beside it on the floor. As I look, a white cat jumps to the head of the couch and arches its back. The man says with a kind of strange flatness to his voice, 'She's at the house.'

'The house?' I say. And as he pauses, he takes his hand from where it presses against the wall as he watches me, and his fingers dabble in the pocket of his flannel shirt for the cigarette he draws from it. I tell him it is important that I see her.

'Urgent, then, is it?' he says. He holds the cigarette and rolls it gently between his stained fingers, then places it back in the pocket.

'Someone's died.'

That seems not to bother him. He looks past me to the roadway. 'You know the house, then?'

'I don't know where to get her except here.'

'I'll put money on that, too,' the man says. He comes out and stands barefooted on the rubber mat at the top of the concrete stairs. His face is so close to mine I smell the tobacco on him, and a sourness behind that. His finger jabs past my shoulder and I turn to follow its direction. He explains to go to the end of this street here, to turn right there at the corner, to walk a hundred yards down the hill. 'You don't know round here?'

'No,' I tell him.

'Five minutes,' he says. 'It's five minutes at the most.'

'I'm sorry I woke you,' I say.

He moves one foot and then the other, as though tamping down the mat. 'You're a friend are you? Friend of Missus?' And before I have time to answer him, 'Where you from, then?'

'Herne Bay,' I tell him.

'The buggery you are,' he says. He laughs so the row of his bottom teeth shows like a low brown fence. And as I go down the steps, turning from him, he calls, 'You haven't heard of me then? You haven't heard of Darkie?'

'I don't think so,' I say. 'I'm sorry if I've forgotten.'

'Thought you might of from the boy.' He goes inside, and I hear his deep coughing as he closes the door.

Kate opens the door to Number 23. She looks at me and says

nothing, and I follow her along a passageway, between the fall of heavy red drapes, through to a kitchen at the other end of the house. A tall young woman in a dressing gown is about to lift a hissing kettle from the coal range. 'Leave us for a minute,' Kate tells her. Without looking at me, the young woman passes through the bead curtains, which stroke against her as she passes. I sit down on a low sofa, and Kate sits beside me. For a moment her hand touches her forehead, then comes back to join the other on her lap.

'Tell me,' she says, before I have told her why I am there. 'Tell me how it was for her.'

And I lie. I say, 'It was not distressing for her, I think.'

The woman beside me looks at the window above the sink, the latticing of branches outside it. We sit like that, neither of us speaking, for several minutes, until she turns to me and asks me again, 'Tell me how she was.'

I hear movements in a room beyond the curtain, the sound of women's voices, what I think is a burst of crying that is quickly subdued. I go across to the range, to the bright kettle, and finish making the pot of tea that the tall young woman had begun. I take the pink cup with its gold rim, thick as a bangle, and give it to Kate, and sit beside her with a cup of my own. I say nothing of God's will, nor of the dead being spared further suffering. None of the phrases, the consolations, I have used heaven knows how many times. I feel no urge to do so, no regret that I do not. I look through from the kitchen to a kind of sitting room, heavy and red with curtains like those in the hallway. There is the dull glint of a large copper pot, and the black leaves of an aspidistra, on a table just inside the door. There is a picture in a dark frame which I cannot quite make out. Then strangely, I thought, she turns to me and says, 'You put sugar in your tea, didn't you? I've never seen you do that.'

And calmly she begins to ask me what she should do about the funeral. There is no one else she knows to tell even, she says. Miriam was a woman she really knew nothing about. 'I loved that in her. Her toughness. Her making a go of things on her own terms.' And what she says to me then is as surprising, I suppose, as anything that has been said to me in my life. 'You remind me of her, now I've got to know you.'

She smiles at the look she picks up, the look of bewilderment, I suppose, and I feel the heat rise beneath my veil. It is not embarrassment, not in the least, that she has compared me to a whore. It is a sense almost of happiness — yes, I can call it that — that she has paid me a compliment so deep, for I know how much that woman meant to her, how much she loved her.

I tell her, 'That is the kindest thing anyone could say to me.'

The delay, the long silence, has been too much for those in the other room. The tall young woman, and another, a little older, squat, yet also pretty, brush through the soft jangle of the bead curtains. The smaller one calls out, 'It's Miriam, isn't it?' while the taller girl's voice, deeper and more agitated, cuts across her friend's as she runs towards Kate. 'Miriam's gone, that's what she's telling you, isn't it?'

Her eyes seek mine with an intense resentment, and as the two women now openly burst into tears and Kate stands to comfort them, it breaks on me, as it had not really done until then, where precisely I am, why the women wear only dressing gowns above their dark stockings, that the scent of incense from the red room beyond me is the odour of enticement, of simple vice. It comes home to me. I am a nun, drinking tea in a brothel. It is a joke that would have delighted my grandfather, who was a moral man, and distressed my father, who was a hypocrite and *roué*. It is thinking that, I suppose, which makes it seem more ridiculous than awkward. The man Darkie's sly glance as he had asked me was I a friend — there seemed some point in it after all. What game was I playing at?

The younger women are sent back again, through the tinkling curtain. Kate opens the front door to a sky that is grey yet luminous: the rain has stopped, the light spread there like a paste.

'Thank you,' she says. 'It was a long way to come. So early. To let me know.'

'It was important.' For so it was, that she should hear it from me. And when she asks me, 'Shall I see you again?' I say yes, before the funeral, surely?

'You'll want to go to it?' she says. Then she sees how it is impossible for me, that Miriam is, at this point, hardly our concern. She says, 'I couldn't bear a funeral myself. But I shall still go.'

I am back at the Home soon after eight. At once I detect the discomfort, a brooding within our silence, that comes on the other patients when they learn there has been a death during the night. Two of the sisters are active in the kitchen, preparing something special for morning tea. There is nothing like a cream sponge to distract the old from the lengthening shadows of mortality. I pour a mug of tea from the large enamel pot and go through to my room. I hang my heavy coat behind the door, then sit at the small table and rest my head in my hands. I am so tired, so early in the day. My eyes clench against the bright morning light. I wonder if I should, at last, have my eyes tested. Then there is a soft tapping at my door. 'Yes?' I call out.

Young nervy Julian looks at me with her small, tight frown. 'These,' she says, 'these were under her mattress when we took her away.'

'Miriam?' I say.

'Who died this morning.' Julian holds out her hands and gives me the two small figures that had disappeared from the crib. I take them from her, the carved sentimental toys where faith fixes itself so simply. I think of how God was not so much as mentioned in Kate's bright, neat kitchen. I think of the woman who lies now in the mortuary, waiting for Mr Opie to call for her body and take it to his chapel in Grey Lynn. What on earth will they say when they bury her?

'Thank you, Sister,' I tell her.

'How on earth could they?' she begins. 'Who was it even?'

'I'll put them back where they belong.' I move my hand for her to leave me be.

When the door is closed I sit again at the table, and put the figures in front of me. The child, with golden snips of straw emerging like rays from its tiny head; St Joseph, who looks like an old man who will put up with anything, as I suppose he did. The swirls of steam from my tea rise up between them. I look at them for a long time. I am as close as one gets, I suppose, to having nothing at all in my mind. Until I hear a telephone ring and ring, far down the hall, and I am irritated that no one answers it. But at the same moment, the first sharp tugging in my side as I stand up. I close my eyes, as my finger runs over the chunky block of the tiny saint.

Here I am then, lying to my Order, asking my dear old friend Dr Flynn to lie for me as well. Which he will do, bless him, without a moment's doubt. All I say to him is that I have a friend I would like to spend time with, now that time is so short.

'She does not believe as I do,' I tell him. 'Yet it means as much to me as it does to her.' To say more than that, I know, would be melodramatic. 'I would like a few days with her,' I say. I even have a friend of my friend (why do I lie even further where I have no need to?) who will drive me there, to Napier, will drive me down, across, whatever it is one says for heading out, three hundred miles, south and east together. And I add, shamelessly, superfluously even, for I know Dr Flynn has set enough views on the harshness, as he thinks it, of my life, 'You know how Mother is, Doctor. She would agree at once if the idea came from yourself.' There is a bright young Australian sister who now directs us, outspoken and quite unfrench! It is to her Dr Flynn will speak.

He smiles, his thin lips, his sketch of a moustache, flicking towards me. 'I believe some would call this blackmail, know that, Sister?'

I take refuge in my old ploy, which of course he knows is pure show, my pretending I do not know English well enough (after forty years!) to take in what he means. Dr Flynn's aging eyes hold mine for a moment. His middle finger dabs at the bridge of his spectacles, raising them a fraction.

'I mean,' he tells me, 'I mean, Sister, that as a life-long friend you know I shall not say no. I shall also say the journey is essential for your health. And I shall say, moreover, that Mrs Cooper is a Catholic widow much given to good works.' For a moment, at least, he enjoys the irony of it.

'Ah,' I say, knowing how I trust him. 'So *that* is what blackmail means.'

A week later and we are walking up and down the lawn at the side of the drive. It is mid-summer, the long grass is drying to tangles of yellowish-green beneath the hedge. Every local child I see passing the Home is carrying a crushed towel beneath her arm, or flicking it at the child next to her, as they make their way towards the small sandy beaches at the bottom of the streets that pour down, hot and wide and stark, towards the harbour on the other side of Jervois Road.

Dr Flynn and I walk slowly, and then stop, side by side. There is a fig tree where we stand. For some reason, which slightly irritates me, its wide coarse leaves make me think of stretched, distorted gloves.

'It would be as well if I mentioned it to the Bishop,' Dr Flynn says. 'If I tell him — you know — the break was on my advice? Mother thought it a good idea.'

I agree with him. 'It would make things simpler. Yes.' To the Bishop, at least, he will be quite frank. She is carrying her death around with her this very moment, let us not beat about the bush. He will say he recommends it strongly. And the young austere Bishop, his voice like a warped, lingering tuning-fork, will join the tips of his fingers, and say, Ah, doctor, yes.

We say goodbye at the far end of the drive, virtually on the street. We can hear the young voices, high and taut and teasing, from the tennis court which is out of sight, beyond the school across the road. We shake hands, for the first and only time. The car burrs so smoothly, only a hundred yards off, a fat descending bee.

My lie, I realise, is such a trifling thing. The doctor carries my small black suitcase from the verandah. He jokes with Spicer, so aware of himself in his cap with its slanted leather peak. He tells him, 'Watch out for villains, now, won't you? Never know who you might meet in foreign parts.' The boy takes my case from him. But his lie, I know, his lie which Dr Flynn does not burden me with, is a matter of agony to him when the car turns away, the daylight slipping on its butter-coloured panels, and makes its ascent back up the slope of the road. He will — I so clearly imagine he will — stand with his hands deep in his pockets, like two heavy stones. He will think how he has done a very decent thing, yet a very wrong one too. I doubt if he has lied in his entire life, and he has done so to please me. My sin will be the harder to forgive, because it is taken on so much more lightly, taken on with more purpose. For I have, now, such a sense of clarity. I know exactly where I stand, and the fault is entirely mine.

Kate moves about behind me. The breeze slips over my neck, over my shoulders; it is living as a hand. She stands for a moment beside me and we look out to the sea together. It is tilted and brilliant with the morning, like some great sheet of tin. To myself, quietly, I say, 'Star of the Sea, pray for us.'

Kate's skirt brushes against me as she moves past. 'What?' she asks. She smiles down at me. She says something I do not quite hear — something I think about a drink, would I like one? I close my eyes against the rising tide of pain in my side. I lean forward, but it stays with me, my enemy. And I open my eyes again to the dazzle, and the distant arc of coast. I imagine I see a young girl, breathless, watching it beside me. She is thinking, 'God is a wider sea than ours.'

Spicer

You AND YOUR BLEEDING FUCKEN NUNS! DARKIE SHOUTS AT ME, HIS gob open like when he's gone berko and screaming so the street looks, everybody looks, and this bit of spit jumping out at you and the brown scraps from his roll-your-own on his dirty tongue there, and I looking straight at that. Thinking what a rotten old mouth inside there, a yellow streak down the middle of his tongue like someone pissed down the middle of a carpet. I watch him working himself up, his eyes red like he's bawling just about and a squeezed-out tear on one side starting to move down his rooted old face. I don't know what to say to him like I never do and he spitting all over me now, spraying on me while he shouts, his face so close up against mine while he's carrying on to Jesus. I think, why you just never shut up you old cunt, but all I do's look at him, I think out the words inside all right but they just there shagged out or something soon's I get near saying them. Then next thing he's on that again, saying high and mighty, aren't I just, give a bloody rangatang a cap like mine, why doesn't she? Might look a bit more like a human about it too, although better not start bringing that into it, he says. Me, he means, me in my uniform and my cap and having the car look spruce and all like it does. Christ in heaven, Darkie says, just get a load of yourself some time, give some poor fucken mirror a chance to put you right. Spawn a thing like that, Darkie says, one finger juts out at me, enough to make a man take a dive off Grafton

Bridge. The new brown suit and the shine on the cap and all, as if I don't know what's narking him and he knows I know that too, that what winds him up.

It was her idea about the cap, I say, I never wanted a cap, it was Mrs C tells me I got to wear it, got to look the part. That's important looking the part, she says, after she tells me, want the job? Next to I drive all right, that's number one, she doesn't want to end up against a telegraph pole now, does she? Laughing all the time she saying it. So I tell him now, Might be smart all the time you think but you're wrong about that one, Darkie, I only got the cap because Mrs C tells me, okay? Because she knows a good driver when she sees one like.

But Darkie never let it rest. As if you don't know when youse been taken for a ride, he says, fruit of my bloody loins tarted up like a whore's monkey which he fucken is and now a clapped-out bloody old nun's monkey as well, just stand aside while I throw up, will you? And then there's more tears bumping down over his crunched-up cheeks and it's the shame he's telling about. Shame you brought on the family, he says, thank God your mother's dead's all I can say. He closes his eyes as he saying that, and clips the top off of a beer bottle just going thwack, his fist sharp down on the top he's set against the edge of the bench so a bit of bench flies off too, then he sucks straight from the bottle. Soon as he put the bottle down after his first half dozen sucks with his adam's apple going up and down like a half-berko lift or something he belches so he makes it sound like a quick bark and rubs his hand across the front of his shirt, pleased as punch, then grunts again, only a fart this time, make you disgusted just to hear it. You're a proper pig, Darkie, Rita used to tell him, in front of the boy. Only he'd do it again if he could when she said that, let a snorter go like that was paying her back. And some friend of hers I don't even remember who it was said, He's as uncouth as they come, God knows how he got any woman, let alone. It was on the verandah of the old house, the first house. And Darkie laughed out at whoever said it and told her, Bother to think of what I done for him in my time, think about that one? Brought this half-quid's worth up, that's what I done, reckon it's worth a medal for humane fucken practices.

Stuff like that I been hearing now for ever, just about. Even to Mrs C one week when I forget to bring the rubbish bin in at Number 23 and someone flogs it, so she tells him better tell his son to take a bit more care can he, and he hollers out, Son, is it? Son! I'd been better off someone give me a foxie didn't piddle inside and at least knew how to go for a burglar's arse. This rooster wouldn't know that much, wouldn't know shit from clay if you shone a torch on it. Screaming that out like he done that other time just after I get the job down at the Home. Knows about as much about anything as old top mick there in Rome in his fancy get-up knows about pussy, that's how much he knows. His face so angry that time I think he's going to keel over, nobody's that pissed off and still standing up. But that other time Mrs C opens the back door when he's in full rant and did she give it to him, did she ever! Get out of here, she tells him, get back to the other house while I make up my mind whether you're even worth keeping on. Whether you're even a human being! So that's when he does this limp round the side of the house and I never seen anyone look more like a dog's been booted in the ring. Talking like that though, that's how it is I reckon half the time at least, people say why haven't I laid one on him? That Spicer, everyone says, they don't come much stronger for a boy of his age do they? As if I'd belt him, belt Darkie who's my dad. Think I don't know how wrong that is, belting your old man, whatever sort of prick he is? As if I never seen the other side as well, seen what he's like when he comes on quiet, when he sit there sometimes, days on end, so down to it you think the whole world give him a bloody great wallop.

So it doesn't bother me that much like you might expect when he carries on mad as hell for days that Mrs C telling me how she wants me to drive her when she goes away, wants me to wear the special cap as well, then tells me on top of that the nun's coming too. That's all right I think, she's one of them I like, but it's the bit driving Darkie over the top. Long as I'm doing jobs around the Home these last couple of years that doesn't bother him, picking up the slops in the barrow and sneaking half them down near Cox's Creek where old Digger Martin's got his four fat gutsing pigs and gives me two bob a week for all the old mush and swill I can get for him and a load on late Saturday afternoons as well from the Chink along Richmond Road, the throw-out half-stinking cabbages and stuff won't last the weekend. Darkie takes half what I make, even what the nuns paying me too. He tells me what kind of recompense is that in any case I ask you, all I done for you in my time? I give it to him, the money, although I don't know what for, he never pays Mrs C a bean for us staying there in the big house, what's it called, that word on the brass bit at the top of the steps? *Carrickdown*. Whatever that is. Not so much as a penny, I know that. She says he works for her so how can she take rent for that. Work, I think, he just lies there half the time out in the lean-to or sitting in the chair at the end of the passage like some old thing stuck at the back of a cave and that creepy green eye in his wireless on the ledge next to him. Sometimes in the dark that's all you see, that eye changing when he moves the knob, it scares the shit you come on it sudden and not expect it. All that sitting about and lying down and supposed to be caretaker or whatever, never seen him do more than a bit of sweeping and bullshitting the ladies down at Number 23. They safe as a bank he tells them if he's there those nights when any trouble likely, after footy games and the Auckland Cup say, days like that. Once or twice I never ask him because he never tell you anyway but he comes back from 23 with a cut lip or something, a fat cheek, his shirt ripped about so the buttons gone. Personal security, that's what he says he does, half-pie bouncer more the gist of it, the other half hanging round the bars up Symonds Street, across in Newton Road, matey as you like with off-duty Sergeant Carroll, trying to pump him when the bulls lined up to raid Mrs C's next time round so she's off the mark good and early slipping a backhander and keeps them off in time. But I ask him the least thing about all that, Never you bloody mind, he tells me, you just cut the doolans' lawn there, leave the men's work to the men. But all the time pissed off when Mrs C taking a bit more notice of me than he ever want, knowing I going to look good all right once she buys me the fancy gear. Knows there's any trouble I handle that all right too, I just about twice as strong now as Darkie ever was. Darkie hates all that.

I think about that time, first time she knows I sleeping in the wood shed out the back behind the lean-to, and Darkie comes on with his father stunt, half blubbing the old bugger while he's spinning her this yarn once she's asked him who I am then, what am I there for? The talk hardly mattering that much to me anyway because I just taking her in, her lovely long gown thing, not blue like any other blue but a different kind of light off it every time she move, her fingers on the ornament she sometimes has there on her front, red stones and the silver bits between going out like streaks of light. Look Missus, that's what he's lying to her, look I'm on the very verge of telling you today and here you are, simply beaten me to the draw. Grinning at her, like that makes it less bullshit than it is. My first born, he tells her, not the brightest by any means and God knows if I didn't always keep an eye on him. Not a word about the money he takes from me and then the extra tanner on top of that, taking it from me every week to let me sleep out there where it isn't even his to say whether I can or not. Parents will do sly things if it's their flesh and blood, you must know that, Missus? While I'm standing there, just watching her. No idea have I if she's going to tell me to shoot through, she's not running a doss house for no-hopers, is she, like Darkie told me she's bound to say if ever she finds me out. I'll sneak you in, he said. She's down the other place half the time as it is, that's the best I can do for you, what's three bob to put aside if she arses me from the job, that's the risk I'm taking, all right, aiding and abetting?

Only then she's laughing at him, he doesn't know what to make of it, Give it a rest, Darkie, you'll have me in tears. She knows him through and through, because first thing she's asking him is how much he been charging the boy? And I say, Three shillings and sixpence, the first words I ever say to her, the same instant Darkie says, A bob or so, doesn't cover what he eats. She tells him then, half having him on I reckon, that because it was her house and she was certain the one thing he wasn't doing was trying to put one across her, and she quite understood his motives, simply to do his best for his son, she'd only take two shillings and sixpence from him out of what he was copping off of me, Half a crown, she said. And then put it to me straight out,

131

not to him, If you'd like to help yourself to what's in the kitchen whenever you feel like it as well? My goodness Darkie seething for weeks after that one, not making a dinar out of me any longer and having to treat me right because she'd be keeping an eye, she said, make sure he was treating me proper.

I'm glad you're a good father, Mrs C said to him. Then to make it worse she tells me seeing she is the only other one living there as a rule anyway and Darkie as I know is caretaker round at 23 there which makes this place good as empty half the time, I might as well move right inside then mightn't I, take the room just off the landing? And she sees me looking at the thing on its chain around her neck, this big dark stone the colour of blood when it's nearly dried and bits of other brighter things coming from it like the lines when people draw the sun. It *is* lovely, she says, isn't it? And she holding it out from her and then I touch the biggest stone, that was warm from where it lie against her. Then when she gone Darkie with the stuffing properly knocked out of him like, says how a serpent in his own bosom was what he had nurtured, his own fucken bosom, he realised that now oh didn't he just.

So I'm more important than he is this once anyway. The car done that for me all right, he knows it too. I make sure when I go with Mrs C to Seabrooks, into that big palace place all shine and mirrors to get the car with its yellow panels so it sort of slips along the street and the black hood and yellow flicking wheels I hardly believe it, believe it's me up there on the shiny leather smells so new as all that. I drive it back along the street with the big old church there on the corner, kids stopping to gawp from inside the playground and I lean on the horn that Mrs C calls the klaxon and when I know Darkie's there, pulling the velvet curtain to have a gander at his one and only, I toot so loud one burst and then another burst and then another the whole street's sitting up I can tell you that. Then for a second before he push the curtain back he's there at the window, his hand inside his shirt scratches at his armpit like when he's thinking hard but not even ordinary angry by now, I see by his face he knows his splutter and his bawling won't make a shagger's difference, not now it won't, him just sneaking a look because that all it is, straight out sneaking from behind the curtains, stand there in his bare feet even, I bet you that. He got to watch me toot at him and look across, the moronic fucken fruit of his loins all right, up there with my cap and my shining boots in the motor, not just in it, mind, *driving* the motor like Darkie's never parked his bum in all his born days. Then I look out the window again and the shifting curtain and Mrs C leans forward close against my neck, she tells me, All right, Spicer, for goodness sake, you can give it a rest! So I just looking ahead again along the shiny bonnet and the high polished mudguards and the whole street slipping past like somehow that been polished too, never felt anything so good as that. Only if I been able to lean out and shout up at him, I'm going to pick the nun up, Darkie, then we're buggering off. If I been able to do that and watch him, Jesus, that would of been it all right. Because I beat him not just this time, but going back and back, know what I mean, as if I turn a hose and everything behind me washed out clean as well. Darkie knows that too. That's what biting him so bad. I think of him sneer at me last night when I try on my cap, my brown new jacket Mrs C herself pick out for me, Flash as a rat with a gold tooth, aren't we just? Cut me down, that's the idea, like he always done. Only now the horn there a minute ago running in and out between the houses, bouncing back after we already gone on past, it must shine out there like it's in the sun and everything around it dark. Knows what flash is now, Darkie does. Knows now, the old bugger, when Miriam gone and everything else got to fill what isn't there. Why we got to do everything like it's so important. Driving Mrs C and the nun half way round the world it might as well be. Drive away from everything ever been.

She's going to ask me, sooner or later, I know that, she going to ask me where you live, who you live with, everyone's always asking aren't they, sooner or later? Everybody always into other people's business. So I think when Sister ask me I just tell her I got no mother, no father, she so used to orphan kids round that place she not going to bother give it a second thought. Just an orphan, I reckon that what she thinks then, won't bother me again. But then that day not long after I start there, she's touching my hand, the blood dripping all over the place where I rip it on some loose tin. She turns my hand over and there's the rip, the skin pushed up and blue like on a plum skin and hanging there, a little hinge. Dear oh dear, she says. She looks at it quick but so careful, touches the little hinge so careful could be her own hand just about. Then a bit of cotton wool and the bandage this way and that way she winds round and round it, her fingers so soft the way they moving I think there for a second, Jesus how she fucken do it, although I shouldn't, not there, not one of Darkie's words. Her eyes close up this nice colour, big and looking at me, nice although she that old as well. She's a friend, she sort of telling me, but not saying that, not saying nothing, no God talk, nothing, just my hand hurt and bleeding and she fixing it up. Asking me nothing not her business, so that orphan bit, I don't tell her that. And glad because I don't want to tell her what's not the truth, like I don't want to tell her about Darkie either, tell her where I come from, where I live while he works for a place where rooters go, day and night that's what it's there for, only that, for rooting, dirty as you like. Don't say that to the nun. Not that I live there mind, I could of said, that's another place, Number 23, that's a knock shop. Darkie even tells me soon as I move in the big house, ever he catches sight of me round Number 23 my arse won't forget for a month of Sundays, that sink in, he'd wear his boot out if he had to. Even later when Mrs C tells me go down there to clear the gutters, she doesn't want the old man up a ladder with his wonky foot, Darkie can't tell me not to but he hate it all the same. Watches me like he think I'm going to rob the girls or something. They so snooty that lot, anyway, they so flashing this and that in the clothes they wear and the place always high as a kite with scent and stuff they keep in little jars. I don't like there even. I like to get away. Only Miriam I like and that's a long time later. The silly bitch, Darkie says, put out because Mrs C tells me that about his gammy leg, I was working the scaffolding he says when they build the new Post Office, I was more at home up and down them bloody ladders than you are walking on those two flat feet of yours, boy, don't you worry.

I try to tell Darkie sometimes how he's always going on too much about anything, to lay off Mrs C anyway because where either of us be without her? Oh, he says then, oh? Next thing he's belted the top of his wireless so the green eye goes out and he's hollering at me Suffering Christ, talking like that to get at the nuns I work for. I can see through him all right. And none of this telling me, he says, none of this fucken telling me what I must and what I mustn't talk about, thank you very much. And then it's Jumped-up little prick, he calling me, don't mind being rouseabout for a houseload of whores, never mind that, but respect for his own father, not on your life! While the old man knows I know he the one spreads the word about for the drum anyway, touting for 23 and the other place off Mt Eden Road as well, talking to likelies in the Astor then across at the Edinburgh Castle. He's the one down there too like a shot ready for a stoush minute there's any trouble, some customer not coming across with his half quid or whatever, some drunk forgetting they're ladies even if turning it up wholesale is what they do for a crust. The Missus, like he always calls Mrs C, the Missus she won't abide trash, I'm round to make sure none get in. Or if they do, the bastards, they don't get out without something to remember us by. He likes talking that way before he leaves the big house and he slips on the heavy knuckledusters and flicks his fingers in and out, likes the look of them with the chunks of lead across them. As if when Sister asks me where I live and that, do I have a father, as if I going to say, Yes, Darkie, that my dad, he helps out in a knock shop. Why I'm ready with the orphan bit even though I don't need to use it. In case she ever asks.

So long ago I don't remember that clear even when I try, when it's still and quiet down the paddock behind the Home and hot enough, it summer all right, hot enough to lie in the cut grass smelling like it fresh and dying together, the best time when I always thinking what was it like at the beginning. Best of all I like it when the two cows hardly any way off, the munch in your ear good as, the stink of them sweet as well in the hot day, and you just lying there with your eyes closed and it all pink inside your head and the swish-swash close to you, lovely like that, the quiet, and you kind of part of it, the paddock and all, so hard to say it, say what's happening but it's hardly you even any more, is it, the way you sinking, slipping into everything else? And sometimes Mumma in my mind those times, so close like she standing at the window in the old first kitchen. She turns from the curtain and where she sees down the long road to the bush right off far as you can, where Daddy works, she says, where Darkie. She got the sun behind her, round her head. She saying to me, Soon now, he coming soon. Her hands in close against me, touches me very quick, down my face, down my side, like that, like that. So light it nearly hurts, my own hand sometimes touching me that quick, that light, only there, the place you never talk of. I think better the nuns not see, and rub my hand clean inside my shirt. Then I sit up sudden in the paddock and the special colour gone from things like it's fallen somehow back to how is ordinary, one old cow pouring muck down on the grass and the other the colour of big tea leaves spread all over her tits, her juicy spit when her head come up and looks at me, spit like long soft shiny wires nearly hit the ground. But nothing else there, only the Home across the paddock and one sister on the long verandah holding some sick old bugger, walks him up and down so slow might as well be dead and call it quits. Bloody everybody nearly dying up there I reckon sometimes, or loony kids can't walk can't talk, nothing, only the orphan kids anywhere near half-way right, look nice all right those ones in their shiny clothes, the new ribbony hats.

She so clear those times, Mumma. Only three or four pictures in my head, never more than that. At the window like that the best one, I think, the sky all blazing up, must be nearly right behind her. And this one too, I can't never of really seen it, can I, but real as looking at someone straight in front of you, real as Sister up that close the day she does the bandage on my hand, the little fine hairs on her lip you never see unless you up that close. Real as that Mumma walking along a track, the house with no paint on it, maybe no real windows in it either, the house up there behind her, the yellow banks slashed open, the wet running down them. Holding me on her arm. I am a baby but I know it is me sure as I know when a knife cut in against your own skin. Along this path she walks that slow, that slow. And I never sure either who it is watches her come that way. Not Darkie, I sure enough of that. Mumma in a long dress, maybe this grey colour is the real colour of the dress or maybe just looks grey because the afternoon's so late.

I got that picture there half the time, give me the chance. Mumma when I lie like that, sometimes at night-time too just before I go to sleep and warm all over when I thinking of her, see her at the window, on the path. Darkie never seen her like that. Never tells me but I know. Darkie's trouble he doesn't never see her. Mumma dead when I only so high, but none of that in my mind, the sad time. Only after that. Miss McAuley, the slut, the raddled bitch, that double-dyed shag-artist by Christ, Darkie calls her, the whore and a half to end them all. I remember her all right though, Miss McAuley. Because she the one comes to live with us after Mumma, after Darkie's accident does his leg proper. I don't know where I stayed some of that time, I'm so small a wonder I remember any of it, the time when my old man's in hospital it must be and then I see him one day. I'm held up, that's all I know of it, held up on a high building and someone tells me, Look down there, Spicer, see your dadda come to get you back? And Darkie looks up at me, I look at him, I'm going down this long staircase, someone still holding me, and he waits for me at the bottom because his leg is buggered and still in white, big and bandaged, and that's all I want to look at. First time I look at him since he left the bush, half his foot sliced off so I hear later, this joker swinging an axe beside him, Monty fucken Evans. I hear that so much later. That day though Darkie grins down at me and his big hands under my arms and I'm up higher then than he is, Whoosh, he says, swings me up and out and whoosh again, swinging me back down. I'm above his head and his hair so shiny I think it's black paint a moment, the light flicks along it. As I come down again my hand goes out and I touch the top of his shirt, first time ever I remember I'm laughing, happy my hand going out, touching the foamy black hair where his shirt's unbuttoned at the top. He carries me out to a mate sits waiting in a car. Me and Darkie close like that there for a bit. I get new clothes, Lord bleeding Muck he calls me, tapping the buttons on me that look like money in Darkie's pockets. The coat with the silver buttons the first time he takes me with him, We're visiting real class, he says. Miss Fuck-for-a-quid McAuley she becomes soon after, but this day My dear he calls her, moves one hand on my head and tells her, This my dear the fruit of, believe it or not, and they laughing then, and Miss McAuley slaps his arm and licks her lips, always licking her lips so they wet and pretty. His hand in my back and pushes me to go forward but my feet stay where they are and I fall over, I remember that, fall right in front of her so my face right against the big buckles on her shoes. That's when her hand come down, so white and long and red material around her wrist, and I'm crying and Darkie grabs me at the collar and jerks me up and says, Get sense out of this one, that'll be the day. Miss McAuley's hand on mine for a minute, her voice I can tell angry with my dad, Leave the boy, she says.

Even now a jumble all that time there, something to do with money from Monty fucken Evans' slicing axe and ladies here and there and then him pissed off with me, more and more all the time. Miss McAuley and Darkie and me living in one house for how many years, not that I call Miss McAuley that, I call her nothing all that time. And Darkie although if you know him now you hardly think so but bow and scrape to her, tells her all the time once the big compo money's through then they're home and hosed. On the pig's back, Darkie says. Just play our cards right. That right, Spicer? he says to me sometimes, so close I see the little veins all over his face, I want to put my fingers up and touch them. I tell him, That right, Darkie, and he and Miss McAuley they laughing like I say the funniest thing you'd ever, and his open hand comes down slap across the top of her leg where she's sitting close up beside him and she grabs his fingers and pulls them back and says, What can you be thinking of, the boy there? I don't know how many years but it must of been enough for me to nearly be at school. She so nice to me that time too, long as it's Darkie my love from her and Twopence he calls her, Treasure, then one day like a door slams shut, sudden as that, it's Fucken slag-arsed twat he tells her, and she's shouting back, and he takes the frilly top of her dress and one quick tug and rips it away, the crushed-up bit in his hand, and she stands there her tits all falling out and her hands cross over so I won't see how they are and Darkie yelling, Give the whole fucken street a decker, why don't you, youse showing the rest of Auckland aren't you? That kind of talk all the time then when Miss McAuley leaves him, shot through with Monty fucken Evans' axe money and not a thing, a lawyer tells him, not a thing you can do about it, you give it to her as de facto as they say, you signed a bit of paper, you've no recourse. I hear him tell it over and over, that's how I know the words. And that not bad enough, she's haring off with Monty fucken Evans himself, who chopped half the old man's foot off then scarpers to Sydney with this slut, this God-forsaken drab and that's a word too good for her, them living it up on Darkie's money. The whole thing one bloody rig-up all that time you wouldn't think butter, Jesus Christ!

Then the night before she goes, she and Darkie shouting across the kitchen, spit jumping right out of Darkie's mouth and hanging there like on the cows down the paddock from the Home, poor bugger, tears and slush all over his face and Miss McAuley cool like a cucumber, that's what they say, stands there white as a hanky on the other side of the table with the glass vase in the middle Darkie gets her last time for her birthday. Next thing she's the one not screaming her swede off like the old man but quiet as you like picks up the vase in both her hands and holds it up nearly to her face, makes me think now how the priest bloke at the Home holds up the silver cup like I seen him do through the open chapel windows in the summer, she holds it up like that and next thing, *there*, both her hands held out open, white like they could be a bird's wings, and the vase falls down from her this quick flash of shiny glass before the crash on the wooden floor. A big slice of glass jumps up from where it crashes, goes across my face so I start to cry, although hardly scratched, but Darkie grabs my hand from near my cheek and pulls it away and sees the bit of blood and the nick against my face. Even children, he says to her, stops his bellowing out and says it to her so quiet you hear the crunch when her foot moves over crumbs of glass, What we done for this, eh? Then she does the worst bit. She looks at him first, and then at me, and this new kind of smile on her face, not the nice one, not the Twopence smile, not the Treasure love, just this one like she hangs wire on her

139

face, and very slow she points at me but turns so her face is straight in front of Darkie's and says to him, That kid there wouldn't feel it if you belted his head in with a hammer that's how thick. Thick's not even in it. He's so dumb he makes plain dumb sound smart. And Darkie like he's almost scared or something asks her, What the hell you on about now, you slut? On about, she says. She's laughing at him now, her finger shaking at me, her voice getting louder. On about? Ever try him on colours, Darkie? Ever see if he can read? How old is he? Eight or something? You got a half-wit on your hands only you're so god-almighty thick yourself you never even noticed, penny never dropped. Miss McAuley turns around then and her shoes crunch again over where the glass is, and at the door she turns and tells him, tells it to both of us, I can't abide the sight, that goes for you both.

Then Darkie changing after that. No more jokes, even when he wins a double chart or a tote ticket, sixty smackers once, he says, So fucken what? Whenever he can he talks bad about her, about Miss McAuley. Tripe guts, he says, a root rat from way back, Christ knows why he never clicked. Not just her either, just about everybody comes in for it. Women, he says, honest to God boy if they didn't turn it up you'd throw stones at them. And starts on me as well until all the time practically he's got me crying. I'm hoping he won't talk to me, won't even see me if I shut up in some place he won't think of looking. But some nights I'm that hungry I just got to let on, and when he opens the door I ask him, Where's something to eat then Dad? And he looks at me like I'm someone he never wants to see and says, Wasn't for you she'd be here now, know that? Wasn't for you driving her distracted gawping at her half the time and the other half just sitting there thick as pig shit, tell me what woman's going to put up with that one? Suppose I think that's part true, even suppose it is, still not nice is it, Darkie saying that? And I thinking of the time we were dinkum cobbers and he'd say it so everybody hears it, everybody knows, Cobbers aren't we sport? and jogs me round on his shoulders and says, Grab that branch there, and I do, I grab it quick as that and hang there while he snorts and runs around again like a horse he's playing at, then runs under me again as my legs slap across his shoulders and Let go!

he hollers at me and we're off. Got to be smart to do it good as that, eh Spicer me lad? Then all that's over like I say, quick as a slammed door when Miss McAuley scarpers, when my dad sitting there quiet, not a word maybe all night, then kicks the table half way across the room and says I don't know who he's talking to because I'm the only one there is, Sorry, he says, sorry he ever called her a fucken trollop, what did your ordinary toss-their-quim-around trollops ever do to deserve *that* thing being dumped in with them? More bitter all the time. That's what Rita says, Talk about time healing things, tell her another if you please.

Rita is Darkie's sister who comes then to look after me because her husband has gone to reap the harvest, she says, gone to gather his reward in the only kingdom that rules for ever. And because you can't drink yourself to damnation and drag the boy up at the same time, she says to Dad. I won't pay you, you needn't think that, Darkie says, I haven't got a brass razoo. That's when Rita laughs at him like she knows a thing or two he'll never click to and tells him, As if filthy lucre comes into it. She talks like that nearly all the time, Rita. Oh never mind, she laughs, shows her big square teeth like it's a joke she wouldn't miss for worlds, *Vita brevis*, she says, as if we need to be told. She watches me look at her when she uses her words I never heard of, and winks at me and says, Never know who your relations might be, that's a fact now, Spicer. But she got so much to keep her busy, church and work at Turners and Growers the fruit-box factory and never anything at home except polishing and scrubbing and if it's not that baking for those who are less fortunate, God's plan is beyond us all, she says, but the helping hand will be there to clap his praises, come the day. But she leaves me just about alone. At first she talks to me about am I saved and I look at her I suppose like I'm everything Darkie says about me, and after a while she just taps my hand sometimes if someone's there, one of her friends from the Assembly and she tells them, He's a good boy, this one, doesn't know what evil is. But when she's by herself, her eye there on me sometimes if I look up sudden, and she smiles like it's making her sad to smile and she says, I don't know what we'll do with you, Spicer, coming on fourteen a boy's got to earn a penny at something. And once she says like she's had it out with him and he laid it on the line, The Lord Jesus can't solve everything for us and that's a fact. It isn't fair to expect him to.

So fifteen by now, I'm bigger than Darkie just about. Mr Coffey in the chemist's shop at the top of College Hill says to me, My you're a fine big lad now aren't you Spicer? You want a part-job it's ten shillings a week, you won't do better than that. My auntie Rita tells me Beggars can't be choosers, you don't go to school half the time as it is and when you do God help us what's the odds? Even the men back from the war can't find jobs half of them the poor devils, she says. So I get this bike with a basket on the front for deliveries and I ride round on it all over the show, Hargreaves Street this time maybe, then along Summer Street the next, nearly Surrey Crescent sometimes. People ring up Mr Coffey, ask him, Send this on round will you? Something for the old lady's cough, liniment seeing some codger can't walk, and he puts down the telephone after he's written on his little pad and calls out, Spicer, be a good lad will you, shut the old girl up?

When I'm not out on the bike I help Mr Coffey at the back of the shop, weighing out from a bin into the small purple packets or stacking tins too high for Mr Coffey to get to himself, and once, a couple of weeks it must of taken, I paint the whole storeroom for him, shift everything over this side, then shift it back over that, talk about fuss. Mr Coffey himself there half the time, telling me, now could he suggest this, Spicer, perhaps if we did it *this* way, eh? Never seen anyone so polite, I think. Never raises his voice. Lah-deh fucken dah! Darkie says when he hears I'm working there. Lay off him, will you? Rita comes in then. And when Darkie grins at her and puts his middle finger up she turns on him full bore. If a rat came out of your gob one of these days it's no more than I'd expect, she says.

Six months then after the storeroom Mr Coffey says, Made such a job of that one we'll essay the sun porch, shall we? It takes the best part of a week to clear it out, then he tells me, Trundle over to Victoria Street, will you, lad, Mr Shroff's an intimate. But Mr Shroff, the woman says, isn't in this week, you wouldn't believe how many are going down with flu. So she helps me find the colour Mr Coffey has written down and when I put the first few strokes of it along the wall he makes out he covers his eyes at the sight of it. Buttercup! he says, call that buttercup! On the second day it's a scorcher and the little sun porch picks the heat up like it's an oven. Mr Coffey stands at the door and says, You're wringing, Spicer, you'd be that much more comfortable with your shirt off. Your strides too. No ladies round here to shock.

I got enough paint on me anyway so I think yes, how it would be better like he says. Rita'd go off the handle as it is, sees me come home with yellow bits all over me. So I keep on painting in just my underpants and Mr Coffey laughs, Gene Tunney, he says, my my! That's the good thing working for him, see, I say to Rita. I never seen anyone in a good mood all the time before. You don't get a boss like that every day, you can put a ring round that, she says. When she tells Darkie he looks up from the *Truth* he smooths over with his opened hand and says, Good men out of work and the likes of that lands on his jaxie. Auntie Rita leans over then and gets him a fair flick with her tea towel that might of been a joke maybe with someone else but not Darkie. He's up and across the kitchen and the wire door smashes back so one spring goes and he's off down the side of the house, and Rita cool as you like simply folding up the paper, then there's this yelp and racket from the side of the house where he's gone arse over kite against the rubbish bin she keeps tucked in behind a hydrangea bush. It's hidden there like that where you hardly see it because she says you're low class like the Ellises next door if you have your bin out for the world to see, outside their fence one week to the next. So Darkie anyway picks himself up and throws the whole bloody bin down the back lawn where I tidy up the chucked round mess later on but for the moment there's only dead quiet. I don't know what to say because Auntie Rita's good as in tears by now. Where do people get the words from, that's what I'm saying to myself, just hundreds of them pouring out like Darkie, like my aunt most of the time? And that's when Rita stands up and clicks her tongue like she does when she finds dog shit on her lawn. If it hadn't been for that damned leg, she says, he might have made a fist of things, had a decent life. Then quietly she hoists the fly door back in against its hinge. Mr Coffey's good to you, she says, don't you go letting him down. Kind as well, she doesn't need to tell me that. And Mr Coffey thinking about her too although I don't tell her that when he sees me standing there dressed just like that, just in my underpants, and he says, Not that your aunt would take much joy from you going home your skin covered in paint either, I can appreciate that. So he gives me this apron with the material crinkled round the edge of it. I must look at him a bit surprised because it's then he laughs and slips the apron over my head and ties the bands behind me, quick as if he's tying a packet in the shop. God, he says, you do look a sight in that, my dear. He watches me and laughs even more and says, Talk about startled rabbits. And like it's part of the joke his finger catches at the elastic of my underpants and snaps it against me before he turns and says, There, I know how modest you are, just carry on, and he leaves me to spread the yellow paint across the boards that are this ugly crusty green before I paint over them. It's a nice feeling, doing that, the paint thick like syrup or something and the brush flowing over the walls, the clean shine on it where all the muck used to be. Hardly any job can be as nice as this, I think.

An hour or so later Mr Coffey brings in the metal advertising stand from the footpath and props it like he always does behind the locked front door of the shop. I hear the clatter of it from out here, in the sun porch. I stop for a moment and the doors must be opened right through the house, because I hear the long blind pulled down over the gold writing that always surprises me when I see it walking through the other way, yəffoƆ written backwards like that, and underneath, the smaller letters to tell you what exams he's got. A minute or so later he comes through to the sun porch. He is carrying a black tin tray and a bottle of beer on it and two glasses. Time the workers got a bit of attention wouldn't you say? And as he puts the tray on a little cane table and fusses with the opener, Speights, he says, I don't remember when I drank anything else. So I pull the string at the back of the apron because work is over I think, but Mr Coffey says, No, don't bother about getting changed just yet, eh, Spice? The first time anyone's called me that, called me Spice, and I think I wish he wouldn't, I don't like him saying that. I sit on the apple box I been resting the paint tin on and he taps his glass against mine so the two froths tilt into each other. I can hear the fizz of it when I lift the beer up to drink. Mud in your eye, Mr Coffey says. He winks across the top of the glass. I say I never had this before. Beer? he says. Never tasted it, not even once. There then, he says, I knew there was something to celebrate. And we talk about this and that. He asks me how I get on living with my auntie, and how often I see the old man, although he calls him not Darkie or my father but your esteemed sire. I raise my own glass the way Mr Coffey raises it and say Cheers, then, when we start the second glass. I think, I wish Darkie could see me now. I'm drinking beer like a man and Mr Coffey's my friend. I'm not some no-fucken-hoper am I, some throwback, like the old man calls me? I am a painter sitting here in my painter's apron, drinking beer from a long posh glass. Mr Coffey is telling me what chances there are for a lad like myself, a bit of application, he says, a touch of luck. By God, he says, it was different in my day believe you me, there was no work to be had for love nor money. And suddenly he says to me, You're a cute one, mind, aren't you, there's no telling what's ticking over in here, and he taps the side of his head. He nods his own head sideways at me, tells me, You'd have to start moving early to catch you out, young feller-me-lad. As if he knows some joke or other that I'm not wise to. I get lost that quick when talk starts whizzing around, I just say to him, I don't know about that, and he looks at me as though I'm a shrewd one even saying that. After a while he leans over the tray and picks up the emptied bottle, holds it against his eye so the world must look for a moment that smoky-brown colour, then he puts it back. My God, he says, the wonders of evaporation!

He goes through to the room behind the kitchen, the one with heavy curtains and the glints and gleams of things in the half dark, and then comes back with another bottle. Caused no pain, that last one, did it? he asks. It didn't, Mr Coffey, I tell him. And this time when he passes me my glass he sits next to me, moving his chair so it's near the apple box I'm sitting on. He says, What's this Mr Coffey now, I ask you? He tells me to call him Simon, the way his other friends do, for goodness sake. He laughs like he clears his throat at the same time. Formality, he says, we don't stand on that round here. When I say, But I only work for you, Mr Coffey, he laughs louder and shakes his head. Is there anything like the honesty of youth? he says. His hand slides over my shoulder the way Rita's does sometimes when she's talking to me, only now I've got no shirt on and Mr Coffey's hand moves so slowly, right across to behind my neck. The other bottle is nearly finished and the sun porch moves round a bit like it's living by itself, starting to breathe or something. He goes out again and this time when he comes back he is carrying two black shoes with straps across them instead of laces and bits underneath that hold you high and tilt you forward when you walk. He puts them down where a bit of shelf is still not painted and pours what's left in the second bottle into my glass and says, Here, Spice, how about you put these shoes on, just for a lark? I ask him, What for though? and he tells me he found the things out the back, they must of been there for years. They look your size wouldn't you say? And when I say, They're not men's shoes though are they? he says, Who's so particular about that, all feet are the same hadn't I noticed? Here, he says, I'll do it for you. Next thing he kneels in front of me, he holds one of my feet in his hand and slips the shoe on, a perfect fit, see? And then the other shoe. He rests it on his knee and does up the thin black strap not much wider than string and smooths his hand across the shoe and my ankle and up my leg nearly to my knee before he stands up and takes his own glass of beer and sits down and begins to talk again like nothing different happening at all, just two friends together like he says, chewing the fat, passing the time of day. He's talking about football now, about the Marist game last week at Victoria Park. He follows third grade, he says, those first grade are just a bit too savage for his taste, and the trek to Eden Park, he says, it might as well be Cape Town. Like this is something everyday, me sitting there like this in my apron and the tall black shoes really for ladies whatever Mr Coffey says. You don't follow the big games either? he says, because I don't say anything. I can't think of what to say when he asks me what I think say of Cookie and Nepia and Porter. Divine though, he says about Nicholls, have you ever seen him run? When I say I never even watched the games down the bottom of College Hill he looks for a moment and shakes his head and says, I cannot believe that, Spicer. Boy of your age never watched the loveliest game on God's earth! Then he thinks of something he meant to bring in from the kitchen and asks me, Be a good lad there will you, bring those empties in for me? And he lets me walk down the passage way ahead of him while he carries the tin tray sort of thonking it against his leg, saying to me, You'll get used to those in no time, believe me, because I bumble round a bit when I first walk in those high shoes, I think I'm like a calf just learning how to walk. I have to touch the wall on the way through to the kitchen so I won't keel over. But once I lean over and put the empty bottles in the crate at the side of the bench and move back towards the porch he's right behind me. I know without even needing to look round. He touches behind my leg and he tells me, My goodness, the muscles are tight there, lad, I've got just the thing for that. I say, I can take the shoes off, it must be that, the way they tilt me up. I put the toe of one shoe against the heel of the other and go to slip it off. No, Mr Coffey says, don't do that, don't take them off. Next thing he's holding one hand opened flat and he tips from this small bottle must of been in his pocket all the time. Just lean back, he says, against the shelves. He puts the bottle down and rubs his hands together so the stuff smoothes over both of them and he's rubbing and sliding them up and down either side of my leg. That's the story, he says, that's the story, gives your muscle great tone this does, Spice, all the good athletes use this. Then, Smell, he says. He lifts his hand towards my face and I get this whiff like peaches or something, and the oil smell as well, and then his hands go back, they stroking smooth and regular down from my knee to just about the lady's shoe, then back up again. Then he takes the other foot and lifts it up, opens my legs so a shoe is either side of him, and both his hands now smooth and nice but just one on each leg this time. I look down on the bits of hair stuck sideways across his bald head and next thing Mr Coffey's face comes forward and his cheek leans onto my knee. He sits up again after that, resting back on his heels, and pours more stuff from the little bottle into his hand and looks up at me and says, Feels pretty nice, does it? Invigorating? Then, Almonds, he tells me, cloves, tincture of this and that. And camphor, that's the deep heat part. He says, Your legs'll feel different for it tomorrow, I can guarantee that. Saying as well, Spice you should be an athlete yourself, ever thought of that? I've pictures of Greek ones somewhere, next time you're here. Lovely strong legs like this, my goodness. And his hands feel good all right, got to say that, moving and slipping and pressing nice way above my knee by now, long and slow and careful the way he strokes me, near my underthings by now then back down again slow and easy to my knees. Secret is, Mr Coffey says, you go with the flow of the blood, the pressure's always away from the heart. That's the knack you see. The rhythm. Brushing now against me there as well. I don't want him to stop but I tell him, That's fine for now then, Mr Coffey. Simon, he reminds me. Simon then, I say, I think that's fine. There, there, he says, tapping the frilly edge bit of the pushed-up apron where his hand keeps brushing. We don't want oil spoiling that now, do we? Hold it up, Spice, like it's a dress, eh? He laughs. So I take the apron and hold it up out of his way. Under your arms there, that's the lad, he says. So I hold the apron bunched like that and Mr Coffey laughs, he says, My you are like a girl aren't you just, holding your naughty old dress up?

That's when I feel the hot rush behind my eyes, the first time I tell him Stop. Stop? Mr Coffey says. His hands already along the insides of my legs. As if you want me to stop, you old silly! His head right in close against me now so I feel his forehead on me, right in close against me. It is five minutes maybe ten minutes, I hear myself making sounds but not real words. I lean back so hard against the shelves the wood cuts in against my neck, the next day my neck is sore although I hardly worrying when Mr Coffey's hands that high and his breath warm that's how close and saying, That's it, Spicer, lovely. Covered with oil, yes, got my eyes closed tight, I nearly screaming out. I all of me everywhere, like that, so sudden. And Mr Coffey too last thing his head his mouth moving his hands down rubbing over my shoes, my ladies' shoes, his hands right under them pressing up like the stirrup bits on horses hold the jockey's feet. Then just as sudden him standing there, folding his handkerchief away, looking now like something's wrong, like someone's coming to the door that very minute. He tells me, his voice gone weak all right, Better you get changed now, eh, maybe your auntie's wondering where you are. And I think, How come he so different, just like that. Is Mr Coffey angry with me or what? I put the ladies' shoes on a bottom shelf and the apron on the hook behind the door and when I'm ready to go Mr Coffey, just before he opens the door with the gold writing backwards, his hand brushes over my shoulder and he's saying, Only us two know, keep it that way, now, all right? And then for days after that not a word at work any different to before, just polite and ordinary, then maybe one week later one afternoon he's calling to me quietly out the back of the house and when I stand there next to him, Look here Spice, never finished that painting job out the back here, did we? And so soon enough, soon as he shuts the shop and pulls down the blind, the holland blind he calls it, he brings out the apron all ironed neat again, I can tell that, and this time a different pair of shoes, ones the laces go right up across my ankle and even part of my leg and today it's all so quicker, the rub my legs bit and his hot mouth and his tongue lick right up from my knee and he's telling me again, Never a soul else know this, okay, not a soul? Course not, I tell him, not a soul, Simon.

He likes that too, I know, when I say Simon to him. And I know all right men not supposed to be doing this secret and all, but never mind his hand so nice there full of oil and his jokey tug against the apron when he says to me, Be a good girl, eh, lift that dress up for me, Spicer. He forgets though we supposed to go to Victoria Park together for the footy, lots of times now on apron days Mr Coffey says we going to do this thing or some other thing, see the negro boxing in the Town Hall, go to watch the parade, but come the day he's too busy, and I ride the delivery bike like nothing else ever happens and Mr Coffey says Thank you at six o'clock, time to call it a day. And one day I see him in the office part behind the shop and his head right down on his arm across the desk. When I come in quiet, he's moaning as if something hurts. Not six o'clock yet and the front door open still and the blind not even down. Mr Coffey's been talking to this man about an hour at least. Then I go out the back door same as I do any ordinary day but then I come back because I forget the bag I bring my lunch in, Rita goes butchers I forget to bring it home. Only then I see for certain Mr Coffey crying to beat the band. His head up and looking straight at me a minute, this look I never seen. I ask him, You sick or something Mr Coffey? He shakes his head, he says laughing, crying, hard to say what's going on, Not a care in the world, Spicer. So I say with the picked-up bag in my hand, Well, better go then. I say to Rita when we're having tea, Nearly forgot my bag today there, Auntie. Forget your head if it wasn't screwed on, she says. When she make my lunch next morning like she always does because she says you don't want to go eating that nun's tucker up there at the Home before you go to Mr Coffey's in the afternoon, one thing I always said, she tells me, was I made as good a lunch as any man'd wish for, good enough for my late lamented Tom then good enough for you, she says, and smiles like it's a bit of a joke as well. She asks me though, What's this oil muck you got in here on the lining? She opens the bag out wide like jaws so I see how the shiny material inside's got these yellow stains about the size of two bob pieces where the stuff Mr Coffey rubs on me must of got in on my clothes, on a shirt I took off and put in there or somehow. I just tell her must be something I got on my hands at work, I can't remember. Well that was Tom's bag too, she says. For years he took it in to work every day and never got a spot on it so you just keep an eye on it, all right? I tell her, All right, I'll do that. Then she puts her arm round me and squeezes me and tells me, God love us, Spicer, I don't know what'll become of you.

But no need to worry, not her, not like poor Mr Coffey. Next afternoon I walk up from the Home after I done the things I always do, the cows first thing then clip the long hedge and rake the path beside the windows where the loony kids slobber out of and decide I'll do the new wood pile tomorrow, the nice old nun couldn't give a stuff. Today, tomorrow, she says, Rome wasn't built in a day. The afternoon's so warm and nice so I walk up slow across the criss-cross back streets and come out near the Maple furniture shop and turn along towards the Lamps. Then I see the people outside Mr Coffey's shop. I always think it's like a joke, like those fat and thin blokes in the pictures, the way Mr Coffey's brother about two times as big as Mr Coffey, not a hair on his head and shiny as a tin and Mr Coffey, this bit of hair he's always patting, touching with his hands when he talks about something and not even notice that he does it, when they stand together most afternoons. But today I see the other people standing outside the shop. Mr Coffey's brother in the doorway talking to Mr Halpin the policeman and someone else. Before I get up close even I know something pretty crook going on. Mr Coffey's brother says without even hello Spicer, Come round the back will you? He closes the high wooden gate so the gawpers got nothing to look at and says in this voice so quiet I just about miss it, There's been some trouble here, you'll have to talk to Mr Halpin. He touches me on the back as if I don't know how to turn into the side door beside the sun porch where the paint still smells fresh as when it's done. I see the shoes still there on the shelf where I put them but the apron's gone from on the nail behind the door. The apron's nowhere round.

Mr Halpin stands at the table in the kitchen. He looks at me friendly enough I reckon, not as scary anyway as Darkie warns me often enough. Fucken cops, he says, never trust them an inch, the bastards, nicer they come on sneakier they fucken are. Mr Halpin asks me, Step in here a minute, I'm glad you're here. Even his hand on my shoulder for a bit until he closes the door and says to Mr Coffey's brother, Don't disturb us will you unless Flynn turns up? He asks me to sit down in the sitting room that's nowhere near as dark now as I always seen it because the big light is on over the table. Mr Halpin sits down across from me with the wide green cloth between us and his hands for a second like he's going to start saying prayers. He tells me Don't be frightened now, okay, whatever he asks me, there's only us in the room, remember that, not another soul ever going to hear what I tell him. I understand that, do I? Yes, I say. Then he starts straight in with all his questions, his pencil flicking across a pad he got in front of him. How long I work for Mr Simon Coffey, what kind of work I do for him, how much money he pays me. Half the time he talks Mr Halpin's finger scratching on the fat part of his ear. He keeps on saying, Very good, very good, his pencil never stop moving. Then a knock on the door and he gets up like it annoys him and opens it an inch, nods at whoever's there, comes back and says straight out, his voice the same but I know he watches me as careful as I ever been watched, Mr Coffey, now, did he ever touch you, Spicer? Touch me? I say after him. Where he shouldn't, you understand? No, I say. So then the sergeant scrabbling at his red lug all the time, the skin on it flaky like it's been sunburned. He didn't ask you to do things to him, things he shouldn't? No. Or say anything? Not anything either, I tell him. I think how Darkie's wised me up.

Mr Halpin taps his pencil, the soft rubber end, tat tat on the green cloth beside his pad. He waits a bit then again he says, You do know what I'm asking, do you? He waits for me and then he says, Like told you take your clothes off, Spicer? Or some of your clothes? When I paint, I say, that's all. Paint? he says. Yes, the store room. And the sun porch. Mr Halpin stops his writing and says, He told you to take your clothes off? He told me to be careful, that's what I say. Not to get paint on what I wore. And touched you then, did he? he says. Saying it over again, Touch you like he shouldn't? And it's then I ask him, Where's Mr Simon Coffey now?

So he did then? the policeman says. Forgets about his itchy ear now, both his hands laid flat, the fingers make me think of sausages on the table by his pad. You're saying he did? For just a second like he's nearly shouting at me, but then back to his talk to me like a friend, You know there's nothing you can be in trouble for, don't you, lad? You needn't have any worry on that score. But I know him now all right, I know what he's up to, the bits he is wanting me to tell him. The apron days, I know that, the ladies' shoes. Mr Coffey's little brown glass bottle with the ridges on the side and the oil smells like peaches, his head in close against me. Our secret, that. I say, Mr Coffey's good to work for. Mr Halpin sighs and looks at me and says, I'm quite sure, Spicer. He pushes his fat fingers on his eyes and says, I know he was very helpful when jobs are scarce, I know that boy. But even Darkie's onto that one too. Have your arse shot off for your country never mind your fucken king and think that gets you a job these days? Saying it to

Auntie Rita only the other week. Not on your lonesome, Darkie said. And to me he said, Don't know how lucky you are, men out of a job and you with two of them, first those bleeding nuns and then Coffey chemist, if you please. Simple Simon's right. And Auntie told him, Lay off him for once will you? Your soul may be beyond redemption but the boy's thank God isn't. So no, I say to Mr Halpin now, every time he asks. No. No. No, he never.

Mr Halpin's back at his ear now, tugging away on that like even his lug doesn't want a copper near him and is trying to get away. Next thing he shoves the chair back and drags the door across the carpet when it opens too slow and shouts to someone maybe another cop, Anyone know anything else about this boy here? Is he the full quid, do we even know that?

There's talk then I can't make out between the men in the passageway. One man looks in over Mr Halpin's shoulder and they both stand back when a thin man with glasses that make his eyes look like wet stones comes into the room. I seen him in the shop tons of times. He's the doctor down the Home and a friend of Mr Coffey's too, I seen him stand and talk to him in the shop. He closes the door. You mustn't be scared, he tells me. So I tell him I not scared, don't think that. Good, he says. He squeezes me on the arm. He says, You know I'm a friend of Mr Coffey? And I tell him yes, I know that. And you understand what Mr Halpin asks you? Yes, I understand that. But I know inside whatever else I mustn't frighten Mr Coffey, make him cry even worse against my knee. I tell the doctor he never done that. He never ask for me to do that. Dr Flynn straightens the white bits of his sleeves below his studs. He says, I know you like Mr Coffey and he's told me what a good worker you are. He tells me how everybody likes you. But you know I'm his friend too, don't you? he says again. You know that? Yes, I know that. He would want you to tell me what's true, Dr Flynn says. But no, I say again, never nothing like that. Then the doctor stands up and takes his glasses off and rubs them this long time in the biggest hankie you ever seen before he opens the door and says, Nothing here I'm afraid. And the policeman says it was worth a try at least and Dr Flynn tells him while he puts the wire bits back across his ears, You won't be short of evidence from other quarters, that's the pity of it. Then the doctor looks at me and says it straight out. I'm sorry to tell you, Spicer, Mr Coffey's dead. I go back down past the sun porch again because the men are at the other end of the passageway near the kitchen, standing beside the trolley with a hood across it the undertaker that very minute's carrying in. Has to be, surely, one of the men says, all I hear any of them say. I still smell how fresh the paint is. I think the first time I put the ladies' shoes on for Mr Coffey and tilt up high the way he likes my legs to look and I got the apron on and he's standing there where I'm standing this very minute. Smiling, saying to me, Oh my God now, that's the story, isn't it?

I don't much like that time do I, thinking of it, finding out, Darkie going on about things he doesn't know? And Auntie saying over and over like time stops there in her silly gob, We know not the day nor the hour. Sick of all of it, because everyone talks about it, even the nuns, I hear them when I get the slops. The *Auckland Star* got his photo even, and big letters to tell you Chemist at Three Lamps Dies By Poison. Prussic acid, someone says, burns your mouth out, think he'd know a better way than that. Gums and everything so you only see the bone. Darkie says, Makes a nice change from what he usually has in his mouth the pervert. So my auntie tells him, You don't make jokes about the dead. Oh? Darkie wants to know. Who can you make them about then? He looks round the kitchen like he waits for someone to pick a brawl. What, then? my Auntie Rita says. I'll tell you what, Darkie says, I'll tell you, all right, into any kid he can get the daks off, bugger me! And seeing how Rita hates talk like that he says, An act of providence I suppose your own flesh and blood here wasn't given a burl at it as well?

My auntie's quick on that one. Mr Halpin, she says, Mr Halpin himself assured me, there was no question of that. And Darkie tells her more luck than good management in that case. And laughing like he does, showing his square brown teeth, telling her, The offending member's roasting for it now, bet your sweet life. My Auntie Rita sighs and comes at it again, like it's something clever she just thought of there and then, We know not the hour nor the time, she says. He knew it sure enough, Darkie says, didn't he stop the shagging clock himself! But another time just the two of us together Darkie tells me, Look here, mate, any bastard ever tries to come that Coffey lurk with you eh, you just let me know? And another day we're walking up past the vinegar factory so the whole air stingy with it, that smell I hate, and he says to me out of the blue, You're shaking down all right down that mick place so I hear, Spicer. You keep it up. He never says much like that, Darkie, saying good on you or that, so I feel good then, don't I? Only when he gives Mr Coffey a going over I tell him I wish he'd stop, I say, Better not say anything, Dad, poor old blighter's dead. That's right, Darkie says, how could I ever forget it, first fucken chemist in history doesn't know prussic acid from Irish Moss. It tickles him all right, he says, wouldn't it anyone, Mr Coffey selling aspros to that outfit of froggie nuns I work for and can't lay his grubby fist fast enough if a kid's koozer pops up in front of him. By God, next thing, he says, next thing they'll be telling you the Holy Ghost's a front for some sly grogger.

People love it when Darkie talks to them like that, the blokes against the wall outside the fire station or near Nat Gould the Jew bookie's barber shop. And here's Spicer, he says, my only beloved you might say mowing lawns for the fucken sisters and helping them cart their stiffs out, making a joke of it, because I told him that once and never should of, how the nice old sister called me to help her lift a dead one and she knows I don't mind doing it, poor old buggers most of them, pick them up in one hand. So Darkie's onto that all right when Nat Gould leans forward red in the face, his eyes wet with laughing at it, and Darkie saying, There's no shit in this story, Nat, he lays the dead ones out for the RCs and here's his father, here's yours truly in the watches of the night, helping to lay the live ones out for half of Auckland to bounce on. You wouldn't in front of Mrs C, I tell him, wouldn't have the guts talking dirty like that in front of her, would you? Should of been a mick himself, Darkie says, mad with me I can tell when I butt in in front of them, the cobbers he shows off to. Still thinks it's for fiddling with between rosaries or whatever, he says, not the quickest, is he? Break it down, Darkie, the white-haired bloke from the bacon factory says, lay off the boy a while. And I know, Darkie knows, the whole room standing round there while Nat clips away at some joker sitting in the chair with the cloth across him, they all know the man's suddenly dead serious, Darkie had better lay off or he'll dab him one.

But if it's not his mates he's with and anyone asks Darkie how he makes a crust he tells them, Caretaker, I keep an eye on a couple of this lady's properties. Full board included within walking distance of the premises. Always making things sound worse or better than they are. But I'm pretty much onto Darkie now. Pretty much onto everything. Bullshit's everywhere, see, spread so you don't click to it first time, maybe not for ages, but just about everyone making out one story and all the time something else going on as well. Because bit by bit after Mr Coffey kills himself with the stuff from his locked cupboard with the black bones painted on it like one big X, It's a pirate mark for a kiss, he used to joke, after that I begin to hear the dirty things they say everywhere. Like one day when I cut up through the Pottery and past the Bedstead Company some man must run a furnace or something because he's leaning on his long rake and just a black singlet in the heat, and he says to his mate but loud enough for me to hear, Don't tell me this lovely lad was part of old Simon's team? The gift of tongues, he says, isn't that what they pump into them in church? And when the police bit comes out in the *Herald* I read it, very slow like I do but understand it all a darn sight better than my auntie thinks or anyone else think either. Perversion, it says, a series of offences only now coming to light. I begin to see it then, Mr Coffey just lying to me, I'm not special like he used to say, his best friend, all that. And Rita talking quietly to her friends like I'm too dopey to catch on. How someone's father been to tell Mr Halpin and then someone else's, three or four boys round Herne Bay to begin with, Mr Coffey down the bathing sheds at Shelly Beach handing out five bob here, five bob there. All right I think, all right then, when I hear all this, but they not the ones with the job are they, Mr Coffey's not asking them to do his deliveries, ride his special bike because I do that properly, never wasting time, never muck up the orders? They not the ones with the apron.

The shiny ladies' shoes. Not everybody knew him real as that. Then for a while there are jokes everywhere about him, in the fruit shop even one day when I'm emptying the old stuff into the barrow so it must be Saturday afternoon, and one man in a round black hat and a watch chain over his stomach says while he holds this lettuce in his hand, says to another man, You heard what Simon Coffey wrote on his labels did you, John? But the other man says, I did not now, what was that? And the man in the round hat leans close because that very moment a lady walks into the shop, but I hear him say, Open wide before swallowing recommended amount. And the other man rocks backwards and forwards on his heels and turns the money over in his pocket and says, My God now, John, what'll we be hearing next? And the other short one, serious now, says, We live and learn, that's a certainty. And even my auntie with her church ladies, the Chosen of the Assembly written fancy on the card they stand against the fireplace when it's her turn for them to have their prayers at her place, after the prayers one night they're having supper when one of them takes a slice of cake, the fat old bitch, she stuffs it in her mouth and says, Just what Mr Coffey ordered, and they're all off laughing at that, bad as at Nat Gould's barber shop, and my Auntie Rita saying Quiet to the others, Not in front of his lordship. Mr Coffey in his kitchen, I think, still crying maybe, sorry even after he drunk the stuff because he so scared when it starts to burn him and wants to stay alive as well, just another ten minutes, maybe, no one wants that last bit ever, do they? Still smells the paint maybe we done that afternoon.

Then all the time there for a while I keep thinking about being dead. And thinking about that bullshit too, the lies just everywhere, the true things and the made-up things just so mashed up, how you ever going to sort them out? The old froggo nun, she knows that too I reckon. She tells me one day very early, before the place even properly awake, when I help her shift a dead one. This old joker I never hear him talk, not once, long as I been working there. Makes a mess all over himself every bloody day, can't even hold a spoon so some sister holds one hand behind his head, and like he's a baby too small for anything she slowly push his food in with her other hand.

He goes and chokes on something anyway this morning while he still asleep. The nun comes on down to the outhouse where I stay about a week that time I remember, because burglars they think hanging round — the vestment thing she calls it gone missing, but that's another story. She ask me can I help shift him on the trolley, she rather not wake up the other nun should do it? So early the sky's hardly pink when I go across the lawn. Then she tells me at the edge of the verandah, take my shoes off, walk quiet as I can, the other old ones get upset if they see what's going on. Although half them I reckon woken up already, sitting up in bed, watch us with eyes like big holes in their old white raggy faces. Behind the screen Sister's got the old joker all brushed up, clean shirt on him and that, before she come to get me. I say, Never looked better, this one. No dribble, grunts, no flopping over, just nice asleep. Then Sister makes me some tea and hot toast after I wheel him down the morgue room and lift him on the board cold as ice. She sits there over the table from me, both her hands round the blue teapot while she says, We can never tell just by looking what the truth is, Spicer. You see poor old Harry, you think what a sad thing, how much better if he's dead. We can't help thinking that can we? But that's only half the story isn't it? I say that after her, Only half the story? So she tells me, Like looking at the chapel windows at night time, think of it like that, the windows black you never think they anything much else. But then you look at them in the morning, all the colours there, the brightness over everything, we've only ever seen Harry at night time. You understand what I mean? she says. Now it's Harry's morning. He just dead, Harry, I say to her. *Just* dead, she tells me back. That's what I mean. We've never seen him properly. Now he's in the right light, at last.

I'm watching her as she talks, her hands white on the teapot, her face too nice somehow for that ugly crumpled stuff fences in her face. I ask her, Why we never see your hair, eh, Sister? She says, How long have we got for me to tell you? I think why does she ask me that, the clock with the fat wood frame right above there where we sit, she must see that, must know it's nearly six o'clock? But she stands up then, tells me no need for me to rush, eat the other piece of toast still there on the plate. She should have ask me sooner, would I like an egg as well? Then a little bell sounds somewhere. The world's on the move again, she says. And as she tilt the pot up to give me the last bit of tea, she says, The sisters will pray for Harry so I'd better go. Pray he rests in peace.

I remember that, clear like in a picture her talking to me that morning, remember it when the trees flick flick over the top of us, the light and shadow wash across us as we bump on the clay road. Seems so long ago, my Auntie Rita dead now, dead as old Harry. And that day Sister told me about lunch time, Go home early, you've been such a help. I walk along Jervois Road it such a warm still afternoon. The sea like someone pushed a roller over it, so quiet, flat. I cross from near the Post Office to the other corner because my auntie ask me pick up the ham she got on order at Hellaby's just down the hill. I see the blinds pulled down in the window of Mr Coffey's shop, the gold writing on the door scratched off. This empty square in the middle of the door, waiting for someone to put another name.

So three, four years, I go down Kelmarna Avenue nearly every morning. Even sometimes like I said I stay there in the shed if some special reason. Another time, that's right, not burglars this time but an orangeman or someone, that's the talk, starts a fire up behind the kitchen one night but luckily an old lady sees it and squawks out to the nuns. They run out with buckets and catch it in time, so only this black streak up the wall and some boards underneath a window got to be replaced before I paint them. Another time someone pissed as a fucken chook like Darkie says runs right through the wards, shouting out, pushing things over, then out again, and they never catch who it is. I stay there then a couple of weeks but he never shows up another time, the loony bastard.

Most of the time it's okay though, working at the Home, living at Auntie's, then sudden as that she dies. Darkie that angry with her he even sits at the back of the Assembly Church, just this old shed really with a tin roof that pops and cracks all through the time they praying for her. He won't even go up near her coffin where the family supposed to be, Next of kin, the parson bloke says to him, if we can't be forgiving to our next of kin then what hope for any of us? So Darkie tells him straight out, Kin be buggered, never had that in mind did she, hoarding her sponduliks all her life, going without for what, leave it all to *him*! Because last week when she knows for certain she won't make her next birthday, If only I'd got to fifty, she cries, and she leaves whatever she got to me apart from the house which isn't hers in any case, all the rest though, the furniture, the bit she got stashed in some fund, whatever they call it. Providential Fund. Only thing she leaves Darkie's this big coloured-in photo of some old bloke in a beard and a collar looks sharp as a knife, supposed to be his father. I wouldn't cross the room, Darkie says, to piss on his boot when he's alive, what's the bitch coming at? Stuff her, he even says to the parson when he talks to him in the porch, stuff her's what I say, Reverend, she can carry herself out, that's how much she thinks of her brother. The whole world of course ashamed he's carrying on like that, but when that ever worry Darkie? You can hear him carry on all over this little church. May Watkins who is my auntie's best friend says, Where's he think this is, Christ's home in the heart of his people or one of his low boozers? But then near the end of the parson's talking about new and shining somewhere or other and angels attending the beloved, Darkie starts sidling along the wall so when it's lift her on your shoulders time there he is, red eyes and all, like he's been his sister's nearest and dearest all along. Bloody hypocrite, Mrs Watkins says loud enough for people to look at, like she's the one now doesn't know her place. While at the front of carrying Auntie out my cheek against the smooth shiny wood about where her feet must be and my arm stretched under the weight of her and Darkie's arm stretched over from the other side, us gripping each other like a footy scrum and the front end of the coffin between our heads. Down the church like that to the back of the long black car, and an hour later in the sitting room with the picture that pisses Darkie off and cakes and sausage rolls. And here's Mrs Watkins letting on Darkie's the biggest card she's talked to for years, patting the front of her big ugly tits like he's going to make her choke if he doesn't lay off, and he's saying something now, his mouth half closed to make her lean even closer. Lean a bit more, I think, you'll tumble over yourself, you round old bitch. Because she's the one supposed to be Auntie Rita's friend, supposed to be sorry wouldn't you think? I watch both of them, my father and Mrs Watkins. I know how much bullshit all right floating round in this world.

Darkie though he's different to me from now on, apart from when I get the cap and the brown suit later on. Struth, he says, just look at you will you? Eighteen and next thing to self-supporting especially if you count the unearned savings from mentally deranged relatives but all the same. And I buy myself this new sports coat that Darkie helps me decide what one, and he says like pretending to be looking at someone else, Get a load of this swank here will you? Son of mine all right, he says, his own mother'd vouch for it, credit that? And pretending to answer as well he says, Same sense of style, same good looks, dead ringer's not it. But it's a joke, I can see that, it's Darkie my father trying to be nice. That's when he says, Now Rita's shot through, son, like it or not, then why not take the shed out the back here at Mrs C's as permanent residence, shall we say? Cheap at half the price until Mrs C hears of it like I've said and she tells him, That's daylight robbery, Darkie, you're not getting away with that one. So that's how Mrs Cooper come into things far as I'm concerned, before her and the nun team up, before all the worst sadness ever, when Miriam get sick.

Like two halves of the world, I think, the two halves I got. By now everyone down the Home knows me like a friend. Dr Flynn talks to me whenever, different sisters say, Don't know what we do without you, Spicer. Even the one not quite all there stops me one day when I come down from a ladder. The night before the wind belts all over Auckland, rain in buckets and the storm bashing the whole town round and two bricks clunk down on the roof, frighten all hell out of the loony kids. So the minute I get to work next morning I see the blown-down branches along the drive, there's Sister, my friend by now, dark under her eyes like she get no sleep. She says, Am I glad to see you, Spicer. So I saw the big branch that's broken the corner of the verandah, tidy all that stuff up, then I make a new part along where the rail snap, rough as guts things I patch up like that, but that's okay, the nun says, slap paint over it, good enough to last the next storm anyway. Then I see where the bricks are out near the top of the chimney like a rotten old tooth, and Sister laughs when I say that. She helps me mix the tin bucket with cement from the back of the woodshed and I get two new bricks from where they're stacked under the edge of the verandah. I spend half the morning on the roof. When I come down there's another funny old nun just about hide her under the bucket if I turned it upside down. She's watching me like she never see anyone on a ladder before. She hopes I'm happy, am I? she says. Well nobody here telling you lies, that's one thing, I tell her. She shakes away like it's a real joke I come out with. But then a young nun with a face looks like a piece of Sunlight soap it's that yellow comes out and tells her, You shouldn't be wandering round like this, Sister, we were worried stiff. And quiet so the old one won't hear her, she asks me, Ever see her outside just bring her back, will you? Shows you how things have changed if I say when I told Darkie about the damage the storm done and the real old nun watching me and talking all he says is, Christ, sixty bleeding years or whatever in an outfit like that, imagine! It's like he's even laid off the fucken micks once and for all. Sometime it's like he wants to be my cobber. One day he even says to me, first time ever anything like it ever, Thirstier than a camel this afternoon, know that? Yes, I say. Well don't just sit there, he says, if we make tracks now we'll hit the Astor before six. So we go and drink beer together. And when I walk down to do some job Mrs C wants at 23 Darkie doesn't mind how the ladies there talk to me, the one I like special, her hair black as coal and floats out behind her when she walks about. Although he says to me one day when she laughs and I'm looking at her and she says, I don't mind it if you touch my hair, Spicer, and the other woman who works there and Mrs C they both look up from where they're playing checkers because she so quiet as a rule, Miriam is, they never hear her say something like that before — and it's after that Darkie tells me, By God boy I don't mind a bit of talk and that, but I pick up a flicker of how's-your-uncle round those tarts I'll crown you. And he says as well, It won't be your swede I'm putting the boot into neither. I don't even know what he means when he says that until the other one, the little one with reddy hair I don't like, jerks this laugh out, she says, Come off it Darkie, doubt he'd know a hard-on if he fell over it. Only it's her Darkie turns nasty on then, tells her he's not having that kind of talk in front of the boy. Boy, she says, the little red runty one, knowing how she makes Darkie mad as all that, Boy! I know some, she says, give their right leg for a slice like that. Then Darkie says to me, Right, Spicer, we're off, we're not wasting time with tripe like this. And to the sawn-off slut he says, It's the last you'll see of us round this place. This used to be a class house. So Mrs C has to wade in and calm everybody down and Miriam, the lovely quiet one, when all the fuss is going on, the checkers by accident knocked off the table, she says quiet and nice so no one hears except me and then only hardly, You can touch my hair, Spicer, whenever you like.

Oh I know all right lots of people think Spicer here's thick as two planks. You don't talk much then people think that, don't they? Even Rita who tried all the time to be kind because Jesus is inside everyone, she thinks, like something good inside a cupboard, she said to me sometimes when her friends from the Assembly going to come round, Just try to say something when people talk to you, do that for me will you, love? But what if there's just nothing to say, how come nobody thinks of that? Miriam's about the only one the penny drops with. She knows that inside herself the same way she breathes. She just *knows* it. She talks to me soon after I first start to go down to 23 instead of Darkie, one time when he takes the whole night off to go to the Buffs dinner, My God, he says, expect a man to even *remember* when those leer-ups finish? So he asks Mrs C for the first time, Surely Casanova here can hold the fort? He's not much more than a boy, Mrs C tells him. Boy? Darkie says, suppose the hau-haus arrive the same time as the Australian navy, just watch the boy there tear them apart. Look, he says. He gives me his empty Three Castles tin and I spread my fingers over it and close them slowly and the tin folds easy as a bit of silver paper. See my point? Darkie asks her. And very quiet like he doesn't want me to hear, Doesn't have a tendency to the female line, if that's any comfort, Missus, so far as a father can vouch for, anyways.

Then for most of the night I sit in the little room next to the red sitting room where the ladies sit and play cards if it's quiet, if the rooters aren't rising to the bait, or doing jigsaws just about big as the table is, or play the gramophone and drink from long thin glasses, something special, one of the girls got a birthday, Miriam says. That night too Mrs C, the only time she ever talks about what goes on there like, at 23 and her other house. She tells me, One thing Spicer maybe your father's not made quite clear. But there are young ladies work here, you understand? *Work*, Spicer. They're not sluts. People out there can say what they like but here we all treat each other with respect. That's what work means. Yes, I say, work all right, Mrs C. So I sit in the room that night and some other nights when Darkie's crook as a dog from Bluff oysters he picked up from a bloke in the Edinburgh Castle — Never trust a bargain from strangers, Mrs C tells him. Or another time he's got the flu so bad he totters round like he should be down the Home himself, that's how bad, so I stand in for him that time as well. Then more and more until I'm nearly there about as much as he is. Like it's become my other job. At first just a matter of sitting in this room with the slide-back screen so I see into the red room where the men go in sometimes when they arrive, swanky buggers half of them like the old man says, you don't get trash at 23. Mrs C tells me too what Darkie himself never mentioned, The worst trouble, she says, your father ever got down here was when one poor fool shot himself right in front of the girls. That true? I ask Darkie later on. And because he likes to make out always there's something he knows but never tells me, all he says is, What do you think they've got that room painted red for? Hazard of the job, Spicer, that's what for.

And this rule there too, not a rule but what you know is proper, you don't look at the girls, not dirty like. Although Miriam never minds too much if things not busy and I sit in her room. Sometimes I touch so soft you can't think softer along her black stocking, or she let me put my mouth on her white shoulder, on the edgy bit of her tits. Sometimes just sit there like real friends, not say a thing, until the bell rings and she got to start work. She tells me, Funny thing you know isn't it, every man comes in here gives me a screaming fit, I wouldn't give you tuppence for the best of them, the ones here or anywhere come to that. And here's you, and I think of you like a brother or something. Even when you're doing that. Yes, I say. Only don't let Missus know, Miriam says. And then one day, Touch it if you want to.

Breakfast with your nuns, supper with this lot, Darkie teases me, don't tell me some people weren't born with a tinny arse. Knows everything, he thinks, old Darkie, but never knows that, the way Miriam and me good mates like this. Nothing dirty anyway, not Mr Coffey lying bloody stuff, just us sit there when she has the time. And doesn't mind where my hand is, Miriam, I touch that soft I think she hardly notice. Her eyes closed when she doesn't feel so good and my mouth moves slow along her arm and that. Like a holiday, she says. That's what it's like, being here with you. Like I'm your sister. And she rubs my hand and holds it in close and tells me no need to cry, Spicer.

You should have everything you want, know that? I tell Miriam. My she says, if we all had that! Then the little bell through the wall and she stands up and flicks her hands over her black lace top that shows her tits off something. Nothing ever lovelier than that I think, and she smoothes down her dress and gives this smile I never quite sure how it means. Fit for the finest in the land, she says, go along with that? She makes the other girls smile too, even Olive who sits so gloomy sometimes and the tall one, Chick or something, she never say anything to me that one, and the others. Vera who looks too big I think to be nice, but Taste bestows, Darkie says in a put-on voice, taste bestows its own charms. And Lily nearly black as your hat and always wears purple, purple stockings, everything. How many? I ask Mrs C once, and she says, Over the years? and I say yes, and she says, More than I could count.

Quiet times since you work here, Mrs C even tells me, you must be our lucky charm. Because only once the cops come and beat the door in the middle of the night and the girls squeal, pretend they're scared but more like a party, and two men run out of the rooms and go through the door that looks like ordinary old wallpaper but the whole thing swings back into a tin shed you think just an old garden one and then you're out in the trees in next door's back yard. Slips the old goat over the fence a free one now and again, Darkie says, does Missus know how to run a shop, eh? But this bull beating on the door this night who was a customer the day before and still in civvies and two constables in uniform. Beating hard with his fist like he thinks that does a better job than the knocker. And Mrs C you never seen anyone more quiet, more on top. She talks so polite to the bull and then the uniforms come in after him and she says, Mr Carroll, so nice to see you again so soon, and you see he doesn't like it that she use his name like that, I thought you were here to protect people's peace of mind, not frighten them out of their wits in the middle of the night. And when Vera stands there behind her, half behind the curtain, Mrs C says, My niece's nerves are a problem at the best of times, what on earth do you think this is going to do to the girl? And after one of the cops noses around and says, Pretty fancy boodwars for nieces, mind, his boss Mr Carroll tells him, Shut up, will you? And Mrs C says to the cop like she doesn't mind his question at all but it's important he knows the truth, Motherless girls, Constable, one tries to make up for that. And then, I'll certainly let Mr Quin know how sensible you were. Quin! Darkie says when I ask him that, Who's Quin? He's only the head wallah in the force, that's all. Don't tell me Missus is giving *him* a kickback! Then once Mrs C shuts the front door on them, black Lily says, Calls for some fizz, Missus? I think it does, Lily, she says. So Mrs C goes to her own room and comes back with a big bottle with gold paper round the top and she undoes a twist of wire and it goes off whoosh and even surly Olive perks up, she says when the bottle splashes everywhere, Hasn't had it for a year, I'd say, and laughs with Vera and Lily, and Mrs C turns on them and says, More talk like that Olive and it's down the sink. But two in the morning now and everyone drinking from skinny glasses and Miriam doesn't give a stuff who sees her sit down beside me and puts her hand on mine. Cheers, she says. And later when everyone's gone to bed Mrs C tells me, Anybody knocks, tell them the house is in recess. So I sit there, only me and Miriam. She looks that tired, she says her head hurts and she hardly touches her glass. I make her a cup of tea and she drinks it slow without talking then says, I'm sicker than I let on, you know, Spicer. I don't know what to say, like when the words won't come. So I just touch her arm. And she touches my wrist, her finger goes this way and that like a brush on it. Damn everything, eh, Spicer? That's when I think I got to get her something special. Something not even in the shops. And it's clear there in my mind, sudden like someone else just put it there and all I have to do is see it.

When I know it's right on morning tea for the nuns and the wards done up and the corridors shining to show your face back good as, and the kids in the little classroom even the ones never learn to tie a shoelace, I know that's the time the chapel's empty too. So I leave my shoes off at the back door like I always do anyway and go through to that mixed-up smell, candles and polish and just a touch sometime of that old pissed-clothes smell from the hopeless ones, and this morning big white flowers they nearly turn you sick they smell that sweet, the feast they say of somebody or other important. Only one I ever know about is this dark joker in a little picture stuck up in the kitchen, Maori or something, he's wearing those old-time clothes just about like a lady's and I think I must be turning mean like Darkie because Mr Coffey, I think, as soon as I see it, he'd have fancied that lot, lifting that dress affair right up. And the sister sees me having a gander and she says, Saint Martin, that's who he is, Saint Martin de Porres. He's far more at home in your world, Spicer, than in the tired old one I come from. But this morning that churchy stink makes me half scared before I do a thing, though I tell myself I know where everyone is right now so why worry? In the little room where all the priests' stuff is kept and the locked cupboard with the wine and the long drawers with the folded clobber, the green and red and yellow with the gold thread thick all over them. But I know the one I'm after, that I seen them ironing in the laundry. Like a white cut-off shirt then lace right down to underneath your knees, the bishop's favourite the young nun tells me when she sees me looking. The lace as pretty I reckon as you'll ever get. So I take that one from the drawer where so many of them anyway whose going to miss it? And I roll it small as I can under my shirt and make for the shed out the back where the bunk is when I stay and no one ever comes in, never, far as I know. I hear the loony kids going

167

their da-da-da making out they're singing and someone laughing down in the nearly snuffed it most of them old people's part, the nuns got special morning tea down there because it's this feast day. When I go through the kitchen on my way out the whole room seems so big and white and empty, even creepy, and him looking straight at you, Jesus is, carrying his heart like he just catched a cricket ball only it's on fire too, a wonder he can bloody hold it. And in the shed I cut careful as I can the lace from the shirt half, then throw that bit in the incinerator where I do the burn-off every couple of days. And that night when I give Miriam the present she puts both arms round me, I tell her, This better be our secret, right, and she runs her fingers on it, on the long bit of lace. Of course it is, she says, as if I'd say a word. Doesn't ask me where I got it, nothing.

Then a week say later Mrs C's out one night and Darkie's got a tooth out that afternoon and Olive's night off and the other two with gentlemen so only us in the red room by ourselves, Miriam and me. Quieter here than the kitchen, Miriam says, and she goes out to her room. Then the nicest thing ever. I'm reading the page in last week's *8 o'clock* about the wrestling, I got to hold it right under the lamp, the print's gone smudgy on the pink paper, like Darkie says every other newspaper in the world's on *white* paper, for Christ's sake, what's this pink shit? So I'm reading and I hear someone else come in. I think it just one of the girls, she'll say if she wants anything. And then it's quiet again and I think nothing of it, and Miriam says, What would your considered opinion be on this lot, Spicer? She's standing there near the door, her back against the wall with her long black dressing gown and her big shoes but the gown right open, and nothing on only what she made from the bishop's lace I nicked her covers her there but I see through it as well. I feel like something jumping alive in my throat. All so soft against her, the top of her legs, so lovely, it makes me say out loud, God, Miriam! She reaches right across to me like that, she holds back the dressing gown again and stands still in front of me, like a statue that's how lovely. Next thing I kneel in front of her my head goes right down against her, you think I'm a nun in church or something and Miriam's hands on top of my head and now my own hands the way Mr Coffey did to me and she tells me, Here, wait on till I sit down. And she kiss me then, not my mouth but on my eyes. And she leans back on the sofa and I put her big shoes round the middle of my back and I sort of lost then, like only this, now, ever, and nothing else, only this Miriam, the smell and dark and taste of her.

Only things go bad, so quickly. First Mrs C got so much trouble with Vera stealing in the shops up Newton Road, and then worse the bitch she tells the police everything about 23, about the Mt Eden house as well, this big row the night before she leaves, Vera shouting out, I'll make that much trouble for you, you old cunt. Only time ever, Miriam says, she hears anyone talk to Mrs C like that. And I go through into the sitting room when I hear a window smack with something and glass rattles down on the path outside, there's fat Vera stands there, her fallen hair stuck on her face like someone tossed water on her, the other girls not knowing what goes on, and black Lily crying out, Don't Vera, don't. And a bit later a man comes then for Vera. He waits outside in an Essex the colour of water in a drain while she grabs things in her room and nobody says anything and she slams the front door, it so quiet then inside the sitting room just this dripping noise on the carpet where a vase of flowers been knocked across the table, and Mrs C says to me, Get that window fixed soon as you can, there's a lad.

Miriam tells me the next day or so Mrs C sees her important friend, a friend of Mr Gunson the mayor, so there'll be no trouble like Vera promised when she goes to the *Herald*, to the *Star*, she's got a list of customers, she said, blow this whole place sky high. Mrs C looks worn out. Then everything else goes wrong. First Darkie slips and breaks his good leg at the Mt Eden house, so for ages I stay every night at 23 and walk across to the Home first thing. Even Sister says to me one day, You need a tonic, Spicer, you're starting to look run down. She gives me this medicine the old boss nun who's dead now made up specially for the other nuns. It's got more iron in it, Sister says to me, than you get in a foundry. That's nearly a year ago I talk about now, I suppose, seems shorter though than that. Miriam just a bit sick at first and then Mrs C makes her go and live in the St Benedict's Street house, there's no point she says staying on at 23 when there isn't need.

They together nearly all the time, those two. Darkie's put out when Miriam comes to one of the spare rooms. He says you'd hardly expect a madam you'd no more put one across than drive the proverbial through a needle's eye, expect her and one of her straight-out whores if calling spades is still allowed in this fucken world to chum up like those two, would you? And for the first time I say to the old man, Just give it a rest about those two Darkie will you, leave Miriam out of it or I'll lay one on you. He give me a long look and he knows I mean it. And I say to him then, Why not have that holiday then you always talking about with that mate of yours? Because it crops up all the time, this mate down Murupara, same one as carried him and cared for him the day that weasel fart Evans half chopped his foot off, who floored Evans too in a pub years after when he spotted him and the bastard's living then with the monkey wrench like Darkie calls Miss McAuley later on. And his cobber tells him after, You done yourself a favour getting shot of that one, sport, know what she used to look like, well you ought to see her now. *Fat*. The word's not up to the job, he says, that's the only trouble. So when I say that about the holiday Darkie cries a poor mouth like he always does, Love to see the old cobber, he says, but times aren't easy are they, so I tell him there's Rita's money, I can give you some of that. So the other side of Darkie then, it's By Christ Spicer, you're a better son than a man deserves, not every lad these days is grateful for what their parents done for them. That's all right, I tell him. And he goes off then to see his mate Tommy Roseman, now there's a fucken whiteman if ever there was, and after a week a telegram comes, it says they're pushing on to Tommy's sister's down Wanganui. It's four weeks before he's back, he looks fitter than he ever done, his hair even dyed round the edges on the grey bits. Tommy's sister, he says, she's a fine lady if ever there was one, she advised me on my deportment, you might say. Even wearing new clothes so I know he's put the nips in there as well. But Tommy he says, he shakes his head, poor old Tommy, sworn off the turps would you believe it. It's that the quack tells him or a dead man's liver inside six months. Then every second day he's writing letters to Tommy Roseman's sister the widow, watching for the postman to work his way along the street from the corner. Takes you longer to write a letter, I tell him, than those jokers down McNabb's Monumental Masons at the corner take to chip out what they write for you on graves. Darkie's in such a good mood he grins at me, his little brown teeth, tells me, Play my cards right this time boy, just wait and see. But best thing while he's away is Mrs C buys the car, the Chevrolet. She gets me taught to drive it proper, I pick it up just like that. I hear her tell the girls I'm a natural with motors, that's why she invested. You could make that thing talk to you I expect, the doctor down the Home says to me when I fix his own car up one day. Open that bonnet, he says, I'm lost.

She gets the car most of all so Miriam goes for drives on good days and Mrs C always along the Home now, there or the St Benedict's Street house, doubt if she's down at 23 more than once a week. The Chev purrs like a big cat. The bonnet's this shiny pale yellow and the black hood I got it polished up like a pair of shoes, better than. The nuns seem surprised I got this other job and I lie to them, I say, Because Mrs Cooper meets me there, that's how. The nice one later on she laughs when she finds out I'm down at 23 all that other time as well, that Darkie's my old man even. And at the Home I push Miriam in a wheelchair sometimes. She's going down that fast, Mrs C says. Next to no time and it's no good in the car even any more, She's not up to that, I'm afraid, the sister says. The day Mrs C throws a cup and the stain there on the wall like someone sicked on it. But if the sun's out warm enough it's all right for the wheelchair, round the paths outside, down to the hedge and along the front and back. Some days now hardly says a thing, Miriam, then sudden she says to me, What's that one we liked on the gramophone, Spicer? Moonlight one? I say. She smiles when I remember. So I sing quiet so no one else hears and when the words run out it doesn't matter anyway, just the music bit she likes. That's nice, she says. And then hardly talks at all except in this lingo no one knows. She loses so much weight I think I can't stand that, I wish it was me, I think, I wouldn't mind what it was if that help her out. Coming on Christmas by now and weeks I reckon since she even goes outside, even looks at the window. I kick the wall in the shed so bad once my boot gets stuck there and I got to take my foot out before

I work the boot back out from where the wall opened like this big mouth. But I don't let on because bad enough for Mrs C. Neither of us hardly talk now, I just drive her down the Home and back and walk along there myself for what I always done there, but never any time I'm not thinking Miriam, how soon she going to die? And I go in their chapel place only the second time ever, the first time I flog the bishop's lace. I say, Why aren't you doing fucken something then? And I stand in front of the little hayshed shows you where he was born and do it so quickly it's no more than a minute, I take him and this older joker, they only half the size of my hand. I go down the verandah and into her room from the outside door so no one spots me inside. Miriam just lying there, sweat all over her face. And I put the little carved bits underneath her mattress then go back out on the long verandah, the cane chairs empty, it's still not six o'clock, and the grass too wet to walk across because it leaves a trail to the shed. I walk right round the path where no one sees behind the hedge. But no use, whatever is?

I get the car ready for us to go away and Darkie carries on like he used to all the time, once he sees my cap, my special suit. But I'm not listening to him even, when he flaps the *Herald* out like wings and says, That mad bastard running round the country, what about the milkman he fucken kills then drinks his milk? Just shot him beside his cart, he says, wonder he didn't do in the horse as well. Christ, Darkie says, he knows what he'd do, give him five minutes and a sharp knife. Then he shuts up again like at last his rotten old tongue's run out.

Now the letters stopped coming every few days from Tommy Roseman's sister Darkie turns like he's suddenly that old. He sits by his wireless and this whoosh whoosh sound half the time like he's shoved it under water while he moves the knob one station to another. Or he stands there at the window behind the long curtain and likely as not when he sees a lady walking past, Cows, he says, fucken cows the lot of them. But I go on getting the car ready for the trip and buy the things up Symonds Street Mrs C gives me the list for. We've got to plan this down to the last peanut, she says, this isn't a jaunt over to Herne Bay, Spicer, this is an *expedition*. And she tells me, more talkative I reckon than I ever heard her, tells Darkie and me together how she's throwing it in at 23, giving the game away. Closing shop, she calls it, smiles at us like there's a joke to it she's got the hang of but me and Darkie haven't. I'm closing shop, gentlemen, she says, we're calling it a day. So next thing I'm round there helping put the furniture on a truck to go off to Coakley's auction mart at the top of Queen Street and Mrs C is folding the big curtains from the red room and sending the beds and mattresses off to St Vincent de Paul so Darkie laughs like there's muck stuck in the back of his throat. Know how much grinding gone into those springs, he says, fucken bring St Patrick's down on top of them, wouldn't it, eh? The laugh coming up like he's going to hoick. I go along the carpets with a claw hammer edging up the tacks. After a day the place is empty as a box, the windows look too big for the place there's so much light pouring through the rooms that echo out behind you when you walk on the boards that never seen the sun. The walls all got these squares and different shapes from pictures and shelves where the wallpaper hasn't faded like the rest. A long measly streak on one wall where champagne flew all over it just after the war, Mrs C tells me. She's standing beside me like we're dumped in a crate together. She holds a lump of dirty soap in her hand she fished from behind the bath with its four black claws like it should of been an animal instead of a bath. She raises the soap that's dry and cracked as a piece of wood and licks her finger and rubs it then puts her finger beneath her nose and says, Ruth, I'm certain of it. Would you believe it, how many years ago was that? And at last she turns the key in the front door and drops it in her bag and I open the door of the car for her and close it, and walk to the other side, and then I'm beside her and I let out the big brake between us. She says as we drive away from 23 and the place without its curtains stares at us like a dead face, I hate the look of that, I tell her, and Mrs C straightens her sleeves that way she does, taking the cuffs and pulling down at them, and she says, Never look back, Spicer, that's the secret. That isn't where life is. So from then on Mrs C lives permanent in the big grey house along from the church. Although first thing she does is say to Darkie, I know you think I'll want you to move out. And Darkie says, Well it would seem the logical thing, Missus. But she calls me into the front room and tells me to sit there beside my father on the sofa no one scarcely ever sits on and says, I'm certainly going to want you to drive me round, Spicer, it's no good having the Chevrolet as an ornament is it? And she tells Darkie, You're such a fixture, Darkie, I haven't got the heart to turn you out. Next thing Darkie the old fart he's grabbed Mrs C's hand and slobbering over it and carrying on until Mrs C tells him, More of that, Darkie, I'll take it all back. And mind you, she says, Spicer is the senior one as far as responsibility goes, and Darkie's face cracks open the old bugger like nothing'd please him more than that, It goes without saying, Missus, he says, I always knew he had the makings.

The day before we go off for the trip, As far as Napier, Mrs C tells me, because this time of year the sun there is like the Riviera, and then she stops and laughs and says, I was never further south than Ramsgate anyway so why do I say a thing like that, you'd think I was Miss Belle! I go on packing up while Mrs C stands at the table and checks the things I bought on her list and says, That reminds me. She goes to the new black and gold telephone and I hear her say, No Miss Clifford, there is no need to disturb him, there is no message. And to me she says, Ham and cordial, Spicer, we'll have had enough of these I expect by the time we get there. If the car stands up to it. Safe as a train, I tell her. The Chevrolet, the man at Seabrooks said to us when we walked round the car in the big showroom, you're safer with this car, Madam, than you are in your sitting room at home. Figures will bear it out. The man's a fool, Mrs C said to me, size it up for yourself. But she had laid her own hand flat on the lovely curved mudguard that looked like light was coming up somehow from underneath the polished shine of it, and I know already this is the one she's going to buy. And I feel a beat in my head and the insides of my hands are sweaty because I want that too, I want that to be the car I drive for her, so big and butter-coloured and the metal bits so glittery I think of jewels, and yet it's nearly breathing too, know what I mean, as though a heart's in it and the beat in my head is part of it already? Mrs C stroking the bonnet now, tapping it with her fist and smiling back at me, we're all part of the same thing. And something like that feeling only twice again. Once when the hard barrel jams in against my neck and I know it's not just me but all of us, Mrs C and the Chevrolet and the nun by then as well, we all beat together. And the other time when the girl with titties like thumbs pushing out the front of her shirt when she leans across the mudguard and the light through the big gum tossing scraps of brightness all over everything when I lift the bonnet for her, Yes that's something now, she says, and she licks just one finger and runs it along the fan belt, I tell by the shine in the girl's eyes she knows the beat as well. Another day though, that.

The night before we go Darkie watches me. He makes out to read his paper and turns the wireless knob and for something to say he tells me the school kids go back to school next week, the little pricks'll be everywhere. Why people travel in the holidays, he says. They're not walking in the middle of the road Darkie, I tell him, I'm the one knows how to drive. And next thing he pulls his last card the old bastard, crying like it's because he's losing me, telling me, Spicer you don't know how it's going to be here, mate, the Missus gone, you gone, everyone taking off in that bloody motor out there. And a minute while he hopes he's sucking me in. What do you think, he says, what do you think it's like to get where I am, nothing left for you to do, no one gives a toss?

So I know I got to say it now whether it's putting in the boot like a decent person never does, don't think I never listened to what Rita tells me. I know Rita's right and the Sister's right too about love like she says sometimes, Love's the only reason for anything or where are we? I know all that. I know Mrs C as well wouldn't like me saying it but I turn round while he's snivelling. I look at him and I know I'm done up better than Darkie ever looked in his whole life, and I tell him so he has to see me like for the first time, I tell him, You're down your leg about that one, Darkie mate, you're down your leg about fucken everything.

There, the first time I ever say it. And I walk out of the room away from the green eye on the wireless drives you porangi just boring at you all the time, and out to where I used to sleep before Mrs C tells me to come inside. But I can't see the sky or the trees at the end of the yard or the chimneys between us and Symonds Street. I can't see a thing. Because I can cry as much as Darkie can any day. More than.

Enter, the Chow

THE FIRST TO BE RATTLED BY THE CHOW, BY THE SILENCE AND inscrutability that she knew had nothing to do with race but something deeper and more troubling, was Marie-Claire. The difficulty began at the moment the Chow demanded their names. He pointed to each of them with the crop he had taken up from the still panting side of the man who lay behind the counter of the newsagents in Otahuhu and had not let go of since. He held the whip towards each of them in turn and said simply, '*Who?*'

The boy responded first. 'Spicer,' he said, his answer direct and clear, a strange and solid remnant from the world that already, in its order and ordinariness, receded from where they were. He understood at least that he must give his name. The two women had not yet come to realise it, as if the flattish face and its oddly angled planes in itself deterred them.

'Spicer,' he said. For the moment he was more curious than disturbed. He understood already that he lived in an adventure as far from anything Darkie had ever known as it was from what Missus knew of either, or the nun, you could bet on that. He absorbed the women's bewilderment and the new element their lives now moved in. He was elated yet wary as well, as though cunning if not intelligence enabled him to take things in with a clarity he had never so much as guessed at. He knew the women were afraid and at a loss, as the Chow asked them their names, his lips as straight and thin as though drawn with a ruler hardly seeming to move but the high soft hooting as the word 'Who' came at them with the raised and pointed whip. He knew that the figure who had stopped them would also kill them, quick as that. And because he understood it without a flicker of doubt, it was as though fear was pointless. Kill them just like that.

A person more at ease with words, less habitually anxious that whatever he felt would lead in some way to confusion, might have said, or have wanted to say, I have never seen things so clearly, I have never noticed the hard reality of things with such precision. But Spicer was not bothered by any such push to definition. He looked along the black shine of the riding crop's handle as it dipped and rose towards him, and then towards Mrs C. The frayed thong of leather at the whip's end, the three cuts into small leather strips, was like a soft claw at the end of a skinny arm, a long black bone. He looked down to the punched holes in the leather that ran across the caps of the Chow's filthy shoes a few feet in front of him. He saw how the hairs of his own hands as they rested on his knees were picked out by the angled, brilliant sunlight as if on purpose, while the rest of his arms moved in the flowing shadows. It was like one living thing slid across the other, the scraps of light between the trees for a moment and then the mottled bluish spill of the leaves. Like he had never looked at things before.

'Kate,' she said. Kate, which Spicer had never heard anyone call her, ever. Yet he knew it was her name. Yes, he thought, Kate's right, it's what she ought to say. As if out here, standing like this beside the car, to say something else would be so wrong. He had never thought of her apart from one or other of the houses, apart from the girls or telling him and Darkie what to do, or now even apart from the nun, the two of them together in the car's high seats, those two, the nun and Missus, like Darkie always called her. But now by herself entirely as she says her name, the only true one.

The little floppy claw moved again, the light skidding on the black casing of the whip's thin shaft. It pointed at the nun. As soon as the Chow had ordered them to step from the car, she had leaned back against the mudguard. For a few seconds she believed she may have been about to faint. She felt the curved press of the mudguard welcome her haunches.

'She's sick,' Kate said. 'If she doesn't sit down she'll fall.'

The man said nothing and Kate took her friend's arm and said, 'There. Sit there on the step.' The nun lowered herself to the broad running board with its patterned rubber matting. The warm smell from that — or was it from the tyres? — filled her nostrils. It made her think for a moment she might even vomit. But she leaned her head back, shifting it slightly to avoid the door's brass handle. She closed her eyes and held down her nausea.

'*Who?*' the voice demanded.

Why do I think of it like that? the elder woman thought. Why do I think that voice is somehow other than whose it is? And she was puzzled further by the utter distaste that came to her as she opened her eyes and took in the figure who stood in front of them, the small round head, the almost invisible eyes, the puffy arm that held the stick towards the boy. Spicer's answer came so quickly, so confidently, she wondered what it was she failed to understand. Then again, the question. The voice like a note on an instrument almost, a reediness, the sound of breath behind the word and around its edges: what was it she was trying to describe? She watched the figure in its khaki shirt, its khaki trousers and filthy shoes alter position slightly and put the same word to Kate. Then it came to Marie-Claire with a force that was stronger even than the nausea she had beaten back, as she acknowledged what it was she felt. It was something she had never so much as guessed at in her life before. It was loathing that was rising in her, a thing she could not control even as she detected it, as she stood in judgement on herself. She knew it was the first time in her life she had felt an actual, searing shame. She moved her buttocks against the sharp edge of the running board. And with the shame she also felt confusion, which was almost as painful to her. In less than a minute, in perhaps thirty or forty seconds, the solidity of her life, her firm conception of herself, had swayed and bucked, as though she stood on a narrow rickety bridge like the one the children up the river, all those years ago, had jiggled on in exaggerated terror. As though she stood there now and the Chow's puffy arms reached up from their khaki sleeves and tugged at the wires of the bridge, swinging its flimsiness above the gulf. The image was so vivid that only her friend's declaring 'Kate' forced her back into the immediate clamour of the cicadas in the bush behind the car, to the awareness that her hands slipped with sweat against the metal edge of the running board. To the stick that now swung and halted within inches of her face.

And the voice that this time she thought of not as an instrument blown by a child but more as something actually inserted into the speaker's throat, and the force of air wheezing past it, the voice itself as an impediment, an intrusion, against breath. Later that night, lying huddled on the back seat, moving carefully against the long bruise across her left breast, it played over and over again in her mind, her obsession with the sound which was husky and thin and high-pitched together. So that the first *Who?* that came at her was ignored, and the second as well, as she looked up into the face that seemed almost flat from where she sat beneath it, looking up at its tilted plane, the nose not more than a minimal raising of the flesh, the hairless brows above the hooded eyes. The moment then, the split second, when she knew she had left it too late to answer, her awareness of the deep fury she provoked in the mind that demanded who she was, and waited, then asked again, then struck. The small, almost pitiable leather paw dangling in front of her so quickly raised, and the entire stick blurring in its fall and the vicious sting across her breast, through the thinness of her summer habit and the loose halter-like garment she wore beneath it. Her head flung back and clattered against the handle of the car door.

Kate turned and called, 'For Christ's sake!' to the khaki figure which so quickly resumed the exact position it had started from, the puffed arm with its totally absent wrist between forearm and the thickish hand that held the whip as still again as it had been a second before. Kate felt the heat of her anger flood over her. It was so obvious that what struck at her friend, whatever it was that stood before them in the now motionless figure with its wisps of hair moving in the late afternoon's slight breeze almost as a child's might stir against a fancy-worked collar, was beyond her normal comprehension. It was mad and lethal and unfathomable. And at the same instant, as part of the clarity of things he had never expected to possess, Spicer came to a decision that all this could end in only one way, that given the time, and the place, his will was already up to it. He could kill the Chow with the same decisiveness, the same naturalness as the arm had flickered out and slapped the whip's length down across the woman on the running board.

'*Who?*' the voice repeated, its tone exactly the same. It was impossible to take from the sound alone either impatience or endless calm. It seemed so unrelated to the violence of the act between those two identical queries.

The nun raised her right hand and laid it across the stinging track of the blow. It had shocked her, as freezing water might, to a sharper awareness of herself. As well it was as if years, as if decades of habit and usage as Sister Martine were peeled back to something more deeply herself, for she answered at once, and with amazement even as she spoke it. For that second, then, looking along the lines of her future, a girl in a white frock with an amber-coloured bow gathered at her waist, with black stockings and black polished boots. From there, from the ten-year-old who had been as fascinated with her own name as she was with each door that life seemed to fling open before her daily, sighting towards the distant aging nun, her cancer raised in her side like a partly buried sphere, gasping now as she moved her hand to cover her pain, giving out her name, the name of a child fifty years before, 'Marie-Claire,' she said.

The Chow looked from one of them to another, silently, and then lowered the whip against the side of the shapeless khaki trousers. There was a curt nod, as if in approval that names had been given and stored in mind, although in the next days none of these would be used, as if possessing them was no more than a formality that had to be got through, a first clearing of the terms between them.

The next day was oddly calm. Odd as well, so Kate thought, that so great a change in their lives had taken place in the middle of the afternoon only the day before. Yet here they were, as if this was how things were meant to be. It was a day when the two women and Spicer and their captor spoke very little.

The nun had been given the back seat of the car to spend the night in. The weather was mild, and one of the checked Mosgiel blankets from the boot was enough to keep her warm. For most of the night it lay rucked about her waist. Only towards dawn, and without moving from the angle she lay at, did she draw its warmth up about her shoulders. Although every morning for the greater part of her life she had been awake and active by six o'clock, she slept on to past eight. But when she woke the nagging was immediately there in her side. As she sat upright her hand moved to her right breast. The bruising from the crop ran from her collar-bone. Later in the morning when she looked at it, in the privacy of the bush a dozen yards off from where the car sat square and larger than it ever seemed on the road, she saw the reddish-blue welt sloping from her shoulder, across her breast. She pressed against it with her fingers, a soft curious pain that was almost pleasing as her touch moved towards the less discoloured edges. I have grown heavy, she thought, I have hardly looked at my body with this attention for an age. *Mine*, she thought. It is such a strange thing, when one thinks of it. *This body is mine.* And how different that was from thinking, *This body is actually me.* All that I am, she meant. To think that, and really believe it, that would be a greater burden than she could bear. Yet it must be what people thought who do not believe in God, not believe in the soul. She remembered Kate telling her of girls who made their whoring possible by saying to themselves, as Marie-Claire now said to herself, This is only what belongs to me, this body, there is so much more to me than that. Those girls under the animal rut or whatever. What consolation there must have been in asserting that, what freedom from what they did!

For the first morning in her life, Marie-Claire looked not towards a ceiling or an oblong of light or darkness through a window, but directly at the sky, at the fringe of trees when she raised her head to the expanse above her. She was amused at the strangeness of it. Even the dull tug in her side seemed, at least for the moment, not such a massive threat. She turned to Kate, who approached her with a mug of tea in her hand. She smiled as she caught the concern in her friend's drawn face.

'I suppose,' Marie-Claire began. Her sleeve fell back to reveal the thinness of her forearm as she raised her hand and gestured to the wall of bush in front of her, the racket of the birds and beyond them, through them, the sound which must surely be water, or was that the sound of the trees, the tops of them in the breeze that plucked at her skirts as she stepped down from the back of the car? 'I suppose the bathroom is somewhere in there?' she said. Her fingers flickered towards the bush. She laughed as she said it.

'I'll keep your tea, then,' Kate smiled back at her.

Both of them for those few seconds were unaware of the khaki figure that had moved from behind the car and halted and watched them, the face, Marie-Claire thought as soon as she saw it, with its single tilted plane from forehead to chin, like the heads her brother used to carve from soap. François had been very good at them. He whittled them quickly and set them in rows, three or four at a time, along the window sill of his room. Some were remarkably like servants or relatives or friends. But all of them of course bore the same sallow complexion. And whether he intended it or not, there seemed something maliciously deranged in their expression, a slyness, a cross between repose and cunning, that made the grown-ups who looked at them both diverted and uneasy. She had not thought of those small clever carvings for years. Then the sense of loathing returned to her, as she looked at the head above the open shirt.

The brightness fell away from the morning as she entered the press of the bush, and forced through to where she felt her privacy was certain. On her way back, as she adjusted her deep petticoat and ran her hands down the length of her habit, it occurred to her that for the first morning in perhaps fifty years as well she had not said the prayers that she began each day with. She dragged a small springy vine from where it tugged against the cloth that covered her arm. And she was then sharply aware of the irony of 'returning to society', as she put it to herself — to Spicer, spruce so early in the day in his shiny peaked cap, to Kate, balancing her tea for her on the steep bonnet of the car. And beyond them, crouching down so that the khaki-clad buttocks rested on the back of the dirty shoes, their captor who,

185

she had no doubt, would destroy them the moment their usefulness ran out. Christ help us all, Marie-Claire said. She stepped from the edge of the bush into the clearing, where the smoke from the fire whisked and blurred the trees at the other side. Spicer raised two fingers and briefly touched the edges of his cap. 'It's warm today,' he said to her.

The figure squatting at the fire, edging the stack of broken sticks towards a more compact centre for the enlarging flame, turned and looked up at her. Derisively, was it, she thought? But no, not even that — as though registering who it was, at once putting her aside and out of mind, as of neither consequence nor alarm. We are only shapes in those eyes, Marie-Claire wanted to say, we are not people at all. But she took the cup Kate raised from the bonnet of the car and held towards her, and instead said lightly, 'That tea's so hot.' She noticed that the figure with its small head and chunky shoulders, and the hair so like a child's — or a very old person's, even — was now jiggling a black pan about on the flaming sticks. The deep drift of frying bacon came across to her.

'We've enough tucker in here for a week,' Spicer said. He stood at the large opened trunk at the back of the car. Kate had instructed him they would be stopping for picnics on the way across to Napier, to stock up on all the things she thought they would need. 'Get the nicest stuff you can,' she had said. So he had walked up to Symonds Street and carried back enough black pudding and bacon and sausages, ham sliced from the bone and pressed tongue, enough bread and chunks of fruit cake in brown paper, fly cemeteries and coconut roughs — Mrs C after all had told him go the whole hog, hadn't she, told him she'd expect him to run up a decent meal for them when they stopped for lunch or tea — that Darkie said when he saw him packing the trunk, saw him shoving down the two ice-filled rubber hot-water bottles he stacked at either side of the meat, 'Loaves and fucken fishes for the dying micks, that's the caper now is it?'

'She isn't dying,' Spicer said. 'She's old and a bit buggered with all the work she's done and Mrs C is giving her a break.'

'Her guts is swelling up every day,' Darkie had said. 'Do you think

I never listen to what Missus is saying or something? That I don't take in what only a bleeding half-wit'd miss out on?'

When Spicer hadn't answered, his father went back inside, across the footpath in his blue socks with a gap the size of a plum in one of the heels. Wear your shoes, you old fart, before you start mouthing off. Spicer had wanted to say that. He knew it was what he should say. It was so simple, he had realised by now, to say things that shut the old sod up. And yet he didn't. It puzzled and irked him that he didn't. But there it was. Darkie would always rule him, he supposed, in a kind of way. But it's because I let him, Spicer thought. That's the difference now to the way it used to be. It's because I *let* him, not because he decides to, off his own bat, like he used to once. But all that was days away — a lifetime, good as. And now the Chow calling to him, 'Here. Get some plates for this.'

The nun returned to where she had sat the day before on the running board. Kate leaned across the bonnet, making a table from it where she balanced her plate when Spicer handed it to her, and where a moment before she had cut a loaf of bread into the thick slices each of them now had with the rashers of bacon. She had carried a plate across to the Chow, who instead shoved the strip of meat onto the end of the carving knife. He ate without altering position, still crouched like that, as if his legs would never ache. He turned his head into his shoulder to wipe a smear of fat from his chin against the khaki shirt.

That was their first breakfast together. No one spoke as they ate. For ten minutes it might have been something ordinary, something normal, for four people on a drive through the centre of the island, taking their time about it, the quiet pleasure of early morning in the open, the smells of sizzled meat and wood smoke and the taste of strong sweetened tea. He had made that first, before cooking the bacon. Chai, he called it. 'Get some chai here if any of you want it.' It was the first thing he had ordered Spicer to bring him from the trunk. And the cups, he had said, once he had the billy balanced above the flames. 'Bring the cups and wake the old tart, will you?' Only three mugs between them, which is why Kate had given her own to Marie-Claire.

The day would pass as if to an unspoken timetable. It was not obvious at any given moment that it was the khaki figure's will that so ruled the other three, but the fact of the gun, the quick retributive whip, imposed a pattern to time that was entirely his. There was a creek twenty yards from where the car was parked, and the pale band of smoke lifted and weaved from the crackling branches. The four ate eagerly, even the sick woman leaning back against the smooth, reflecting door. Without being told, Spicer took the mugs and the enamel plates and let the creek run across them. The water was cold and brown apart from the few coins of early light that jogged on it through the mass of leaves. The grease lifted and ribboned off, although the plates felt slippery still as Spicer took them from the current. He rubbed them with the red checkered tea towel he then folded neatly and wedged between them. He wrapped the unused bacon in its greaseproof paper and slotted the bread in its tube-like container, BREAD written large along the side of the tin cylinder, a design of smudgy roses worked between the letters. He took his leather hat from where it lay on the front seat, and looked briefly in the tilt of the mirror extended from the side of the car. Behind him, in the silvery pool of the reflection, he saw the Chow. They were the two who kept an eye on each other, Spicer quite knew that. As he knew that sooner or later, when the time was right, it was between themselves that all this would be worked out. It was like they were on rails. There was nowhere else for them to go, nowhere else to end up. Spicer tipped his cap to the angle he liked. With his other hand he flicked the edge of the mirror so the figure observing him was dismissed. He knows as well as I do, Spicer thought. He smiled at Kate, who was watching him.

'Things'll be all right,' he said. 'Give it a day or so and things'll be all right.'

The Chow walked across towards the car, the gun hanging casually from his hand as though it were no more than a garden trowel. It seemed to grow straight out of his partly rolled-down sleeve. He's even pinched that shirt, Spicer realised. If he let the sleeves right down they'd cover half his fingers.

'I know they will, Spicer,' Mrs C told him.

The Chow sat on the broad back seat beside the nun. As soon as the back door closed, the engine jumped as though it had waited to be asked. It turned over loudly and the car's framework juddered into life. Spicer felt the energy, the eagerness to press ahead, move along his legs and into his thighs. He thought it just about the loveliest feeling in the world. He moved the vehicle forward, slowly at first so they could hear the brush of the long grass and then its gentle swishing lost in the roaring surge as the bonnet tilted steeply, and the clay ramp was crossed and the tyres welcomed the smooth asphalt.

'On our way, then,' Marie-Claire said. She closed her eyes. If she thought of something else, perhaps the throb in her abdomen would not become too insistent. She owed that at least to Kate. To the dear dim boy who drove them as well. The last thing she wanted was to make her own discomfort an additional fret for either of them. She turned to the flattish face, the expression it was impossible to read. 'So what do you have in mind for us today?' she said.

Kate wished her friend would stay put and not attempt to converse. It did not ring true, she thought, it would not ring true for the creature who for the time being was all that you might have in mind if you spoke of Fate. But how could any of them know how to act at a time like this? The Chow alone was certain. And yes, the nun's words had rankled him. He said, with the gun swung loosely in the gap between his knees, 'I can blow the face off any of youse, at least that must have sunk in?'

Don't answer, Kate wanted to call out. For God's sake, don't. But Marie-Claire seemingly had lost interest. She was looking from the window to where a carcase of some kind, a thing of fur and black paws, lay gutted at the side of the road, its innards smeared to a red swirl in a patch of sun. Spicer turned left as they came back to the main road. There was soon a sign that told them, 'Taupo'. They drove through farming country with patches of bush and farm houses, some of them partly concealed by trees, most of them as though dumped starkly in the middle of cleared paddocks, a rawness about them, a box-like ugliness that Marie-Claire took in with vague distaste. So long in this country, yet it still was not her idea of how countryside should look.

Watching only the car's bonnet nose out along the road ahead of them, Kate took no notice of what they drove through. She was not afraid of the mad creature who sat behind her, beside her friend. She refused to be that. She thought only of the silliness of it, their holiday held to ransom, what should have been a delight for the three of them turned to something else. She thought, almost indifferently, of what the Chow might have in mind. Whatever might take place, it was so obvious that Spicer must be the one spared until last. Without Spicer there was simply a killer on the run, and two women, and a half-ton car that none of them could drive or so much as move between them. Spicer was the one who was meant to be saved. There was the unexpected memory of her Gran in the kitchen, tutting in irritation at her son who sat with his damaged leg concealed beneath the table while he slapped the racing pages flat, and said, 'Can't you pray for a winner there for me, Ma?' And her Gran flaring back, 'There's some as meant to be saved and some as not.' Uncle Stan catching her eye, winking at his niece, calling through again to the kitchen where the large black kettle clanged against the range. 'Give us a song there, then, if you can't stack the odds. You know how I likes them Wesley ones.' And his head dropped down while his fingers tapped at the paper, *What a friend*, he himself sings quietly, *what a friend we have in Jesus*. Spicer, she said to herself with such utter certainty. Spicer will outlast us all.

The young man's hands held firm against the wheel as the heavy Chevrolet took a long curved corner. Then Kate felt, even before she realised why, the fresh tenseness in the car. She turned her head to see the dark barrel of the gun against the back of Spicer's neck. Not pressed in against the flesh but brushing, backwards and forwards, the way you might flick a pencil across the neck of a cat. It was the playfulness that chilled her. She saw Marie-Claire, her hands folded together calmly in the dark blue shadow of her lap. Then, almost like a child, the Chow's chin leaned against the other arm, which he had laid along the back of the front seat, his elbow in fact nudging softly against Kate's shoulder. The flattened face was inches from her, while the barrel lowered and nestled on Spicer's collar.

'Just an idea,' the Chow said. The husky reed of the voice, like the playful movement of the gun, drawing them again to the volatile and erratic madness that sported with them.

Spicer slowed almost to a stop. Their captor's head nodded to a rough track ahead of them, a grey indentation turning from the tar-sealed road into the high motionless gloom of the pines, a logging track that quickly disappeared between the close-spaced trees. The car rocked over the hardened clay ruts and further on between the closing trees. The first of the branches began to whack and strike against the body of the car.

'Those branches scratch the paint,' Spicer said. It worried him what the stiff fingers would be doing to the panelling, to the shine of the mudguards where his polishing brought his own face towards him out of the dark pool of the paint.

'Never mind that now,' Kate told him.

He eased the vehicle back to the slowest it would go, an inching through the bleached corridor of diminished light. He felt the tip of the gun, gentle almost as a finger stroke, play across the back of his neck. As the car dipped into a rut then rode heavily out of it, the bodywork creaked and strained. At the next dip Marie-Claire was flung across, her upper body pressed close against the set of the figure next to her. Her right fist opened and her fingers braced against her captor's thigh. It was a moment of strange, disturbing intimacy. The other body took her weight for those few seconds, neither resisting nor receiving it, but nothing could prevent the nun's being aware, so closely, of that simple animal warmth, the mould of shoulder and of thigh, a bond so quickly made and then dissolved, and yet a violence in it, she could not help thinking that, a violation. It was the closeness of another being for whom one's own existence was a thing so trifling that a gust of impatience, an unprovoked flurry of ill-will, could provoke annihilation without a qualm. She knew words trickled away, inadequately, in trying to bring it into comprehension. More than that, she knew and feared that her years, her decades of vocation, the attempted sincerity of her dealings as a creature with her God, might not prove up to whatever final challenge was brought to her. 'I'm sorry,' she said. Like a child, she knew that was what she must sound like.

'You all right, my dear?' Kate said to her. Her friend turned to face her, her hand on the shiny leather at the back of the seat.

'I'm all right,' Marie-Claire told her, her own fingers lightly finding those of her friend. And laughed a little, 'This is like being on a boat,' as the car rose and sank across the waves of hardened mud.

The barrel of the gun tapped again at Spicer's shoulder. He drew back on the heavy handbrake, the last clicks as the ratchet engaged. He lowered his hands to his lap. He saw how his sweat stains shone on the wooden steering wheel. Beside him, the woman in her long fawn skirt, her cream summer blouse, looked ahead through the square framing of the glass. They were now in a small clearing between the pines. The regularity of the planting was broken here for some reason, some lapse perhaps of the workers twenty years before. Is that how long these vile, brooding trees took to grow? She had no idea. But the silence now in the car was like a physical weight. Then came the quick click of the handle beside the Chow, the flinging out of his door as far as the hinges would allow it to open, and he jumped it seemed in one decisive movement so that he stood there, looking at them in the enclosed tension of the car, his gun no longer visible, both hands on the fattish hips. Ordering them, with the decisive calm of a schoolmaster instructing a busload of pupils, 'Out the front here. Out here in front of the car.'

None knew what to expect. That he no longer held his gun at them was a temporary relief. As he walked ahead of them and waited in front of the car's high grid, they saw the weapon tucked in the back of his belt, the handle squat and colourless, the barrel bulging in the lift of his khaki trousers. What he ordered then was so simple, so unexpected, Spicer laughed at the absurdity of it. The Chow held his eye and said in that breathy exhalation, as though the sound somehow came from further off than the throat that uttered it, 'You'd better do it, that's all.'

Spicer went to the trunk at the back of the car and lifted down from the top the large case Mrs C had brought her clothes in. There were half-torn scraps of paper stuck to the leather sides, a word he could not read in a kind of wreath around the picture of a ship. All so faded and old. How long's she had this thing? he wondered, a car like this you'd think she might of got herself a new bag as well. He put it down on the layer of rust-coloured pine needles, where it slipped on the slight slope. He reset it again where the ground levelled out.

It all took place so quickly, like it was a game or something, Spicer thought, a game kids played with a stack of clothes. Mrs C came and knelt down in front of the case and her two thumbs pressed at the metal clasps. The lid snapped back with a sound that like all others in the heavy, uneasy light seemed louder than it would anywhere else. She raised up by the shoulders a black dress, and shook it out. The lower part of it, from the waist down, wasn't black at all. As she moved it and let its length fall along the suitcase, it stirred almost as though it were a living thing, and the colour swam green for a second and then as its length slipped again it moved like a purple tide.

'It's three-quarter length,' her friend said. 'At least it won't drag.'

'Don't muck around,' the Chow said. 'You hear?'

She lay the dress across her arm and asked Spicer to close the case for her.

'Give it to her, then,' the Chow told her. 'She heard what I said.'

Kate handed the dress she carried to the nun. It was clear now what was intended, a line they were to cross that would take them even further from what any of them had assumed to be a set and stable world.

'Go on,' he said. His head flicked towards the concealment of the trees a few yards further on. 'Don't muck around.'

Marie-Claire moved into the dim corridor between the scabbed trunks of the trees, her dark habit a smear against the drab, buckled earth and the pluck of the rigid branches. Then she was gone from sight.

Kate and Spicer and the smaller figure who compelled them continued to watch the overlapping, receding wall of trees. Kate touched the watch that hung by a short chain from her leather belt, but did not look at the time. There was little in the light where they stood that might tell them whether it was morning or afternoon, if the day receded or grew more intense beyond the oppressive clutter, the motionless, dead underside of the row upon row of pines, the smoky, lustreless depth that might end in fifty yards or go on for miles. The Chow ran his fingernails along the grille of the radiator behind him. A cone clattered down several yards from where they stood. Those were the only sounds.

Then the woman emerged from behind the concealing trees. There was at once something so pitiable about the way she stepped towards them, and stopped like a child unsure of what she should do next, that Kate gasped at the sight of her. She seemed in this crude transformation from nun to frail, aging woman to have been reduced, humiliated, exposed so she stood and blinked at them as though facing an unexpected light. Her hair, grey and shapeless from its perfunctory clipping a month before, was the thing that startled her friend. The shapeless cap of hair and the utter pallor of her throat and arms. For the dress Kate had taken from the trunk and handed her a few minutes before was meant to be worn in the evenings. Its sleeves reached to only a fraction below the elbow, the neckline dipped to expose the ridges of the woman's collar-bones and that appalling whiteness of her throat and neck — the feeling they should not be seen. For that word, appalling, came to Kate as soon as Marie-Claire returned their gaze. There was even an indecency that seemed to flood between the viewers and the hesitant woman, observed as she had never been for forty years. Again, like a child, she held her hands together in front of her, then raised them, as if about to begin a song. Then one pale arm swept down and bunched a handful of the dark shimmering skirt, raising its hem but not far enough, so that when she stepped forward she hobbled, no more able to control the garment she wore than a child, again, dressed up in some parody of adult life.

But then her boldness surprised them. She stopped in front of the small head, the tilted face, the eyes level with her own.

'If you want my clothes you can get them,' she said. 'You will not use me to help you insult God.'

The smooth, hooded face a few feet in front of her own raised slightly. The Chow's head jerked twice, and a sound like a dry rapid bark came at her, a laugh that was dismissive of both her words and her appearance. It carried a contempt that reduced her to what he saw — an ugly, helpless woman whose shred of asserted dignity served only to make her ridiculous as well. He stepped forward and past her, the dress she clutched in one rigid fist hissing for the merest second as his khaki trousers brushed against it. And Marie-Claire turned and took his place in front of the car's ridged grille. He moved into the trees, as if this were some game they played where one after the other must go and hide and reappear, transformed. The two women and Spicer stood side by side without speaking, while the other figure slipped from sight. They heard the crack as the Chow's movement broke an extended raking twig. And then, as a few minutes before, only the smoky, directionless blur of diminished light between the trunks until the entrance, more dramatic but less pitiable than the last, of the Chow togged up in the nun's habit and wimpled veil. Again there was the quick bark of his laugh, cut off almost as soon as it had begun. The bottom of the long gown touched the tips of his shoes.

Spicer thought with a sense of shock, Jesus, look at him. Like that he could be fucken one of them just about, no one'd tumble to it until he spoke. The Chow looked at Spicer and took up what he thought. He said, 'No one's going to shoot a nun, go along with that?' And once again, a single sharp rasp of amusement before he told them to pile back in, they'd mucked around for long enough.

Spicer rocked them back across the corrugated ground and down the verge onto the road south. A cattle truck clattered past, a trail of greenish shit running ahead of them from its guttering where the packed animals scoured. A dark stain ran down the centre of the road.

'They pack them in too tight,' the Chow said. 'See how they pack them in?' Again he sat next to the frail, huddling woman whose clothes he wore. No one answered his observation.

Kate turned in the front seat and glanced behind her. 'You're cold?' she said.

'I'm all right,' her friend said. 'If Spicer puts the window up.'

'Put it up,' the Chow said.

Their captor was no taller than the nun. The habit fitted him as well as it had her. But Marie-Claire continued to look so ill at ease in the only other garment she had worn since she left France. It was not the cold that troubled her, that drove her back into the corner of the back seat as though she cowered from some impending blow. The exposure of her arms in their three-quarter-length sleeves disoriented her even more than the unaccustomed movement of air about her neck, the sides of her head. Her arms were thin and not simply pale; they were as though buried from light for decades, and now exhumed. That was how she thought of them. The image, its macabre associations, revolted her. She felt the rising of bile at the back of her throat, the revulsion at her own flesh. She knew this, if ever, was something she should attempt to offer up, turn from its immediate misery and humiliation to the positive acceptance, the grace, she should readily make of it. Yet that was something, at least for now, she was unable to do. There was only the sense of distress, the dismay at those white thin ugly arms, the exposed and thickened wrists, the fingers which struck her as so coarse, and on her left hand, the silver band of her religious marriage pressed in against the puff of flesh on either side. She could compare it to nothing, this feeling of disgust at how she looked. Her hand rose, and her opened palm ran along the slope of hair at the back of her head and then drew down across the naked ridge of her throat.

The Chow watched her, as her eyes turned to the passing rise and fall of the farms. A boy at a milk stand rolled a churn that was more than half his size. The boy's tongue was held between his teeth, his eyes lowered to the heavy metal container he concentrated to control. No more than a couple of seconds, the boy's life and her own, that flickering past another human being, two souls of all the countless millions that had lived already and would live in the future, so close and so distant, the chance brushing of time and place, and that was that. What more could one say of it? Marie-Claire had felt it before, this mysterious awareness of what was whipped by as on a different stream of time, she had felt it so often at the Home, as she laid out the recently deceased for burial, as a dying patient grabbed at her hand and then the pressure was released. I know nothing, she thought, after all this time, God keep me from the terror of all I do not know. And even this drifting off into such vague apprehensions as these, this attempt to touch beyond the wall of strangeness that surrounds us all, she knew was itself a luxury she would not have access to for much longer. The demanding tug in her side drew her back, almost savagely, to where she knew more and more of her time would be concerned. The body. It was that she thought of now. How well she knew what to expect. The way it will become like a funnel, that unexpected comparison suddenly coming to her, the drawing and siphoning of all attention, all interest, towards the descending, inescapable centre of pain that we finally become.

Marie-Claire began to pray, hoping for the comfort that did not arrive from the old familiar words. She closed her eyes to blot away the nakedness of her arms. Then she must have slept, for she realised the car had halted, that there were voices outside, there was a clatter against the side of the car. She looked out to see a large young Maori with the heavy metal head from a benzine bowser hanging from his hand.

Spicer stepped down from the car. He removed his peaked cap and ran his hand across the line it had scored on his forehead. The early afternoon had turned uncomfortable and sultry. Kate wound at the knob on the door beside her, and the window lowered. There was a slight puff of breeze, heavy with the stink of benzine. A disconsolate mongrel with a scab as large as a saucer on its haunch held her eye for a moment and moved casually away, crouching into the shadow beneath a parked truck. Kate's mood had swung from the deep sense of helplessness that so pressed on her a couple of hours before. She was now alert and angry. She turned to her friend but did not look at her directly. She knew Marie-Claire would not want that. It would take more than today for that dear bewildered woman to accept how things had fallen out. And she knew the shame the nun would be going through in that incongruous fashionable frock — 'the best we have', the woman in Smith and Caughey's had told her, showing her the label that was now so ridiculous.

The Maori looked at them with interest as they drove away. He raised a large hand, palm outwards, and Spicer returned the wave. Kate held in her lap the opened bottles with yellow straws rising from their necks that Spicer had handed her as he came back behind the wheel. They must have been standing in ice because their tartan labels were soaked through. As the car again took the road south, the sheet of the lake which all of them had heard of but none seen until this instant, revealed to them its distant steely stretch. Kate said, 'That's the first test then, Spicer. You passed with flying colours.' He was not sure what she meant. Getting by with no one noticing them, was that it? No one clicking to the fact that the woman with her ugly grey hair and the shiny dress shouldn't look like that at all, that the nun sitting next to her was the crazy bugger half the cops in the country were supposed to be on the lookout for? Who likely as not would do for the bloody lot of them.

'Give us one of them,' the Chow said. 'One of them bottles.'

Kate passed one across. She felt the warm blunt fingers touch quickly against her own.

'No,' Marie-Claire said. She shook her head when Kate held a bottle towards her. Although her throat was dry, the thought of the sweet drink sickened her.

'You then?' Kate said to Spicer.

He took the straw from the bottle with his teeth and spat it from the window. He tilted the bottle up and his throat jerked with the pleasure of it. He then passed it back. He had bought only two bottles from the Maori man's wife, who had reached them up from a deep bin and pushed them across at him and taken his money and never said a word. She had looked out at the car and back to him. He had bought only two bottles because he didn't want the Chow thinking he had got one especially for him — he might swing his gun round as much as he liked, but Spicer wasn't coming at that. He wasn't buying lemonade for him. But he didn't buy three bottles either because he wasn't prepared to provoke the Chow like that. If he'd brought back three the Chow would know Spicer was saying, None for you, you bugger. Two's the story, he thought, as he stood at the counter and ordered. You could take buying two any way you liked.

They drove through the main street of Taupo. Then ahead of them they saw the police at the corner, just past the big hotel where the road divided off, leading west into the hills or south along the edge of the lake. The cloud had shifted and the lake lost its cold greyness. Light sparkled off it now like hundreds of turning knives. It would have been nice, Spicer thought, to keep on driving along beside that. But Mrs C had said a hundred yards before the roads diverged, 'Watch out for the Napier road here, Spicer.' And then the cops there, waving them into the kerb.

The Chow said, 'This is pointed right at your swede so remember that, won't you, driver?'

The cop tapped with the knuckles of his closed fist at the side of the bonnet as the car came to a stop beside him. As he tapped again he leaned forward and Spicer lowered the window. One of the man's eyes was so bloodshot it looked like a red marble. But the other eye moved across them and he said, 'You know we're on the lookout for that feller from up Hamilton way?'

'Someone mentioned it back there,' Kate said. 'They said we should be on the lookout.'

'Lookout's right,' the cop said. Both his hands were now across the lowered window, grasping the ledge. 'We don't reckon he's down this far, but you never know.' His one good eye roved over Spicer's shoulder to the women in the back seat. A thick forefinger raised to the brim of his helmet as he saluted the nun. 'Sister,' he said, politely.

'She's not well,' Spicer said.

'Not surprised in this heat,' the policeman said. 'It's over eighty out here. You can add ten to that inside a vehicle.'

Kate said, 'The road's all right, is it? From here on?'

The policeman laughed as though making a joke. 'Road's all right,' he said. 'How's the driver?' Then removing his hands from where they rested and standing back from the car, he asked them, 'Going all the way?'

'The ladies are tired,' Kate said. 'We'd like to get across as soon as we can.'

'Don't push it if you don't have to,' was the policeman's advice. 'The country's worth taking a squizz at anyway.' He nodded and Spicer turned the engine over. As the car moved off, the cop flicked his head to the side. He told them, 'Don't pick anyone up.'

They drove several miles before the Chow's voice put it to Spicer, 'You know what I'd do, don't you? Come any funny business?'

'I know,' Spicer said.

'So long as you do,' the Chow said.

Marie-Claire looked at him directly, with a graver attention than she had so far done. Why the Chow, she wondered? Why call him that? She saw how the face was strangely flat, how at a distance the skin appeared more sallow than it was when you were closer to it. She had seen cases enough of jaundice that looked like this. There was only the faintest marking of eyebrows. The eyes were small but no more slanted than her own. There was a kind of haze in them if they looked at you directly, a sense of blurring as well as scrutiny. From a few yards away they were greenish, pale clots. To take all that on now, the face surrounded by the framing habit of her Order — it was impossible not to feel disturbed. Although was that quite it? So many definitions had begun to slip. Then something both delicate and yet oddly violent occurred. The Chow became aware that the woman in the shimmery dress, with the ugly jagged line of hair, was paying such attention. The phlegmy eyes moved towards her before his head was turned. Then the arm nearest to her, covered in the garment that had been her own for so long, raised and came towards her, slowly and without any sense of threat. The raised fingers rested gently enough against her chin. They then pushed quickly, firmly, so that her head jerked to face directly in front. And the hand again withdrew.

What came into her mind was the hand of the novice mistress at Lyons, the older nun's stealth as she came behind the postulants, her fist suddenly pressed between the shoulder blades, her palm sharply lifting their chins. Demeanour, she instructed. Posture. These are part of obedience. These too are part of your vocation. The fraud in her own clothing now reminding her, commanding her, to that same acknowledgement, as the car picked up speed and for almost half a mile passed beneath high overarching trees, and the windows, the movement of light inside them, were a dappled variegated rush. Then the sun, hard against the back of her neck. Marie-Claire closed her eyes. She recited lines she had carried with her from that same time at Lyons. And an image coming into her mind that amused her — the long iron bar attached to the wall beside the bath at the Home, a support for the old, the frail, the doddery to cling to. The words of the Psalms were like that. To help her keep her balance. For that, she knew, would be the hard part. Not the pain — she was confident she could cope with that. Dr Flynn had told her, hadn't he, she would not suffer beyond what she could endure? Pain at least made you more certain of who you were, a driving in, a drum-beat whose refrain was *me*, this indeed is *me*. That was one fact nursing the ill brought home each day. But that other loss was what she feared, to lose the balance she had worked at all her life — to serve, but to serve with dignity, decorum. She feared the loss of that. She reached for the supporting rail of what she knew by heart, the words whose consolation was such a simple, animal thing. They held fear back for the moment at least, a flame against the dark. *Au jour du malheur l'Eternal le délivre; l'Eternal le garde et lui conserve vie. Il est heureux sur la terre. Et tu ne le livres pas au bon plaisir de ses ennemis.*

The words came to her so easily, although they were not ones she had said for years. Our past pours through us at every moment, she thought, we are the funnel of ourselves. *Mais c'est ta droit, c'est ton bras, c'est la lumière de ta face* . . . What Marie-Claire believed she recalled in silence was now a low, sustained murmur, indistinct but constant beneath her breath.

'Shut up.' The figure so close to her did not move, did not even raise his voice, simply commanded her to silence.

She must then have slept again, for all the confusion in her mind. When she woke the sun was much lower in the sky. Her mouth tasted unpleasantly of copper. The road was so smooth, the tyres hissed softly across it. The body of the car seemed scarcely to move with the motion, simply to be drawn with such ease towards the hills rising ahead of them. On both sides there was low, scruffy, uneven ground, mounds of flowing tussock. A painted sign was tied to a post. 'Store', it said. '1 mile'.

There was nothing ahead of them on the road, nothing behind. The Chow coughed into his sleeve. No one else spoke. Perhaps they had said something while she slept. For Spicer knew to slow down and ease the car across an iron cattle-stop and follow a drive down towards a low wooden building with 'shop' written large along its side. Three figures inside the shop-front window watched them bump across the yard. An old woman and a younger one, and a girl whose hair was so vividly red it was a splotch of colour in the dim interior of the shop. The three stood in a line, as if waiting like this, watching out to the open space above the one tall gum that soared over its pool of shadow, was something they always did. Hine and Chook and Mrs Campbell. Mrs Campbell was the mother of both of them, of Chook who was as gaunt almost as the older woman beside her, and Hine who was twenty-three and looked seventeen, a girl no more than five feet tall, her flaring mane as though some deep anger in her had broken out and burned above her.

Chook laughed as the arrivals stepped down from the car. 'What's this we've got?' she said. 'A freak show?'

Spicer looked towards the shop-front window and the trio of dim figures. He removed his cap and placed it on the heated metal of the bonnet, and ran his palms along either side of his head.

'He likes his hair smoothed down, that one,' Mrs Campbell said. 'Thinks he's in the pictures.'

'You've never even seen him,' Hine said. 'You've never seen him in the pictures because we never go to the pictures. There's no one in this place could even spell pictures.'

'I've seen him in magazines,' her mother said. 'I've seen his sort enough to know that rooster.'

Hine looked at her sister. She then said to her mother, 'If you'd seen anyone else in a magazine and could remember his name you'd say he looked like him as well.' She eased her shirt out from where it rubbed against her breasts. She hated the way her skin itched with just about anything against it, once summer started. A doctor in Taupo said she was allergic to pollen and things — her skin was allergic to it the way other people got hay fever. Sometimes she had blotches on her legs so bad she wouldn't wonder if people thought she lived at the pa.

'He's a nice-lookin' feller,' Mrs Campbell said. 'What I can make out of him.'

'You never get past it, do you?' Chook said. 'There's some people as'd root a tree-stump even when they're ninety.'

'Language, if you don't mind,' the woman said. But she grinned too. Chook could make her laugh, that was one thing she'd say for her. Damn all else, mind. Never learned to cook even, nothing you'd call cooking, anyway. Couldn't iron a hanky. Doubt if she'd touched a spade in her life. Who was it planted the spuds round here you might well ask, tied the beans up, watched the tomatoes and doctored them with blood and bone so truck drivers pulled in here for a plate of sandwiches when there was a posh hotel half an hour on towards the lake, a tea-rooms flash as a chink on a bike, but it was always here they wanted to stop? Like this lot out here now. A woman in some kind of dress didn't even fit her and a haircut like she was trying to outdo a shagged mop got out of the car so careful you'd think she had boils. Then that other done-up tart from the front seat held her arm like she was going to keel over and began staring over here to the shop, hobble, hobble, those little steps Mrs Campbell hated no matter what your age was, you should walk proper or just stay put if it was her you was asking. 'Looks like a dose of rat bait,' she said. One of Blue's sayings, that.

'Look at that!' Hine said. Her head jerked as though a hand had spanned her neck and driven her forward.

'One of *them*!' Chook said.

'One of what?' Mrs Campbell knew her eyes weren't up to much these days, but be blowed if she'd let that on to the girls. But she couldn't help it, the tone of their voices now. 'One of what?' she said.

'Not blind, are we?' Chook asked her. 'Could see the trousers all right though, couldn't we?'

Mrs Campbell watched the figure in dark blue, top to toe, covered up the way Hindus were. She'd seen them once with Blue it must have been, three Indian women walking beside a cart stacked with mattresses and tables and God knows what, and this little darkie perched up on the top like he was riding an elephant through shit river — that could only be what Blue said too. Couldn't see a thing except their eyes glittering there like specks of glass, the rest of them covered like the world was just waiting to have a gawp at them.

'It's a nun, Mum,' Hine said. 'I've never seen one up close, have you?'

Kate, though, was the one who came to the doorway. She paused, her eyes not yet adjusted to the swirling half-dark of the shop. It was so bright outside, in here was like a cave.

'You do teas?' Kate asked. 'Do you?'

'We *serve* teas, Missus,' Mrs Campbell said. 'The tomato sandwiches are what we're famous for. But there's all kinds. Cheese. Ham. You just ask for it.'

Then this woman who must have been forty-five if she was a day smiled at them and she looked that lovely, Mrs Campbell thought. Her thick dark hair and that smile. Bit of a honey pot in her time, that one, she'd put good money on that.

'That sounds perfect,' the woman said. Teeth like that, for Christ's sake! Mrs Campbell couldn't help but grin back at her. Lucky to have half a dozen left herself.

'You could sit over here,' the elder of the daughters said. She was lean and pale, you didn't expect to see someone in the country look like that.

'That's perfect,' Kate said again. And addressing herself to the daughter, who she felt was the one to get on side with, she said they had a sick friend with them, was there somewhere she might sit comfortably for a bit? Might lie down even?

'It's only a tea-rooms,' Chook said. 'There's a doctor in Taupo.'

'There's a sofa,' the younger one put in. 'There's a sofa there, see. Against the wall? She could lie there if she liked.'

They couldn't be sisters, Kate thought, those two, yet there's something — what is it? — the timbre of their voices. Close your eyes and you'd know they were, open them and it seemed impossible.

The small figure darted in front of her to the doorway and said, 'Over here, then,' to the nun.

'It's the other lady,' Kate said. 'The one behind who needs to lie down.'

The red-haired girl plumped up the cushions. She so enjoyed the activity, the diversion of it. This place was a morgue most of the time. She noticed there was sweat along the small hairs on the sick woman's upper lip. There was a gleam too along her neck, beneath the grey straight hair. The girl said, 'It's a bit hot in the car, rest'll do you good.'

'Thank you,' the lady said. Although something not quite right about the way she spoke, was there?

Spicer was the last who stood in the doorway. The roomful of six women looked towards him. Chook stood at the bead curtain through to the kitchen. It was so still for a second. The little tinkle of the beads, that was about all. The cicadas racketing away, but they seemed far off. The sick one lying down there, the nun and the other handsome one standing by the table, about to pull out the chairs, Mum and her sister turned towards the door, the dark figure of the driver, the daylight behind him so he was a cut-out shape. That'd be a great drawing if you could fit it all in. You never could though. Not all you wanted — the silence bit and what you looked at, the dark and light of it, the way they all were held there, just that instant like. As if time was a flower spread about them that might collapse at any second. But she'd draw it all the same. She'd remember it and later on she'd draw it.

'You're a fine figure,' Mrs Campbell said to Kate. Then she laughed and wiped at her mouth with the back of her hand and said, 'You'll excuse us then while we get youse all tea.'

There was the sound of pouring water, plates clapped together, the strident voice of Mrs Campbell telling her girls to get a move on, couldn't they, how often did they have four people in at one time? Three, she corrected herself, that sick one's not going to eat a thing, you don't have to be Truby King to work that one out.

Marie-Claire, now that she lay outright, had drifted into a light restless sleep. One hand moved up and down her other arm, as though prompted to feel about her for something she expected and did not find. Kate's chair was placed close to the end of the sofa. Her own hand stretched out and touched the older woman's head. She raised the damp neckline from where it lay, clammy and stained, against the top of her breast. A mottled bruised streak, livid at the centre, ran up from one breast towards her shoulder, a reminder that the Chow ruled them even as he stood there, nun-like, demure, looking through the grimed window panes to the expanse of paddock behind the house, to the slight elevation of the land where the tussock poured across in messy clumps. They could be so many heads lopped off if you wanted to think of them like that, the hair streaming down around them. Things could be like anything you wanted if you decided to think of them like that. The trouble with people, that's the thing, the Chow thought; they think things have to stay the same for you all the time. That's tripe. What you like to think's always stronger than people ever say. You think they're heads cut off, they're floppy gingery mops with just the tops stuck up; they're helmets like those guards, you must have seen pictures of them outside the King's palace in London; or they're plain old tussock if you want to see them like that. Things become confused when you push thinking too hard. The Chow knew that.

The nun looking out the window, standing so still. That's what nuns are meant to be like, Hine thought. Quiet and that. She clicked rapidly through the bead curtain, cradling the stack of saucers and the nested cups against her breasts. She set them down on the counter and spread the table with a sheet of clean white newsprint she reeled off from its roller near the till. She'd done it a million times but she loved the burring rip of it against the heavy metal bar. Her small hands smoothed across the paper and edged it down neatly at the corners of the table. A few minutes later she came out again through the glassy rustle of the curtain and set a plate of cold scones and butter in a tarnished silver plate-stand in the middle of the newsprint. Mum had told her take the tea out next, by the time it drew in its white enamel pot with the deep-blue handle Chook was always going on about, such a lovely colour that, she'd say, that's the loveliest thing in this goddamn house — by the time the tea was ready to pour, the tomato sandwiches would be ready as well, a tower of soft bread and the brilliant glistening red Chook was stacking up this minute. The loveliness of that too, she'd think, just look at that crumbly white against the vivid streak between. Only it was no good saying that, what was the point of saying it? People just thought you were off your rocker.

Chook brought her hand down flat and the pile of bread sank beneath her palm, then the green-handled breadknife sawed through them. 'You can take these through now,' she said to Hine.

The young woman who looked like a girl flicked in and out between the kitchen and the other room. It was the closest she'd been for ages to what she thought of as 'the world'. Something more at any rate than boring lorry drivers and loggers and farmers with stains down the front of their trousers and bits of string tied below their knees. They'd grab at you given half a chance, and Chook sometimes said to her the one thing they owed their mother, the one thing she'd given them without intending to probably, was the wisdom of that — you didn't go giving it away so you'd finish up like her. She's all right, Hine tried to defend. 'All right is it?' Chook said. 'You never saw the way she went on. You don't remember what it was like when the old man shot through.'

'*Your* old man,' Hine reminded her. And Chook saying, not with accusation and certainly not with any attempt to put her down, but simply recollecting, 'I remember your one all right,' she said, 'the day they rode over that paddock out the back there and this snooty bitch hardly out of school asking me about my drawings and all of them ballocky naked in the river before they came in for tea. Mum was a pushover, even I could take that in. The old man gone for months.' And Chook saying nothing then, even when her sister spoke, looking out on the rise of tussock the nun's looking at now while the old one sleeps on the sofa and the flash woman with the nice hair sits next to her and the man in the leather cap there like a cat on hot bricks giving her the once-over. Hine knows that, him watching the way she moves and the rasp of the material over her little tits — little all right, but that doesn't mean men don't like the look of them, Chook had put her wise to that. You don't even *need* tits, she had said, men still want to jump you.

Hine watched them avidly. The old one with the god-awful jaggy hair muttered something in her sleep. The younger woman stood up from where she sat beside her and moved towards the table. 'I'm famished,' she said. And then, without turning but raising her voice in a way that struck her as both a boss giving orders and an auntie, say, simply pointing something out, the woman said, 'Spicer, sit down and eat something, will you?' The young man did as she directed and laid his cap across his knees beneath the edge of the paper cloth. Spicer. There's a name and a half for you, Hine thought. She smiled at him and he held her eye a moment and the woman pushed the sandwiches at him.

The surprise, Hine thought, and Chook thought so too, who saw it as she came through from the kitchen with the teapot, was that the nun turned from the window and came to the table but did not sit down. She behaved like a hungry shearer, Chook thought, someone who had never been taught a thing about manners. She snatched up half the sandwiches and turned and went back to the window and shovelled the food into her mouth, two sandwiches at a time. Then she ran one hand down the length of her dark-blue dress affair, wiping tomato juice off her fingers. That's not the way she should do it either, Chook thought.

There was a clang from the kitchen, where the tin tray Mrs Campbell knocked from the bench rolled like a hoop and clashed again as it hit the slop bucket and woke the sleeping woman.

'I'll bring a cup over,' the other woman said.

The old one slowly sat up. 'I'm not quite a cot case yet.'

That dress she's got on, Chook thought, does she think this is one of them nightclubs or something? Not even a fit either, the way her hand rose up and bunched the loose fall of the bodice as she moved across to the table.

The nun turned again, the strong glare of the window washing over the oddball angle of her face, silvering it, Chook thought, like she'd been dipped in something other than ordinary light and was rising from it. And that voice as well, like her breath was forced through a tube but there was a leak in it somewhere, hissing along the sides of what she said. 'Tell them to make as many of those sandwiches as they can. We'll take them with us.'

There was something so queer going on, Chook felt, it was like the room was suddenly a stage: there was what she saw and heard but there was more to it than that, shadows that were there but you couldn't quite make out. Things it would be lovely to try to draw. When she went back to the kitchen, the door to the back porch was open and Mum was sitting on the steps.

'I'm not going in there with that rum lot,' she said. 'You two girls can take care of them.' She was easing off her slippers, one foot working against the other. 'You can pass me them bluchers there,' she said. She nodded towards the row of boots set close against the wall of the porch. Her daughter moved impatiently and dropped the boots before her mother.

'No one calls them that any more,' she said.

Her mother instructed her without looking up. 'Look, girl, this is my place here and I call things what I want to. Those who don't like it,' she said. She stamped on the verandah to settle the laceless boots. 'I'm up the shed,' she said.

She looks like a bad sketch stumping across the yard, Chook thought. I've drawn the old bag often enough but never quite catch her, do I? The way she's stiff and gaunt but a springiness to her for all that. You could imagine her bent like a willow twig but you'd never see her snap — it wasn't in her. She'd be the same at ninety. When I'm sixty. The thought clouded Chook with a dull, useless rage. As if she had anywhere to go. She'd grown up with these oppressive hills, their scatter of trunks like so many bits of huge bone, grey and stark and enough to drive you crazy. Hine would push off one of these days — she never said she would, but you could feel it coming, first chance she'd be off. She would shoot through and they'd get a card from her at Christmas time and that would be that. But Chook herself never would, she knew that with a leaden certainty. She'd move round this tussocky dump for ever, there was nowhere else she belonged. Or even wanted to go to, if it came to that. She'd become as mad as Mum in time. She'd become as ugly and ramble on to herself and not know if something really happened or if it was only in her head.

She wished that mob inside would get on and out of it so she could get to the shed and the stacks of cardboard and the big sheets of newsprint she spread out and worked the brushes over and brought out the shapes, the ranging sinuous lines that were the hills, only ochre and magenta and the colour of everything she felt inside, and the dead trees were bones all right, and the whole lot of it was her, it was her as well as what she looked at, she would draw the inside and the outside too of everything.

Chook hadn't heard her move, but the nun was there, sudden. Why did they make themselves into some draped secret done up like that? She'd do the face once they'd left, a face and hands and the inky stormy smear of everything being covered, not allowed to move, not allowed to beat, the face she'd make like the exit from a tunnel because everything about her had to come from there, just rush out from there and nowhere else.

'Where's the old tart?' the nun said.

'You mean her?' Chook said. Her head nodded at the bland, dirt-coloured yard, the blaze of her mother's pink dress in the corner there where she sat on the chopping block outside the shed.

'What's up there?' the nun said. 'There's not a telephone up there?'

'There was one down here for a while but they cut it off years back. You can't make a phone call from here.'

'I don't want to make one,' the nun said. 'And we want more tea. You better get back inside there and make more tea.'

'Who's ordering?' Chook said. Is this the way they go on, is it?

'I'm telling you,' the nun said. 'That's all.'

'Where's Hine?' Chook said. 'Why haven't you asked her?'

'She's getting water for the car. You're the one who'll make the tea.'

The other room rang with nerves when Chook went back into it. The two women sat at the table still, the scones had gone and the second lot of sandwiches, but the cup of tea in front of the older woman looked as though she hadn't touched it.

'Could I just have hot water?' she said. 'I'd be grateful if you'd give me a cup of hot water.' There was a little container thing beside her saucer, with a scatter of white pills.

'Denying the flesh,' the nun said. She spoke in the same even, breathy tone that could become a laugh and you'd scarcely notice.

'She's dying,' the prettier woman said quietly. 'Anyone can see that.'

'She's breathing,' the nun said. 'What do we do, pray for her?'

'It's of no concern,' the other woman said. 'Please.'

The nun kept watching through the open window to the front of the store.

Spicer had asked the young one, 'You must have a bucket somewhere, have you?' He had stood up and smoothed his hair on either side with his palms and placed his cap back on, adjusting it to some notion of exactness. Hine knew he looked at her, and that he liked asking her and not the others. He was tall when he stood in front of her, not just tall the way practically every man was because of her own size, but tall in another way as well, it was like the *idea* of him had a tallness of its own. He was younger than her but she could tell that meant nothing to him either.

'There's one out the side there,' she said. 'I'll show you where the tap is.'

She went out through the entrance to the shop. The big car sat there in the pool of shadow beneath the gum. 'That's a humdinger,' she said. 'That car there.'

'You think she's alive, you know, when you're driving her.'

He liked it that she was nice about the car. He wouldn't have thought he'd say that, but then he was glad he had. Because it was exactly that, sitting there, the wheel fat beneath his fingers, the dashboard telling him things only he could understand about her, how the car feels at different times. He liked the leathery creak when someone got into the back and the softest of rockings when a foot stood on the running board and the vibration moved right through him. It even excited him sometimes so he thought of the girls back at Number 23, like the car knew it was doing that even, making him hard.

'Alive?' the girl said. And then, 'Yes. I bet it does too.'

She liked him telling her that. The car with its shine and the brass, the firm squareness of it, dark and light together there. She could see what he meant when he said it was alive.

'The bucket, anyway,' he said.

'Here it is,' she told him. She turned the tap and the twisting column of water rang and broke in the aluminium bucket she shoved beneath it.

'You forget the radiator you're in trouble,' he said. 'The radiator's where you put the water.'

'I know about radiators,' Hine lied to him.

He looked at her seriously then smiled. 'Course you do,' he said.

She stood beside him, holding the metal cap he passed her before he hoisted the bucket nearly level with his shoulder and carefully measured the rate he poured at.

'Do it too fast,' he said, 'the whole thing can swell back and chuck the water over you.'

'Sounds alive all right,' the girl laughed.

'Bet your life it does,' he said. He was laughing with her now. 'Listen,' he said. 'You can even hear her drink.' He made a gurgle in his own throat at the same time. He wanted her to laugh again.

Because she was so small and didn't wear anything under her shirt, you'd have thought I'd have got used to all that kind of thing, the girls and that, Spicer thought. He had sort of, too. Apart from Miriam none of them meant a thing to him, it was part of his job to make sure they didn't. Hadn't Darkie warned him first off, by Christ boy, you go pushing a prong round that place Missus'll have you out quick as look at you. Not that he needed Darkie mouthing on about that one either. Miriam was the only one he'd given a thought to. She had told him things like, One day, Spicer, you'll meet up with just the right person. But all that was so distant now, Number 23 and the grey stone house along from St Ben's, the clatter of doors and the little spyhole he slid back some nights to make sure it was one of the boney fideys as Mrs C called them, the dinkum rooters, Darkie said, not the bulls trying to set the house up. But a thousand miles away, all that. He liked the way the girl's shirt stood out like she'd eaten down to about the last couple of inches of ice-cream cones then shoved them down there. Pointy like that. And the way she held his eye as she laughed with him. When he took the radiator cap back from her he felt how warm her hand was. Then he unlatched the side of the bonnet and flung it up for her and said, 'There, see what makes her tick,' because he knew she'd lean across the mudguard to look at the arrangement of wires and tubes and metal casings, and she wouldn't mind when he leaned across beside her and their shoulders pressed together. Neither of them spoke then because they knew they wanted to lean into each other. Her bright twists of hair brushed into his eyes. He stood up and she turned from the motor as well and looked at him and told him that leather cap he wore wasn't half flash, was it?

'She likes me to dress up for the job,' he said.

'She's your boss?'

'It's her car,' he said. 'The other one's her friend.'

'The nun?'

'The other one,' Spicer said.

Then Mrs C was at the door. There was a ping as something fell from the tree onto the store's corrugated iron roof and rattled down towards the guttering. Hine saw him look up.

'Everything in this place is falling apart,' she said.

'There's only the three of you?'

'There's been blokes one time or another. With Mum. But they've all done a runner.' The small shoulders shrugged, the breasts pushed against her shirt. 'I won't be here that much longer,' she said. 'First chance I have.'

Kate called again from the doorway. 'Can we get on the road?' She knew the Chow was agitated and she feared to provoke him further. Her friend appeared then behind her shoulder, the cap of grey mottled hair, the sickly whiteness of her throat. Then the Chow pushed through.

'Get on. All of youse.'

'We're coming back this way,' Spicer said. There isn't time, he thought, there isn't time for me even to get the words right — the rest of them were at the car now, they were getting into it, the creak when the Chow and the nun who should be dressed like one rose back into the rear seat and Mrs C spoke quietly as she moved close enough beside him for her dress to brush against him, the soft flicker against his knuckles and the smell that was always there. It made him think of Number 23, it must be something she put on.

'Let's get moving, for God's sake,' she said. 'I don't know what's going on.'

'I'm here,' Hine said to him. 'I'm here all the time, if you do come back.'

'Yes,' Spicer told her. 'I reckon I will, Hine. I reckon I'll be back.'

The car throbbed into life. Spicer felt its force along his legs and in his thighs. He turned his face towards the girl. From where she watched in the big pool of shadow the car changed colour as it took the sun, its brass shone out and the panels, oiled and shiny, flared so much lighter. And for a second the sun winked along the peak of his cap. She hadn't said his name, even; he wished she had said it to him. But he knew her name was Hine. He had said it to her. 'I'm here all the time,' she'd told him. That must have been what she meant, Spicer thought, she meant she wanted me to come back. He saw her standing in the centre of the round mirror that angled on a bracket from the side of the car. She must have meant if he wanted to come back, then she would be pleased to see him, any time he came back.

The Chow raised both hands to his head and pulled at the cloth that enfolded his face, freeing him from the confining veil. The draught lifted the pale wispy hair that had reminded Marie-Claire of a sick child's. He opened his mouth as though to take in more air. The wimple, now grey with fingering and sweat and pulled askew, hung around his neck, a grubby, comic horseshoe. Then his right hand entered the deep slit beside the skirt's pocket. He tugged at his waist and brought out the gun. He lay it in his lap and placed both hands lightly on the metal, warmed from its closeness to his body. There was the sound of his breath, the rasp that preceded his speech, but that was all that came.

It's relief, Marie-Claire thought vaguely, that's all it is, he does not want to say anything, he is simply so glad to be back here, back moving with the long grass whickering against the sides of the car and that smell of benzine, stronger now in the warm afternoon. Why on earth should she care about his comfort, she wondered, now that he no longer pretended to be what she herself once was, a woman in the dark habit of self-denial and service? Because he is my brother in Christ, one part of her answered, as if by rote — the answer of habit as much as grace. Yet *why*? persisted a contrary voice, a mild indifference. Did it matter greatly either way? She closed her eyes against the afternoon and the spinning flow of landscape. She wished she could sleep again, but knew she would not. The tug in her side throbbed softly. She thanked God it so seldom drove on to deeper pain. It is a knocking at the door, she thought, it will soon expect to be asked in. Amused, a little, at this dredging from how far back — five or six, she could not have been more? She was standing on a chair, leaning against her grandfather. He let her turn the pages of a big book. There were no words in the book, but pictures of how it was so long before she was born. Her grandfather smelled of smoke, and something sweet. It was nice to press against him. Then there was a picture of people inside a room, laughing, having their dinner, and a skeleton stood outside, his frosty knuckles almost tapping at the door. Her grandfather stood above her, his big hand over hers, and turned the page. 'Nonsense,' he told her. The tugging now in her side. The knuckles ready to tap.

From the elevation of the main road Spicer and Kate looked back down towards the store. The girl — she couldn't be more than a girl, Kate thought — stood still in the shadow of the gum. Twenty yards beyond her the elder sister also stood, thin as a stick, her blue smock falling shapelessly. And there behind the store itself, at the steps of the shed, on the edge of what seemed mile upon mile of tussock, the old crone who watched the car turn from the top of the climbing loose-metalled drive onto the big road east. Kate looked down the bank to the three women, each isolated from the others — three worlds she supposed that barely touched, yet packed so near together each was driven mad by such closeness. She imagined the endless nights when they must sit in the same room, eat together, the mother watchful and ridden with resentment. And the one who said she painted, whose bits of cardboard were stacked around the wall. Not that Kate would know if it was brilliance or lunacy, those dense strongly coloured pictures she had found her eye drawn back to in the airless room with its three dark tables and their perfunctorily smoothed-out sheets of newsprint. There was one of a horse stuck in a pond of clinging mud, men dragging at it with ropes. The animal's head was properly finished, and then a smear of pinkish-red clawed across it, a picture whose pain was so immediate you wanted to avoid being drawn back. She is the most interesting of them, Kate thought. The young one is more desperate. She would have eaten Spicer. The boy would have let her, too. She is probably the first young woman he has ever talked to who is not a whore. Who has made him feel he is something. Not as Miriam had done, as an erotic pet, but as a man. One who does not have to pay.

None of the women below them attempted to wave. It was like a picture itself, the stillness of it, the great reaching gum, the squat box of the store with its unpainted roof, the corrugated shed at the back, ochre-red, rickety. Then with the elevation of the bank to the side of the car, the view snapped closed, a hand might as well have been clapped across Kate's eyes. A bend in the road and they were gone, the women, the buildings.

The place stayed on her mind. She could not conceive of living there in such isolation, in such a brew of female edginess with only the tussock, the rise and fall of the hills on the skyline, the dispersed wreckage of ravaged forest. Waiting, she supposed, waiting always for the crunch of wheels on the steep driveway from the road, the slam of doors, anything that would break the appalling monotony, lives caught in the slow intricacies of decay. The girl especially disturbed her. She guessed that at another time she might turn up at Number 23. She would be brought by a friend who already worked there, who had convinced her — had she needed convincing? — that to sell herself for a while was better, for God's sake, than the lives a lot of women had. Kate would have talked to her in the room with the scarlet drapes and the deep comfortable settees. She would have told her, as she told all the women who approached her, that she must have no moral scruples in doing what she did. If you go into this with guilt or some hovering religious fear, then forget about it, she would have said, don't mess up your life. But if you see it as she did herself, an act of freedom, a choice that was a damned sight better, more dignified — even that!

— than giving your life to some man who confined you, bred from you, took your slaving for him as a matter of course, who as likely or not patronised houses such as this. 'Bring me a doctor's certificate,' she would have said, 'behave decently to the rest of us here and you've got a job. It's a fifty-fifty cut which is better than you'll get anywhere else, believe me.' And the girl as likely as not would have become her friend. She would have advised her to save and walk away in three or four years' time with a tidier amount than she ever dreamed of. The conventions would be transgressed, wasn't that Sir William's phrase for what she did? But Kate wanted her girls to feel as certain about themselves, as uncaring about the names tossed at them, as she had herself when she first knew 'the world', as it grandly fancied itself, survived on flesh and blood; as she first knew that afternoon when the world of men went through its games and a black handkerchief was spread across the judge's wig, and the journalists and the gallery and the junior counsel watched not the judge but herself. She had waited for that moment all along. And she had refused to gratify them when it came. She had stood and raised her glance to Peter, and walked from the court and the implacable ticking of its dominating clock, walked from the theatrical, feline antics of its tapping to and fro with the living flesh of love. Each girl who worked for her earned with her body an independence, a defiance, that was part of her own slow recompense against that world. The girl at the store may well have been one of those. But the vividness of her standing beneath the tree, the vibrancy of her play for Spicer's regard — the animal tug of one towards the other, so open, so innocent — that was not part of what Kate wanted to take into account. It ruffled her that she had so much as picked it up. Spicer should not be part of this. That is what disturbed her. She disliked it that her certainties had begun to slide, like ice running, slipping, on a tray whose sides had thawed.

The road began to climb into heavy bush. The road itself was narrow, the loose metal sliding beneath them at the steeper inclines. The sky clouded over. It became cool inside the car. 'Can you turn that window up?' Kate instructed Spicer. Cloud shredded along a crest, high up to the right. The bush was dull, depressing, pouring into the distance as one ridge rose beyond another.

'It's been raining up here,' Spicer said. The cloud was now low enough to look like pockets of steam where it sat in gulleys above them.

The Chow spoke, his voice tensed as though with anger. 'Get us out of here,' he said.

'You can't just get out,' Spicer said. 'We've got to climb these hills before you get out of them.'

'This is shit in here,' the Chow said. 'This is shit, all this.' He meant the gloom, the grimness, the dark oppressive vegetation across hill after hill. You'd be lost in there all right, Spicer thought. You could walk for days and no one would be any the wiser. There'd be dead blokes in there. If the Chow stopped them now and made them walk into that. The idea of it chilled him.

'A couple of hours,' he said.

'What for?' the Chow said. The voice was urgent, petulant.

'Until we cross over,' Spicer said. 'We've got to cross this lot or we won't get anywhere.'

And the Chow for some reason laughed at that. 'You'd better not break down then. It mightn't be much fun for anyone.' As if revived, he raised the gun and brushed the barrel's tip lightly across Spicer's neck, running it back and forth along his collar. It was playful, and the terror was in the play. Spicer turned his head and confronted him directly.

'Do that,' he said, 'I'll go off the road.'

The Chow laughed again. 'You just worry about the driving then,' he said.

There was no talk among them for a long time. The late sun came through again, splashing across the bushed gullies and along the hills. Where the trees pressed in close the road ran with quick shadows and sickles of light. Spicer thought how it might have been so marvellous to drive through here as the three of them had planned to do, the freedom they might have felt as the car rose and rose, the views broader and more extensive, the hard green fading off into remotest blue. Sometimes a stream, a passing dash of running water, flashed up at them like a mirror tilted at their eyes, a flash and then again the dense packed extensiveness of the bush, as though one could imagine nothing else, bush the way it must have been in the beginning, before roads were even thought of.

He saw Mrs C's eyes were closed, her body rocking softly with the motion of the car. The Chow didn't like them talking together anyway, he had picked that up. His dislike for the figure behind him came over Spicer as strongly as a physical weight. Mrs C who had worked for this holiday and tried to do the sister there a good turn, to help her enjoy something anyway in these weeks when she was dying but before the pain yanked at her like a great chain, dragging her down, insisting to her, like it did with Miriam, Go on, die then, don't you know it's time? Spicer thought of death as something more or less like that, a living thing that wore you down, that knew what it was doing. When he'd seen a cat run down by a truck outside St Ben's he had watched its final minutes with the fascination he might have watched a fight between two healthy men. As the cat's crushed rib cage seemed to tear and gasp at the air it could not take in, as the animal lay then convulsed and the pinkish foam rushed out from its mouth, its eyes narrowed and defiant and even contemptuous in these last rapid minutes, Spicer had imagined the force moving in against the cat's mutilated fur. That's what dying was. This thing that covered one part of your body maybe to begin with, and then another, until it lay on top of you, on every side of you, its darkness seeping until you and it were the same. Its darkness and force until you were only a glove that it wore and then put down because it was no longer there, it had gone on to someone else. He knew how the Chow dressed up in the nun's dark outfit behind him was part of all that — he felt the presence of it move towards him through the flattened face, the fiddling nervous hands. This is death, he had thought, while he watched the cat in its gasping throes. And as the agitation subsided he heard the drawn-out wail behind him of the child whose pet it was, running towards the broken and damaged pile at the side of the road. *It is gone now*, he had thought, *death has moved through it and gone on somewhere else*. The thought mazed and circled in his head as he drove on, uneasy, sweating, in the pressure of such puzzlement. He edged at his collar with his hooked forefinger. He must do what he could for the two women even more than for himself. If only he knew what it might be.

Twenty minutes later the motor began to hiss, shreds of steam rose from the front of the bonnet. Spicer told them they were overheated. That's why he had filled the tin with water before they left the store. 'You can't touch it for a bit, though,' he said, 'it'll shoot all over the show.'

'How long?' the Chow said. 'How long you got to wait?'

'Ten minutes,' Spicer said. It was a figure he guessed at.

Kate left the car and walked into the bush at the side of the road. Marie-Claire told her no, she was comfortable for the moment. She had only sipped at the tea back there in any case. She stayed in the car, alone.

The Chow stood close beside Spicer, as though it were essential he kept his eye on him. 'Do it now,' he told him, 'we haven't got all day.' He leaped back when the driver, a wad of bunched tea towel in his hand, turned the cap of the radiator loose and a rod of boiling steam jerked out. Spicer took no notice. Did the Chow expect him to talk or something? He attended to the car carefully, slowly.

'That bitch in there stinks,' the Chow said.

'She what?' Spicer was fitting the tin back in its metal bracket beside the trunk.

'Makes me want to toss.'

'She's sick,' Spicer said. 'You can't be sick and not smell.' He knew that from the Home, from when the sisters sometimes called him to help shift furniture, to heave an old mattress out for them and load it for the tip. You could always smell them, the sick ones, beneath the soap and the medicine and the disinfected floors. There was that other smell as well, so faint sometimes you nearly missed it. The dying ones.

'Not her,' the Chow said. So close to him now Spicer could feel the nun's dark cloth rub against his sleeve. 'It's not her, it's the other one, the one who fancies herself.'

'Mrs C?' Spicer said.

'Whatever you want to call her,' the Chow said. Grinned at him even. 'The stuff she wears.' At that moment Kate brushing through from the bush and holding her skirt so it didn't catch at the clumps of tea-tree in the scabby yellow earth.

'There should be a town. A village anyway,' she said.

'Where?' Spicer said.

The Chow, still close beside him, asking that as well. 'Where?'

The woman back there, Kate said, the tall one. Two hours, she had said, two hours on from there. From the store.

'How big is it?' Kate had asked, 'the town?', and the woman had looked away, losing interest. 'This is the sticks,' the woman said. 'This is nowhere.'

'It's got baths there. That's all I know about it. Tourists go there for the baths.' Kate pulled at her cuffs and picked a burr from just below her waist.

'We're not stopping,' the Chow said. 'Don't think we're stopping.'

'We've got to stop sometime. We have to buy things now there's four of us.'

The Chow's face was close against her own, so smooth, hairless, his eyes holding her own with an expression she was unable to define. As if it was fun, almost.

'Get back,' he told her, 'just get back in the car. And leave your window down.'

Several minutes later she told him, 'It's cold. The window like this.'

'Leave it down,' the Chow said. 'I don't like the smell.'

Until now Kate's moods had swung between anger and calm, and back to anger at those times when she sensed his enjoyment of what he did, the lift he took from commanding them. Now, with the early evening's breeze whipped by the car's movement to a gale that tugged at her clothes, brought her flesh out in bumps, she felt depression descend on her. Is this what it will come to? The first time she had allowed herself to contemplate it. Is this what life will seem like at the end, whenever the maniac behind her decides it is the end? To feel merely as flat as this, so dull? And fear, of course. She crossed her arms and rubbed her fists against her upper arms. It was how she had stood as a child, rubbing at her arms exactly as she now did, while Gran reprimanded her, told her to stop fidgeting, girl, for sweet heaven's sake. Uncle Stan defending her as he always did, knowing the old lady's irritation would then flare at him, and so release the girl. And his great gusts of laughter at how easily he provoked. From there, the Clerkenwell kitchen, to here, this afternoon, this moment, the other side of the world. There was no link between any one thing and another. She was coming to see that so clearly. Chance. Even that is too strong. I am there or here. I am this age and then I am another, I am happy or I am not. Those are the things one can say. Beyond that there is nothing.

'She's cold,' Spicer said. 'Both ladies are cold.'

'Just drive,' the Chow said.

Kate was sick with the cold. The Chow had not allowed her to raise the window, even after she asked for the second time. Marie-Claire had said nothing, but Kate knew she must feel it more intensely than herself. The dress she wore was hardly made to keep out the evening chill that hurled in at them as the car crossed the highest ridge and began the descent on the other side. The land ahead of them and out to the east buckled into further ridges, the bush blackened under the night that now came down on them quickly. Kate shrank from the loneliness of the place, its sense of total remoteness. It was the country of nightmare. For twenty years, she realised, she had sat on the edge of it, the narrow crust of a city along a stretch of coast. There was the rare pricking of farm lights, the occasional sweep of headlights from some vehicle in the distance, the dazzle for fifty yards as it approached and passed. Once an animal, a ferret she supposed, small and lithe and panicked, dashed from the scrub at the side of the road. Spicer dragged the car sharply to avoid it. The slewing of the wheels, the quick purchase of the tyres reasserting their grip, jolted the Chow and Marie-Claire against each other. The shoulder the sister leaned against was strangely warm and soft.

'You're freezing,' the Chow said, a note of surprise behind the breathy rasping of the words.

Marie-Claire told him it didn't matter. There were worse things than a bit of cold.

But the Chow leaned forward and his knuckles rapped at Kate's shoulder.

'Wind that window up,' he ordered her. 'Can't you put it up?'

Kate did as he instructed. The interior of the car then seemingly so still, without the racketing of the wind, the force as it whipped at Kate's fluttering collar and swirled around them. But with the silence that now rode there, a different dimension above the living motor and the constant chirr of the tyres, a new fear came over her. It struck her, what should have been so obvious to her already, that the man so grotesquely hidden in the garments of compassion, on the run from God knows what, was utterly irrational as well. It is in his gift, she thought, the gift of his unpredictable malice, whether we suffer or survive. While there was another thought, as much intuitive as reasoned, which she held at bay. 'I will not think that.'

The Chow cut across her discomfort. 'There!' he commanded, his voice raised, the high rasp in his throat, his fingers jabbing against the back of Spicer's neck. 'In there.'

The white trunks of the birches flickered in the headlights as Spicer turned past the milk stand and the tin letterbox and along the curving drive.

'Stop here,' the Chow instructed.

Spicer took the car against the edge of the drive and cut its motor.

'And the lights.'

The Chow then stepped from the heavy door and eased it back, careful not to slam it. He walked to the back of the car, catching his shoulder against the corner of the trunk. Inside they felt the impact, a break in his step, but no other sound. He walked round and opened Kate's door. She stepped from it without either of them speaking, it was so clear that she must follow him. Before he closed that door with the same care as he had the other, he spoke to Spicer. 'I've got the gun, so you just sit here, right.' He pressed the weapon where he held it through the deep pocket of the habit, raising the dark material as if in some parodic erection.

'How long will you be?' Spicer said.

The Chow ignored the query. He and Kate moved into the dark. A flag of expanding light was thrown from a window at the side of the house, across a mown lawn with high clumped shrubs at the edges of the square. Spicer waited to see the figures cut across it. But the Chow must have told the woman to walk out beyond the reach of the pale falling light. Spicer strained to hear some hint of where they moved. A dog, he thought, a place like this must have dogs. But underneath the silence, only the ruffling in a nearby hedge and the clipped hollowness of an owl, until Spicer picked up the low thrum, a dynamo somewhere from the hill rising behind the house.

'Will you get something for me, Spicer?' Marie-Claire broke in on him.

He turned towards the old woman. 'What is it?' he said.

She told him. In the trunk. In the small basket inside her black bag inside the trunk. There was a brown bottle with ridges down its side, there was no label on it. 'Just bring me that,' she said. Dr Flynn had insisted she take it with her, although at first she had moved it back towards him with a quiet smile. 'It won't come to that. I'll be back home well before that.' The doctor, as though it were a game they were playing, moved the bottle towards her again, across the thick plate of greenish glass that covered the top of his desk. 'One never knows,' he said. His spectacles flashed for a moment as his head inclined towards her. 'For me, then,' he said simply. 'As a favour to me.' And wryly, he added, 'Your Brompton cocktail,' so that she knew exactly what he gave her, the mixture of morphine and gin and sweetened tonic that at least took one towards the brief consolations of sleep. She had held the bottle in her hands while they finished their conversation, let her nails rasp across its milled sides. How the patients — the desperately ill — sometimes looked first to her hands, she had noticed, as she came to their bedsides, hoping to see the bottle she now held on her lap while poor Dr Flynn knew there was nothing useful to say, yet felt that he must try to say it. The bottle she now took from Spicer's outstretched hand.

'That's medicine?' Spicer asked.

'For indigestion,' she said.

Her fingers hesitated at the cork. She had not expected pain as severe as this, nor for it to come so soon. She felt the sweat at her breasts, at her throat. She had the vivid image of Miriam, her flesh glazed like something in a kitchen. How often she had seen it, that final sweat! And now, her own. She felt it break along her forehead. She had always thought, always hoped, that when the real pain began she might nevertheless hold it at bay, that she would bear it with fortitude, opt for clarity and discomfort rather than the fuddled consolation the drug would bring. And here she was, already, so anxious to receive it! One afternoon, no more than that, and she was demanding what she had rather despised, that quick cringing of the flesh calling to be lulled, to be edged from its own intense presence. *Like a knife.* That tired old phrase, yet how serviceable it now proved. The pain in her abdomen turning, probing her, an assault that knocked the breath from her.

'You're all right?' Spicer said. He felt a new fear looking at her, at the smear of her paleness against the dark.

'I'm worn out,' Marie-Claire assured him. 'All this excitement. And the worry of it.'

Spicer said, 'He's all so much shit, you know? He won't get off with this. He fucking won't.'

'No. I'm sure he won't, Spicer.'

It was so important to agree with the boy, to make him feel the fury of his language was itself of some use. She suspected that his being the male among them, the youngest, the one most suited to some final physical resistance, must weigh on him. Several times she had seen him watching the plump yet oddly frail figure of their captor, as though weighing when he might best make his move, when to overcome if not completely destroy that intense malevolence which she knew the boy himself did not comprehend, and that even Kate did not detect for what it was. All afternoon, as the car had progressed over the uneven road and the turning blade in her side took on a deeper thrust, her mind insisted on distinguishing between the forces that ravaged her. It is so simple and wrong to think of what our bodies suffer as evil. Hadn't heresies risen from that very thought, armies fought to affirm or deny it, cities burned in the infernos inflicted by those who took one side or the other in that belief? The most natural thing for the suffering to call out, *Father, let this evil pass from me*. Even He was tempted with it. She must not think that. And even more, must not think of the figure who looked back at her from her own clothes, who with his face concealed could indeed have *been* her, sitting a few feet from the grotesqueness of how she now appeared — she must not for a second believe one ill was of its nature the same as the other. The corruption of her body was a thing simply of this world, no more nor less than what we have in common, all of us, thrown into light, wrenched out of it, the mystery of what we are. When the figure turned and she took in the clotted drift of the eyes, the curious and slight quiver at their almost colourless centres, she forced herself to hold his gaze, so far beyond the coldness or fury we see in the gaze of a caged animal. She had been held by that as a child. Her brother beside her, the reek of the tigers, the iron carts hauled into the square at New Year, and the fired hoops and the rest of it, the tenseness, the incredibly swift release of coiled fur and muscle as the creatures leaped from one high stool, then settled on another. It was the eyes she had always watched, the feeling she could apprehend but not explain that everything she valued, everything from her singing class to the smoothness of tablecloths to the very words she used for things, *tigre, sauvage, la jungle*, those eyes would hold and burn away in one endless gaze of retribution. She could not tell that to Father or to her grandfather, least of all to François beside her who yelled and clapped at the vast lifting of that resentment when the whip cracked and the animal's eyes winked, and the tiger hung in the air, circled in flame, then thudded back to the wooden tub on the hoop's other side. That memory returned and circled, vivid and drifting between the waves of pain. She was determined not to let the naturalness of her pain, the clawed raking inside her, confuse her when she held the gaze of the tilted, soap-smooth face, the cold and deliberate focus of what she knew was evil. She knew the blaze of its purity was of a different order from anything dear, innocent Spicer might pit against it. The contest was between themselves — it would come to that; between their captor and herself. She knew that as clearly as if it had been handed to her and written down. And the unfairness of it flared over her, the doubt that she could bear it, as the moments of clarity blurred with the returned vigour of her pain, until she had weakened and leaned forward and asked Spicer to go to the trunk at the back of the car, to bring her the syrup that would drench her in relief.

She attempted to ease the cork from the top. She would have to ask Spicer to do even that for her, she did not have the strength to budge it. The young man reached back to take the bottle. He placed it on his lap and began to work it with his thumb nails. 'Whoever shoved this in,' he said, his voice almost querulous.

'The doctor,' she told him. Pain alters time so profoundly. As though it were weeks since she had seen him. His narrow strong wrists. His coat sleeve riding back and his white cuff, the jet cuff-link, as he insisted she take it with her, the escape she now yearned for. 'The doctor can unscrew jars no one else can move.'

Then both Marie-Claire and Spicer jolted with the sharpness, the unexpectedness, of the gunshot from behind the house. It seemed the night cracked apart. A second later Spicer flung from the car, his cap torn from him as his head scraped against the top of the door frame, the bottle clattering against the brake.

'Don't go there!' Marie-Claire shouted at him, surprised at the panic and agitation of her call. Who knew what danger the boy would be going to? Then only after that first moment of fear when he had already run across the lawn at the side of the house, and across the fall of light from the window to the darkness on the other side, did she think of Kate. She heard the single crunch as Spicer's foot landed on a narrow path that cut across the lawn, and then the heavy brushing of branches as he broke through the line of shrubs. And the silence after that, the utter stillness and her own heart pelting in her ears.

'Kate!' she called. She tugged at the door handle, catching it in her sleeve. There was the dry ripping of cloth as she jerked free and opened the door. She stood at the side of the car, unsure what she must do.

She shivered at the cold. She stretched out her hand and felt along the length of the car to the great bulb-shape of the headlight. Her body swayed in against the mudguard, her legs so inadequate for what she wished to do. She waited, her chin raised, aware of the dark line of the house's roof, and then, beyond its sharp straight edges, the chips of icy stars. She waited for another shot, for at least a shout, a cry of some kind. But none came. As though she had been scooped empty as a gourd, she was aware of cold, immensity, silence pouring in on her, filling her. She was aware of nothing but those things. Even fear was a diminished throb beneath their weight, and her pain retracted. 'Kate,' she said again. Saying it quietly, beyond hope or expectation, or apprehension for herself. Simply a sound she made.

Then the door on the house's darkened front verandah dragged back so forcefully it banged against the wall. A light far down a hallway behind her flung Kate's shadow hugely out across the steps, setting her outline clear and sharply in the square of the doorway.

'My dear!' Kate called. She looked over towards the car. The steps rang as she ran down them. There was the rush of her feet across the lawn. She grasped Marie-Claire and drew her close to her, their faces rubbing at each other in relief, in consolation. Marie-Claire raising her hand to brush aside the crush of Kate's hair against her eyes. 'There's nothing wrong!' Kate said. She kept repeating it. 'There's nothing wrong. There's nothing wrong.' And the smaller, older woman's hand running the length of her friend's neck, beneath the mane of hair, the nun not speaking but making the small meaningless sounds of comfort one uses with a child, clucking and burring, her lips against Kate's throat. And Kate, for only the second time in her life, sobbing, her face smeared with her tears, her hair stuck against her cheeks, her mouth, allowing herself to be comforted. Saying over and over, 'Yes, yes.' The quick soft dabs of the other woman's lips along her throat, her forehead. And the words she did not comprehend, which Marie-Claire now chanted.

The Chow had said nothing when they left the car, but Kate knew she was compelled by him as surely as if the press of his gun's barrel was in the small of her back. She knew her will was subservient to his. And a mild surprise, which did not even distress her, as she realised her own weakness, realised that in fact she had never been tested in all those years when she believed she was so much in charge. There was a sense even that she followed him because it gratified her to do so, as though something were fulfilled in accepting his mastery.

He had led her in a deep curve across the lawn, avoiding the pool of light from the window at the side of the house. Then he told her to go ahead of him, until they were through the line of rhododendrons. Moving fragments of light dabbed through the stir of the shrubs. 'Keep going,' he told her. She stopped beside the pole of a clothesline, her hand running along its smoothness. An engine, a pump or something, throbbed from a shed some distance from the house. Beyond that there was another building that loomed against the expanse of sky, the broad vivid run of stars. A weak bulb burned there, in the shed. Then something that struck her as extraordinary took place. She looked up to see a large dog, the light from the partly opened door throwing its shadow in front of it, enlarging it. Its skin was an iridescent blue as the light slipped across it. Why doesn't it bark? she thought. Why doesn't it attack me? Instead its attention was completely held by something of more importance to it than herself. The animal was tense, anxious. It raised one front paw, then placed it firmly beside the other, its body swaying slightly. She knew nothing of dogs, but she felt its uncertainty, its puzzlement even, in the low whine that came from its throat. Then she noticed another sound, a kind of soothing wordless purr that came from the man she now turned to and saw crouching, his hands held loosely in front of him, his own attention fixed completely on the animal in front of them. The dog shook its head briskly. There was the soft rapid flap of its ears. And then it moved forward, past Kate as though indeed she were invisible to it, and lowered its head to the knees of the crouching figure. The hands from beneath the dark sleeves were at the sides of the dog's head, assuring it, controlling. He then stood and the dog shuffled beside him, a rapport beyond Kate's comprehending.

'Go inside,' he ordered her.

Kate crossed the back verandah, passed the rack where shoes and a pair of gumboots were neatly lined. The back door was open. She entered the house which she felt was empty. A pot boiled on a coal range. Its lid rose and fell in a soft repetitive clatter. A slow froth ran down the saucepan's side. Kate looked about. The kitchen was simple, tidy, the colour of stale butter. A calendar with the small print of tides and sunrises beneath the squares of the months was tacked to the side of a cupboard. A milk bottle on the mantelpiece held a trailing clump of white flowers that had begun to shrivel. A sideboard with willow-pattern plates, a worn armchair with a piled stack of washing. There is no woman here, Kate thought. There was a colourless male tidiness about the place, apart from that tumble of shirts and towels and tea towels. A ham covered in cheesecloth waited on the table, a carving knife and fork beside it.

Kate turned, expecting the Chow to be close behind her. She knew how quietly he moved. She walked back to the door, to the row of boots, the three hats on pegs against the wall. There was no sign of him. Then the gunshot from near the shed forced her instinctively against the wall. 'My God,' she said. And after her words, the echo ringing back at her from the high dark slope beyond the house. She was held by an indecision which she knew was also part of the will she had succumbed to. She was standing there still when she heard the sound of Spicer running across the grass and onto the concrete between the clothesline and the porch. He stopped when he saw her. 'You're all right then?' he said. 'Missus?'

And before she answered, the other shape standing there, the black flowing figure of a nun, only feet behind Spicer.

As if the Chow's appearance in some sense released her, she turned and ran along the corridor from the kitchen towards the front door. She was aware, remotely, of heavily framed pictures, a dark velvet drape she brushed against before she flung open the door, and saw her shadow expand and pour down the steps. The car was a solid pale block at the edge of the lawn. She ran towards it, towards the shape that detached itself from the darkness and lurched towards her. 'My dear,' she called, grasping at her. She helped the older woman to approach the house. One arm enclosed the thin waist, her other hand crossed and clasped where Marie-Claire's fist pressed against her chest.

'I'm close to spent,' her friend said. Kate felt the slump of her weight against her.

Kate said, 'Think of once it's over. Once he's gone.'

'He'll never be gone,' Marie-Claire said, a declaration of such certainty that Kate flared against it.

'He has to sleep. He can't watch all of us all the time.'

'He'll stay with us,' her friend said again.

Kate said, 'He'll make a mistake and when he does we're ready for him. Spicer's ready for him.' And she realised as she spoke that this was the first time in days the two of them had been together by themselves. 'My dear,' she said again.

There was a clatter from the top of the steps that led up to the verandah. The Chow stood there, framed by the panes of coloured glass surrounding the opened doorway. The glass was lit by the lights he had switched on in the long hallway, so this figure with its long gown, standing between the bright blue vertical panes and beneath the red strip that ran across the top of the door jamb, seemed to Kate a parody of a religious picture. She felt hysteria work in her throat, the panic of knowing the creature above them controlled them utterly. And she felt as well that the woman beside her in the evening gown with its three-quarter-length sleeves and her feet still in the firm black clogs of her vocation was at this moment so certain of a God Kate found inconceivable, as certain of order and divine will as she herself felt, even more pressingly now than she had as she turned from the Caledonian Road and out through the courtyards from the tracking journalist within minutes of the doctor's death, that there was nothing to existence beyond mere chance, the utter indifference of everything to the tiny flicker of one's own irrefutable self. As if that painful moment had rushed in to merge with this, and her life between had not occurred.

They mounted the steps, Kate still supporting the smaller, weaker woman. The Chow stood back to let them pass into the house. At the far end of the hallway, beside the dark velvet curtain, Spicer stood and watched them enter.

'Up here,' he said. 'There's a place to sit up here.'

They moved towards him and the yellow glow of the kitchen. Then the Chow ordered from behind them, 'There,' he said, 'that room where you are now.' So that Kate and Marie-Claire, obedient as schoolgirls, turned into the large room where only a standard lamp in one corner threw a cone of light across a space steeped in a pervasive gloom. There was the sense of heavy furniture and what seemed in the obscurity an enormous table whose almost black covering reached to within a few inches of the ground. It was a room whose attempt at grandeur had finished up sepulchral and depressing. Kate touched the thick brass light switch, and the room sprang into a more illumined gloom. The black cover on the table was a deep emerald plush. The settee and the two armchairs were tan moquette with random orange stripes. The carpet ran off into squares and semi-circles of tangerine and brown. The room revolted her.

'Whose house is it?' she said.

The Chow ignored her question. He turned back to the hallway, speaking across his shoulder to Spicer. 'We'll eat in here,' he said. Then she heard him open another door.

Kate thought about the shot. Whose house were they profaning? It took so little to dismiss other people, such a slight shift of perspective, after all, to take another's house, another's life and assume it as one's own. She heard a noise from the room across the hallway, a scraping of something heavy along the floor. This was followed by the banging back of a door, a rattle which for a moment she could not place and then recognised as coathangers pushed along a metal bar. Why has the dog not come back? she thought. Is that what the shot was, nothing worse than that, the trusting sleek animal that had licked the Chow's hand, that was taken behind the shed, its skull shattered with the oblique precision and suddenness their captor brought to whatever he decided on? At least not the man who lived here, she thought, let it not be him.

Spicer came into the room. He carried a tray with a stack of plates, the top one piled with sliced ham. He placed the tray on the table and transferred the plates onto the cloth. 'That's pickles,' he said. He went back to the kitchen several times, returning with a plate of steaming potatoes, a loaf of bread, a breadboard with a deep rim of painted roses. There was butter under a china cover shaped like a lettuce leaf. There was a pot of jam and a plate of tomatoes and a block of fruit cake. 'That's about it,' he said. 'There's nothing else so far as I can see.'

'You can take your cap off, Spicer,' Kate told him.

He laid it down on the arm of the large chair. He laughed, like an embarrassed child. 'I just went back and got it.' Then, bareheaded, he went to the kitchen yet again. The cups and saucers he brought back he set carefully by the four plates Kate had arranged around the table with the knives and forks. The pewter teapot with its curly black handle he placed at the centre of the table. He then moved it again, as though its positioning must be exact.

'You're good at this,' the sister said, smiling at him. She guessed his fear was deeper, perhaps more simply physical, than either Kate's or her own. 'If you get tired of driving you could get a job like this.'

Spicer was not sure what she meant. He stood, his hands loose and awkward at his sides, uncertain of what to do next. Eating with Darkie or by himself was such a straightforward thing, just grabbing what you wanted, half the time taking your plate to sit somewhere else, Darkie with his lug stuck against the shiny circle on the wireless. Or if it was fine Spicer would take his own plate and sit on the back steps, hardly noticing what it was he ate, just liking the feeling of out there, quiet and by himself, the roofs and chimneys and a few scraggly trees growing harder, darker, as the sky dimmed. He had never sat down with other people like this.

'Shall I get him?' he said. They could hardly start without the Chow there, could they?

Spicer saw the women move their eyes beyond him to the doorway. He turned to see the figure move across the hallway into the room where they waited. For the second time that day he had taken off the veil and the headgear. His wispy hair rode up against the back of the habit. At first it was not clear to any of them what he carried in his arms. He was cradling an animal, was it, almost as dark as the garment he wore? Then they saw it was a jumble of hats.

The Chow stood at the end of the table. 'They were in a box,' he said. He grinned. The smile was not at them, even Spicer understood that. It was like the smile of a child lost in its own game, a pure attention to what absorbed it. One by one he laid the hats on the table. The first was the kind Kate recognised as fashionable before the war, a shallow brown expanse with a clutch of felt flowers crushed against its side. The Chow put the others down beside it, a deep-green cloche helmet, and the kind of square-set black straw hat she remembered Gran wearing. The last hat, the one the Chow moved about in his hands, and then lifted and placed on his own head, was a turban, a simple swathe of deep turquoise with a marcasite clasp splayed out like a tiny black glittering hand.

The figure at the head of the table was terrifying to the rest of them, not simply for the fact that beside the array of hats appeared the squat authority of the gun which he had laid as well on the dark cloth before he raised his hands to settle the turban. The terror was not in the gun, which God knows, Kate thought, may only ten minutes before have killed the man whose table they now sat at, but in the grim ridiculousness of what their captor imposed, the grinning and flattened face between the simple exposed neckline of the nun's habit and the slipping of the too-large turban that the raised arms, the stubby hands, worked to settle squarely.

'Put them on,' he ordered. His short thick fingers nudged the hats towards them.

He drew back the chair and sat down, and leaned across and took up a wad of the stacked ham. The others watched him, Marie-Claire even moving the breadboard and the uncut loaf to within his reach.

'Put the rest of these on, will you? I told you that. These hats.'

Then he began to eat, one slice of bread after the other, until he raised his gaze, grinning again, a wedged mush of bread congealing about his gums, telling them, 'This is like a party.' Spicer's face was shadowed under the broad hat handed to him, the cloth flowers bobbing at the front. Kate sat beneath the widow's square-cut plainness; its smell, as she had raised it, was the very smell of Gran's when she held it in front of her face as a little girl, looking through the stippled, meshed obscurity of the black straw, the dry clutch of its smell at the back of her throat.

'Pour that tea, will you?' the Chow said to her. And turning to Marie-Claire, 'Does this shine when my head moves? This badge?'

'It's like a little fire,' she told him. And again reminding her of a grotesque child, the Chow repeated what she said, as if the words were exactly those it wanted, 'Like a little fire,' he said, 'that's how it moves.'

Marie-Claire closed her eyes. The pain was less intense. The felt hat pressed close against her ears. I must look a sight, she thought, this gown, this hat that feels like a helmet, my own clunking shoes. She supposed this too might be offered up, it was part surely of what she was meant to endure? 'The world', they had always called it. Everyone had called it that, to cover whatever it was her chosen life had put aside. 'That is what you will give up,' hadn't her grandfather said, as they stood in the great iron criss-crossing of the Eiffel Tower? The world down there, he had meant, everything they could see until it shaded and hazed off in the ruffled line of the Bois, the remote towns. What the novice mistress had said, emphasising it so differently, meaning all that they were saved from, the snares that were always set, but which they were chosen to be spared. While all the time the world was this — what waited for her on the other side of the globe. To be sitting, dressed like a buffoon, in a room that seemed submerged in this thick, treacly light, with a handyman and her friend who kept whores, and this creature who intended — that was never in question — who intended to kill them, whenever that moment and his will might coincide. She supposed it must be her illness, or her sense of total tiredness, that prevented fear being uppermost in her mind. Although there was fear too, she had no doubt of that, an animal apprehension that lay perhaps as the ground to everything, below all else. But for this moment, now, with their captor's arm the colour and even the consistency of putty, as it stretched out towards the plate of ham and the sleeve of her habit rode up his forearm, what came on her so strongly was the weight of sheer absurdity, the thought that perhaps *this*, after all, was as close to the grain of what existence was, as anything she might ever know? She pushed the plate towards him.

'Your sleeve's dragging in the butter,' she said. And the Chow surprised her — surprised Kate and Spicer as well — by saying, 'Thank you.' Saying it simply, as any person might do. Yet the rasping rush of air that cushioned his words, that gave yet again the impression of air being let from a tyre, his speech a thinner, strident thread in its flow. But the one normal remark that would ever pass between them, the fragment in their intertwining in which there was neither threat nor compulsion, nor even condescension. Spicer laughed and tapped at the straw box on his head and said he could hardly tilt his head to eat, the thing kept slipping that much. Marie-Claire smiled at him. The heel of her palm nudged against the felt encasing her head, pressing against her ears. 'The Germans,' she said. 'The Boche. They wore ones like this.' Only Kate stayed outside the brief flare of ease. She had looked up when Marie-Claire spoke, and beyond Spicer who sat opposite her, and saw herself in the dim, tarnished mirror on the wall behind him. She was taken back by her own image, rising as it seemed from a discoloured pool, the hat, solid as fudge, darkening her face.

It struck her quickly, forcefully as a slap. How vulgar she looked! How like — and that came at her too, swimming up at her, disgusting her even before the thought had quite taken shape — how like a shadowed version of Miss Belle! The heaviness of her own cheeks, the silly extravagance of what she wore, the lift of her eyes beneath, as though even in that there was something fetching. The same heaviness, she thought. Am I as gross as that? She had always felt so slight beside Miss Belle. Now look at her. It was the heaviness the doctor had hated. It is like being drowned, he had told her, it is like being crushed by so much — so much *pressure*. That last word, how American he sounded when he said that. When he had told her what their lives might be if that crushing presence were no longer there. How they would float without its weight! The click of his collar studs as he let them drop on the marble mantelpiece. That odd habit of his, rolling them in his half-closed fist like dice before he put them down. Then the collar placed there too, the high starched band. Yes, she had said to him, although she had never told the court, Peter had forbade her to, 'Yes, imagine if she wasn't there.'

The Chow stood up abruptly. He told Spicer to take the things out to the kitchen. He then sat in one of the armchairs and his hat tilted up as he leaned his head back. Marie-Claire thought he was like a boy at a picnic. The children up the river loved to get old hats from the men of the pa and curve the brims up at the front or angle them to the side.

The Chow told them to go to the lavatory if they needed to. He then said to Spicer that he wanted them to be ready first thing, he wanted them moving early. The young man must have looked unsure, because the Chow said with obvious, reedy irritation that early meant what he said, *early*, they had better remember that. He then closed the door on the dining room, and a key turned in the lock. They heard him dragging the big wooden chest in the room across the passageway and then another sound, a tapping followed by the sharp splintering of wood as he ripped at something he couldn't open.

Spicer was the first to sleep. He had watched as they had eaten, how the gun lay there beside the Chow's plate, how casually and yet carefully it was shifted whenever their captor moved. He had thought, should he spring at him with the carving knife? But the Chow was quick, silent when he moved. Spicer guessed he would be stronger than he appeared. What, then, if he shoved the knife into his back? But was there time for the gun to be grabbed and swung around? Or fired wildly? Things could be even worse than they were now. If Mrs C was hurt, say, and there were two sick women for him to watch. Or if he only injured the Chow, would he make a bungle of finishing him off? Or held the gun right in against his head so bits and pieces went over his shoes, onto his clothes? He knew he would be sick at that. But once we are near a big town again I know that is what he will do to us. Spicer closed his eyes against having to work it out.

The marvellous comfort of sleep, Marie-Claire thought, watching his head loll back against the raised back of the other armchair.

'He's terrified, poor boy,' Kate said.

Marie-Claire told her, 'I think he's muddled. I don't know if he's afraid.'

'We're all afraid,' Kate said. Why did Marie-Claire so want to argue such a thing? She slapped her flattened palm against the cushion on the chair behind her, and leaned back against it. There was a luxury in that, whatever else. She looked over to her friend, who lay with her bare feet raised on the padded arm of the sofa. White as two cats, she thought, looking at the naked feet. 'You'll get cold,' Kate said.

Marie-Claire's arm moved slightly, the back of her wrist across her eyes. 'They feel hot,' she said. 'My feet feel so hot.'

Then there was only the sound of breathing for several hours.

Kate startled at the quick grating in the lock, and the door flung back. The Chow ordered them to get out to the car. 'We have to go,' he said. He had replaced the neckband and the veil. In the oppressive light the exaggerated angle of his face was like a varnished board. His spread hand closed on Marie-Claire's shoulder. 'Just get moving,' he said. He shook her sharply.

'It's dark,' Spicer said. 'If we go now we'll have to have the headlights on. People will know.'

The Chow told him, 'It's daylight in an hour.'

No one thought to turn the lights off in the house. As the car curved to the broad end of the driveway, Kate felt an enormous sense of emptiness, as though the desolateness of the house, its yellow kitchen with its glare flagged out across the lawn, the brown embalmed light of the dining room where she had turned at the door to see the disarray of the table, the cold dismal strewing of their meal, the strange isolated hats discarded on the chairs, was in some vague yet pressing way the last remnant of their old lives. The memory of Miss Belle had come so close she had hated it, as though twenty years had collapsed between them and they stood side by side.

For the few brief moments before Spicer sprang life back into the motor and the car jolted with its power, she had heard the hum from the dynamo in the shed above the house. Out there somewhere was a dead man, surely, whose house they had possessed, whose food they had eaten. And the dog, she was certain of that. The dog whose tongue had licked at the Chow's relaxed and enticing hands. The dog would be there, somewhere, its blood black and sticking, its fur as though stiff with paint. Then the lights from the house were no more than a flicker, a diminishing rush of brightness through the trees as the drive angled away, and the night was there, black and solid about them. Spicer clicked at a switch. Two great scoops of light leaped ahead of them. It was as though the car was drawn along a tube of light.

Marie-Claire held the bottle Spicer handed back to her. He had dropped it, hadn't he, oh such ages ago, when they had heard the shot, when Spicer had run off and Kate dashed from the door above the steps and flowed towards her across the dark wet grass? The loveliness, the safety, when they had grasped at each other, the bewilderment of love that fear can bring to one! It was as though she had passed some boundary, moved into a garden where winds that had pelted her were suddenly stilled. She would not take the drug, not yet. For the time being at least, she thought, she could tolerate the discomfort in her side. It came and went, that at least was a blessing. She knew this sense of composure could hardly continue, yet it seemed so important that she draw from it what she could.

The dark continued to rush by outside, the great claws of the headlights reached out across the ruffled floor of bush and into a fading blur of space when Spicer took the car round high sharp bends. For a long time they lost height.

The car gripped on steep descents, the banks were so close that ferns brushed against its sides and roof. And then light began to edge the line of hills, at first a mild dull grey, and then quickly poured above them; the sky lightened to the palest blue, the bush rising towards them with a sense of drenched freshness that startled Kate with its strangeness. Twenty years in this country, she again thought, and she had never seen the day begin except through windows, or occasionally on the verandah, after some night when business had kept the girls on call until all of them were dog-tired. She would stand with Miriam or one of the others, and watch the strange calm of the street as dawn raised it up to them. While every morning was like this, she supposed, up here, an emptiness that was tolerable only because one sped through it so quickly.

Spicer cleared his throat. His fingers scratched above his collar. The country below them billowed in dark waves and hardened into ridges, hills, the expanse of land falling away to the east. And far out now, the sea, a pale, perfect line. His hands tightened on the wooden steering wheel. It would have to be today, he knew that. He knew the Chow was like a cat, that he must have done things like this before, over and over, that he was clever while Spicer knew that he himself was dumb. People had said so for ever, everyone except Mr Coffey. Mr Simon Coffey who touched him and laughed with him as if he said clever things and kissed the ladies' shoes he made him wear. But he could drive, couldn't he? He could drive and knew about the car and he looked snazzy as they come, because he saw the way Darkie took him in these last few weeks, and he knew Mrs C depended on him and the sister crook there now, crook as all hell in that dress he knew she hated and her hair for everyone to see. He wanted her back in her proper clothes. He'd make the Chow pay for that too. He thought of the mouth that was like a slit, not even proper lips, and the teeth that weren't right either, not a grown-up's. He would smash those all right. And then when that was out of the way he would tell Mrs C they had to drive back to the store. Hine was standing in the clump of shadow underneath the gum, while everything around her burned and faded with the summer. She had asked him if he was coming back. She wanted him to. She had asked him. After the Chow he would go back. Go back to Hine.

The morning was brilliant now, the colours sharp and fresh. The big wheels of the tree ferns were lighter than the rest of the bush when the car crossed above a valley. Sometimes in the dark green there was the rapid glint of water. Spicer spoke for the first time since they had left the house. 'I don't know where you want me to go,' he said. It was like he had made a joke. The Chow's breathy laugh that sounded like a gasp and stopped, and then gasped again as he said, 'There's nowhere else is there, except this road.' The quick amused expulsion of breath inches away from the driver's neck.

A few vehicles passed them going the other way. One was a rust-red truck with sheep on the wooden-slatted back and a dog leaning from the window. It came up the slope towards them so slowly it seemed always about to stop. The driver raised his hand and Spicer touched the peak of his cap. He had seen it done like that in the pictures. When you drove a lady's car and someone spoke to you, that was what you were supposed to do. The dog's head stuck out above the driver's arm on the edge of the lowered window. Its tongue jerked and dribbled, you'd think it had run up the hill, not driven up in style. Then twenty minutes later one of those long posh Vauxhalls that purred up the hill towards them, sweet as pie. The driver and the woman beside him looked straight ahead. There'd be no wave from them, Spicer thought, ramrods up their arse that outfit, Darkie would have said. A bus passed them with the name in the glass box on its roof wound only part-way round so you saw the half of two words and you couldn't tell what either was. And a long time after that a motorcycle with a passenger car that buzzed towards them, you saw only the mouths beneath the goggles and the leather helmets. They looked like mason bees stuck together. Spicer touched the bulb beside the steering wheel when they passed, a quick blurting stab of sound. Behind him the sister opened her eyes and moved her tongue across her lips and said, 'Are we stopping now?'

No one answered her. How everything except just sitting here, the sky brighter and more intense, the country racing past them, seemed so remote, so *unlikely*, Kate thought. The sea was ahead of them again for a little, the horizon so much sharper now, the water itself a streak of broken mirrors where the sun mounting behind them picked it out.

'We'll stop for breakfast soon, can we?' Kate said.

'I have to put more benzine in anyway,' Spicer said. 'There's the can at the back. I'll have to put that in.'

'I'll say when to stop,' the Chow said. 'I'm the one tells you when to stop.'

The farmhouses were now at closer intervals, the tin mailboxes on their wooden stakes at the front of their drives. The dense packing of the bush had given way to cleared blocks, the hillsides dotted with sheep, and on lower paddocks herds of black and white cattle. The names for so many things that we never learn, Kate thought. Even at home it had been like that, the different kinds of instruments and tools for every trade there was, even things Gran used in the kitchen — there were words Gran came out with she had never heard since. It is such a scrap of life that we ever know, nearly everything goes on outside the little circle where we sit and think ourselves so important. Yet how everything ended so quickly in a question. Peter had thought that too. They had thought it together, when she sat with his head on her naked lap and she leaned forward and brushed her breasts across his cheek, the sad rawness of his face when he removed his steel-framed spectacles. When he had said to her, There is a way, you know, and she had said nothing but turned his head towards her and crushed his mouth against her stirring breasts and run her hand the length of his body, the white smoothness, her hand closing and resting on him, there was no more said than that. Sometimes his quietest of smiles when his head turned slightly in the courtroom's high cold light and he saw her, for that moment excluding everything but her. The artists from the papers sketching her day after day, her own innocence mounting as the trial took its course, Peter made sure of that. The gloat of justice as the crowds muttered and stared when she left the court. See, the girl the monster pawed and rode and slobbered. She knew the thrill she gave them, walking past, so close some of them touched her sleeve. She smelled their eager pressing. She was like a relic with the Catholics.

Kate opened the large black handbag that lay across her feet. There was the folder of banknotes she supposed the Chow would take, eventually. There were the papers for the car she had slipped in beside her pocket mirror and her two combs when Sir William's friend had handed them across to her and told her she would never regret it, a car like this would change her life. There was her notebook with addresses, and initials beside phone numbers. Q. for Detective-Inspector Quin, H. for the Home. The bag could have carried so much more had she been the kind of sprawling, cluttered woman she so despised. She knew her neatness was not quite what it seemed, that Miriam had put her finger on it when she joked, 'It's a compulsion, isn't it? You can no more break it than if you were an alkie.' How right she was! Some women drink to make life tolerable. And that was what simplicity, tidiness, was to her. It kept the clutter at arm's length. And yet the nonsense of thinking we can ever quite do that.

Her fingers dug past the folded banknotes and the address book and touched the hard spikiness of the sunset brooch. The impulse was direct, decisive. She had taken the brooch into her hand, let it lie on her palm when the doctor passed it to her and the knocking began again on the cabin door. He had told her, 'Keep it until you need it.' The dull stones and the seam of small diamonds between the blood-coloured petals. It had lived in the light as though she was holding a flame. The doctor kissed her cheek, and pressed her against him. Then he turned from her and opened the door to the captain in his elaborate uniform and a man standing at either shoulder. It was the last time the doctor spoke to her with only the two of them, alone.

She reached out her hand towards Spicer as she continued to look straight ahead at the descending road. Her fingers found the pocket in the side of his jacket. She let the brooch slip into it. She then put the handbag back down beside her feet. 'There,' she said. As if something she herself did not quite understand had been concluded, a termination of some kind.

The car turned a wide slow bend and Spicer said, 'They're stopping people up there. The police are stopping people.'

It was as though an electric current charged the car. They heard the rustle and a clink as the Chow arranged his clothing, the gun tucked against the belt beneath the habit. Marie-Claire sat upright, her thumb rubbing the smooth surface of the door handle.

'Any of you,' the Chow said. 'It could be any of youse if you don't do it right.'

A motorcycle had stopped at the wooden barrier set across the road. A young Maori in a yellow singlet lifted one end of the barrier and opened the road for the motorcycle to pass. A stoutish policeman, with sweat below his eyes although it was still so early in the day, patted the bonnet of the car, and from Spicer's lowered window took in the passengers.

'On the road early,' he said. He moved a peppermint about in his mouth.

'The sister isn't well,' Kate said. She smiled at the bluff and suffused face. 'We don't want her travelling once the day warms up.'

'You've come from where?' the policeman asked. 'You couldn't have left Taupo this morning.'

Kate smiled and told him, 'We left last night. We slept in the car when our friend became ill. She has medicine to make her sleep.' She felt her palms moisten, the flutter of the pulse in her neck as though an insect had suddenly landed there.

The policeman took a notebook from the top pocket of his uniform. He licked the end of the short pencil he drew from the fold where the notebook flapped back. 'We're confirming everyone's details,' he said. 'You'll appreciate that. You know the Chow's still on the loose?' He looked at Kate with bulbous blue eyes.

Kate said of course she saw that, it must be a great worry until they picked him up.

'Reports from Te Kuiti. One from Tokoroa. We're at sixes and sevens, truth to tell.'

His younger assistant walked round the back of the car. He undid the leather straps on the trunk and swung up the lid, which thudded against the bodywork. Marie-Claire turned, she saw the brim of the young policeman's helmet conceal his face as his hand flicked across the containers of food, the folded blankets, the squat thermos. 'Picnic stuff,' he called out, 'holiday stuff in here, sir.'

When Kate remembered the letter, she leaned forward to take up her handbag and clicked it open. She handed the stiff envelope with the embossed seal across in front of Spicer to the blue-cuffed hand that rested on the lowered window. The policeman read it, his head moving slightly with the lines, and folded it back into its envelope. He handed it back. 'Well we know who you are then,' he said. He also glanced at the driving licence Spicer offered him. He looked across the driver's shoulder to the women in the back. Marie-Claire diverted his scrutiny. She said to him in some bloody accent, as he would tell the younger policeman later, this accent he could scarcely make out, she asked him if he knew how far they were from some convent or other. Could be sacred arse she said for all he could tell. He touched the knot in his tie and nodded. 'Keep an eye out, then. You see anything suspicious you'll inform the authorities, right?' He called over to the Maori in the bright singlet, who now leaned against the barrier, a cigarette cupped in his hand. 'Let them through, Joe.'

The car moved slowly forward. The younger policeman said, 'Those new Chevs take the climb lovely.'

'How do you know how it takes the climb?' the older man said. 'Have you been across in one?'

The policeman watched the Maori swing the barrier back so that it blocked the road again, and the car picked up its pace. Trust the left footers, he thought. Letter from the only Jew minister in the government saying do what you can, et bloody cetera, carting crook nuns one end of the country to the other, wonder they didn't order him to salute while he was about it. He looked up at the sky. In for a scorcher, he thought, you didn't need to be Rua the bloody prophet to know that much. He'd be out of peppermints too if he didn't pace himself.

Inside the car there was a sense not simply of relief but of complicity, a virtual elation that they had brought it off. An absurdity they should think that, yet there it was, Kate thought. She laughed at the strangeness of it. While, It must be today, Spicer continued to think, it has to be today, and yet he had done nothing. He might have swung round and thrown himself at the figure behind him, he might have said to the policeman with the rivers of sweat beneath his eyes that the engine was shot, they needed to pull over and wait until a mechanic could come through. The Chow might have fired but they would have overpowered him — it might all have finished in a few crammed, random seconds. And yet here they were, as they had been before the barrier came into sight. In the mirror Spicer watched the dwindling figure of the policeman. They had been that close to the normal world and now they were driving away from it. He heard behind him the exhaling breath of the Chow, and the nun too breathing out, as though in relief.

Marie-Claire, who had leaned forward while the policeman conversed at the lowered window, her discomfort forgotten in the excitement of their danger, now eased back into the padding of the seat, her eyes closed, the pelt of her pulses scaling down. They hadn't heard then, she thought. No one has heard about the farm, the strewn hats in the brown light, whatever it was that had been shot before the carved ham, the delicate gold-rimmed cups of tea. But then nausea swept her body. Her mind concentrated utterly on keeping it back from the point where it might overwhelm her, possess her so fully she would be reduced to a mere spasm of rising bile. She felt the prickle of sweat along her forehead. She leaned her head on the back of the seat in front of her, its leathery pungency grasping in her throat. She would take the medicine Dr Flynn had given her. She had held off doing so long enough, God knows. She felt the altering intensity in her side, as though the pain had shifted into a different gear. Mother of God, she said. She felt the taste of copper rise in her mouth. Everything reduced, shrank, before the pressure in her guts. Her fingers closed and gripped on Kate's shoulder. Her friend's hand at once rose and laced tightly in her own. 'She's sick,' she heard Kate say. 'We have to do something.'

Marie-Claire raised her head. 'It comes and goes,' she said. 'Once it goes it isn't bad.'

Kate put her cheek against the hand she held and said, 'We can't be that far now. Not that far from Napier.'

'We're twenty-five miles,' the Chow said. 'I know exactly how far it is.'

The car shuddered and veered, as though something pulled from under it, slewing it to one side. At first Kate believed it was a ditch they had skidded into. Spicer called, 'Hold on,' unsure himself for several seconds that it was a tyre that had blown beneath them. They were on a shallow dip of road, the land sloping off on one side, on the other rising steeply into dry grassy slopes. The bush was well behind them. They were in terrain where farms had broken open into tilted wide paddocks, high tawny stretches where sheep ran sparsely in rough, ugly scrub.

The Chow was alert, distressed. His voice rose thinly into the command that Spicer must not stop here, not on the main road, the whole world would see them. Kate said cars got punctures every day, nobody would think twice.

'We don't want them thinking once,' the Chow said. Both his hands were on the back of Spicer's seat.

For the first time, Kate saw, he was close to panic. She spoke with deliberate calm. She knew it was now he would be most reckless. She said, 'We could drive off over there. There must be somewhere along that track.' She hoped there would be a farmhouse, a lone farmer who spotted them, who might even guess there was something about them worth telephoning the police for. 'Somewhere we can just stop,' she said, 'where Spicer can do something.'

Spicer said, 'You drive on a wheel like this you'll wreck the rim.'

The Chow's finger tapped at Spicer's collar, a curious unaggressive touching that almost seemed concern. He said, 'You can guess what's round there. That bit of hill there. You see down the valley and out towards the sea. No one's going to bother us round there.'

'What about the wheel?' Spicer said. An almost girlish plaintiveness in his query, as though they were about to damage a living thing.

'Do it,' Kate said. 'Drive off there to the left.'

He moved the gears into bottom. He nudged forward as slowly as he could. Once off the main road, the car's body swayed and creaked with the rutted surface of the track. The Chow turned and looked from the large rear window.

'There's nothing coming,' Kate said. She placed her spread palm on Spicer's knee. She said to Marie-Claire, 'There's nothing, is there?' The car rose slowly on a hardened ridge of clay and thudded back. A graunching scrape came from the back wheel. Kate said, 'Twenty yards. Only twenty yards and we'll be round that bend.'

The Chow's head was still lowered at the rear window. The cloth of the headpiece whisked against Marie-Claire's cheek, a disturbing touch of intimacy in which the sister smelled the dry, distinctive odour of her own clothing. The Chow then sat back, his eyes closed, his hands palm down on his skirt. It was a gesture of weariness, a slumping of his entire body away from the vigilance he was obliged to maintain.

The car rocked and dipped as it took the curve that opened up the falling of hill country towards the plains and, beyond those, the sea. The city showed as a distant smear on the shoreline; the morning sky above it carried the faintest haze.

Kate stood now beside the car and gazed out. She said to Marie-Claire, 'Come and sit here. I'll put a rug on the ground.'

Spicer was already at work with the heavy jack. He had told them they would need to get out of the car anyway, it was the first rule, he said, the first rule if you knew the first thing about cars.

'What is?' the Chow said. The nun's clothing rose in a fresh turn of breeze, the veil levelled out almost horizontal and his neck was exposed above the cut of the neckline. He slapped down at the rising skirt, and then the gust was past, the morning still and hot.

'That you never use a jack with someone in the car. In case it slips off.'

The job took longer than Spicer thought. He told them the track was not as level as it looked, he'd have to hunt out some rocks, or maybe a chunk of wood, to hold the jack properly firm.

He was not aware the Chow was so close to him until he heard the wheeze, and then the thin, grating voice. 'I'll come with you, then.' The Chow ripped himself free of the nun's headgear, then raised his arms and tugged the long smock over his head. His hair stood in tousled wisps. He was again as they had seen him when he first stepped from the footpath and into their lives, the sleeves of his khaki shirt rucked back untidily towards his elbows, his cotton pants held by the black snake-clasp belt that bulged with the gun shoved in behind it.

'I'm not bolting off,' Spicer said. He began to climb the hill's steep side towards a clump of trees that stood almost black against the tawny summer grass. 'It's only some rocks or something.'

'I'll come with you,' the Chow repeated. He stayed ten yards or so behind the younger man's eager climbing.

The discarded habit lay on the track behind the car. The veil had tangled in a low clump of gorse. Kate went from where she spread the rug and picked up the garment, shook it out and lay it across her arm, and retrieved the veil. She stood in front of Marie-Claire and held them out. She said, 'You could always put them on again. While they're up the hill.'

Marie-Claire raised her hand to touch her friend's wrist. Her fingers lay briefly against the draped habit. She laughed and surprised Kate with the lightness of her tone. 'He might want them back a second time. I couldn't go through all that again.'

Kate went to the trunk at the back of the car and worked the broad straps loose. She said she wasn't up to boiling the billy the way Spicer was but there was this orange cordial they hadn't even touched. And ham and biscuits and some fruit. 'We won't starve,' she said.

'Something to drink would be nice,' Marie-Claire said. Kate handed her the cup and she took one of the biscuits held out to her. As she raised her hand she noticed the gap, the glimpse of her own flesh, where the sleeve had ripped along the seam beneath her arm.

'There. I've ruined this for you, haven't I? I've worn it for a day and now it's a rag.'

Kate sat beside her. She gripped her own cup between her palms. The drink tasted too sweet. She supposed it was really made for children. She should have bought limewater, or lemonade.

'This is awful,' she said. She flicked the cup, and the drink leaped in a dirty ribbon and splashed into the pale grass.

Marie-Claire dipped her biscuit in the cordial, then sucked at it. She knew she must force herself to eat, even a little. Inexplicably, the pain had gone off. She could feel the thickening in her stomach, but luckily that was all. It would be back of course. She saw Dr Flynn's wry smile.

'I'm exhausted,' she said. 'As though all my life has somehow piled up on me and now I have to shrug it off.' And then catching her friend's eye, 'What nonsense I talk!' she said. 'It's because I'm so tired.'

Kate put her fingers across the harder, tougher hand of her friend. With her other hand she smoothed her own skirt. Her collar that must be filthy by now, she supposed. She had avoided the little mirror on Spicer's side of the car when she walked past it with the cups. And as though picking up her thought, Marie-Claire said, 'I must look a sight.'

'You do,' Kate said, stroking her friend's hand. 'So do we both.'

Marie-Claire looked out and caught the distant flash of the sea. Was it haze, or simply her eyesight, that she could not make out the horizon? It was the only time she felt the infinite, she supposed, when she looked far out at sea, her own tiny apprehension of what drew her, enticed her, however one wanted to put it. God, she had thought, as a girl. And she had run down the slipping rush of sand. God had pulsed at her from as far as she could see. It was the way God and the world should always be. She knew it was no more than a comparison, what she felt; her elation was simply *like* being close to Him. She did not, even then, think to know Him closely was that easy.

'I'm not frightened of him any more,' Kate said.

There was nothing Marie-Claire thought she might say.

'If he'd been going to do anything.' And after a pause, turning her hope into a query, 'Don't you think he would have? By now, I mean?'

The nun said nothing because she knew how pointless it was even to guess. Goodness we always know in such tiny parcels, such immediate facts — this good act or that good person. Goodness is so transparent. But evil is like a cloud, even its direction eludes us until it hardens and we strike against it. She supposed Kate spoke as she did to buoy them both along, to comfort her especially. Sin which is only sin, she thought, swerves into error and weakness, which is why God forgives so readily, how could He not, understanding us as He does? But evil we cannot grasp, we cannot point to as we can to sin. It pervades, like sunlight. As if it is too pure to quite grasp — is that too silly a thing to say? Evil. But she hated it more than she feared it. She knew that, at least.

She said, 'I'm too muddled to think, my dear. You'll have to ask me later.'

Spicer heard the sweep of the Chow following him through the dry grass, the heave of his breath as though even a climb like this was an effort for him. 'Wait,' the Chow called. He leaned forward, one fist on his knee. With the other hand he undid another button of the shirt that was too big for him. His breathing now came in flat racking gasps.

It has to be this morning, Spicer put to himself. It has to be before we get back to the road, because after that we'll just about be in the town, he won't want us ever to reach there. Hine back at the store would have told the cops by now, she must have. Must have clicked there was something so wonky about the whole set-up of them, the sister looking like she'd been dragged through Christ knows what and even Mrs C looking utterly buggered and the Chow like something you'd never seen except the drawing of in some comic book or something. He'd get the spanner from the tool kit and have it ready on the running board, it would look like it had to be there with him changing the tyre. Even the Chow wouldn't think twice about that. How you bring it down's the important thing. On the back of his head, the way he'd seen it in the pictures. Swing it round and down and crack. Hine would read about it more than likely, it would be in the newspaper, half the country looking out for the Chow as it was. And whatever happened last night at the farm, they must know that soon enough. Even if it was only the dog, they'd know it was some loony done that too, who else would shoot a dog?

The Chow called up to him, 'You can go on.'

Spicer said, 'I need to have a piss first, right?'

He climbed the next twenty yards and went into the tall dim light inside the stand of trees. When he did up his buttons he turned to see the Chow only a few feet behind him, rubbing his hand along his other forearm, watching. Spicer picked up what looked like a sawn stump of fence post. There was a clump of rusted tins so someone must have camped here at one time or another. Fencers, he supposed, a long time back now because the fence line he spotted coming up the slope had sprung loose in places and some of the posts were on a lean. There were a couple of bricks wedged together where they must have done their boiling-up.

Spicer said, 'I'll take this wood and two of the bricks. Reckon you could bring the other?'

The Chow said nothing but stooped to loosen the brick from a clutch of weed that tangled it. It could be now, Spicer supposed, just belt him one on the back of the swede with the sharp edge of the brick. But if something went wrong, if the bugger swung round at him suppose as he went down? Better to wait until Mrs C was nearby in any case. He wanted her to see it. He wanted her there in case the Chow wasn't knocked out proper and she could swing at him as well, whatever she had in her hand. And even as he thought, That's the story, that's the way to do it, he's cunning as a rat and only the two of us up here in this scrap of bush, I got to be dead certain it comes off — even as the images ran through his mind, his own falling arm and the sharp snap of bone, Mrs C looming above the Chow with her own arms raised as if with an axe, he knew too that he delayed because he was afraid. That he did not want to kill.

And then something that stopped utterly the drift of his fantasy so that for several seconds he felt spiders of panic writhe across his flesh. As Spicer stood above him, above the shirt that fell forward as the figure leaned, he saw the tits. They were soft and small but unmistakable, the nipples two blunt peaks. Spicer stepped back and turned away. A pressure of vast confusion welled against him. *Tits!* The realisation then came on him, but it was as though he wanted to keep it back, to resist what was inevitable and repellent to him, the thought that beyond the malice and danger and exhaustion of the Chow's constant threat, there was this further thing, this revelation that so startled his thinking. And anger also now welling in him, this deception that he took as something directed at himself, as though the Chow's intention had been simply that, to humiliate and outrage him. He knew he was caught in a tangle of responses, a ravelling of feelings for which the words would never come. But there was a net or something — the image that came to him was precisely that — a net that lay across these last three days and now was suddenly hauled away from him, a femaleness that firmed against him and caught up Mrs C and the sister as well, a collusion he was at a loss with.

The Chow was looking at him, standing within touching distance.

'I said what's holding you up?'

'What?' He looked away. He had to make out he didn't know.

The Chow said, 'Get back then and fix the wheel.'

'The tyre,' Spicer said. 'It's the tyre, not the wheel.'

The Chow snorted and raised a wrist and wiped it across the dry, perfectly level lips, then stroked one arm against the khaki pants. 'Just get back and fix it.'

Spicer moved out from the stand of trees. He walked several yards in front. He held the chunk of thick sawed wood in against his chest, the burned bricks lying on top of it and balanced with his other hand. He stepped cautiously, eyeing the slope of the terrain. His shirt front was smeared with the black stain from the bricks. 'Shit,' he said softly. He hated things that marked his clothes. He hated Darkie's bloody untidy duds. If you don't look the part, his auntie used to say. It took him a long time as a boy to know what she meant. But Miriam liked it. Miriam said she liked it when he came in spruced up, after he'd come back from down the Home and had a wash and put on a white shirt before he went round to 23. He could tell Hine didn't half mind it either, the cap she kept looking at when she leaned next to him over the big mudguard and he smelled the softness of her and he'd showed her the shine and gleam when he raised the bonnet back. And now the brick had shagged the look of him good and proper, the black rubbed stain that was just the latest part of all this muddle, this rotten bitching mess of the Chow.

Marie-Claire looked back from the hazed sea, from the rising memories of her girlhood and the consuming, comforting certainty of God which the line of horizon stirred in her, and watched Spicer pick his way down the slope. The smaller khaki figure moved behind him. This was, she supposed, the major event of her life, a thrusting into the great plain of placidity and service of this ragged unpredictable peak, a place she could not comprehend and yet refused to fear. Perhaps it was this that so struck her, as if clarity and order had been such overrated things, so totally assumed, and yet here in front of her eyes, a young man edging slowly down a dry hillside with an armful of dirty bricks, and a lunatic behind him, someone who had murdered already and no doubt planned to do as much again. She was drawn back by the dry tap of glass as Kate moved about at the back of the car, clinking the tin cups and the tall bottle of orange cordial. Kate called to Spicer as he drew close to them, 'There's a drink here if you want it.'

Everything is so simple, Marie-Claire thought. Everything happens because we choose, or because it will happen anyway, in spite of us. She stood to ease the pins and needles that stirred in one of her legs. She stamped her foot and ran her hand along the back of her neck. It was still so unfamiliar, this movement of breeze directly on her flesh.

Spicer dropped the bricks and the length of post near the back wheel of the car. He said to Kate, 'I can stack these bricks see and the bit of wood underneath the jack. I reckon that'll do it.'

Kate asked how long it would take.

'It better not be long,' the Chow said. 'You better get it done.'

The brick he carried was placed beside the others. Spicer knelt and was already packing the sloped angle of the track to take the hunk of wood. Kate balanced a mug on the front mudguard while the Chow brushed both blackened hands on the grass at the side of the track before standing and taking the gun from behind the snake-clasp belt.

Kate said to him, 'Do you want a drink then?' It was as if she were steeped in some element of intense attention, yet her movements seemed sluggish, her thinking slowed. She realised she could imagine only a little ahead, and then her thought was lost against an oppressive wall. She supposed the Chow would try to kill them, and when it came to that, in the flurry of their numbers, at least one or two of them might survive. She saw Spicer crouched in his litter of tools, his arm nudging the black heavy jack to where he wanted it placed on the supporting wood beneath the car. The hillside sloped sharply down beyond the car. She could not imagine what else the Chow might do. It did not occur to her that they might simply be let go, that their captor might leave them at a certain point and tell them to drive on, as direct and casual a separation as their coming together when they picked him up.

Kate saw her friend's slow rising from where she had placed the rug a few feet from the car. A bee burred close to her head, and Kate's hand moved quickly to brush against her hair. The nun hobbled slightly as if troubled by a stone in her shoe. The Chow stood clasping together the S-shaped buckle after tucking the shirt back into his trousers. He laid the gun on the bonnet as though it were a table. Spicer's movements beneath the car wobbled the cup that was balanced on the waist-high mudguard.

'That's going to fall,' Kate said quietly. She spoke to no one in particular. But when she spoke Marie-Claire looked up at her, and in a quick brilliant clarity, like that of a theatre almost or the illumined sanctuary of a chapel, she took in the tableau of the car, its brasses and mirrors and sheen so luminous in the morning's sun, Spicer on one knee and half obscured beneath the car's bulk, and beyond it a little Kate's fingers moving from her hair, shaking her head then turning her face towards the sliding cup, and the Chow's own hand darting out to arrest its slide. There was an abrupt grunt of satisfaction as the cup was scooped into his palm. A dab of cordial splashed across his wrist. He and the nun now stood on opposite sides of the bonnet with its neatly notched sides. The Chow's tongue darted at the spilt liquid, cleaning his hand. His teeth showed in a rare smile as he raised the cup to his mouth and drained it. His throat was exposed and pale, his head tilted back and the muscles moving in his throat, and Marie-Claire's hand stretched out to the gun lying on the bonnet. It was heavy and firm and fitted her palm as though shaped expressly for that. The weight of the butt tipped her hand slightly back.

Kate's hands were clasped in front of her breast. The Chow lowered the cup and placed it on the broad curve of the mudguard, his face immobile, passive, but the body tensed as a spring, a soft dry rasp of breath as the seconds of inattention came in on him. There was a knocking from beneath the car as Spicer pumped at the extension rod of the lifting jack. His mind swirled still with the image from up the hill, the undoubted and dislocating glimpse of the softly moulded tits that threw the Chow not simply into a different aura of attention, but beyond comprehension altogether. The job in hand, he told himself, I must think of that, of raising the car and wedging the chunk of fence post and the bricks against the sloping ground. Beyond that his mind was blank.

The shot rang out with astonishing sharpness. Spicer's head jerked and caught against the car's open door. But he forced himself upright and saw first how Mrs C's hands were at her mouth, the flesh of her face distorted in both horror and relief, although it was not these that Spicer took in, only the enormity of some emotion unlike anything he had seen in her. And then he felt the shudder of the car and saw the swishing slide of the khaki body down the mudguard's smooth slope, the bump of the Chow's head on the running board before he lay, one arm angled back, beside the car. The nun seemed to be looking at something in the distance, her eyes almost closed, when Spicer saw her at the side of the bonnet and heard the clunk of the gun dropped back, the shiny stuff of her dress moving and shimmering as the breeze rose and tugged at it. And from high up in the surrounding scoop of hills the echo of the shot came back at them with an isolated, vivid directness. It is only a second, Kate thought. It is only a second and I have seen all this. And again, from further off, diminished, the shot coming to them for a third time, as the car now slid and jolted from its block, tilting with what seemed an almost courteous slowness. Marie-Claire saw its bulk descending, a paraclete of shining surfaces and brutal weight.

After the end

SERGEANT STAFFORD REFUSED TO BE RUSHED, ALTHOUGH IT IRKED HIM that young Hansen, raw as a carrot, sat there and gawped across the paper he was meant to be taking evidence on prior to typing it up with two concentrating fingers. The sergeant raised his hand palm outwards to the witnesses and turned in the swivel chair which his superior across in Napier had always thought something of an irregularity, his own station boasting no more comfort than a schoolroom.

The sergeant said, 'You do have every word, constable? Every second or third is not enough.'

Young Hansen coloured to his reddish spiky hairline. This too irritated the sergeant. Hicks, he thought, they will think we're hicks, Aucklanders always do. But he swung the chair back towards the witnesses and attempted a smile at the woman. 'Please go on,' he said. But the woman slapped her hands in her lap and said if she did not have tea immediately, she would faint. So the sergeant called half an hour's intermission to the line of questioning, and knew his first mistake was not to let her rest longer at the farm and proceed with his queries out there. It was Joyce being present that had put him off. He was embarrassed at the thought of working where his wife would see him. He knew this was unreasonable, how touchy he was at almost anything. But that was the way things were. Sergeant Stafford was a man who looked facts in the face, he could say that much about himself.

He and the witnesses sat in silence. He sharpened two pencils, then went to the door and shouted to Hansen to get a move on there, couldn't he? The young policeman turned, his face slick with the sweat of confusion as much as summer heat. He silently mouthed towards his superior. 'Sugar?' he said. He held up the jar with its scatter of remaining grains. The sergeant's impulse was to snatch the object and heave it from the opened sash window where at that moment the gauze curtain wafted in and webbed around the constable's shoulders and head, a comic illustration of a ghost holding an empty jar.

'Very good, constable,' he said. He closed the door and faced the witnesses. 'You miss a female's hand around the station,' he said. And knew at once they would have no idea why he had bothered to say so. But the woman looked through the window behind his desk and seemed not to hear. The young fellow was licking his finger then running it across the shiny peak of the cap that for most of the interrogation he had been stroking where it lay on his knee in the slow absent-minded way a man might stroke a cat while he thought of something else.

When they had first arrived at the station from the farm and passed through the door he held open for them, Sergeant Stafford had, for one necessary moment, leaned back against the door jamb and closed his eyes. He did not like to think the case was getting out of hand. The last thing he wanted was to have to telephone Napier Central and ask that bastard McGibbon to take the matter up. So far he had done everything as he believed he should. According to the book, as they say. The moment Joyce rang through he had sent the lad Hansen to the farm and set out with the police doctor to the reported scene. He had supervised the removal of the bodies into the ambulance after the photographs, and then proceeded forthwith to the farm where he lived. He instructed that the witnesses be taken to the station for questioning. For this, as Joyce had said to him as he walked down the back steps to the waiting car, was certainly not your run-of-the-mill enquiry.

The sergeant's fingers dug deeply into his trouser pocket and scrabbled at the dermatitis that gave him what for at this time every year. It was only the beginning of February. By the end he would have a patch on his groin the size and colour of a cricket ball, and Joyce would move into another bed. Jumped at the chance, he sometimes suspected. But today he scarcely registered the raised welt of his itch. He came back to the thought that if he did things right, if he was the one to break the story, then he'd come out of it impressively, no two ways about that. There was no doubt either this was headline stuff. Although when his wife had rung through and her normally level voice poured at him like a siren, less than a minute after the kids came pelting in, he had thought he would not half mind if she had phoned someone else instead. Phoned McGibbon even, because he knew you couldn't make mistakes with a story as big as this. And he thought even now, supposing the witnesses weren't giving him the entire facts? Had cooked up some kind of yarn? He'd be like that copper down at Waipuk years ago soon after the war. Someone fed him the line that there was gold in the Tukituki. They set him up with a couple of planted nuggets and the fellow had rung through to the Wellington papers. Within hours the Otane road was blocked with cars and horses and even those on foot before the malice of it all came out. The man had left the force and six months later, so they said, he was two stone lighter than he'd been before he ever heard of gold, and then a year later, practically to the day, he was dead. That story too had flashed by his mind before he placed the receiver back on its gleaming hook. But it was a gamble he had to take. So Sergeant Stafford instructed Junior Constable Hansen to drive hell for leather the few miles to the farm and place them under closest scrutiny until he arrived, whoever they were. Who had walked, so they now said, from the foothills and across the bronze haze above the stubble of the paddocks, eighty-two degrees out there according to the thermometer on the back verandah and anything more than fifty yards away shimmered in the heat, and that was when the kids had seen them.

'Just coming through the hot wobble down past the hayshed,' Jackie will tell them later — tell anyone he can, over and over, the adult world for once absorbed in what he has to say. The ten-year-old lingers on the detail. The man with the white shirt and his coat held over his shoulder by one finger, and the shine on the front of his cap bright as a bit of glass. And the posh lady hobbling along beside him the way a horse does when one of its shoes is half gone. She was leaning into him and hanging on, and his arm was round her helping her stand up. 'She'd have come a cropper if he wasn't there.' So Lucy and the Hopai kid leading them to the back verandah while Jackie tore on ahead and raised the alarm and knew this time it was a big one, they'd have to believe this one, because there they were, the lady collapsing now onto the old rocker on the verandah and the man in the shirt that had fluttered like a flag when they first moved into the heat around the side of the barn, throwing his coat across the rail and sitting on the steps, asking him for water. Jackie hopping about in his excitement so his words at first meant nothing to his mother who had been resting in the heat of the day, so that when she gives her own account she will say, to Jackie's fury, that it was like he had a mouthful of marbles, she had no idea what he was on about, she thought there must be a fire started out the back. Until Tom Hopai told her exactly what was going on, and told her she ought to ring the police. That's when she went to the back door and saw the witnesses for herself. She said it was like there was a crack in ordinary things and something else had stepped through.

'Tea, sergeant?' Young Hansen stood in front of his superior, holding towards him a cup and saucer. He already had placed two cups in front of the witnesses, and a bowl of sugar he had obtained by dashing from the back entrance of the station to behind the barber's shop a dozen yards along the street. The shop's back door had been open and he took the silver bowl from the table, his huge hand coming down and concealing it in an act a casual witness might well construe as petty theft. There was not time to shoot through and explain matters to Bert Gray, whose scissors he could hear snipping away in empty space in that way the barber had of never ceasing to move them about even as he stood back from the chair to size up his work, or pause to complete a fragment of local gossip. He had taken the sugar and dashed back. The constable felt the rare satisfaction of initiative as he placed the bowl on the low table between the witnesses.

The sergeant said to him shortly, 'Put it there and clear out.' He returned to the face that illustrated the poster lying across his desk. 'That's him,' the woman had said, before her request for tea.

'You'd swear to that?' he said. 'Quite beyond doubt?'

'It's exaggerated, of course.'

The woman sounded surprised that the drawing was not a better likeness. Were they supposed to be clairvoyants or something, the police? 'It's an approximation,' he informed her. 'At that stage of a search you can't expect more than that. An approximation.'

'His eyes weren't slanted like that, to begin with,' she said. 'They were narrow but not slanted.'

'And his voice,' the man beside her said.

This time the woman turned her sharpness towards the other witness. 'His voice has nothing to do with the picture of him, Spicer.'

The sergeant looked again at the poster. Something wonky about the face anyway, whatever it was. The whole country didn't call him the Chow for nothing, surely? But the woman interrupted him. She said, 'The face. The face was more like it was pressed against glass. Does that make sense?'

Sergeant Stafford did not bother to answer. He was not one to encourage impressionistic evidence. He checked off to himself the facts of the rampage as they were presently known. A man killed in a newsagent's shop in Otahuhu, eight days ago exactly. Two days later a milkman found beneath his cart, shot at close range in the chest, half a bottle of milk standing within a few feet of the corpse. The murderer must have drunk the milk after he killed the man. No other assumption was possible. And a policeman wounded in Hamilton was still fighting for his life. You could get that much from reading the *Tribune*. Confidential information sent to all stations in fact said little more than that. Although he was called the Chow by the press on the evidence of two brief sightings: five feet seven, high cheekbones, hair as pale as straw, which did not sound Chinese, but then it took all sorts. Reports claimed he may have travelled north from the West Coast, or south from Whangarei, or indeed east from Australia. There were all kinds of chows in Australia, the sergeant refrained from remarking. His own professional suspicions were scarcely the concern of the witnesses.

'The general feeling, certainly,' Sergeant Stafford said, 'is that he's not one of us.'

'You've seen him too,' the woman said.

Again, he had the unsettling feeling that the woman was not taking him as seriously as she ought, and that the young fellow's mind was not focused on the enquiry in hand. Pansy enough name that, Spicer. He might have sworn there was a touch of the tarbrush there too, if push came to shove. The young fellow had said he suspected from the first few minutes that their passenger was the Chow. From the minute in fact he stepped from the side of the public lavatories near that big park in Cambridge. The driver had thought at first it was an old person because of the sunhat pulled down over his eyes and a newspaper hanging across his arm. He had moved across from the edge of the footpath and stopped beside Mrs C.

'Mrs C?' the sergeant asked.

'Mrs Cooper,' the witness said. 'When I say Mrs C I mean Mrs Cooper there.'

He had watched, he said, from where he sat with the nose of the car pointed in towards the kerb, because when they pulled up there had been a lorry with planks of timber sticking way out beyond the edge of the tray and there wasn't room to park any other way. 'There's a law against a load sticking out like that.'

The sergeant said, 'That's not the law we're concerned with at the moment.' There was something lumbering and slow about that young bloke that was beginning to grate on him.

'They pull you up in Auckland if you got a load like that.'

'Never mind about Auckland,' the sergeant said. 'Would you care to go on?'

The figure there beside Mrs C, he said, he had watched him suddenly take off his hat and put it in a rubbish tin near the entrance to the Men Only, then next thing because he moved that quick, didn't they say that, the Chow moved like a cat? Next thing he's beside her when she's ready to step back into the vehicle, he's hitched the newspaper back along his arm so the witness saw the barrel of the gun the paper concealed. No one spoke, as far as he could remember, no one said a word until they stopped on the side road past Tirau somewhere and the Chow had the whip in his hand that he took from his sock when he raised the leg of his khaki trousers. 'When he hit the nun across here,' and the witness made a sawing motion with his arm angled across his chest.

The sergeant turned over the poster so he would not be obliged to examine any longer the face that was sketched in thick crude strokes. He looked up at the clock. It surely could not be long until the doctor telephoned about the inquest? Not that any new photographs would get closer to how that face had been, even before the doctor's instruments began on it. The head was opened like a split melon when the sergeant had stood above it a few hours before. The flies had risen in a dull heavy drift, it was like a black seething veil was lifted up from it. He had felt as though a finger hooked into the back of his throat. And the dead woman they said was a nun with the toppled car on its side lying half across her, her eyes still open, although the witnesses had laid a blanket across her before they moved down the slopes towards the level paddocks and the distant speck of settlement. When the blanket was raised there was no mark of distress on the woman's face. Her head lay turned to one side, as though she merely rested, looking across the blur of scorching country towards the sea.

Two mechanics hauled on the ropes and pulley they had rigged behind the breakdown truck driven out from the town with the police car and the ambulance. The biscuit-coloured car, its hood crumpled on one side, raised slowly upright, exposing the length of the woman stretched beneath it. The bulk of the Chevrolet juddered as it planted down on its three solid wheels. The younger mechanic moved quickly to adjust the jack beneath the exposed socket of the fourth, the taut ropes holding the car against the slope of the hill. The dress the woman wore shimmered as the rising breeze twitched across it. It was a dress made for parties, the sort the sergeant saw in the pages of the *Mirror* when Joyce lingered on the pictures of what she called the crust, the upper crust, the way people were in Auckland. As the car rocked back on its springs, he leaned forward across the woman and drew down the rucked-up dress. He could make her look decent at least. It made him feel queer to see the sudden nakedness of her legs, the paleness that made him think of floured dough. Only the knees were discoloured, a kind of horny roughness that puzzled him until he clicked, until he thought, That's it, if she was a nun like they said then you'd expect her knees to have done overtime. All that effort getting through to God and this is how they ended up. As he smoothed the long skirt down across her thighs he felt a brief intense tenderness that was yet another puzzle to him. He must be the only man who had ever done that. He clicked his tongue in irritation that the thought had so much as come to him.

They put her in the ambulance beside the man she had shot. A sheet, almost as heavy as canvas, was laid over both of them. Sergeant Stafford turned from the slammed door at the back of the ambulance and bawled across to the farmer whose land they were on, who was shoving his arm through the lowered driver's window of the Chevrolet and tugging at the steering wheel so sharply the front tyres scraped against the dirt.

'Leave that bloody car will you!' he ordered him.

The farmer looked across and paused, then drew back his arm.

The mechanic at the rear of the car kicked hard against the jack. 'She'll hold,' he said. It was the first thing he had said since he took the ropes from the tray of his truck and arranged the hoist to haul the car upright. He had turned his back and checked his gear while the police and the ambulance driver attended to the bodies. He now paused long enough to fetch a thin cigarette from inside his shirt pocket and lit it with a match he scraped several times along its box before it flared.

'Don't go throwing that down,' the farmer told him. 'It's like tinder round here.'

The mechanic walked across and stood by the copper. He said, 'Whoever tried to change that tyre didn't know shit from clay.'

'Is that so?' the sergeant said.

'That's what I'm telling you,' the mechanic said. 'You couldn't expect the car to hold firm the place he tried to raise it. Not if it was bumped.'

The farmer had joined them. He said, 'That your place they walked down to was it? Down Shepherd's Road?' He nodded vaguely to the expanse of country below him. 'The driver and that other woman?'

'The brother-in-law's,' the sergeant said. 'We rent the house from him.'

The farmer gave a curt, amused grunt. 'Bit of a coincidence.'

'What is?' the mechanic said.

'Turning up. Them turning up like that at a cop's house, first one they pick.'

'They do happen,' the sergeant said. 'Coincidences. They do happen.'

The mechanic threw down his half-finished cigarette. He held the farmer's eye as he ground the butt beneath his boot. 'Well,' he asked the sergeant. 'How long until I can drive this back into town? The apprentice can take the truck.' He gave a shrill whistle as though to a dog, and a heavy lad sidled over towards them from the truck. 'Get that other wheel on,' he said to him. 'Sooner the better.'

'My photographer is still taking pictures,' the sergeant said. 'Of the vehicle. As soon as investigations are complete.'

The farmer walked back to the horse tethered near the stand of trees. The mechanic looked down at the boy crouched by the wheel. He told the sergeant he might look thick as they come, that kid, but he was a natural when it came to motors. He winked at the copper. 'Not that I'd let him in on that,' he said. 'He'd be off to town and twice the pay.'

'No, I don't expect you would,' the sergeant said.

That was at two o'clock. The hands on the large clock with its thick roman numerals now moved to six. There was a soft ping as the hour was passed. The sergeant had put an end to its chimes the day the thing was hung, yet each hour ever since there was this slight admonitory reminder of what he had done.

'We've taken rooms for you in a hotel,' Sergeant Stafford explained. 'It's the best hotel we have.'

'My friend has not telephoned back?' the woman said.

'Your friend?'

'I gave the young man the number,' she said.

'Hansen?'

'The constable.'

The vein pounded in the sergeant's temple. 'Perhaps you might have asked me?'

'While we were having tea,' the woman said. 'You seemed occupied enough.' She smiled slightly. 'I'm sorry,' she said. 'I didn't mean it to annoy you.'

Sergeant Stafford laid his palms flat on the desk. The young fellow fiddling with his cap glanced up at the clock. He put his hand in one pocket of the jacket that lay across his knee, and then in the other. He did this several times, his eyes now level with the sergeant's own. I have no idea what is going on, the sergeant thought, there is nothing about this whole God-damned business I understand. He had just laid down his pencil. It seemed there would be another body too, on the farm above the valley. And all that stuff they had talked about hats. The driver had talked about them until the woman told him, 'Do keep quiet, Spicer.' But she had put her hand across his as she spoke. She added, 'There was also a dog. He shot a dog.'

For several minutes there again was silence between them in the room, until the young bloke said, 'I'll go back by bus if that's all right then. I'll go back as far as the store.'

When the telephone jangled through from the other office, both the sergeant and the woman rose. Hansen opened the door. He saw the woman coming towards him and he looked past her to the squat, compact irritability of his superior.

'Sir William?' the woman said.

Hansen did not take in what she said. He announced simply, 'For you, sir.' He closed the door between the rooms after the sergeant had walked through.

'It's the doctor,' Hansen said.

He watched the older man's damp face. The sergeant stood stiffly as he listened. The doctor explained he had been held up with a sudden delivery ten miles out. He had only just had a chance to examine the bodies. No, he said, although Stafford had not in fact questioned him, no, no one else had seen the bodies. He spoke briefly and rapidly. The sergeant had always admired that, the quick professionalism of the man. Young Hansen saw the sergeant's hand rise and sweep slowly across his forehead and back along his thinning hair. 'Yes, doctor,' he said. 'Yes, doctor. I think so too.'

He replaced the squat earpiece on its hook. He then sat at the desk and leaned forward, pressing his knuckles against his eyes. Young Hansen watched him, as concerned as though he watched the distress of a parent. And the sergeant, when he did at last raise his head and look across to the younger man, had about him the bruised luminousness of distress.

'Sir?' young Hansen said.

The sergeant rose slowly, as though surfacing back to a room that had altered and become strange.

'That was the doctor,' he said.

The constable waited for him to go on.

'He's examined the bodies,' he said.

'Examined them?'

'Looked at them.' Then the sergeant laughed in a way that Hansen would try to describe later as he told the story and could never do better than 'spooky'. He looked at the younger man so intently the constable lowered his eyes and thought, Something is wrong, something has to be wrong.

Then the sergeant told him. 'You won't believe this, Hansen,' he said. 'The Chow isn't a man either. Any more than he's a Chow.'

The constable was slow in taking in his superior's words, while the sergeant undid his watchstrap and rubbed at the pink welt where another itch had flared up. Young Hansen then put forward what seemed the only thing to say. 'A woman, you mean?'

'Not that either,' the sergeant said. 'Not one thing or another. Would you credit that?' His face now flushed and disconcerted. 'The doctor's got a name for it.' And the constable too felt a thick pumping embarrassment as he tried to comprehend what the sergeant meant.

'I'd better phone Napier,' the older man said. He stood again before the shining black apparatus on the wall. 'I'd better get McGibbon in on this.'

Which is the very thing Joyce will say for years that she can never forgive him for. There was not the least thing McGibbon could do or needed to do but swan in, the one thing he was good at, swan in and take it on himself to make the announcement to the press and get his name in every paper in the country. That fool, Joyce says, that fool of a husband of mine hands fame on a plate to a man he's hated for years, since they joined the force together just after the war and McGibbon married a detective's daughter and here they are, what is it, twelve, fifteen years later? *Sergeant* Stafford, she insists, still sergeant and stuck in a burg like this and then makes damn sure they'll never move from the place, not now. Who'd want a cop who can't sniff the difference between his own best interests and handing over a gift you might as well call it, handing over the *one* story the whole country's got its tongue hanging out for?

For weeks the rumours seethed of the killer who was neither man nor woman. 'Hermaphrodite' entered the vocabulary of a nation, while with an authority no one at school dared question, Jackie Stafford informed his closest friends under vows of utter secrecy that the police would never know who it really was, the Chow. Never. The police knew that and were ashamed to say so. And more than that.

'More than what?' The smallest boy in the group was the most urgent. He fizzed with the excitement of it.

'What it was like. Down there.'

'What you mean, *down there?*' one of Tom Hopai's cousins shouted, an aggrieved note in his curiosity.

Jackie quickly touched the front of his school shorts. To heighten the moment, his head flicked to either side, the heads of the boys surrounding him following his own. Making sure, as he said, the coast was clear, that no one would get a whisper of it apart from them.

'Tell us, then!'

'Like a fish,' he said.

The effect was as much as he had hoped for. There was a long pause of bewilderment. The smallest boy's face contorted with it. He tugged at Jackie's shirt. 'Scales?' he said. 'You mean like scales?'

'He means like a *fin*,' another boy said. 'That's right, isn't it? No balls or nothing. Just this fin.'

'Like a fish,' Jackie repeated. 'That's all I can tell you.' He could not be drawn further than that. There were some secrets even his mates could not expect.

Only Lucy seemed unbothered by what she had been part of. She said nothing at home or at school. 'But then *Lucy* —', as Joyce's friends sometimes said, and left it at that. Lucy who was so slow at reading that even after her first year in Tiny Tots she could not get through the alphabet. Her mother liked to say there were well-documented cases of slow learners developing with a dash by the time they reached matric, Lucy could well be one of those. But no one was taken in. 'Could be Madame Curie in that case,' Joyce's brother said. 'If you're going to measure things by what they aren't.'

Not that it mattered a jot to Lucy whether they made jokes about her or teased her the way they did, the other kids. They were not much more to her than shadows moving behind the frosty glass in the front door. And sometimes when everyone else was talking while they ate their tea, she would sidle from her chair and edge from the kitchen door and someone would suddenly ask, 'Where's Lucy? Where's that child?'

With her rabbit, they would say, with the broken-down sheep dog no one else gave a toss for. Jackie might make a joke and say, 'She's trying to tame that locust in the jar in her room. Trying to teach it tricks.' While by then she had reached the barn and dragged two bales of hay so she could lie one down and put the other on its end and lever it with her weight so it fell forward and balanced on top of the first. She then stood on the bales and put her hand into the dark behind one of the barn's rough wooden supports where a bird's nest used to be, and lifted out an Edmonds baking tin with the pattern scratched off to show the dull shine underneath. From the tin into her warm expectant hand she then tipped the treasure from the pocket when the man had put his coat down on the verandah rail and the lady sat in the rocking chair. It was like a huge spider with silver glittery feelers. Its back was nearly black until she moved it to a roadway of light that poured between the chinks in the boards, a hot shaft like she had seen at the pictures in town that left the hole in the wall behind where people sat and threw the whole bright world up there in front of them. She sank her hand slowly in the angled brightness and it leaped to life, the burning spider brooch that was the nicest thing she had ever seen. Even when it wasn't a summer day and the sun wasn't making the dusty pouring roads between the boards she could still close her eyes and think about it. Close her eyes and the spider burned.

The summer ended. The fruit was picked and sent off from the orchards along the network of side roads, and the leaves shrank and fell and the hot suede paddocks and the yellow hills turned lush within days, once the season changed. The sergeant's dermatitis vanished as quickly as it had appeared three months before and Joyce, although she did not say so, liked having his heavy breathing back next to her as she listened to the rain needling across the corrugated iron roof. The district talked of other things. Even Jackie's audience craved something new. He sat on the verandah steps and rubbed at his footy boots with slabs of dirty mutton fat and thudded the rugby ball for hours against the side of the barn. Lucy was put up into Primer One without it seeming to make the least difference to her reading. McGibbon wrote a letter to the Commissioner commending Stafford for the way he had handled the initial stages of the enquiry, but it lay there on his desk for more than a month, until there hardly seemed much point in posting it. Although he did think young Hansen was a likely enough lad, and arranged for his transfer to his own station in exchange for a dour Southlander who was proving far too eager in his pursuit of after-hours drinkers.

And at four o'clock one afternoon towards the middle of the year, when it was almost too dark to read without the electric light in the thick dusk of the kitchen, Joyce looked up from the Auckland weekly spread in front of her on the kitchen table while she waited for the range to stoke up.

'That rich one,' she said, 'remember? In the purple car who came down and got the woman?'

'The 1928 Hudson Eight?' her husband said. His memory for vehicles was a credit to any officer. Even Joyce knew that.

'Sir William,' she said. It was nice to say his name like that and to think she'd actually seen him, with his yellow gloves but his eyes too small to be really handsome, and his features — swarthy, that was the word. Owned half of Auckland, her brother had said. Sir William's lot, he meant. Auckland was swarming with them.

'The Hudson,' her husband said again.

Joyce said, 'He's gone to Germany.' She ran her palm over the page and leaned close to read it and said in a different voice for reading, 'To try to assist relatives whom he believes may be in danger because of recent political events. One cousin, a journalist in Munich, has already been arrested.'

'No one's arrested without reason,' her husband told her.

'This is Germany they're talking about,' she said.

'Take your pick,' her husband said.

'*And* his recent wife.' Joyce raised an eyebrow, as though alert to rather more than her husband might think. 'Two and two!' she said. 'You don't have to be Sherlock Holmes for that one, do you?'

She turned the page and stood up, and ran her thumb inside the collar of her dress to ease the strap of her brassiere. 'Is there anywhere I'm not putting on weight?' she said. She seemed not too bothered by her question.

Her husband adjusted the damper on the range, and clanged one of the iron rings. A sharp drift of manuka smoke blurred across the kitchen.

'For God's sake,' Joyce said. She brushed him aside and attended to things properly. But her husband stepped close behind her and his hand rested first on his wife's waist, then slid up to enclose the firmness of her breast.

'Worse places than that to put on weight,' he told her.

Joyce laughed and partly turned towards him. 'Always the gentleman, our sergeant.'

He ran his tongue behind his wife's ear.

'That drives me mad!' she said. 'I've told you that!' She shook her head as though something was caught in the mass of her hair. But she did not mind that he tilted her forward and pressed against her. The kids were across at Hopais so they wouldn't see them for an hour. She heard his breath catch, and his face touch gently at the back of her neck. Her haunches firmed against him.

'That's it,' her husband said. 'That's the story, then.'